Quotes from Readers a

51HL00: I'm a college English pr
graduate level. The author of "Sha
capturing the feel of medieval Franc.. .... classes, genders, and
beliefs are well-handled. . . . Many readers will be captivated by the young man, the
young woman, and the hawk.

12MS01: Awesome, fantastic, fabulous! I recommend this to everybody. There is
not a flaw in the book it had just the right amount of romance, action, humour [sic],
and history in it.

14FA01: Shall Die By the Sword [is] one of my favorite books, right up there with
The Lord of the Rings. There was a good balance of romance and action and I loved
the poetry. I would reccomend this to all readers looking for a great book.

57HL02: I liked the way that the author made the story fast-paced. . . .

00MSXX: I think it was an amazing book! The character development was very
good. I got to know the characters and got attached to them. T.S. Beckett is a very
good author, I can tell he's done a lot of research and knows what he's writing
about. I strongly recommend this book.

46MS01: I liked Shall Die by the Sword because there was plenty of action, the
characters were interesting. I especially liked the foreshadowing us[ed] in the
begining of the book in the dreams. . .

48HL00: Beckett has an amazing gift for developing character. . . .

45HL01: I really enjoyed this book! My 16 year old son liked it as well. The
characters were well developed and believable, and I liked the fact that the heroes
were real people with flaws but yet doing their best to live honorably. The
descriptions made me feel like I was right there in the middle of the action. I started
reading it late one afternoon and read into the wee hours of the morning, because I
was so caught up in the story.

64MS01: [T]his book is fantastic, keeps your interest, can't put it down.

79HL00: I liked the fact that it was based on reliable history of the period.
It was an exciting story that held my interest to the end. I especially appreciated
the high moral tone and the implied biblical emphasis.

39MS01: The characters were great. . . .

54MS02: Overall I thoroughly enjoyed this book and will read more from this
author. . . .

00FA01: . . .I really enjoyed reading this. . . . Great book!

34MS03: GREAT JOB!!!!!!!!!!!!!!!!!!!!!!!!!!!!! Definately looking to read another
novel.

41HL01: Although the book has Christian themes, it also appeals to the general public on the basis of an active plot and beautiful descriptive language. The poetry is an added bonus (and my favorite part!).

51CF01: I thought the book was well written and easy to follow. I've never been into historical novels but I couldn't put this one down. Very good book!

15FA01: It was a good mix of action and romance. Well written characters that the reader could connect with. You really come to care about the characters. Wonderful combination of happiness and sadness. I couldn't put it down. Easy story to follow, easy read, very, very enjoyable. One of my top favorite books. Would make a good movie!

38MS01: I THOUGHT IT WAS A WONDERFUL STORY AND WELL WRITTEN. IT HAD ENOUGH ACTION IN IT TO KEEP THE STORY FLOWING WELL.

You, too, can impact our publishing decisions!

Go to **doubleedgepress.com** and click on Public Library. There, you will find manuscripts submitted to *Cutting Edge Literary Services* by writers who are looking for publication. Make a choice, read your selection, and then fill out a report. It's free!

As we see manuscripts that grab readers' imaginations as this title did, we'll publish them.

Shall Die By the Sword

T.S. Beckett aka mo Brauer

Double Edge Press
TM

Double Edge Press

ISBN 0-9774452-0-8

For Cassie and Sasha: Your wit, your charm,
your beauty—both inside and out—your
intelligence, your perseverance, your kindness,
your grace, your elegance, and your desire to be a glory for Christ
make me proud to be known by you as:
Daddy.

Acknowledgments, Comments, and Historical Notes

I will address the historical notes first. I have long been a student of medieval history and lore, which is not to presume the title of medievalist—No, I am far from that. And while I have done much diligent reading on this subject, I have also taken creative liberties. For example, to my knowledge there never was a Duke of Gascony. As another example, Mont St. Michel did not have a statue of the archangel until several centuries later. What is more, those of you who wish to place this tale in a particular year of the late 14th century will not succeed. You will never find the proper confluence of the King of England, the King of France, and the location of the Pope. This was intentional. The medievalist may also find other errors; some of them I knew and ignored, others I never knew. But Shall Die by the Sword is first and foremost a novel. I have tried to create mood and setting; details of history are correctly relegated to history books.

It is not within the scope of a few short paragraphs to list all my research and reading for this book, but I will mention three sources. Those of you who are interested in this period cannot go wrong with Barbara Tuchman's *A Distant Mirror*, to which I am in great debt. For the mood of the period I found Johan Huizenga's *The Autumn of the Middle Ages* invaluable. Third, Henry Adams's classic *Mont Saint-Michel and Chartres* was a great delight to read.

Regarding the poetry in the book, all of the chapter and subchapter poems—unless otherwise credited to scripture—are original works of mine. Having said that, however, I freely admit to being influenced by a wide variety of poets in creating my gems. Let me explain my methods: sitting in my leather chair listening to the ancient choral chants of Hildegard von Bingen, I would study the chapter heading and read the masterpieces of poetic literature. When I found a poem that I liked, I would read it through several times, close the book, and then I would let the mood of the music, the melody of the muse, and the overarching theme of the French title push the pen. One of my readers, a great scholar of poetry and medieval literature, pointed out a very close similarity between a line in one of my poems and a line of John Donne's, and he was quite right. For those of you future scholars who have been assigned to discover the influence of the masters on my 'modern classic,' I give you this hint: find the volume *The Top 500 Poems* edited by William Harmon and published by Columbia. To those of you who just like poetry, I give the same advice.

Regarding the scripture quoted in this book, where credited it is mostly taken from the English Standard Version. However, where it is part of Henri's speech I have taken liberties with several versions to write what sounded best to my ear. The vicar's sermon at the beginning of the book included a number of introductions to the text. I have not included chapter and verse because they would have distracted from the intent of *Shall Die by the Sword*, which is to tell a story.

And now I come to the acknowledgements. As a reader I have often read these 'credits' with passing interest. As an author I now understand the indebtedness others have felt. In no particular order I want to acknowledge those who have been so instrumental in bringing this volume to fruition. (Please, please forgive me if I fail to mention someone I should never have forgotten.)

Ed Christian, a friend of huge intellect and colossal literary skills, voluntarily went through my manuscript and provided a wealth of editing comments. My gratitude cannot be properly expressed. J. Mark Bertrand (this is a name that will soon soar among the reading public) and Jaime Hathaway (she has published a small classic gem) also read my manuscript and gave many excellent comments. Michael Cooley, after reading the book, sat me down and gave me a very encouraging analysis. His input came at a critical time for my self-esteem. Then there were the many other readers including my partners Richard Milligan and Beth Cardwell; my office staff Teresa Borden and her sister, Tracy Lam, Peg Crook; my friends Mike and Linda McCabe; and my brothers Robert, James, and Ronald. All of these provided encouragement. It would be impossible to overstate the encouragement of my biggest fans: Lauren Byrd, Andrea Milligan, and Kristy and Joel Kurtz. Neither can I forget my friends among the online literary group Faith*in*Fiction, nor the readers on cuttingedge-literary.com, who by their praise of the book got the attention of an editor. And how does one thank an editor, Rebecca Melvin, who on the merit of my book accelerated her plans to start up a publishing company in order to publish it? To inspire the launch of a publishing house is a huge honor.

Finally there is my family: my daughters to whom this book is dedicated and my biggest fan and most faithful friend, my wife, Judy. By the way, Judy, Molly is beautiful.

To God be the glory.

--- T. S. Beckett

Shall Die By the Sword

T.S. Beckett

Prologue I

Henri woke with a start. His shirt was soaked with sweat. Shivering, he groped in the straw for his blanket. It was wadded up below his feet. As he rewrapped himself in it, he listened in the darkness. The calm breathing of the horses in their stables reassured him. He lay back down and closed his eyes. For a couple of minutes he could not remember what had awoken him, and then the memory returned; it was fuzzy at first like banks of fog rolling off the nearby Bay of Biscay, and then it grew increasingly vivid. He had dreamed of the wolf and the greyhound bitch again, third time this month. In the first two dreams this sleek greyhound, leading her pair of puppies, had visited a mangy wolf. The gray he-wolf, growling all the while, licked the frightened puppies. They were disquieting dreams, but tonight's was worse. This third dream was hideous. In this dream the bitch, looking sleeker, coat shining, eyes gleaming, carried the puppies out of her lair. She laid them down before the glowering wolf, and he ate them.

Prologue II:

Coal black rain clouds threatened as they rolled off the bay and over the marsh. The wind chilled Renée. With one hand she pulled her white coat close around her slender shoulders; with the other hand she checked her prancing gelding.

She was worried, deeply worried. Not of the impending storm; that was the least of her concerns, for they were near their destination, the small fortress of Anwar-de-la-Bay. They would find shelter there. No, her worries stemmed from her mother, the Comtess Elaine. She looked back. Her mother did not ride well and was overmatched by the spirited, white mare. A squire was even now fastening on a lead rope. She looked like an olive stuck stiffly on a stick, albeit men would have added that she was a very luscious olive.

Why had her mother insisted on this trip? Why had she forced Renée to come? It was not as if they were close. Her mother had ignored her from the day of her birth remaining distant and cold. Renée had no fond childhood memories of being rocked to sleep or of receiving affectionate embraces. And why Anwar? Why this marsh laden, mosquito-breeding, forgotten corner of Guienne in southwestern France? Yes, she knew her uncle, Sieur de Bixmarch, was here, but he was of no account, a worthless man whom she had met once and did not wish to meet again.

Something was wrong; she had first suspected it when her mother had given her a white, intricately embroidered, satin dress, a dress fit for a aughter of the king and yet given to her. She had known something was wrong this morning when her mother had not only personally brushed her hair but had also suggested Renée might practice her walk "To be a little more womanly." All of this deeply troubled Renée.

Now, as they approached the little village, Renée turned her head toward the clouds and began to pray, "St. Catherine, protect me. St. Catherine, they say you have a special place for unmarried girls; watch over me." She stopped her prayer and looked at the unkempt huts. Dirty-faced children watched as the armed escort passed, but she felt no peace, no sense her prayer would suffice. She must seek a higher power, the Virgin mother. "Mary, mother of God, watch over. . . . " She stopped her prayer in mid-sentence. It too felt powerless, and her sense of need loomed. What could she do? She had never felt this sense of danger before. It almost choked her in its intensity. Could she approach the Savior, Christ himself? Was that allowable? Would he listen? Even to one like her? She had missed mass the last two weeks and had not been to confession for a month. But she must approach him; her need was too great. Wrapping her hands tightly around the reins, she dropped her head and whispered, "Jesu, Jesu, Jesu Christus, I am in trouble, in danger. Jesu, help me."

Then she was silent, not knowing what else to say. When she raised her head she saw a shaft of light piercing the stratus. It fell on a small wooden building to the left of the gates. It lasted a few seconds and then faded.

As they passed through the wooden gates of the fortress and dismounted, she looked toward the building where the light had fallen. A knight stood in front of it, and within the shadows a tall youth was throwing down straw. The servants led her horse to the building. It was the stables. The light from the clouds had fallen on the stables. A warmth filled her.

Chapitre Un
Au Commencement

The sun rose in its climbing path before
The moon and stars were spread upon the sky; before
The land, the waters, and the deeps were cast; before
The fish both large and small went wiggling by; before
The limbs of trees, bushes, and growing grass; before
The robin, the crow, the dog, and horse did pass; before
The breath of life was given to you and me; before
His plan of love was ever there, us to restore.
- Sir Thommas the Hunter

Bells tolled in the twilight. They echoed off the castle keep. Their clear tones spread to the surrounding village. While the first tones passed the town and reverberated on the bay, new tones rang sharp. The bells faded; they diminished into the emptiness, into the stillness of coming night, and as they did young Henri rose from his knees. He was the last to leave the chapel. With his feet wrapped in tattered cloth he steered away from the other worshipers and back to the stables.

As he passed through the rough frames, he saw the mare and gelding: the mounts of Lady Elaine d'Ayes and her daughter, Maiden Renée. They had arrived a little before vespers. Though young, poised at that threshold between youth and manhood, he had an uncommon eye for evaluating horses. These were several ranks above his Lord's herd, a little underweight, certainly in need of grooming, but of fine breeding.

He knew horses. His father, Sir Thommas de Bretagne, Master of the Hunt, lately deceased—may he rest in God's peace—had taught him this and much more: taught him of hawks and hounds; taught him of the forest; taught him of the ways of the hind and the boar. But not only the hunt; Sir Thommas had also taught his only child many other things: how to wield the sword and crossbow, how to read the night sky, and languages. Of languages he could speak Breton, the ancient tongue of Brittany—from which his father and mother had come—French, and Latin. He spoke these fluently. Others, such as the Occitan of Languedoc, the Catalan of the Spanish, and the Arabic of the Moors, he spoke in bits and pieces. Not that his learning in languages did much good now, for though he was Henri, son of Sir Thommas the Hunter, a son of a nobleman, his status had fallen much since his father's death. Now he was a common stable boy.

Henri pitched his fork into the hay and offered it to the new horses, the dappled gray gelding and the white mare. He filled a bucket with water and, grabbing a brush, began grooming them.

He recited quietly what he had heard in chapel.

"'Now, O Lord, please remember how I have walked before you in faithfulness and with a whole heart, and have done what is good in your sight.' And Hezekiah wept bitterly."

Henri knew his father had had little use for the friars and priests of the church, but that was not uncommon. Many protested the illiterate and ignorant state of the common priest. And the blasphemy of the mass sometimes exceeded all bounds of propriety. Thommas and Henri had even heard a choir sing the words from the vulgar "Kiss Me" jongleur song to the tune of one of the sacred melodies. For this and other more personal reasons Sir Thommas de Bretagne had often gone long stretches without uncovering his head in a cathedral or chapel.

"They know nothing about the Scriptures, Henri. Nothing. They are a stench in God's sight," he said. Henri, however, was not his father. He had not studied with scholars as his father had. He had been forced down in social status, becoming a common man. If he was to hear

Scripture it must come at the mass. True, the priest was a liar, thief, and womanizer, but his vicar loved the Word, and this Word was Henri's comfort. It had preserved and soothed him during this year of sorrow and loneliness.

"Yes, my fine lady," Henri said to the mare while combing its mane, "I do understand Hezekiah weeping. I have done that too."

At that moment Sir Petro de Lomange, master of the stables, entered. "Henri, are you here? We have new horses to see to." Observing Henri brushing the mare, he added, "Already at it, as usual."

Henri stopped and looked back at the knight. Sir Petro de Lomange's face was pockmarked, probably from the same outbreak of the pox that had claimed Henri's mother when he was just a toddler.

"Yes, sir."

"What do you think of them?" Petro asked.

"Need a little grain, a little weight, a scratch here and there, some grooming, but they are fine, very fine," Henri said as he finished combing out the mane of the mare.

"Yes, yes those were my thoughts. Of course there is no horse so well shod that he never slips, if you know what I mean, but these, these are beauties. They didn't come cheap."

Petro walked behind both horses studying them. "They have both speed and strength; large hearted; it is a good combination." Then he glanced at Henri. "In your hands they will soon be at their finest."

Henri smiled as he lifted the hoof of the mare to pick it out around the frog. "It will be a joy to work with them."

"I was a lucky man to find you." Petro placed a hand on Henri. "What you have done with Sieur de Bixmarch's herd of sag backs! Remarkable. Sieur de Bixmarch is very pleased. He is becoming proud of his stable, and he believes me responsible. Indeed, I am envied. It was fate that I should have found you; no, rather, it was the providence of Mary the Blessed Mother. I told you of the relic my wife bought just before we moved here, didn't I?"

Henri nodded; he had heard the story several times; how Maria had accidentally found a small pewter box while rummaging through a tinker's trunk of goods. The box was right at the bottom, and in it was a locket of hair from John the Baptist. How it had been hidden there all these years the tinker could not understand, but seeing how she had found it, he gave it to her at a truly remarkable twenty livres—about the price of a horse. Still, for such a treasure as this Petro had been only too glad to pay. Not long after that, Sir Petro had left his plague-ravaged holdings, traveled on foot, and sworn fealty to Sieur de Bixmarch. He had been assigned charge of the ragged herd as master of the horse. Two months later Henri had come, cold, hungry, and forlorn. He had sought shelter at the stables, and Petro had taken him on. The horses had thrived under Henri's care, and Petro had soon turned it all over to him.

"But these two. . ." Petro stopped and patted the neck of the gelding. "Even I can see these are fine horses." He laughed.

"That one is a Camargue from the Rhône delta," Henri said, looking over to where Petro was standing. "You see the wide-set ears, large square head, deep chest, strong hindquarters. Thirteen and a half, fourteen hands I would say."

"Are they always so small?" Petro asked.

"Don't let his size fool you. They are strong and sure-footed. He is an excellent horse for the marshlands. He would do well here in Guienne. If I were Bixmarch I would build my herd with a breed such as this." Henri set down the hoof of the mare and walked to the gelding. He picked up his rear leg and tapped on the hoof. "See how sound his foot is? Very hard."

Petro migrated to the white mare. "And this one, what of it? It reminds me of a Spaniard's horse. Very elegant."

Henri accompanied Petro and patted the mare on the croup. "It's all right, lady," he said as she shifted in the stall. "Notice her thick, rounded neck and intelligent eyes; see the well-sprung ribs, the luxuriant mane and tail. You are right, Petro; this is a Spanish horse from Andalusia. She is a beauty."

Petro changed subjects. "Did you see the grand entrances of the lady and daughter? They were dressed like none other in this bywater village. I wonder why they came." He shrugged. "Well, we shall find out, probably sooner than we like."

"No, I did not see them," Henri lifted another of the mare's hoofs and continued cleaning. "I had my dream of the wolf again last night," he said.

"Really! What is this, the third time?"

"Yes, except in this dream the wolf ate the pups."

"Ate them! Very odd."

"There were two pups, a male and a female. He ate the female first, and then the male. I was the male pup, and he ate me. The hairs of his muzzle scratched me, and his breath was putrid, and then he ate me."

Petro stopped and studied Henri for sometime. He shuddered. "You have strange dreams, Henri. You have not mentioned this to anyone else have you?"

"No, just you."

"Good. Since Sieur de Bixmarch's banner is that of the wolf, mentioning it can only bring trouble. Keep it quiet."

Henri nodded.

"By the way, they call this one Fallaire," Petro said as he patted the mare's rump. "And that"—he pointed to the gelding—"that one is

Heretic."

At that Petro looked at Henri one final time, shook his head as if perplexed, and exited through the rear entrance.

"Don't miss the feast tonight," he called over his shoulder.

Henri had missed the arrival of Lady Elaine and the Maiden Renée. Though their coming had been rumored for the last two weeks, he had spent little time pondering it. Now that he was a commoner, a fine lady and her daughter, other than more work, would be of little matter to him.

Hooking a rope to the gelding, he led him down to the best stall at the far end. He recited the verse again: "'Now, O Lord, please remember how I have walked before you in faithfulness and with a whole heart, and have done what is good in your sight.' And Hezekiah wept bitterly." With such rare access to Scripture, memorizing was the only way to grow his list of stored verses. He only wished it fit him, but he knew his failings all too well. He lacked the courage of his father. And what of his faith? Since his father had died, his faith had too often faltered.

He was taller than most, with long, brown hair hanging over hazel eyes. His father would neither have approved of the length nor of using the horse combs to brush it, but there was nothing else available. Henri was agile, with the sure and strong movements of an athlete. Modest, unpretentious, and reserved in conversation, whenever possible he preferred to remain in the background—very different from his charismatic father. He did have a sweet smile, however, and a kind word for children and their mothers.

Having finished with the grooming, he raked the stables. He kept them clean. Only when that was finished did he head toward the feast in the grand room. Though the sun had nearly set he could still make out the whitecaps of the bay stretching out to the west. The spring breeze had a damp chill. Last spring he had come.

Children were gathering the hens into their coops along the wall of the fortress. Well, wall might be stretching the word, for there were large gaps where there was no wall, large sections where it was just a helter skelter, an improvised barricade of beams; even the front gate needed repairs.

The state of the wall was a reflection of many things in Anwar; more than that it was a reflection of Europe itself in these times after the plague. Southern France, like most of Europe in the fourteenth century, had been devastated by the Black Death. In some areas half of the population had died. Abandoned farms lay fallow; forsaken fields returned to the forest; depopulated villages were deserted; and drought and famine had followed the plague. If that were not enough, there were the incessant wars with the English, corrupt government, oppres-sive poll taxes, rogue outlaw armies, and insurrection. The church split in schism, was devastated with debauchery, hysteria, superstition, and indolence, it could do nothing to relieve the pressures of the times. In short, it was a time of great chaos and darkness.

Indeed, it was this turmoil which had allowed Sieur de Bixmarch and his small band of men-of-war to take Anwar-by-the-Bay. Bixmarch, however, was a fighter and no steward, and the town and fortress had suffered.

La Fête

I remember her. . . and you.
How beautiful she was, and how the men did notice
The way she moved among the tables;
The sway of her dress,
The cleavage of her breasts,
And I just a common boy of the stables,
In common garb and common passed unnoticed
By all, but especially you.
- Henri d'Anwar

The feast was underway as Henri entered the grand room. He stopped at the door and looked. Sieur de Bixmarch sat among his men-of-war by the hearth at the far end of the room. He held a leg of lamb in his hands as he gestured towards his men. He was a dark-haired German with premature gray hairs and well-toned arm muscles. Along either side of the room, among the supporting beams, tables were filled with the lord's men-at-arms and fortress hands.

Sliding through the crowd to the left, the young stable hand took a seat at the end of one long bench. Two of the castle dogs leaned in against his leg. He reached down and patted their necks.

"Yes, yes," he said softly. "A bone for each of you, with a little meat if I can."

These dogs were not like the hounds he remembered from his years at the court of Gascony. Those had been beautiful animals: well trained, white Pyrenees. As a boy he had enjoyed being the son of the Master of the Hunt, for then he had been with the hounds every day; in affection and loyalty many of them had been his dogs. These. . . these were mongrels. Still, Henri loved them.

Henri took his wooden bowl and gathered a couple of bones lying on the table. He took some meat, an apple, and a couple loaves of bread. Feasts in Anwar were not bountiful, not like they had been with his father; his father had always known how to cook a good meal, even when they were traveling beyond Constantinople among the Turks.

"Here you go, boys." Henri slid the bones under the table. The dogs took them and settled down beside his feet.

Bending his head, he said a quick grace. The priest had probably blessed the food before the feast began, but Henri doubted if anything the priest said ascended beyond the range of his voice.

Sitting at the end of the table, he pulled off a hunk of bread. The room was crowded and noisy. The burning flambeaux set in the cressets provided a smoky light. A minstrel strummed on a lute near Sieur de Bixmarch. Henri could not hear a note. He spoke little to the other revelers, and they ignored him. He cut the apple in half, and stored one half in his pocket.

A commotion at the front of the room drew his attention. One of the sergeants was staggering to his feet. Sieur de Bixmarch and the other men-at-arms were coarsely laughing. Henri wondered what had prompted the disturbance. Beside Bixmarch sat Lady Elaine and next to her the Maiden Renée.

Henri looked at the Lady. Her dress, draped provocatively low, revealed a well endowed bosom. Her rich attire indicated high nobility, but how could a woman of her station be at ease amidst this coarseness, this incivility? Having lived in the courts of Gascony, Henri had seen chivalry, high manners, and decorum, the antithesis of this little fort's barbarian, even pagan conduct. Still, she seemed to fit in comfortably with Sieur de Bixmarch and displayed no reserve enchanting the men with her voluptuous charms. It was odd. It did not fit.

Her daughter, however, was clearly uncomfortable. She said nothing, ate nothing, and rarely looked around. It was as if by avoiding her surroundings she could magically disappear. She seemed like a shunned puppy constantly being bumped from the feeding bowl. Henri felt an urge to shelter her.

He pushed that thought aside. Grabbing a loaf of bread, he slid between the crowded tables and headed for the door. Outside the wind had stirred. It was growing colder. He started toward the stables but stopped when he saw one of the village children standing by the oak doors.

"It's cold out tonight, girl. Go on home," he said as he patted her head.

"My daddy is in there, and he promised to bring me something to eat." The little girl pointed inside.

"Who is your father?" Whoever it was would want to know that his little daughter was standing outside in this cold wind.

"Caron."

"The blacksmith?" Inwardly Henri groaned. As a stable boy he frequently had to deal with Caron. Caron was rude, lazy, and disliked Henri, had disliked him ever since Henri had asked him to remake a badly forged horseshoe. Sloppy job.

"Unhuh," the little girl replied.

Henri ducked back inside. He spotted the blacksmith near the front table downing a large tankard of ale. He was drunk, amid a table of drunks. Should he talk to the smith? His quiet nature balked at the confrontation. He went back outside.

"Did you see him?" the little girl asked.

Henri nodded and ran his hands over her hair.

"And is he coming?"

Henri paused.

"If I gave you an apple would you go home and wait for him?"

The little girl's eyes lit up. "An apple?"

"And half a loaf of bread."

"And half a loaf of bread!"

Henri pulled out the food he had planned on eating tomorrow morning. "Here you are."

The girl took them and ran off down the street. He smiled and then made his way back to the stables. He would sleep beside the horses. These were lawless days, and though there were guards at the town gates, he never felt the horses were safe unless he was with them.

He pulled up the blanket Petro had given him and settled down on a bed of straw. As he closed his eyes he recited the verse again:

"'Now, O Lord, please remember how I have walked before you in faithfulness and with a whole heart, and have done what is good in your sight.' And Hezekiah wept bitterly." And as he closed his eyes a tear slid down his cheek. He missed his father terribly and was so very lonely.

Chapitre Deux
Le Ménestrel et La Damsel

Beside the fire, before the hearth,
Where burned still the bitter coals,
You bundled tight, your form so small;
The stars were dim, the moon was cold;
The minstrel his bleary eyes all
Red played on his weary harp.
-   Henri of Anwar

In the darkness of the night Henri was awakened by a tugging on his sleeve. He opened his eyes. Petro was standing over him.

"I brought you something." Petro settled a bag by his feet and then sat down on the ground. Reaching into the burlap sack he pulled out an apple in each hand. "I picked up a couple dozen apples when everyone else was drunk or asleep. I took a bag to Maria, and I bring a bag for you, though I know you will cut them in half and give some to the horses. A waste of good apples. Still, I cannot complain; your care of the horses is what has made it go well for me."

"Oh, but there is more." He reached into the bag and pulled out smaller bags filled with almonds, peas, onions, cabbage, and bread, six loaves of bread. "You left too early," Petro continued as he showed Henri the storehouse of food. "It was a very interesting evening. Did you know that the Lady Elaine is our Sieur de Bixmarch's sister?"

Henri sat up and rubbed his eyes. He looked to the stable door trying to gauge the time. It was dark, with no sign of the dawn. He picked up an apple.

"The Lord is good," he said quietly. "He remembers even the most undeserving of his children."

"You are a good man, Henri. If you get blessings they are justly deserved. But I tell you it was a most unusual evening. I learned many interesting things. For example did you notice that Roland, Bixmarch's chief lieutenant, was not there? Nor were several of the warriors. Where would they be, I ask you?

"And what did you think of Lady Elaine. Is she a woman or what? Oo-la-la!"

"I thought her daughter prettier," Henri objected. "The colors of her face are as lovely as a rose on a May morning, and her body is well made and graceful."

"Really!" Petro chuckled. "Well then, it may interest you to know that when I left she was still sitting by the minstrel listening to him play. He kept trying to quit, and she kept insisting he continue, though it was apparent both were very tired. Very odd, but what business is that of mine. 'He who is silent about all things is troubled by nothing' is what I say.

"But here now, here is the bag. Go back to sleep. It should be a quiet day tomorrow. No one will be up before noon. Certainly I won't." And with that, Petro dropped the bag and left.

Henri rolled over and tried to return to sleep. But sleep would not come. He contemplated what Petro had said. Bixmarch and Elaine were brother and sister. Lady Elaine refined and beautiful, Bixmarch crude and cruel. Then he thought of Renée, thought of her sitting, sitting and listening to the minstrel play. When after several more minutes and sleep still did not return, he arose and left the stables. The only light was a quarter moon and the dying fires from the great room. The only sound was that of the lute and an occasional dog barking from the village.

He slipped quietly into the hall. A dozen men snored on the floor. A-nother dozen slept on the benches. The fire had burned down to a bed of coals. The minstrel sat beside the fire strumming his lute and singing softly. Beside him sat the Maiden Renée. Henri sat down on a rough-hewn oak bench behind her. She slept fitfully. At each pause of the minstrel's music she awoke, wiped her hand roughly across her mouth, and shuddered. She would shift her position and glance all around the room before falling back to sleep. On each occasion Henri would close his eyes and pretend to be asleep.

Henri had seen many daughters of nobles: he had seen the proud, the beautiful, the shy, the homely; he had seen fat ones and skinny ones, loud ones and quiet ones; but he had not seen any like Renée. Though not striking like her mother, still, she was pretty, and the more he looked the more he thought so. She had long, dark lashes and a cute nose. Her hair, though dark like her mother's, was wavy instead of straight. Her figure curved with the incomplete touches of womanhood. But mostly he noted how vulnerable she seemed, a quiet sadness of her mouth as she slept.

He stayed through the rest of the night watching from the background, out of sight, urged by some undeniable need to guard her. He stayed until the cocks began to crow, and then he slid out the door and returned to the stables.

The chimes would soon ring the prime.

He could see the horizon beginning to lighten. He grabbed a bucket and went to the well. As he pulled the rope back up he meditated, "O God, you are my God; earnestly I seek you; my soul thirsts for you; my flesh faints for you, as in a dry and weary land where this is no water. So I have looked upon you in the sanctuary, beholding your power and glory."

The bells began to peal. He loved the bells, the beauty of their resonance as they sounded across the stillness of the morning. With each bell he could feel himself drawn. After filling the water trough he walked across the yards to the chapel. Prime was Henri's favorite; few people came, and never the priest. He did not like to think ill of others, but the priest was so transparently false, so vain, so lusty, so rapacious, that Henri avoided him. Besides, it was people like the priest who had troubled his parents. Lacking true religion, this kind made a show of false piety but had little tolerance for questioning. The vicar, on the other hand, was sincere, and Henri had often poured out his sorrows and doubts to him.

Inside the chapel he knelt in a back row. A few older ladies entered and smiled at him. On the first row sat Maria, Petro's wife. The vicar entered from the left. It was a small chapel and like the rest of the town in need of repairs. The vicar uncovered his head and climbed to the lectern. He looked at the congregation.

Le Sermon
How can I say better what has been written in the Word.
- Vicar of Anwar-by-the-Bay

"Do not think the Lord does not see." He spoke gravely. "Do not think he is unaware of the revelry and drunkenness of the people of Anwar-de-la-Bay."

The ladies nodded approvingly.

"There is a great evil in liquor and the consumption of too much wine. There is a great evil brewing of which I cannot speak."

He stopped and looked at the few people in the church. "You are God's faithful. It is not of you I speak, but it is burning in me. Hear now the message of Habakkuk, for it is for this time, for this people:

"I will stand at my watch post and station myself on the ramparts; I will ask, what answer can I give? See, he is puffed up, haughty; his desires are not upright."

At this the vicar swept his arm toward the hall indicating Sieur de Bixmarch, and then more gently back on his small congregation. "But the righteous shall live by faith."

Shaking his head he spoke softly but firmly. "Moreover, wine is a traitor, he is arrogant and never at rest. His greed is wide like the grave; like death he never has enough; he gathers to himself and takes captive peoples.

"Woe to him who heaps up stolen goods and makes himself wealthy by extortion! For how long? Will not your debtors suddenly arise? Will they not wake up and make you tremble? Then you will be spoiling for them. Because you have plundered many, the remnant will plunder you. For you are a man of blood and violence; have desecrated the villages and everyone in them.

"Woe to him who builds his fiefdom by unjust gain to set his nest on high, to escape the clutches of ruin! You have plotted the ruin of many, shaming your own house and forfeiting your life."

The vicar paused for a moment, letting his head fall in his hands, and mumbling so as almost not to be heard. "What will you not consider? Is there no sin too foul?"

And then returning to his sermon he cried softly, "The stones of the wall will cry out, and the beams of the woodwork will echo it. 'Woe to him who builds a city with blood and establishes a town by incest!'

"For the earth will be filled with the knowledge of the glory of the LORD, as the waters cover the sea.

"Woe to him who makes his neighbors drink, pouring it from the wineskin till they are drunk, so that he can gaze on their naked bodies. You will be filled with shame instead of glory. One day it will be your turn! You will drink and be exposed! The cup from the LORD's right hand will come around to you, and utter shame will cover you. The violence you have done will overwhelm you, and your destruction will terrify you. For you have shed man's blood; you have destroyed lands and villages and everyone in them."

He stopped and looked all around him, at each of his parishioners, at the table of sacrament, at the holes in the walls.

"The LORD is in his holy temple; let all the earth keep silence before him."

Then he came down and performed the mass.

When it was over Henri headed toward the stables. It had been quite a sermon. But what did it mean? He could not say. Still the vicar had been brave, even if he had spoken it to such a small gathering. Henri admired that.

As he entered the stables preparing to muck out the stalls, he sensed a disturbance. The horses were unsettled. Someone or something was in the stable. At the far end he heard the low nickering of the horses. But it was still too dark to see.

"Can I help you?" he asked quietly. He started to light the lantern. But the figure quickly moved out from the shadows towards him.

"No, you don't need to light the lantern. Why ruin the beauty of the morning?"

It was the Maiden Renée. He knew it instantly. She was lithe and light like a lynx on new snow, and a touch of joy ran through him as she approached. But what was she doing here at this time of the morning?

Matin sur la Rive
How the sands passed beneath our fleeing feet
That morning on the strands, on the shore,
When first we met and the sun was at our door;
And you were kind, and you were sweet,
My stable boy, my protector, my lord.
- Maiden Renée d'Ayes

"I thought I might take a ride along the beach and watch the sun rise. Please have my horse saddled."

This he could understand.

"Yes, mademoiselle. How many will be in the party?"

"Just me. I wish to ride alone."

"As you wish." He turned and pulled the saddle for her Andalusian mare. A few minutes along the beach ought to be safe, he reasoned to himself. Maybe. It was never truly safe. And if she was hurt he would be blamed. More importantly, he would blame himself. On the other hand, he was a stable boy now, no longer Henri, son of Sir Thommas de Bretagne, Master of the Hunt, but a stable boy; that was how people saw him, that was who he was, and it was not the place of a stable boy to advise a woman of rank.

"Hurry up. If you dawdle I will miss the sunrise," she said.

Henri finished the saddling and brought her the horse. The mare danced nervously. Henri knew horses reflected their mistresses' moods.

Something was wrong.

"Would you be requiring an escort? It is not entirely safe. I could lead the horse."

He could see the idea had caught her a little, but not totally, by surprise.

"I ride well enough. I do not require a lead, but if you know the area I would appreciate a guide. Saddle up the gelding."

"The gelding? Are you sure? I really do not think. . . . These are horses fit for nobility, not stable boys." A stable boy riding such a beautiful horse could only lead to trouble, and he assiduously tried to avoid that.

"It is not my mother's. It is mine. Both of the horses are mine, and if I choose for you to ride the gelding it is my choice. You can ride can't you?" Renée asked.

Yes, he could ride. He had been raised on horseback. He had not yet met a horse he could not ride.

"Yes, I can ride."

"Well then, saddle the gelding, and be quick about it. If you are to ride with me you will need a horse as fast as mine, and I don't think you have one in your stable except him."

This was getting complicated. A year of keeping himself trouble-free seemed about to end. He would try to mitigate the damage.

"One moment," he said and dashed out the back of the stables and up the staircase to Petro's lodgings. He knocked on the door. Maria answered.

"Henri?"

"Is Petro up?"

"No, he is sleeping."

"When he wakes up tell him that I am riding on the beach with the Maiden Renée. We should be back shortly."

"On the beach? The Maiden? Is that wise?" He could see concern in her eyes, some for him, but more for Petro.

"No, probably not, but she requested it. Tell him when he awakens. It is my hope we will return before then." Henri ran down the stairs, grabbing an old jacket on his way.

Renée was fidgeting by the door. "The sun is already rising," she said sharply.

"We are ready."

He started leading the horses out the front entrance.

"Isn't there a back way?" Her voice quivered.

Henri stopped. Her dark eyes were hidden in the shadows, but her mare's eyes were frightened.

"There is no wall between here and the beach. We can slip out that way."

This was better; if they went out and came back without being seen it would cause less trouble. He led the horses outside the confines of the fortress then helped her mount. Her waist was soft and thin.

. "We ride north," she said.

On the beach, white sands stretched in both directions. She tapped her horse into a cantor. She rode well. That was one less worry for Henri. As his gelding broke into a cantor, Henri felt his power. He reached over and patted his neck. Maybe the joy of riding would be worth the trouble.

Behind them, the sun was rising above the Pyrenees. Its bright rays set the waters of the bay alive with a full spectrum of orange and turquoise, purple and red. Seagulls roosted on the sea. A formation of pelicans flew low. White frothing waves crested in the early morning wind. Farther out towering, nimbus clouds were forming. Undoubtedly a storm would come later, but for now they were splendid. And it was wonderful. He had not felt this alive in nearly a year.

They rode for twenty minutes until the town of Anwar-de-la-Bay was far behind them. She turned her steed away from the bay toward a small ravine that led off the beach onto higher ground. As they slipped into a grove of pines she halted her horse and turned away from Henri. She bit her lip but did not speak. Her horse danced under the restraints. Her slender frame drew smaller. He had noted that for all her stated desire to see the sunrise, she had been oblivious to its beauties.

Chapitre Trois
D'elle Peril

I could not leave she when she quaked—
Her eyes were moist, her voice did break,
Her body clung so tight to rein and mane—
I could not go and leave she when
Her peril called me to defend
Her from the nameless evil of her bane.
I could not go and leave she then,
E'en though she willed to send
Me back upon the traveled lane.
My Lord I could not go.
I could not go.
- Henri of Anwar.

"I shall not be returning," she said softly, nervously rubbing her thigh. "I mean never to go back. I would rather die."

"O my," Henri muttered. A list of problems crowded his thoughts. What had brought this on? What danger could possibly warrant her running away? Was she spoiled or truly in trouble? He did not know. He did know, however, that if he did not get her back to the castle and quickly *he* would be in a pretty pass. Sieur de Bixmarch had a rash and violent temper; for Bixmarch life was cheap, especially a commoner's life, and no amount of explaining would clear Henri. After all, what place had a stable boy riding with a maiden—a fair one at that. Bixmarch had hanged people for less.

"Maiden, you are tired and need rest. We should return to the castle. Surely your mother can help you," Henri reasoned.

"My mother!" Renée interrupted. "You do not know my mother. It is my mother who delivered me into this peril."

"But. . . maiden, if we do not return quickly. . . that is to say. . . you are a noble woman, and I, I am a commoner; if we do not return quickly my life is. . . ." He drew a quick finger across his neck, while under his breath he recited, "Do not be afraid or terrified; the Lord will never leave nor forsake you."

She stopped and looked at him. Her eyes saddened. "What do they call you?"

"I am Henri."

"Henri, an unusual name for a stable hand."

"Nevertheless, it is mine." He did not wish to delve into his background as a nobleman's son. No one except Petro believed him.

"Henri, I give you leave. Return to the castle. As for me, I shall go on. I cannot return. I will not return."

"Thank you maiden. I shall erase the tracks we left on the beach," he replied. "It will give you a head start. And you should take the gelding. These horses from the Camargue are excellent at navigating through the marshes. You will need it."

She nodded at him. "Thank you."

Henri started to swing his leg off and dismount, but stopped. Was this why he had felt such a burden to stay by her last night? Was this what his dreams had all been about? Was she the puppy, her mother the bitch, and Bixmarch the wolf? And if he left, how would he feel? He wished he could have sought advice from his father. Sir Thommas had always tried to protect the oppressed. But it was one thing to protect a commoner, quite another to poke your head into the politics of families and lords. Still, there was something about her that touched him. He wanted to believe. The sadness in her eyes, the way her slender shoulders drooped. She looked so discouraged, sorrow-stricken, like a lamb lost on the heather. Henri had never considered himself courageous like his father, but now there was something in him that he had not felt before. For the first time since his father had died, he felt needed.

Je ne te laisse pas
You will not leave, O blessed thought
O comfort of my periled lot,

E'en though all others pass away,
Leave me stranded when I sway.
When this slender body of mine decays
You will not leave me now or then;
You will not leave me even when
The night has come and day reached end.
- The Duchess de Bretagne

He put his feet back into the stirrups and sat up straight. "I will come with you. I will not leave you. Maiden Renée, behold your servant."

"What?" she replied. "You give me your allegiance?"

"I do."

"But what of Sieur de Bixmarch?"

"I swore no allegiance to him."

"And if he should find us?"

Henri sighed. "It will be ugly."

She stopped and looked into his eyes for a moment, her sadness replaced by a wan smile. "Thank you. . . . Henri, isn't it. . . . I thought I could trust you."

"You did? You thought? How? On what basis?"

"I saw you come and watch over me last night." She chose not to mention the shaft of light coming through the clouds in answer to her prayer.

Henri swallowed hard and turned abruptly away. She had known he was there. He had tried to keep himself out of sight, watching her only because she did not see him. But she had known he was there, the whole time. He felt foolish, like a boy caught with his hand in the sugar. On the other hand, she must have followed him to the stables. She must have planned and hoped that he would help her. And this trust in him, this blind trust was so. . . well it moved him, moved him like he had not been moved before; moved in him a passionate courage—most often found in the young, and especially in young men—such that if she had given the word he would have attempted to slay a dragon for her.

"Where then are you going?" He asked.

"I am heading home. I mean to ride hard and fast. It took my mother and me four days to come here, but we were accompanied by soldiers on foot. On horse we should make it in two."

And with that she tapped the mare into a long, striding gait. Henri swung in behind, noting as he did that the clouds were now gathering faster and growing more ominous. Storms brewed quickly over the bay, and they could be severe. They would need shelter. He knew of a deserted village not far down the path. They could hold up there. As the storm mounted the temperature dropped. He looked at the maiden. She was wearing a white leather jacket over her brocaded dress, not adequate for someone unused to hard living.

Soon the first drops began to fall. The village was not much farther. Then came the rain.

"Maiden, we must stop. We must take shelter. There is a village close by," Henri said as he drew his horse up beside her. Having spent his childhood by his father's side, often in the woods, he knew a great deal about survival and the dangers of being damp and cold. "A few minutes will save us hours. Look, we can put the horses in that stable and sit in dryness." Henri now had lighted from his horse and had grabbed the mare's bridle.

Acquiescing, Renée looked at the deserted buildings. "Where is everybody?"

"No one has lived here since the plague."

She shuddered involuntarily. "Is it safe?"

Fear of the plague would never pass for those who had survived it. Images of the dead piled high on wagons with great oozing sores—and the stench—were not easily forgotten.

After Henri stabled the horses, they sat down together on a bench. At least the rain would wash away their tracks, Henri thought. That was some consolation. Renée laid her head back and closed her eyes. She shuddered and wiped her hand across her lips several times. She was tired. Lightning flashed and then a clap of thunder. The gale and rains intensified. He was glad he had insisted on taking cover. He looked back at her. She had fallen asleep, her head resting against the wall. Standing up, he pulled off his jacket, and laid it down for a pillow on the bench. Then he repositioned her, laying her head on his jacket. She shuffled a moment and then rolled onto her side facing the wall.

La lépres
I was a leper—and so we all—
Disfigured beyond all men's recall,
But you came anyway.

I was a prisoner—and justly so—
My deeds were evil, my ways were low,
But you came anyway.

I was in sickness, my health was poor;
A wanton life of wine and whores,
But you came anyway.
- Brother Matthew

Seeing her comfortable and hoping to scrounge up food and supplies for their journey, he explored the stables and attached rooms. With regret he remembered the loaves of bread and apples he had left behind. He knew he could survive in the forests living off what he could hunt and gather, but it would be easier if he had a good knife, traps, or a bow; besides, there were other dangers: thieves, brigands, bear, boar, even wolves.

Leaks from the roof dripped in several spots as he wound his way through the maze of rooms. He pushed open a door and found himself in the kitchen. A stone fireplace was at the far end, and to his surprise, a few coals were smoldering. Behind him he heard the door open. It was Renée. She rubbed her eyes and then, noting the coals, went to warm herself.

From the next room they heard a rattling. They both knew the sound. Renée shrank behind him and placed her hands on Henri's shoulders. The far door opened. Feeling his way through the opening, a man entered. His eyes were sunken, empty sockets. His nose was ulcerated down to the bone. On his right hand he had lost three fingers; the remaining two oozed pus on a bed of white, lifeless skin. With his left hand he continued to shake the obligatory rattle society had given him, the leper's rattle.

"Is that you, my nephew?" The blind man spoke hoarsely. "I was afraid with the storm you would not come, but as you can tell, my fire is nearly out."

Henri and Renée stood silent. His appearance was like a specter, a skeleton rising from purgatory.

"Nephew? Nephew?" The man repeated then haltingly added, "Who's there?"

Henri recovered. "I am not your nephew. We are travelers. We found refuge in the stables during the storm."

"Oh." The leper groped for the wall with his bad hand. The rattle now fell to his side and an awkward silence hung in the room. Renée turned her eyes away in repugnance as the defenseless leper trembled against the back wall.

Henri looked over his shoulder at Renée and then back toward the leper. "If you tell me where the wood is I will build up your fire and set you a store."

The leper relaxed a little. "Lord bless you." He shuffled to a bench by the fire. "The woodpile and axe are through the door to your left."

Henri glanced once more at Renée and then set to stoking up the fire. He was strong, and the axe was sharp; he split a large pile. By the time he had finished the rain had nearly stopped and rays of sunshine shone through the window.

"There. You have a good fire, and a pile of wood. I have stacked it on the left. We will take our leave."

The leper felt the stack from top to bottom. Checking how neatly it had been laid, he murmured with satisfaction. "You are kind. If I had silver, I would pay you."

"Your thanks are enough," Henri said as he leaned the axe against the wall.

"But I must give you something. Would you consent to some bread and cabbage?"

"We are in need of food. I don't deny that."

"Good, good. In the far room there is a staircase. It leads. . . " The leper struggled, wanting to be generous, but afraid that he would be taken advantage of, "to the pantry. Take three loaves and a couple head of cabbage."

"Thank you; we will not take more," Henri replied.

Chapitre Quatre
Marche à Traverse le Marais

March, march, march through the slough and through the marsh;
Sink deep in the mud, slop in the brackish cold.
Your arms and hands, your legs and feet are frozen and stiff;
Your dress once so white by the grime is soiled,
But still we must march, march, march through the endless marsh.
- Henri of Anwar

They found the loaves and ate them before setting off again. Soon they came to the main road traveling along the Adour River. It was mid-morning and others were on the road: peasants pushing carts to market, a tinker driving a wagon, and a clothier leading a mule laden with cloth. The peasants gave way to the horses and then turned to watch. Odd that a young damsel of rank should be riding with only a stable hand and no larger escort. Odd and dangerous.

Past the Adour they rode through a land of marshes. Blackbirds sat on the dried cattails of last year's growth. Towering reeds grew in patches, sometimes rising even to the level of their heads. Streams rose up and then faded. At times the marshes covered the road, and they had to slop their way through. The gelding proved valuable with its innate sense for finding dry ground. Still, on several occasions they found themselves having to dismount and stomp through knee-deep bogs. Henri, bootless, with only tattered cloth wrapped around his feet, felt the cold mud between his toes.

After they emerged from the marshes they crossed the river. To the south they could see Gascony and beyond that the Pyrenees. Henri knew that land well. He had grown up in the courts of Gascony. Those had been happy years, when he had been inseparably at his father's side. His father had been a great man, a brave man, a man of honesty, humor, and intelligence. Henri had often heard people talk about Sir Thommas de Bretagne, Master of the Hunt. They said he was the epitome of chivalry, a true Sir Roland or Sir Lancelot.

Towards evening they turned north, away from the river, into an uninhabited woodlands. As nightfall descended they found a small clearing just off the road. Renée collapsed in fatigue and fell to sleep where she lay. Henri built a fire and boiled a pot of cabbage stew. Without spices it was bland, but it filled the stomach. He awoke Renée. She ate without comment and then huddled back on the ground with one horse blanket beneath her, the other over her. She quickly returned to sleep. Henri tethered the horses and then stacked wood near the fire. It would be cold, and fire would keep wild animals at a distance. Now that spring had come, the wolves were less of a threat; still, they had been known to attack even into the outskirts of Paris in recent years. Sitting by the fire he saw the occasional flickering lights of marsh gases. Some said the marsh gases were fairies or goblins, or even the souls of unbaptized dead infants. When he finally did sleep he was restless, especially when he heard the distant howling in the middle of the night. Once he thought he saw eyes circling the fire, and he brought the horses closer.

At daybreak he stoked the fire and reheated the stew.

Du potage et le loup
I fear the gray wolf lurking in the shadow of the woods;
His eyes hungry, glowing from the fires.
His tongue, his lips, his teeth drip red
Upon the ground where sleep I dread,
But you, you stand beside me and do not tire;
Your eyes ever watchful beneath the shadow of the hood.
- Maiden Renée d'Ayes

Renée rolled over, groaned, and then slowly sat up. "I swear I did not sleep more than a few minutes, and I am bruised all over. . . and cold; I am so cold. I have never missed my feather bed so much."

"Take some stew. It will warm you."

"That awful stuff again. You are not very clever at this, are you? It is bland and tasteless." But she took it.

"I am sorry, maiden, but I have little to work with."

"Can't you hunt? A little rabbit would spice it up. I saw several yesterday."

"I can hunt, but hunting takes time, and I thought you would want to get going as soon as possible this morning."

Renée crossed herself, tipped the bowl to her lips, drank some, and then continued, "Of course I want to get going quickly, but you could have killed one while you were waiting for me."

"Yes, mademoiselle, but I feared to leave the horses because of the wolves."

"Wolves?" Renée pulled in closer to the fire. "I did not hear any wolves."

"They made little noise." Henri had not meant to scare her, and in fact he had not meant to speak of it at all. The wolves had not worried him overly much, but her expectations were unreasonable.

"It's a lie. There were no wolves," Renée responded after surveying the land in the quickening light.

Henri remained silent. He was wrong to dispute her. She was the mistress, and he was the servant.

But Renée would not let it lie. She got up and started walking around the campfire. "There are no prints, no trace, nothing. In fact there were no wolves, and you were lying to me because you were too lazy to get up and rouse a decent breakfast as you know you should have."

Reluctantly, Henri got up and walked to where he had seen the eyes in the middle of the night. His eyes were well trained in tracking, and he immediately found a strand of fur on the twig of a bush. He handed it to Renée without speaking.

"Oh," was all she said, and then returned to her seat by the fire and sat silently drinking her stew.

Henri picked up his bowl. "Lord, I thank thee," he said quietly and then drank his stew. Afterwards he rinsed the pot, saddled the horses, and helped Renée to mount.

For the first hour at the breaking of the dawn they rode in silence, Renée in front, Henri behind. They overtook a blind man, a wooden stick sweeping before him measuring the road. Renée slowed her horse and watched him as they rode by.

Portrait enluminé de la livide mort

Then dead we all become like living pictures of living hell;
Our futures bleak, our paths fade in a bitter pall,
And futile all our efforts are. Doomed we are,
Doomed we shall be living—if living this scarred
Life can so be named—Or rather shall we lie us down
On river banks and leave this world of pitch and tar,
Our mortal corpse, until by others we are found
All lifeless and cold in dale so fell.
- Maiden Renée d'Ayes

"God's peace to you this morning," Henri said as they passed.

"To you maybe, but none to me," the blind man cursed.

A half mile in front of him two old veterans were limping toward them. One had lost a leg, the other an arm. The legless one leaned on his comrade as they approached. They stopped on the side of the road at the approach of the young riders.

"Look, Michal," the legless one said to his partner. "A young noble miss and her lackey out on a morning ride. It is to keep them in their castles of splendor that I lost my leg."

"And I my arm, Pierre, and I my arm."

Renée gave them a sharp look and pulled up her horse. She thought about reprimanding them for their impertinence but remained silent.

"God will reward you for your service," Henri said quietly.

"For what?" The legless man spat. "Will He reward me as I rot in hell? Is that how He will reward me? I raped a woman and her daughter, and then burned down the village. Will God reward that?"

Henri was speechless. The two rode forward.

Within five minutes they met a mother leading three scrawny children, and in her arms a squalling infant. Renée slowed her horse to look at the mother. The peasant woman, seeing she was watched, dropped her shawl. Her face was disfigured by the pox. "Now is your curiosity quenched, my beauty?" The woman pulled the wrap back over her face.

Renée shuddered and spurred her horse, but a moment later brought her steed alongside Henri's.

"We are cursed to live on this earth. I race back to my castle for what? To avoid horrors, but horrors cannot be avoided as long as one lives. What a world this is! Did you see that baby? My heart goes out to the infant. What life is in store for her? She would be better off to die while still in her mother's arms. Her mother as likely as not will be unable to feed her. The other children were barely more than scarecrows. And if the baby survives, will she catch the pox and go through life scarred, a monster like her mother? And what of her father; does she even know him? Maybe it is best if she does not. If he is a good man, then he will be conscripted in the endless war with the English. Likely he will lose an arm or a leg as did those soldiers, and that is if he is a good man. But it is more likely he is a scoundrel—most men are—and her mother a whore. And if the babe survives, what then? Ah, then she will marry some worthless curl, and she will go to mass, and the priest will molest her. If she works hard to buy a goat, her lord will claim it for taxes, or a soldier will steal it for the army. When she dies and goes to see God, He will assign her to purgatory because she did not have the money to buy a candle in the monastery, did not have the money to buy monks to pray for her soul to relieve her from purgatory. I say she is cursed to be alive."

Stunned, Henri said nothing.

"Am I right?' she asked. She studied him for a minute, waiting for him to respond. When he did not, she shook her head and spurred her horse. After a couple of minutes she slowed her mount and came back alongside.

"You puzzle me, Henri, stable boy. I have heard you reciting your verses. I have noted your manners, your speech, the way you walk, and how you talk to me. You are no simple stable boy." She paused and looked him over from head to foot.

Henri felt a flush as she looked at him.

"I am sorry for this morning. I appreciate the food, even if it was awful, and I appreciate you watching over me. Sometimes I wonder if you are not really my angel."

"No, I can assure you I am no angel."

La Ville par la fleuve
O crystal waters, sea of glass,
Golden streets 'neath ransomed feet
When first those gates of pearl we pass
And see our Saviour, Saviour sweet.

O river flowing, flow through me,
Though life and death our mortal lot,
Shall hold us 'til your jubilee
Redeems all souls that your cross bought.
- The Duc de Bretagne

They rode hard the rest of the day and by evening approached the Gerond River. The road turned west along the river and then climbed a hill. Through the trees they saw the stone castle sitting on the limestone promontory. All around the castle was the bustling city of Ayes. It was much larger than Anwar-de-la-Bay, though nowhere near as large as Bordeaux or Toulouse, much less the fabulous cities of Venice and Constantinople, all of which Henri had seen.

"We must hurry," Henri urged as he glanced back at the sun. Soon they would be closing the gates.

But Renée pulled her horse to a stop. "No, there is something wrong."

Henri followed her outstretched arm. There were two banners, and the lower one was that of the wolf, Sieur de Bixmarch's.

"What does that mean?" he asked.

"It means it is not safe for me." She looked all around and then turned her horse off the road onto a rocky path. She dismounted and led her horse down the side of the white stone. The sun warmed the stone as she came to the bottom of the ledge. "I had not even thought about this, but my mother and uncle obviously have. I am outmatched and outwitted and am now a fugitive." Her voice quivered as she sank against the wall. She wrapped her arms around her slim frame.

Henri began reciting in Latin, "They wandered in the wilderness in a desolate way; finding no city to dwell in."

"You speak Latin?" Renée shook her head in wonder, "What were you saying?"

Henri started again, this time in French. "Hungry and thirsty, their soul fainted within them. Then they cried to the Lord in their trouble. . . . And he delivered them from their distresses."

He sat down beside her; side by side they sat. "He led them by a straight way till they reached a city to dwell in."

He stopped and looked back up the trail before continuing, "O that man would give thanks to the Lord for His goodness and for his wonderful works."

Renée studied him a moment, then shook her head. "But will he deliver me?"

Henri pushed off from the wall and stood up. "I do not know why you ran away, or why your mother is your enemy, or why Sieur de Bixmarch's flag is alarming. You have told me nothing. I am just your servant, your stable boy, and I have no place asking, but if you might tell me I could possibly assist you more."

She rubbed her lips with her sleeve several times and then turned away. "No, no, I cannot."

Henri waited for her to continue, but she said nothing. He began to unsaddle the horses. She stood up and tentatively walked over to where he worked.

"It is too disgraceful, too wicked." Her words came hard. "You are just a stable boy. . . what do you know?" She gave him an odd, quizzical look. "What do you know of the world? What do you know of. . . . "

Henri laid down the saddle. She did not finish but pulled her jacket closer. "I can read you. You are innocent, some would say naive, but I don't say that. I would like to be pure and innocent. Would to God that I were. . . . If I were to tell you why I cannot go to Ayes. . . . You must believe in me." She stopped, looked up at the cliff over her head, then asked rhetorically, "Why should I care what a stable boy thinks?" Fastening her green eyes on him she added, "But I do. Stupid as it is, nevertheless it is so; I need you to believe in me, Henri, stable boy."

Henri watched her. Such complexity he could not understand. She was right though; even having traveled extensively with his father he was an innocent. Deceit, calumny, though they surrounded him, had passed him by. He knew people lied. He had seen his father betrayed. He knew that all were sinners, but it had not blotted him, nor really even touched him. He focused on the beauty of the earth; that was where he wanted to live, seeing beauty as he found it: the beauty of the waters on the bay, the beauty of horses as they ran in the fields, the beauty of a flower closing in the evening, even, yes—in fact more than he realized—even the beauty of Renée, even as she stood hugging herself. In fact, as he looked on her, tears forming on her pale cheeks, he thought he had never seen anyone quite as pretty as her.

"You will believe in me, won't you?"

"Yes, I promise."

She looked at him. "Henri, stable boy, I believe you. You have told me you will never forsake me, and now you tell me you will believe in me. And I have faith in you." She gave him a little smile. "But I still can't tell you."

Chapitre Cinq:
Les Cloches

The bells are ringing, ringing, ringing
From steeple and cathedral singing, singing, singing.
Come worship Him who made the morning;
Come worship Him who made the evening;
Come worship Him, all you your praises bringing.
- Little Henri of Gascony, age five, son of Sir Thommas the Hunter

As the bells of vespers began their melodious tolling over the river town, Henri found himself absorbed with the penitents headed toward mass, his feet traveling on the dusty street. Here, near the center of the city, near the cathedral, the street had widened, and there were open parcels on either side, spots of land where small patches of green were emerging. Above the townsfolk, but below the pinking clouds, he watched two storks flying overhead. He watched them as they flew over the battlements of the castle on the hill and then disappeared behind the tower. The storks returning each spring were a sign of faithfulness. They epitomized the good of the world: the joy of the bells, the clear sky, the first green of leaves on the trees, and the fellowship of mass. In this space of inner calm he almost forgot that he had come into the city to spy for Maiden Renée. She had sent him to go where she could not. She would be recognized, but Henri, a common peasant lad, who would remember him? He was to gain information, and where better to gain it than in the cathedral? Milling among the people as they gathered gossiping and talking, he could learn much. She would wait off the trail outside the town.

The cathedral itself was of Romanesque architecture, centuries old, with rounded ceiling arches and thick walls. Henri entered the massive oak portals and passed up along the left of the nave. Fewer people were near the front—he could never understand why people preferred the back. It was much like many other churches he had seen, not as grandiose as St. Mark's in Venice, or St. Sophia's in Constantinople, but certainly more so than Anwar's little chapel. A canon celebrated the mass.

Back outside the evening was pleasant and people were in no rush to return home. Henri saw one group gesturing toward the castle. He worked his way over near them.

"But who is this Bixmarch?" one questioned.

"Bixmarch is a cousin of our Lady Elaine," a tall, burly man said.

"Cousin? I heard she was his brother," another suggested.

"Really? Brother of Lady Elaine?"

A glover now joined in authoritatively. "Indeed it is so. Sieur de Bixmarch is the brother of Lady Elaine. She sent for him from Germany a few years ago. She bought him several fine pair of gloves from me, and I understand she aided him with some of our men-at-war to join his fight and become Lord of Anwar. They have raped and pillaged many of the surrounding villages. From what I hear he has a great lust for power."

"Which of our fine Christian noblemen do not?"

"None is chaste if it's not necessary."

"That may be true, but he is exceptionally rapacious. Not even Catholic, but a pagan."

"A pagan? Is this true?"

"It is what I have heard, but that should not seem so surprising. The Lady Elaine is no great saint."

Several of the women agreed. "She will burn in hell."

"No doubt, and will take a host of men with her."

The glover spoke again, "So I have heard, but that does not explain why Sieur de Bixmarch's flag flies here. Is he here in the castle?

"No one has seen him, though day before yesterday some strange knights arrived."

"My cousin is a sergeant of the gate," a peasant woman said, "and all he will say is that the seneschal is very upset. Trouble is brewing."

"Whatever her faults, I wish the Lady Elaine were here; at least we would have stability."

"Or the Comte," another offered.

"No, the Comte is worse than useless. He spends too much time at the monastery in prayer and neglects the town, neglects the Lady Elaine, neglects his daughter Maiden Renée, too heavenly to be of any worldly good. He is nothing like the old Comte. Still, I do not think Lady Elaine, when she returns, will make things better. There is a great mischief brewing, and no mistake. I say we will all wish we were living under the days of the old Comte."

"Now on that I can hardily agree."

"And it amazes me that we are agreed on that. He taxed us heavily to build this new castle and did not even demolish the old one."

"True, but that was to preserve us against King Charles's armies."

"Yes indeed, back when we were English."

"And now we are French." They laughed roughly.

"And what will we be next year?"

"We will be townspeople of Ayes."

"'Tis true."

"Still, I feel sorry for the Maiden Renée. To have such a weak and worthless father and mother. . . ."

"If you can call her a mother. . . ." the peasant woman scolded, and with that the group dispersed.

Henri whistled softly to himself. He was beginning to understand Renée's predicament.

He moved toward the gates of the castle, toward the bridge spanning the stream that connected the city to the limestone hill and the castle on its crest. The waters under the bridge passed through the millwheel. As he stepped on the stone archway he looked into the castle. He was surprised; the gates had not been shut. To the contrary, a great deal of activity was occurring: pike men taking positions in the courtyard; guards lighting torches on the bridge sides; archers posting on the wall. Farther back, towards the central tower, knights prepared to mount their horses. Still, they did not have the look of impending war, but rather, they appeared as if they were preparing to receive someone.

By habit Henri studied the horses. These were warhorses, larger and better than any Sieur de Bixmarch had in his herd, probably from the north of France, maybe even from the Ardennes. Without realizing it he approached halfway up the bridge trying to get closer to the horses.

So caught up was he in peering into the castle that the first horses galloping through the town caught him by surprise. It was Sieur de Bixmarch, and Henri had no where to hide. He dropped his head and turned away. Then came Lady Elaine on the best horse of Bixmarch's stable—though nothing like the white mare she had ridden into Anwar—the mare Renée had taken. That must have vexed her. Behind Lady Elaine rode the priest. Though Henri still knew little of why Renée was running away, he did know that if the priest had come something must be seriously amiss. Then came five of Bixmarch's knights. The last rider of the troop was Petro, Bixmarch's Master of the Horse. He recognized Henri; reined his horse for the briefest of moments as he looked between Henri and Bixmarch, now inside the castle, and then touched his finger to his lips, before spurring his horse on, hooves clopping on the stone.

Henri did not watch anymore. Quickly he made his way back through the crowd, heading for the town gate. All the while he realized how close Renée had come to being overtaken. They had only barely escaped. If he had known, they could have ridden faster. He had been in chases with his father, both chasing and being chased. There were things he could have done, if he had only known. Whatever Renée's secret, it clearly disturbed Sieur de Bixmarch.

When he got to the gate he found two of the Anwar men-of-war posted with the guard. In the darkness they probably would not recognize him; still he could not take the chance. He would find another way out. He slipped to a side lane and crossed to the wall. It was not high, and with the darkness deepening Henri scrambled over it and dropped onto the grass. He sprinted downhill to the cover of the trees by the river before stopping to survey the bridge. Would he be able to cross over there? No, it would not do; the guards at the gate were too likely to see him. After a brief hesitation he waded into the river. It was cold. In the middle he swam a little distance before he could get back on his feet. Then he climbed up the bank and onto the road.

De lune au bord des flots dormants
"Lay me down beside the sleeping waters," said the moon one lingering night,
"And I shall send rays, long and glistening, gleaming fingers of silver light
That will guide you cross the stone and path to where she lies a' softly breathing.
Lay me down beside the mountain among the pussy willow blooming,
And I shall illumine with my softening grays the fairest form and face
That dwells among the maiden in all of Aquitaine, Gascony, or France."
- Henri of Anwar

The waxing moon overhead was the only light, and in the darkness it took him a while to find the path that led off the road to Renée. She was pacing back and forth at the base of the limestone cliff, her coat pulled close around her. When she heard his footstep she hid behind a tree until she saw him and then quickly came out.

"Well, what did you find?" she asked eagerly.

Henri did not answer. He looked around their camp and began gathering wood. She was cold. He was cold. And wet. They needed a fire. They were both hungry. He would take care of the necessities first; then they could talk.

"Well? What are you doing?"

"Building a fire. . . drying myself off. . . warming up. I had to swim across the river on the way back. You hungry? I'm starved. You look cold, too. I am going to build a fire, cook something to eat, and take care of the horses. Then we can talk."

"No, you can do that later. What did you find?" She was irritated.

Henri answered calmly, "Maiden Renée, I am your only servant, and I must take care of you and your servant." He started to build the fire.

"All right, but can't you work and talk?"

He paused for a moment, took a deep breath, and answered, "Your mother, the Sieur de Bixmarch, and the Priest of Anwar—they are all in the castle. They arrived while I was there. One of Bixmarch's men spotted me. And. . . there is a pack of unrest in the city, but what can I do? You have told me nothing."

Renée buried her head in her horse's chest, and her shoulders sank with defeat.

"I cannot tell you. Not even you, Henri, stable boy. It is too shaming." She shuttered and wiped her mouth.

Henri rose and came to within a few feet of her. He wanted to hold her, comfort her, but that would be inappropriate for a stable boy.

"Have you been disgraced, Maiden? I may not be a champion, but you have but to say the word and I shall ride and bring honor to your name."

She turned and tried to smile. "You are too good, Henri. I never knew there were people like you in this world." Her green eyes met his. "I believe you would die for me if necessary, and who knows? Maybe it will come to that before this is over. You are too good. Still I cannot tell you. Believe me, I would if I could. I just cannot bear it."

Henri built the fire, cooked the stew, and took care of the horses. Then he made a shelter of pine branches and a soft bed of needles for Renée.

"You will sleep better tonight," he said.

She knelt down and felt the mattress of needles. "Oh this is soft," she said with delight. "Thank you Henri, uncommon stable boy." And she curled up on the bed and quickly fell asleep.

Henri sat by the fire.

In the morning she rose almost cheerful. Henri, having awoken well before her, had caught a couple of trout from the river and had roasted them on the fire.

"May the Lord of heavens add his blessings to what we shall eat." Henri blessed the food and then cut her a piece of fish.

"It is good," she mumbled with a mouthful. "I am a lucky noble. I have only one servant, but he is talented—especially for a simple stable boy."

Henri blushed despite himself.

"I was thinking," Renée continued, "I will go to my father at the monastery. We have never been close, but he cannot refuse to see his daughter, nor can he refuse to help me escape from this great wickedness."

In the distance they heard the baying of hounds.

"Does your father keep hounds at Ayes?" Henri asked in alarm.

"Of course, he has a fine pack."

Henri jumped to his feet. "Then we have to go. Now. Quickly."

Confused, Renée looked around. "What? What are you talking about?"
"The hounds. When my father needed to track someone he would give
the scent to the hounds. I suspect they have given them your scent from
one of your gowns, and it will not take them long to find us here."
"You think so?"
"Indeed I do."
"Oh."
"Put out the fire. I will saddle the horses. We have little time." Henri
worked fast throwing on the saddles and bridling the horses.

The hounds were closing. Henri knew they would quickly pick up the
scent on the road. He had not erased their tracks, and they had camped
only a short distance off the road. But he was quick and strong, and the
horses were soon saddled. With both hands on her waist he lifted Renée
onto the mare, and they rode out onto the road before the hounds were
in sight.

Corps feminin qui tant est tendre
It lures me, O it calls and I can scarcely resist.
Eve, how your flesh is ever before me;
Your legs, your thighs, your wanton breasts—
Woman, from your beauty I must flee
To the sanctuary, where free from you I rest.
- *Abbé Odile of St. Stephen's* (excerpted from his larger work *The Fall of Man)*

They galloped east to the Cistercian Monastery of St. Stephen. Stopping at the top of a hill they looked around. Two teams of oxen were
plowing in the near fields. Behind them lay monks followed, sowing barley. To the right, where the road bore south, was an inn, the Inn of the
Sunrise. To the north was the river lined by plane trees trailing off into
the distance. Beyond the monastery, a copse of ash, cypress, and oak
covered a hill.

The monastery itself was walled. Inside the north wall stood the
cathedral of St. Bridget. Scaffolding supported the nave. They watched
as masons carefully hoisted a large granite block to one of the supporting buttresses. Along the south and west walls of the monastery was the
dormitory, bakery, and library. Beyond the library dozens of buildings
were set up as workshops to aid in the building, and beyond them the
cemetery.

They rode down and dismounted at the open gates. A white cowled
monk met them. He was short with very hairy hands.
"How can I help you children?"
Renée spoke, "I have come to see my father."
"Your father?"

"Yes, Comte Sevestre. I am the Maiden Renée; he is my father."

"Oh," The monk's expression rapidly changed from open friendliness to wariness.

A second monk joined the first. "What is it, Brother Martin? What do they want?"

"They wish to see Comte Sevestre."

"I see." The monk looked at Renée. "So you are the Maiden Renée?"

"Yes."

Speaking to the first monk he commanded, "Stay with them. I will talk to the Abbot. Do not let them in until I return. And it would be better if you were not found talking to her."

"Yes, of course."

Renée handed over the reins of her horse to Henri. "Why can't you talk to me? I don't understand."

But the monk ignored her.

Renée looked blankly at Henri for a moment, and then turning back to the monk she asked, "Is it because I am Renée, or because I am a woman?"

The monk glanced at her agitatedly, and then hissed, "The Abbé has refused to allow any women in the monastery. It is from Eve that sin enters the heart of man." And then he would not speak anymore.

The Abbé came to the gates a few minutes later. He was not tall, but he was imposing; big, black eyebrows and a long, straight nose. His figure, hidden under his white robes, suggested a man of great energy. "Be gone you daughter of a whore, you spawn of the dragon lady, the lady of scarlet adulteries. Be gone and take your sins with you."

Renée was momentarily put off by the invectives pouring from his mouth, but she was determined. "No, I must speak to my father. I am in grave danger. There are those, my mother—the great whore you referred to—who would cast me into a great evil, an unutterable sin. I must appeal to my father to rise from his reveries, his prayers, and deliver me, his child."

The Abbé looked at her intently. Then at Henri. "And you are her servant? Beware, my son. She is of the worst type. Beware of the superficialities of her beauty, her creamy white skin." At that he reached out and stroked her cheek. "For the beauty is that of the skin alone. If men could only see what is underneath the skin of a woman. (It is said that in Bavaria the lynx can do this, can see beneath the skin.) If men could do this, they would find the sight of a woman abhorrent. What are her charms: these pretty eyes, the straight nose, the contour of the breasts, the sway of the hips when she walks? No, no, a woman consists of slime and blood, of wetness and gall. Men are loath to touch the intestines of a slain pig. They cower at the reek of a dead animal lying in the field. If we cannot bring ourselves to touch slime with our fingers, how can we bring ourselves to embrace the dirt bag itself?"

And then, looking back at Renée, he dismissed her. "Be gone. Go to the inn over on yonder hill. I will talk with your father, for he is here. If he will see you, he shall come, but no woman, even one like you—half girl, half woman—shall enter these gates. Indeed, your presence has already caused disharmonic disturbance to the monastery. Only prayers can hope to assuage the passions aroused at just seeing a woman such as you. Now go. Go away."

Turning to the two brothers who were with him, he commanded the gate to be shut.

The two travelers turned; discouraged, they crossed the valley and rode up the hill to the Inn of the Sunrise. When Renée identified herself—though they had no money—the innkeeper gladly sat them at his best table and brought out a board of steaming food: duck steak cooked with garlic, pepper and wild herbs, bean stew, and cherry tarts. It was better than anything either had eaten in sometime, and they ate heartily. They ate and waited, and waited, and waited.

Towards evening a lay brother from the monastery finally arrived. "Your father grieves to hear you are in distress but is unable to help; he is under a vow not to see a woman for a year and a day."

"Is that it?" Renée was dismayed.

"That is all. It is all I was told," the messenger replied, shrugged apologetically, and then left.

"What shall I do, Henri? If I could only see my father, I am certain I could convince him. What they have proposed would horrify him; it would arouse even him to action."

She buried her head in her hands, her long hair falling to the table, her white gown stained through days of travel. Such a slip of a girl, and so young.

"I have no one, Henri, no one. Where shall I go? What shall I do? How can I live?" She shuddered.

Henri stared at the fire for a moment, and then suggested, "Write a note to him."

"Write? With what shall I write? I don't know how to write."

"I can write a little," Henri answered. "You speak and I will write."

"You know how to read and write? French or Latin?"

"Both," Henri replied.

Renée shook her head in amazement. "You are indeed an uncommon stable boy, Henri of Anwar. But for you to write, I must tell you. . . tell you everything. . . and it really, truly is. . . awful. Will you believe me, and what will you think of me?" She stopped and looked at the fire burning in the stone hearth. A log fell and sparks flew out. "Your loyalty and devotion have been rare for me, and I am afraid, afraid that you who are so good will shrink from the foulness in which I have grown up.

I am afraid you will despise me." She rose abruptly and walked away from the fire into the darkness. "Why should I care what a stable boy thinks? I don't know; but the fact is I do care; I care very much."

Chapitre Six:
Une Femelle sans Defaut

It wavers not. It blooms for thee,
Unwrapped and scented fragrant be;
The bush of white, the thorns of rose
Arise from dirt, from filth bestow;
Its bud it grows upon red branch
All pure, all perfect, spotless, blanche.
For whom does the rose bloom?
The rose it blooms, it blooms for thee.
- Sir Henri at Cairns.

"But I see I must tell." She sighed. "I need to start at the beginning. You will never understand, unless I start at the beginning. See, my mother is, or rather she is not of nobility; that is to say, she is the daughter of a Bavarian tanner, a peasant girl, a simple peasant girl, she and her brother."

Henri raised his eyebrows.

"You look surprised. Most people are," Renée continued. "Nevertheless it is true; for all her beauty, she was villein born.

"It happened like this. My grandfather, the Comte Raymond, was returning from the crusades with a companion in arms. They stopped in Bavaria on the eve of All Saints and joined in the festivities. My mother was a vestal virgin. She led the parade, dressed in only a white gauzy gown. Grandfather, like so many men before and afterwards, was captivated by her."

Henri had seen those festivals. In many cases the young virgins were scantily clad; in some cases they were stark naked. The church frowned on this hedonism, but it had been powerless to halt it.

Renée continued, "But Grandfather Raymond did not take her for a mistress. He was a devout man. He brought her home as a present, to be my father's bride.

"It was fortunate, or unfortunate, that I was conceived in the first month, because the marriage was doomed. My mother was ambitious and had a sharp tongue. She was driven by lust: for power, for riches, for fame. She had neither tolerance nor patience for those unlike her. My father, on the other hand, was sensitive, a peace lover, and content to let things lay. Consequently my mother scorned him. As long as Comte Raymond lived, however, her bitterness was checked—my grandfather had a tremendous will.

"To escape, my father turned to hunting—long sojourns into the forest. He was gone a lot, but that too was folly, for my mother took advantage of an empty castle, consolidating her power using any means available— you saw my mother; she has ample means. And if he returned empty handed, which was not uncommon—my father was not a great warrior or huntsman—she mocked him. The knights who went with my father often played into her hands, supplying her with amusing stories of his follies in the field. You really have to watch my mother turn on the charms. She manipulates all toward her plans.

"Some of my earliest memories as a child were watching my mother make a fool of my father. I could not understand it at the time, and I probably tried to break up a few fights, but I soon saw that was futile.

"When Grandfather died, my father tried to apply himself to the management of the holdings, but my mother had already undermined him. Several powerful knights were ex-lovers, and she had a not-so-secret affair with the steward.

"Then my father made friends with the Abbot Odile. The Abbé is a man of strong will and could not be seduced by my mother. My father relied on the Abbé, and that balanced the power. Unfortunately for the estate, my father spent more and more time at St. Stephen's.

"Through all this I have been a spectator. My mother was never interested in me. I did not exist in her eyes. My grandfather looked after me while he lived, and my father would occasionally call me to his side before I began to mature, but as I have grown out of childhood he has distanced himself. He became very uncomfortable with me around and was unwilling to talk. I have not seen him in six months.

"It all came to a crisis when my father suggested he might relinquish his title and take up the cowl. Whether he would bequeath the title to me or give the properties to the church was uncertain; still, it sent my mother into hysterics. She knew the Abbot, and if the church took the land she would be put out, possibly even sent to a convent."

Renée smiled. "My mother in a convent? That is a strange thought indeed." She stopped for a moment and looked around the room. They were nearly alone, seated at the table before the fire; evening lights were fading outside. She looked at Henri across the table, listening intently. Listening to her like few had ever done. It was good to have a devoted servant. She looked out the window. "You know that Sieur de Bixmarch is my mother's brother. She brought him to Anwar several years ago. She supplied him and his men with horse and arms. I was only five when he first came. I never liked him. He was crude, cruel, and unchivalrous, but my mother has always been very fond of him— probably the only person she is truly fond of."

"I had heard Sieur de Bixmarch was Lady Elaine's brother, but I would have never believed it," Henri interrupted. "She is so beautiful, and he is so. . . ."

"Coarse?" Renée supplied the word.

"Yes, although I would have said ugly," Henri agreed.

Renée nodded. "Exactly as he is on the inside. My mother, on the other hand, is beautiful, but inwardly she is. . . I know it is awful to say of one's own mother, but she is filled with hate, deceit, unrest, and bitterness. But now. . .now I come to the horrible part." She shuddered.

"I did not know why my mother wanted to go to Anwar, or why she insisted I go. It was shock enough that she spoke to me, but to invite me to ride with her! And she even tried to charm me, so gracious, so winning, such a delightful smile. She had never done that before, not to me, never. I did not trust her, but I did not imagine the depths of evil they wanted to drag me into." Renée's voice dropped very low. "My mother had decided that her brother should be the next Comte d'Ayes. That is to say, I should be his bride."

Henri's jaw dropped. "Incest? That would be incest. The church would never sanction such a marriage."

Renée dropped her head in shame.

He lowered his voice to a whisper. "What happened?"

"At the feast at Anwar, when I first left the room to return to my chambers, he came after me. He grabbed me in his arms and kissed me. . .kissed me on the lips." She shuddered with revulsion at the thought. "I slapped him and ran out of the room before he could catch me—I am very fast. He quickly gave up the chase, and I went to my mother's chambers. As little as she has cared for me, still I thought this would enrage her. I waited for her on the bed. I did not have to wait long before I heard her coming, with *him.* I hid behind the tapestry.

"As they entered he was laughing coarsely. 'A spirited thing your daughter. She slapped me.'

"My mother was not as pleased, 'Of course she slapped you, but you let her get away. Tonight was to be the night. We could say it was under the intoxication of the feast and impulse.'

"'Do not worry sister, tonight I will marry her. How far can she run? This is not a big castle like Ayes. And you are sure the priest will perform the ceremony?'

"'Absolutely. I have the most wicked of priests. He is the most dissolute man I have ever met, and I know all of his secrets. He will do as I say.'"

Renée stifled a sob. "And there I am afraid I broke down. Learning of my horrible fate, and how my own mother would sacrifice me, I let out a sob.

"'What have we behind your tapestry, sister?' Sieur de Bixmarch said getting up from the bed.

"'Has she been in here the whole time?'

"Sieur de Bixmarch's heavy boots stepped toward my hidden position on the wall. I fled out of the room and back to the great room.

"'I shall go bring her back if I have to carry her.'

"'Don't be a fool,' Lady Elaine cautioned. 'If you are seen forcing her, not even a dissolute priest can protect you.'

"So I came back to the great room and stayed there trusting he would do nothing in front of the others, and that is where you watched over me, though you did not know it at the time." Renée stopped and looked at Henri with thankfulness.

Henri sat motionless for a moment and then quietly said, "He is my refuge and my fortress, my God, in whom I trust. Surely he will save you from your uncle's snare. He will cover you with his feathers, and under his wings you will find refuge; his faithfulness will be your shield and buckler. You will not fear the night terrors, nor the arrow that flies by day, nor the pestilence that stalks in the darkness, nor the plague that wastes at noon. A thousand may fall at your side, ten thousand at your right hand, but it will not come near you. He will command his angels concerning you to guard you in all your ways; 'Because she loves me,' says the LORD, 'I will rescue her, I will protect her because she knows me. She will call upon me, and I will answer her. I will be with her in trouble. I will rescue her and honor her."

"Thank you Henri, truly the most uncommon of stable boys." And a tear fell from her eye which she did not wipe away. "But now that you know, am I not defiled in your eyes?"

Henri did not look at her. "When I was young a gardener came often to the stables and filled his wagon with horse manure. He spread it around his plants. One spotlessly white rose in particular caught my attention. Its fragrance was like none other. I marveled at it; how out of the dung sprang flowers, how out of the dung came such loveliness." He stopped and looked at her. "You are that rose."

Renée, holding back a sob, looked to the fire. "That is what I want. O Henri, that is what I want. I only wish I could."

La parole subsistera

And the word? The word stands.
It stands alone; it will not sit
Nor idle be when there is action for
To accomplish on this earth. Who
Will listen? Who will take his fill?
Of each page, given from above
Until they raise arms aloft to swell
Heaven's court and eat the unleavened
Bread, guaranteed by the stricken Christ's head.

*- Abbot Odile of St Stephen's (*excerpted from his larger work
Trinitarium)

Returning to the monastery the following morning, Henri dismounted
from the gelding and then helped Renée off the mare. He handed the
reins to a monk who guided the horses to the stables. At the gates Henri
presented his sheets; another monk took them and gave Henri a look of
mild surprise. "You wrote these?"

Henri nodded. The monk left. He passed along the east cloister by the
kitchen and then to the library. Henri watched him cross the courtyard
until he slipped in a door. It seemed like an hour before the monk
reemerged. With him now was another monk, an older, taller, thinner
monk. This second monk tapped the rolled parchment in his palm as he
approached.

"I am Brother Matthew." He said with both authority and friendliness.
"You wrote this?"

"Yes," Henri replied.

"Your Latin is good, and your writing is exquisite. What is your name?"

"They call me Henri."

"Henri? That is it?"

Renée drew closer to the gate to hear the conversation.

"I am a stable boy."

"And you write like this?" Brother Matthew looked from Henri to the
Maiden Renée. He had a grizzled gray and black beard. His eyes were
deeply set and intelligent. "Good morning to you, Maiden Renée."

Returning his gaze to Henri, he questioned, "Do you have no other
name? Who taught you letters?"

"My father, good sir."

"I am no sir; I am a monk; but then who is your father?" He did not
wait to hear the answer. "Come along with me. The Abbé will speak with
you."

Henri glanced over his shoulder at Renée and then followed the
brother along the smooth stone-covered walk. As he walked, he
observed the monastery. Across the courtyard the workers were climbing
the scaffolding. Just south of the bell tower, the sun was rising. Out of
the cathedral's open doors Henri could hear the choir chanting. Then
there were the aromas of the kitchen: the smell of fresh baked bread
and meat pies. They passed on to the library. Before they went in, Henri
glanced beyond. The walk divided in three directions: to the dormitories,
to another chapel, and to the workshops for the cathedral. There were
shops for the woodcarvers, metalworkers, stone masons, and glass-
makers. The place bustled with activity.

Inside the library they followed a long hallway. Small scriptoriums on
either side were occupied by monks carefully copying texts. Brother

Matthew, noting Henri's attention, commented, "It is the Abbot Odile's ambition to make our small monastery an important place of pilgrimage like the Church of St. Sernin. He is energetic, filled with ecstasies and mysticism and widely read: Aristotle, Platinus, Thomas of Aquinas, Dominic, Hildebrandt, Gerson de Paris, Bernard de Clairvaux. He can quote extensively from any of them. He writes incessantly. Already his writings fill fifteen quarto volumes, all proofread, improved, indexed, and illuminated. During every activity, whether dressing, or undressing, he is in prayer. Many a time he has quoted the entire Psalms. After midnight mass, when others go to rest he remains awake. He is strong, and his body can withstand most anything. He says he has an iron head and a copper stomach. In fact he will sometimes eat spoiled food by choice, such as wormy butter, cherries partially consumed by snails. He hangs over-salted herrings out to rot. He would rather eat food that stinks than that which is too salty.

"He is a great man. No one has experienced the Four Last Things as he has, and it is because of him that our monastery has prospered. For example we are now fortunate to have several relics brought back by Comte Raymond on his Holy Crusade. We have a shard of the alabaster box that Mary Magdalene used to anoint Our Lord's feet; we have a small portion of Peter's net that he used as a fisherman; but our most Holy Relic is one of our Lord's baby teeth."

Henri nodded, though his father had taught him to be skeptical of relics.

They paused before a door at the end of the hall. Brother Matthew placed his hand on Henri's broad shoulder. "Before we go in let me talk to you. What do you know of the Maiden Renée, the Lady Elaine, and Comte Sevestre?"

"She told me some of the story yesterday."

"And then you wrote this down."

"That is correct."

"Is she speaking the truth in what you wrote?"

"I believe so."

Brother Matthew shook his head sadly. "Hideous to think her own mother would stoop so low. Unfortunate, but probably too true. She has sold her soul to the devil. Bavarians are known for their sorcery. She is doomed and will suffer forever in hell for this. We live in a wicked day. But tell me more of yourself. You were reluctant to speak in front of her, I could see, but it is unheard of for a peasant taught by a villein father to know Latin. There is more to you."

Henri nodded. "If you would know, my father was no peasant. He was Thommas de Bretagne, also known as Sir Thommas the Hunter."

"Sir Thommas ? Of Brittany? Yes, I did hear of him. . . ." He paused and put his hand to his forehead. "We had a troubadour pass through here three months ago. He was looking for news of this Sir Thommas. The troubadour was from Brittany. . . ." Brother Matthew looked gravely back at Henri. "But you are a stable boy, now. Your father is dead then? And your mother?"

Henri bit his lip. "Yes."

"The son of Sir Thommas a stable boy?"

Henri shuffled his feet and looked down to the floor. "After my father died I. . . I really. . . I really cannot remember much about those weeks. They are lost to me, a dense fog. You see my father and I were very close, and I was unprepared. I must have just wandered. I remember being robbed and beaten up at least twice, but even those memories are dim. I ended up in a stable. The stable master and his wife were kind, so I stayed."

"And what is your relationship with the Maiden?"

"I have sworn an oath of allegiance to her, whatever befalls her. . . ."

"I see. In appearance a stable boy, in your blood a noble, and you will be her knight-bachelor: gallant, honest, a true Christian knight. You know, of course, your father's lineage descended from Sir Lancelot?" A pleasant smile came to the monk's face.

Henri replied, "Yes, my father mentioned it once."

"Once?" Brother Matthew raised an eyebrow.

"Well, maybe more than once." At that Henri laughed.

"But as for this," Brother Matthew tapped the rolled sheets on Henri's shoulder. "I am not sure what the Abbot will do. Your cause is good, but what is best? Abbé Odile is farsighted. He perspicuously sees difficulties others do not."

"For the sake of my Maiden, help us," Henri pleaded. "Do not leave her in the treacherous hands of her mother and uncle."

"No. Your words were effective. I have not seen the Abbé so distraught except when someone suggested the Pope should leave Avignon. He is a godly man, a true man of the church; he will shield her from Sieur de Bixmarch's hands."

"But what of her father, Comte Sevestre? You talk only of the Abbé as if the Comte will have nothing to do with her. Is he impotent? Will he not rise and defend his daughter?"

Brother Matthew shook his head understandingly. "To be sure. The Comte has been informed. He has read your sheet. You must understand, however, that he is outmatched by the Comtess, always was; he leans heavily on the Abbé."

"Then her fate hangs with the Abbé."

"Quite right." With that Brother Matthew opened the door and ushered Henri in.

It was a large room filled with numerous leather volumes both on shelves and on tables. There were barred windows on the far side, and a fireplace to the right. Straight ahead the Abbé sat at a large chair engaged in deep deliberations with several monks. To the left another cluster of monks sat on benches copying sheets. At the far end beneath a window sat a monk dressed in more than the standard white cowl. It was trimmed with fur, and his boots were large, leather, riding boots. Henri surmised correctly this was Comte Sevestre, Renée's father.

Henri curiously studied him. He was a good looking man, well toned, and this surprised Henri. He had pictured him effete, weak of eye, bone, and manner. As he looked, however, he saw much of the Maiden Renée in him. Still, Henri could not understand how the Comte had not immediately risen to defend his daughter. Henri intended to energize the Comte.

But Brother Matthew led Henri to the Abbé Odile instead. "This is the author of this morning's message, Reverend Father."

Marking his place with a red ribbon, the Abbé shut the book he had been working on and surveyed Henri. Taking the sheet from Brother Matthew, he laid it down, straightened the corners, picked up a pen, and reread it, occasionally correcting the grammar in the margins. Then he rolled it up and handed it to Brother Matthew.

Brother Matthew took it and then said, "Our stable boy here is really the son of Sir Thommas de Bretagne, Sir Thommas the Hunter."

"Indeed? Sir Thommas de Bretagne? Did we not have a minstrel come through here in the winter mentioning Sir Thommas ?"

"Yes, Reverend Father," the monk replied.

Then the Abbé turned to Henri and switched to Breton. It had been some time since Henri had heard his native language so beautifully spoken. Instantly floods of memories that he had long forgotten came rushing in: memories of his mother, the softness of her hand as she stroked his face, the smell of her hair as she leaned over to kiss him while he lay in bed, the rustle of her skirt, and the music of her voice as she talked with his father late into the evening while he tried to sleep, the pair speaking in this ancient Celtic tongue.

"You come as a stable boy in disguise, when you are really a child of nobles. You write like the best of my monks and carry yourself as one who was well raised. You are a handsome lad, and she is pretty. Do you wear no mottoes of love?"

"I am not her lover, but her servant," Henri replied in Breton.

The Abbé nodded approvingly, and then quoted,

"To wear mottoes of love for one's lady
  Or to wear blue is no proof,
But to serve her with a perfectly loyal heart
  And no others, and to keep her from blame.
. Love lies in that, not in wearing blue,
  But it may be that many think

To cover the offense of falsehood under a tombstone
　　By wearing blue."

He stood up and walked over to the fire and warmed his hands a moment. He spoke again, but now he had returned to French. "This is a very insidious plot, even for Lady Elaine. Do you believe it?" he asked, looking not at Henri but toward the Comte. The Comte did not respond.

"She is the spawn of the devil, to be sure," the Abbé continued. "I have read in Chastellain a story about Duc Philip the Good. He used to marry off his knights to unmarried daughters of the villein class. At one time he met a stubborn resistance from a Lille brewer who refused to consent to such an arrangement. So the Duc kidnapped her. But the brewer moved lock, stock, and barrel to Tournay, where outside of the Duc's territory he could present his case before Parliament in Paris. But he reaped only failure and ill health. The mother then came and pled her case before the Duc. He mocked her and humiliated her, but finally he acceded to her wish and gave her back her daughter." The black brows of the Abbé lifted. "But the Maiden Renée does not have such a mother or father, does she, Henri?"

Henri wondered at this comment spoken in Sevestre's presence. Was it intended to be a backstab, or was it to motivate the Comte from his inaction? Or was it just to prove to the Comte how much he relied upon and needed the Abbé?

"So the question is what to do? She came here hoping to awaken her father from his torpor; hoping her great need would arouse him to be a father to her, which he has never been before." The Abbé stopped and looked at the Comte before returning to Henri. "But you see that is impossible. He has taken a vow not to see a woman for a day and a year. He has made this oath freely before God. So what is to be done? He can do nothing; even though his heart cries to spring forth to action. . . ."

Henri looked back at the Comte. There was nothing that suggested a heart crying and longing to spring forth to action. If anything he was more despondent than before.

"Now *we* could rise and fight Sieur de Bixmarch. The monastery has fighting men at its disposal. But. . . ." And the Abbé began pacing back and forth across the room as he talked. "We do not have the resources to fight Sieur de Bixmarch while he is entrenched in Ayes. Our fighting men are not well armed, nor well trained. We would have to train for war, and war is expensive. And as such it is not in the best interest of the monastery. The monastery will achieve greatness and its place in the earth by becoming great in the sight of God."

"But you must do something," Henri burst forth. "You cannot as a man of God allow this great wickedness to happen. Nor can you, Comte Sevestre!" Henri started across the room toward the Comte.

Brother Matthew stepped in front of him. "Be still, Henri. Let the Abbé speak."

But Henri kept speaking. "Must the innocent die in this way, the big wolves filling their bellies with ill-gotten gain, stolen corn, grain? The peasants by hundreds and thousands die each day, spill their blood, spoil their bones—they who till the soil by the sweat of their toil. Will God not hear their cry, hear the humble, and hear the poor people, hear their spirits cry? Will he not bring vengeance and woe to those lords, who denied justice and withheld mercy?"

"Be still, Henri," the Abbé said. "I recognize the quotation. Be assured we will not allow this wickedness, though you now see for yourself that we cannot do as she wishes. Her father will not rise to help her."

At that moment a monk burst into the room. "The watchers have seen a troop of knights approaching by the road from Ayes. They are riding rapidly."

Chapitre Sept
Au dessous du sol

Comes their worm-moistened earth sprinkling down
Upon the winter white face so pale;
Falls their clay and lime, dirt shoveling down
To surround and cover the head so still;
In that sunset hour, when laid deep in the ground
There shall be no thought of You filling
Me, as gently now, lay me down, lay me down.
The Duchess de Bretagne

"That would be Sieur de Bixmarch," Henri exclaimed. "Maiden Renée! She is outside the gates. They will take her." And he ran out of the room, turned right in the hallway, and out the door of the library. Brother Matthew and the Abbé trailed behind him. The Abbé and Brother Matthew climbed the stairs of the wall as Henri ran out the gate.

Renée was resting against the wall. She jumped to her feet at Henri's hurried arrival.

"Sieur de Bixmarch is coming," he said quickly. "We must get the horses and flee."

"But what of my father?"

Henri did not stop to explain. "We must hurry."

Having scanned the column of horses, Brother Matthew called down, "Henri, you have no time to escape. I can see the troop; they will be here in five minutes. You must seek shelter in the monastery; you and the Maiden Renée; you have no time to escape." Brother Matthew descended the steps two at a time. "Follow me."

Renée looked up at the Abbé. He did not return her look. If he did not see her enter it would be easier on his conscience to allow a woman in the monastery. Henri ushered Renée ahead of him and then followed closely behind, watching nervously over his shoulder.

Brother Matthew led them past the dining hall and into the kitchen. The monks looked at her in surprise and then back at Brother Matthew with wonderment. "Her danger is great," he said as he passed through the bakery and stuffed them in a pantry closet. "Stay here. I will come for you." He closed the door.

The room was dim. The only light came streaming through shutters above them. After their eyes adjusted they could see it was filled with barrels of food on the ground, hanging herbs, small bottles of ground spices on the shelves, bags of onions in the corners, large clay pots filled with oil, and bags of rye, barley, and wheat.

They settled down beside each other on the burlap bags of neatly stacked wheat.

"So what did happen?" she whispered.

Henri told her about his interview with the Abbé and about seeing her father.

"You saw him? Will he help me?"

"No." Henri still had not come to terms with his bewilderment. Comte Sevestre's unwillingness even to see Renée was unfathomable, completely beyond his scope of experience. He had never known anything like it. His father, Sir Thommas, had been so different. Sir Thommas had kept Henri by his side from the time of his mother's death; had always wanted Henri by his side; would have ridden through a storm of arrows to rescue his son. Henri had always known that, but here was the father of Maiden Renée unwilling to see his daughter, even when she desperately needed him.

He could feel her shoulders sag. "Quite a pair of parents I have, wouldn't you say. . . stable boy?"

Henri had no answer.

"So what am I to do? My hope is sinking."

"The Abbé said he would help," Henri said, trying to encourage her.

"Did he?" She was skeptical.

"Yes, but we got interrupted before he told me his plan."

"Well, we shall see." Renée was tentative. "You do not know the Abbé as I do. My hope was in my father."

At that the door swung open. It was Brother Matthew.

"Come quickly. You are not safe here. They found your horses in the stables. Sieur de Bixmarch is searching the monastery. He thinks you are in the basilica and is searching there. Men-of-war defiling the church! What blasphemy! Follow me."

As they wound back through the kitchen Brother Matthew explained the plan. "The Abbé will place the maiden in the safety of a remote convent. He sent a messenger to the leader of our order. We should have a mounted escort assembled by nightfall two days from hence. In the meantime I will show you the entrance to a secret tunnel, which opens into a small wood not far from the monastery. There is a hidden little cabin. Stay there."

They had wound their way back to the kitchen entrance. Brother Matthew peeked out the door. None of Sieur de Bixmarch's men were in sight.

"See that door across the courtyard, just past the library, the one painted black? That leads to the wine cellar, the tunnel starts from there."

He looked doubtfully at Renée. "I hope you can run."

"I can," She replied as she gathered her dress above her knees. The monks averted their eyes.

"We shall see," he replied none to certain. Then, after another quick look, he opened the door and bolted out. "Let's go," he called out over his shoulder.

It might have been better to have asked Henri if he could run, because Renée sprinted rapidly past both of them and into the room. When the door was shut safely behind them, Brother Matthew patted her on the shoulder. "You *can* run," he said. Henri said nothing.

Brother Matthew cracked the door open and looked out again. "I don't think anyone saw us." He smiled in relief. Then he led them down a ladder and into a dimly lit wine cellar. Big oak kegs filled the room in five rows. Moving to the back of the room, Brother Matthew came to the last barrel. Manipulating a concealed hinge mechanism, he swung it open. Inside it was empty and pitch-black.

Renée looked apprehensively at Henri and then at Brother Matthew. She swallowed hard before crawling in. "I don't like this. I don't like this." She stopped and slid quickly back out. "I can't do it. It is too dark, too small." But at that moment they heard heavy boot steps on the stairway.

"Quick. In," Brother Matthew urged. Henri ducked and went in first, followed by Renée, then Brother Matthew, who pulled the barrel door shut behind him. They started crawling and quickly left the wood of the keg. The tunnel dirt felt cold and damp. It was too low for anything but crawling; too narrow except to go single file. Hand after hand, knee after knee. Hand after hand, knee after knee, on and on.

"Mary, mother of God, be with us now and in the hour of our need," Renée repeated over and over.

"Watch out; there are some rocks," Henri warned. Renée tried to avoid them, but her dress caught and tore.

"How much farther?" Her voice was desperate and small.

"I don't know. It's pitch-black."

Henri bumped his head into one of the support posts, and some dirt fell from the ceiling.

Renée gasped. "It's collapsing!" But when the dirt settled, it had not been much.

Henri pushed forward.

"O, I cannot go anymore. I can't stand this."

"Come, Renée," Henri urged.

She steeled herself and forced herself on, suppressing her panic as best she could.

The tunnel got smaller. They had to wiggle on their stomachs.

"This does go through, doesn't it?" Henri asked Brother Matthew.

"O, yes, of course it does. . . Though I must admit no one has been through it in a couple of years."

"Sweet Jesu, have mercy on me," Renée whimpered as she slid. "Now I know what the pits of hell are like. I shall be so glad to see sunlight again." As she said that her knee scraped across a razor sharp rock. She heard the ripping of her dress, and reaching down to her knee she could feel the sticky warmth of blood. "I cannot go on; I am going back." She started to scoot back and bumped into Brother Matthew.

Henri pressed on. The tunnel opened a little. He stretched his hand to the ceiling and then carefully to either side. He could not stand upright, but if he bent he was able to get off his knees.

"Maiden, just a little farther. I can almost stand." He tried to sound cheerful.

"We are certainly more than halfway," Brother Matthew encouraged.

Renée stopped her backward slide and took several deep breaths. "All right, I shall continue," she said, mostly to herself, and started struggling forward. When she got to where Henri was, she stood up and felt around her.

Henri kept leading the way, warning of rocks or stones. He could feel the earth beginning to warm and the soil becoming dryer. "We are nearly there." He stopped and Renée stumbled into him, holding onto him to regain her balance. Henri felt all around him; it seemed to be a dead-end. "We have reached the end of the tunnel. What now?"

"Reach above you and push on the wood," Brother Matthew answered.

Henri braced himself in a squat and then gave a large shove, and the covering slid off. He pulled himself through the hole and then, grabbing Renée by both forearms, delivered her. Brother Matthew came out stiffly behind them.

They were in a small cabin. Looking out the windows they could see only dense brush and cypress trees. Inside there was a fireplace, a table, several chairs, a cot, and beside the cot a trunk on the far wall. Opposite the fireplace was the door.

"You've cut yourself," Henri said with concern, looking at Renée's hands and knees, "And your dress. . . ."

Renée looked at her once white dress, now torn and caked with blood and mud, all the fine patterns woven into the material obliterated by grime. What had once been an exquisite dress of nobility had been reduced to rags. She sank onto a chair with sobs.

"There, there now, child," Brother Matthew patted her on the shoulder. "We must not worry about our clothes. Cannot he who clothed the lily in its splendor also take care of you?"

But that piety did not comfort Renée. She was tired. She was cold and hungry. She was in pain and scared. She had been forsaken by her father, and now her dress. Brother Matthew, not knowing what else to do, withdrew his hand and motioned for Henri to join him on the cot. They sat down together.

"Abbé Odile will see that she is safe. He is making arrangements for her to be taken to a convent. It will be for the best. If Comte Sevestre, her father, willed her the estate she would be no match for Lady Elaine and Sieur de Bixmarch. That is obvious. Lady Elaine would make her life miserable—if not with Sieur de Bixmarch, then with a hundred other devious plots. The Lady is a wicked woman. For the maiden to be safe she must find shelter elsewhere. Many young maidens in similar situations have found safety in the convents, and of course it is not necessary for her to become a nun, though she may choose that if she wishes. She is young, but already she is learning much about the way of a man with a woman. I would think being a nun would be a very attractive alternative for her." Brother Matthew patted the cot. "As I said, you stay here. There is some food stored on the shelves. There is wood stacked out back, and a spring within a few feet. And. . . ."

At that Brother Matthew arose and opened the trunk. "Do you know how to use this?" He pulled out a sword and scabbard.

Henri nodded. "My father gave me many lessons."

Brother Matthew then pulled out a leather breast plate. "Wear this as well. This cabin is hidden, and I don't think you will be found. Still. . . ."

"Thank you," Henri took the armor.

"And as for you Henri, stable boy, when your charge is safely in the convent, come back to the monastery. We need a gallant knight. We have swordsmen and archers but are in need of a captain. You could become that."

Henri smiled noncommittally. "We shall see how the Lord leads."

Brother Matthew placed both of his hands on Henri's shoulders and squeezed. "Never better spoken."

With that Brother Matthew slid himself back into the hole. "It is a long tunnel, and I do not relish crawling through it again, but I must go or I will be missed." In parting he added, "God bless you, my daughter,"

While Renée sat huddled and sniffling, Henri recovered the hole and then brought in kindling and started a fire. He found the larders of food: dried meat, peas, flour. He cleaned off her hand wound in a basin and bound it with cloth. Then arranging the cot near the fire, he suggested she rest while he surveyed the surrounding lands.

Surrounded by shrubs of myrtle and broom, and hidden by cypress and mountain ash, the cabin was sheltered from view. Even if it could be seen, a simple cabin would not cause suspicion. He made his way through to the edge of the small woods. The monastery walls were nearly a quarter mile away across an open field. He turned back, explored through the woods, and found the springs.

When he returned, Renée was sitting on the doorstep. She looked small and fragile, her beautiful hair now all matted, her face still caked with dirt, her dress tattered and torn. She looked more like a chambermaid than a noble heiress.

Henri relayed the plans Brother Matthew had given.

When he finished she wrung her hands together and looked over at the myrtle hedge. "I am not going to a convent. The Abbé says he wants to preserve my life, but what he really wants is me out of the way. He wants Ayes. It would provide a nice income for St. Stephens, but I will not be put away. I will not spend the rest of my life locked up in a convent."

"It would be safer, Maiden Renée."

"I would rather die."

Henri admired her grit. "So what will you do?"

"I don't know. I must hide. I must find someplace beyond the reach of my mother and Sieur de Bixmarch, and probably beyond the Abbé as well."

"There is a little hidden village about two to three days south from here. My father and I lived there for a couple years. You could hide there."

"Take me there."

Dans l'ombre

From the shadows ever growing, gray and black and flicker swaying,
Came she down the nightlane passing, on her warhorse nicker saying,
'Death's hooded figures are pressed close in darkness hiding.
Beware the reaper's bloody scythe this dread night, when moon has set
Below the 'rizon and all is black; beware the front, beware the back,
Lest he catch you unawares, sever head, and dump you sack.
This I warn you—though it does no good—destiny will not let
You slip its noose when first it's gathered its fattened goose.
Still I am the nightlane rider; all is not lost while I am loose,
With quick feet and clever mind, still we may defeat his ruse.'

- Henri of Anwar

First, however, they needed their horses, and that presented a difficulty. If they crossed the fields in the daylight they would be seen. On the other hand, if they waited for nightfall the gates would be closed. The only option—much to Renée's dismay—was back through the tunnel. Henri suggested they wait in the cellar until the midnight matins. By that time Bixmarch would be well on his way, and the monks would be in the cathedral. They might be able to untie the horses and slip out with much less attention.

Thus, despite her dread, Renée readied herself. Looking at her torn dress, and seeing the cuts on her hands and knees, however, she first took Henri's knife and ripped her dress to just above the knees. Then she tore the garment scraps into strips which she bound around her palms and knees. Henri tried to avoid looking at her legs, though he thought they were very well-formed.

Back in the hole they crawled through the darkness, resting, wondering again at how far it seemed. Finally they reached wood and came to the wine barrel door. Henri favored remaining in the barrel until later in the night, but Renée, certain she would suffocate, could not bear that. They cracked open the keg door and huddled up between two of the kegs until they heard the bells for the matins.

As the bells rang, they slipped up the stairs and looked out. The moon had set. It was dark. Keeping close to the wall, they passed through the courtyard like shadowless wraiths. If they could avoid being seen they would have a couple of days head start on a search. Only when the Abbé did not find them at the cabin, two days from now, would they be missed. (It did not occur to them at the time that their horses would certainly be missed.) They tiptoed past the guard house unnoticed— there were advantages to Renée's gown no longer being white. Henri halted just before the stables and held Renée back. He listened.

"The horses are restless," he whispered.

Silently they entered the saddle room. The smell of leather, horse, and hay permeated the room. Henri stopped at the door and looked. He stood perfectly still for a minute watching for any movement. He had already identified where Fallaire and Heretic were tied up. They were near.

Seeing nothing, he grabbed saddles, blankets, and bridles. He would be quick.

"Unbuckle the sword, and hold it for me. I am not used to working with it on," he said and then stood while she fumbled a moment, unhooking the sword belt from his waist.

The gelding nickered as he came up behind her. It was a nervous nicker. That put him on his guard. Just before he threw the saddle on her back he heard a heavy boot behind him. He dodged to the side, thrusting the saddle in front of him. The blade of a sword turned off it and caught the edge of his leather cuirass.

"So you ran off with my niece, stable boy," Sieur de Bixmarch growled. "We figured you would be back for the horses."

Henri backed toward the corner. The gelding stamped, agitated by the activity in the stall. For a few moments Henri was able to keep the horse between him and Bixmarch.

"A pretty young thing that niece of mine," Bixmarch said. "I can see how you would want her for yourself, but it won't do. What were you thinking? You are just a stable boy."

Henri slid under the neck of the horse, hoping to break out of the stall, but Bixmarch stepped back to guard against that.

"Still that was pretty low of you; after I had taken you in—you an orphan—and given you food from my own table. And this is how you repay me? I suppose she has told you we are to be married. You've run off with my bride, Henri, and now I will show you how I will repay you." Then turning his head for just a moment he called, "Petro, come here and help me catch this stable boy."

Petro? Here? Henri wondered at that. And what of Renée? Where was she? He hoped she had had the good sense to get away. Heretic reared, forcing Sieur de Bixmarch to back up. Bixmarch paused and then pushed forward again, slapping the gelding on the rump. The frightened horse kicked and caught the knight a glancing blow to the shins. Sieur de Bixmarch staggered back several steps and rubbed his shins. Taking advantage of the opportunity, Henri rushed out of the stall. Renée ran forward and handed him his sword.

Sieur de Bixmarch saw her. "So there you are," he growled. "You just stay there, you pretty little thing, while I take care of this impudent villein."

Henri whipped the sword out of the scabbard, parried the knight's thrust, and then blocked the second one as Bixmarch sliced for the neck. He could feel the strength in Bixmarch's arms. Henri's father had trained him well, but Bixmarch had years of real fighting.

"Petro," Bixmarch sounded irritated. "Grab your stable boy so I can thrust him through."

Was that a trick, Henri wondered? Did he need to be watching over his shoulder? Henri gave a quick half cut, which Bixmarch blocked, and then he ran toward the other end of the stable. He ran right into Petro's arms.

"I have him, Your Lordship," Petro called out, and then whispering in Henri's ear added, "Trust me."

Bixmarch strode through the dark stable towards the sound of Petro's voice.

"When he gets close, break away to your right," Petro whispered. A moment later Bixmarch neared, and Henri broke free from Petro's loose arms and ran to his right. Bixmarch charged and stumbled over a bench in his way. He crashed to the ground, his sword flying out of his hand. Before he could rise, Henri had one foot on his back with his sword edge resting on the neck.

"Hold or I'll slice."

"Petro, get him off of me," Sieur de Bixmarch shouted.

"One step closer, Petro, and I'll skewer him."

"Kill him," Renée urged as she crossed the room. "He does not deserve to live. Remember what he wanted to do to me."

Sieur de Bixmarch lay limp.

"Bring me rope," Henri called.

Reluctantly Renée fetched a coil of rope and brought it to him. Then he tied him to a cross beam. "Give me one of your knee rags." With that he gagged him. Then he stepped back satisfied.

"What of him?" Renée motioned to Petro.

"We will tie him up in the saddle room." Henri said gruffly. "March soldier."

When they were out of the main stables Henri lowered his sword. "Thank you, Petro. But now what shall we do with you?"

"Yes, indeed," Petro answered. "Sieur de Bixmarch is not a stupid man, nor a forgiving man. Your ruse might have fooled him, but I doubt it. If I go with him he will either kill me or make me wish I was dead. Nor is he above taking it out on my wife, Maria."

"You can join us. The Maiden Renée needs a good knight."

Henri laid out his plans to take Renée to the town of Cairns and suggested that Petro could take the gelding, ride back to Anwar, pick up Maria, and meet them in Cairns.

"I accept. When I am with you the Lord blesses me. I aim to stay close."

A few minutes later they parted ways, Petro riding the gelding southwest toward Anwar, Henri, with Renée seated behind him, on the mare riding southeast toward Cairns.

Chapitre Huit:
Les Étoiles du Ciel

The night's celestial stars and sprinkling lights are passing
From my sight, while dawn comes sprinting. From everlasting
Have I been formed and pondered in your divine mind
That I might seek your face and all true glory, find,
Beauty in your creation. The yellow broom, the rock rose,
Sweet alyssums have come sprouting—fragrant under the zephyr's
nose—
Now blooming, rising petal and stamen praising

> *You. Reaching leaf and petal, lifting trunk and raising*
> *Branch, they like I find joy in awakening to the dawn,*
> *In your presence, amidst your love, singing songs*
> *You have so richly bestowed. All heaven and earth is aglow.*
> *- Henri at Cairns*

It was a night like none other. For the first hour Henri had urged the white mare on, but when he was certain that he was not being followed, he let the horse settle into a steady walk. And they rode on, Henri in the saddle, Renée seated tight behind him, her arms wrapped around his waist. The stars were bright that night. Henri steered by them: Castor and Pollux setting to the west, Regulus and Spica ahead, Arcturus rising. Keeping Polaris over his right shoulder, he pushed on. A warm zephyr blew from the south, turning the night balmy. And as he held the reins in his hands, he remembered portions from the Psalms:

When I think on my ways
   I turn my feet to your statues. . .
Though the cords of the wicked bind me,
   I do not forget your law.

Though in this case, he mused, it was the wicked that had been bound. He thought again of Sieur de Bixmarch tied and gagged to a post. But it was the next part that had brought the Psalms to mind.

At midnight I rise to praise you.

Midnight and the hours that flowed past like a never ending stream, like the stars in their motions, like the white band of the Milky Way revolving again and again on this flat earth.

For your righteous laws.
I am a friend of all who fear you,

O, yes, Lord, I am a friend to all who fear you. And not only that, Lord, but I feel so at home with those who truly do love you. When I find them, those who are yours, they are as my own brothers and sisters.

who keep your precepts.
The earth, O LORD, is filled with your love.

Indeed the earth is filled with your love. And at that he felt this incredible warmth, this joy of life, this bonding with all the beauty of the earth around him. It was good to be alive. Then an involuntary shudder passed through him, a shudder of fear at how things could have turned out. He had never faced someone with a sword before, someone so intent on killing him, but he had passed the test. A hard test to be sure; Sieur de Bixmarch was a veteran and trained warrior, no novice, and Henri had survived.

Yes, it was good to be alive. It was good to feel the mare's smooth gait, to feel the warmth of her flanks and the coarseness of her mane as he reached over to pat the neck. It was good to hear the plodding of hooves on the road and fields as they rode on and on; to smell the winds, and the plowed dirt, and the sweat, and as the night wore on, to feel the young woman riding behind him, becoming sleepy, resting her head on his shoulder, the silkiness of her dark hair sweeping across his arms, and nodding off. Every once in a while she called his name in a way that simply asked if he were still awake and if he were well. It was better than wine, wonderfully intoxicating, to be the one she trusted. Indeed, it was one of those nights in which sleep is unnecessary.

He rode till the eastern horizon began to lighten. Then turning his horse toward a small meadow, he brought her to a halt. Swinging his leg in front of him he dismounted while steadying Renée on the horse. She opened her eyes a moment as he slid her off. She put her arms around his neck until he set her down in a soft patch of moss and grass. Then she curled up and instantly fell back to sleep. Henri unsaddled the horse and spread the blanket over her. After taking care of Fallaire, he lay down, listened for a few moments to Renée's quiet breathing, and then fell asleep himself.

Two things awoke him later that morning. The first was the aroma of stew cooking over a fire. The second was the lyrical voice of a woman singing. It was a familiar children's tune,

Frere Jacques, frere Jacques, dormez-vous? Dormez-vous?

Sonnez les matines, sonnez les matines. Ding din dong. Ding din dong.

He opened his eyes and looked to see Renée kneeling down on the ground beside a fire stirring the pot with a stick. He shook his head ever so slightly, and a smile spread across his face. He sat up and looked a-round. They were near the edge of a wood in a small meadow. It was noon. The south wind continued to blow, bringing unexpected warmth, and it seemed that in the space of the night the whole earth had come alive, greeting spring with exuberance. The grasses were sprouting, the flowers blossoming; there were mounds of yellow broom, and thickets of rock rose, lavender, irises, and sweet alyssum. Beneath a massive oak was a clump of pink bindweed and near a small stream little ground or-chids and lilies of the valley. Where had they all come from so suddenly?

He looked back to the fire and then at Renée in her short, white dress—dirty though it might be. Her movements were graceful, attuned to the bursting spring. Her lashes blinked as smoke swept up into her face. She turned her head, coughing, tears coming to her green eyes.

Seeing him watching her, she smiled. "So you finally woke up?"

Henri rose to his feet. "I didn't know you could build a fire, and cook, and. . ."

"What do you take me for, an idiot?"

"No," Henri quickly defended himself. "But. . . ."

"But what?"

He raised his hands in surrender. "Pardon me, Maiden Renée, I mean no offense, not when it smells so good."

That answer pleased her. "Well, if you want to be helpful, I need more wood for the fire."

"Yes, Mademoiselle," he said, but he could not help but smile over his shoulder as he looked at her. She had turned back to the fire and had started singing again.

She filled his bowl with stew, and they sat down on the ground opposite the fire.

"Where are we?" she asked.

Henri shrugged, "I don't know, not exactly. I never came this way before, and Cairns is a hard town to find; but we traveled a good distance last night."

She nodded as she tipped the bowl up to her lips.

"It's good." Henri pointed to his bowl.

"When her father ignores her and her mother despises her, a child spends a lot of time around the servants. The kitchen staff was kind to me." She shrugged.

He took a second bowl. "It is better than anything I ever cooked."

"Yes, it is," she replied matter-of-factly. "But tell me, stable boy, I want to know something."

From the tone of her voice, Henri expected hard questions.

"How is it that a stable boy knows Latin and can write? How is it that a stable boy can guide his way at night by the stars? How is it that a stable boy has trained with the sword and can fight off an experienced knight? How is it that a stable boy has memorized so much Scripture? Answer me that, uncommon stable boy."

Henri took another swallow and then wiped his chin with his sleeve.

"The truth is my father was a nobleman." He stopped and looked up at her, wondering if she would believe him. "A knight, Sir Thommas, Master of the Hunt for the Duc de Gascogne. My father taught me all of this. He was an incredible man, a good teacher, and a very good Poppa." Henri's voice cracked just a little.

There was a pause as Renée watched him. "He's dead, then?"

Henri nodded. "Yes. He rests in the grave."

"He sounds like a good man. Maybe he bypassed purgatory and went straight to heaven."

Henri turned his head noncommittally. "He taught me that the dead rest in the graves until the resurrection, like Lazarus sleeping in the tomb before Jesus called him out."

Renée looked at him quizzically. "I've never heard that before. Where did he learn that?"

"He showed it to me from Scripture, but I am afraid I did not fully understand."

Renée nodded. "So then, you are nobility." Her voice changed, becoming cool. "Henri, uncommon stable boy, is really Henri, uncommon knight bachelor. Well. . . I am not sure what to say."

She stared at him hard, got up and tugged at her dress in an attempt to make it longer, and then strode away from the fire. Whirling around suddenly, she pointed her finger at him. "If you are a knight, why didn't you kill Sieur de Bixmarch? He should have been dead. You had the opportunity."

Henri spoke without looking at her. "I used to wonder what it would be like to take the sword in battle. Now, having done it, I find I have no love for fighting. I am glad I did not kill him. I do not want that burden."

"Will you be a monk then?" she answered angrily. "Will you be a Francis of Assisi? I have no need of a knight who will not put the sword to use. I would rather have a stable boy than a cowardly knight. Any knight who will not defend his mistress is no knight at all."

Hurt by her anger and accusations he was silenced. Where was the Renée who only last night had rested her head on his shoulder?

She continued, "A knight cannot be soft-hearted like melted butter. Melted butter is spread on bread, chewed, and swallowed. It is sliced by a butter knife, never mind the sword."

Rising to his feet, Henri started to defend himself, but he was cut off.

"Didn't you listen to my story? Don't you know what Bixmarch wants to do to me? Why won't you help me?"

"I fought and protected you," Henri protested. "Bixmarch's sword cut into my leather. I placed my life in danger for you again last night, as I have ever since you ran away. But I shall not kill, not if I have the means of avoiding it. God has not given me to judge who should live and who should die. I will have mercy and pray that at the resurrection the LORD will have mercy on me."

She turned away and began to walk off into the field. Her voice cracked as she answered, "So you will leave me. You will leave me, too. You will abandon me as my father has, abandon me to those who would defile and destroy me." She looked scathingly over her shoulder at Henri. "You will desert me when I need you. You will go off searching for some ethereal world of beauty, when I need a strong protector. Or was it something else. . ." She turned to face him, and her slender shoulders straightened. "Maybe you see me as just a filly that a poor nobleman might use to ride his way back into society; a young maiden, an heiress, distressed, with no one else around, and you thought to hitch yourself to me. Was that it, Henri? Sir Henri." She looked angry, scared, confused, and betrayed.

"No," he said resolutely. "I entered your service as Henri, stable boy. I swore my fealty to you as a stable boy, and if that is what you wish I shall remain a stable boy. But I will never leave you."

He moved toward her and stopped. They looked at each other across the fire for a long while, measuring the change. Now that she knew he was of her station their relationship must transform. Based on past experience, she distrusted her own class and was sorry to know he was not a simple stable boy. Then again, if he was nobility and had given himself into her service, then maybe, just maybe, he could be more than a servant. Maybe he could be a friend, a real friend like she had not known before.

"When I met you," Henri was speaking again, "remember I went with you for a ride on the beach? I did not know your story, your troubles. When I promised to stay with you I did not know you were an heiress, nor did I try to tell you that I was anything but a common stable boy. I came with you because you needed me, and that has not changed. Believe me. Please. . . Believe me."

She did. Though it was beyond her experience to know someone this faithful, still she believed him, and it caught her unawares. She tried to stifle the tears, wiping them away with the back of her hand.

Henri searched for something to give her. "Don't cry. Please don't cry. I won't leave you."

"Yes, I know," she said between sniffles. "I believe you."

Henri felt a small tingle shoot down his spine and a sensation that he could not identify. Confused, he began to pack up the camp. A few minutes later he helped her mount the mare, except now instead of riding with her, he took the reins and led the horse.

"Fallaire needs a rest from the long ride last night, and I need to stretch my legs," he explained, but both knew that it had more to do with the change in their relationship.

They came to a road bending southeast and took it. They made good progress and were content to proceed in silence, each absorbed in thought. The sun passed over their heads, its warmth welcome this spring morning; fields passed by; streams babbled under the rock bridges; bluets of early spring passed unnoticed; swallows and swifts darted through the air around them.

La poursuite pour le hurlement
Come crashing, Come hurling down—
All battered souls beware;
Come coursing on Hades' great hound—
O sinful man, take care;
Come howling, come dread pursuit—
Let not him find you there.
Linger not, pause not on tempter's ground—
Thy bliss he willn't pay fare.
Away then, away on heaven's horses found,
Lest dread under his feral stare

We find you fallen, tromped in ground and root
With all your sins to bear.
- Paul of Brest, Archbishop de Bretagne

Near sunset, they heard a distant howling. It came from their left, from over a wooded hill. Henri knew that it was not the howling of a wolf, but rather the plaintive howl of a hound in distress. As they came closer it did not let up.

"The hound may be wounded. I will go and see if I can help," Henri said.

"It will be dark soon, and the meadows are safer."

"The dog is just over the hill."

"Henri, it's just a dog. Must you save everything?"

Henri stopped and looked back. The howl stopped and then returned with an even more melancholic call.

"That is not the call of a wounded dog, but a call of distress. I must go. I will not be long."

Renée nodded. "Yes, I understand. This is the same as a stable boy promising to stay with a young frightened noble girl, just because she asks."

Henri was embarrassed, but he felt compelled to do what he could.

She slid behind the saddle, and reached down to give Henri a hand up. He mounted, and they turned off the road across the field at a trot. They worked their way over the intervening hill, entering the woods as they did. At the top of the hill Renée turned and looked over her shoulder to the south and then the west. To the south she could see the Pyrenees, to the west the sun. It would set in less than an hour.

The howling guided Henri down the backside of the hill where shadows lengthened. The mare carefully picked her way through the fallen branches and undergrowth until they came to a small clearing in the valley.

"Oh my, Oh my! Mon Dieu, My Father," Henri gasped and slid from the saddle.

"What? O!" Renée replied.

Across the small clearing, in the dusk, head slumped, blood soaking through his jerkin, right leg turned at an unnatural angle, a knight sat propped against a tree; his right hand still gripping a bloody sword. Beside him a large red hound alternated howling with licking the knight's face. A few feet away the knight's black destrier stood, occasionally swaying his large head toward the hound. And on the saddle horn a hawk perched, its eyes covered with leather blinders.

Henri began walking the perimeter of the clearing, looking at the turn of the grass, and studying the surrounding woods. When he had finished his initial investigation he sank to his knees and held his head in his hands.

The maiden went immediately to the knight. As she approached, the hound backed away and then came forward again and began licking Renée's hand. She felt the knight's forehead and then looked at his abdominal wound and the bone protruding from the leg.

"He's not dead," Renée said softly and glanced back at Henri, who was still kneeling in the middle of the field, his head buried in his hands. "He's not dead," she repeated louder to get his attention.

Henri started and rose to his feet. He came over and squatted beside the knight. As Henri's hands touched the forehead, the knight opened his eyes vacantly and mumbled in garbled Occitan.

"He is delirious," Henri said. "He has a fever, and his wounds are festering. There is little we can do for him." He turned his attention to the hound, which had a large cut on the back of the neck.

Renée looked incredulously at Henri. "We must do something for him; he is still alive." She patted the knight's left hand and then unbuckled the helmet from his head. Getting up from her knees she found a water pouch on the knight's horse. She put it to his lips, but he kept mumbling garbled words.

"Do you know what he is saying?" She looked at Henri.

"He is from South France. He is speaking Occitan. His words do not make sense. Mostly he is saying, 'Mother.' I cannot make out the rest."

"Maybe he his praying to Mary," Renée suggested.

Henri shrugged, and after cutting a piece of the knight's garment began dressing the hound's wound. Then he got up and looked at the horse.

"What happened here?" Renée looked up to Henri.

"Wild boar," Henri answered. "He was charged and gored and will die at the hands of a wild boar. He was all alone. No one to help him, no one to distract the boar when it knocked him down." And at that Henri buried his head in his hands, leaned against the saddle of the black war-horse, and broke down sobbing.

"Henri, what is it?" Renée stood up and put her hand on his shoulders. "Henri, we could not have done anything more. It's not your fault. Why are you so distraught?'

Struggling to control himself, Henri turned and swept his arms across the field. "This. . . ." He slapped his hand on the saddle, startling the destrier. "This is exactly how I found my father last spring, save that he was already dead; killed by a wild boar; little more than a year ago. I found his body lying in a field; just like this, face down in a pool of dried blood. My father."

"Your father was killed by a boar? But he was a great hunter. How could he have been killed by the boar?"

"I don't know. I was not there. He had left me some pages to copy while he took a horse to market. But when he did not come back, I sought him. . . and found him." Henri regained control of his emotions. "I found him dead. . . but he had not been alone—that was clear—there had been at least one other, probably two more knights. I do not know what happened. I never heard, but I do know that when he needed help they left him. I was with my father on many boar hunts, and I know that often he aided another knight when the boar charged. He would distract it, but this time the boar got him, and the other knights fled."

"When did you say he died?" Renée asked.

"About a year ago, when we had the big rains. Remember, the rivers flooded after that."

"Yes, I remember," Renée answered thoughtfully.

At that Renée searched the horse. Behind the saddle on the right was a war axe, on the left a bow and quiver, and directly to the rear a saddle-bag. The saddlebag contained a cloak, blanket, dried meats, fruit, and nuts. She put the blanket over the dying knight.

"What shall we do for him? We can't just leave him to die alone," she said with tenderness.

"Of course not," Henri replied. "We can try to drape him over his horse, but I think that will only increase his suffering." At that Henri began re-exploring the clearing's perimeter. He did not wish to alarm Renée, but the knight's bloody sword meant there was a wounded boar nearby, and of all the beasts in the forest, a boar in distress was dreaded most. In pain they became enraged, eager to destroy. He saw where the tracks of the beast led to a thicket; just the place he might seek to recover, or die if mortally struck.

Henri twisted to tell Renée where he was going, but as he did he heard the stir of branches. He did not need to turn back to know the boar was charging him.

La mort pour le chevalier
Is he dead then, no breath, no life, no pulse?
Has he passed beyond our ken
Into that gray nether land where else
We shall not see;
Where his smile forever fades, and his brows
Shall never arch?
Is he dead then, so rich, so strong, so fair,
Fallen dead among the larch?
- Maiden Renée d'Ayes

"Henri!" Renée screamed as the animal emerged from the bush.

He grabbed his dagger and spun around. The boar grazed him, but such was the bulk and power of the beast that it knocked him to the ground. Stunned for a moment by the impact, Henri struggled to catch his breath. The boar stopped and pawed the ground. It was a large male, easily over a thousand pounds, with a full thick coat of dark bristles, a gash on the back left leg, and an angry eye as it snorted. It watched him a few seconds and then charged again. Henri jumped to his feet and sought shelter behind the trunk of a beech tree. Sweeping around the tree, the boar caught one of its large tusks in Henri's calf. Henri grimaced and plunged his dagger into the boar's right shoulder, but the blade turned on the tough hide, leaving only a small cut. Henri knew he was in grave trouble.

Just then an arrow buried into the wild pig's hind. The boar screamed, wheeled, and charged away from Henri. Henri looked and saw Renée running toward them, bow in hand, and notching her second arrow. She stopped only long enough to let it fly. It missed the beast's head, though just barely. The boar had her sighted in its maddened eye.

Henri yelled and ran after the boar, but it was the hound that turned the boar away from Renee. Barreling across the meadow, the hound hit the boar in the right side. When the boar hesitated for a moment, Henri threw his dagger. It buried up to the hilt in the boar's side. At that the boar wheeled back towards Henri.

"Get out of here!" Henri called to Renée. "Flee! Take the horse and ride." Henri knew they were doomed. Fighting a boar was hard enough for several knights well trained and well equipped. What chance had they? Now that he had thrown his dagger he had no weapon, and his only assistance was a slender wisp of a girl and an injured hound. "Go," he called again as he grabbed a large stick lying on the ground.

But Renée did not hesitate; she let her third arrow fly. This one struck the boar in the neck, just as it approached Henri. Henri broke the stick on the confused boar's head, while the hound kept a constant harassment at the boar's hind. Renée was extremely fast at notching the arrows and buried a fourth one in the boar's side. This gave Henri a chance to grab the dying knight's sword from his hand. The boar was now turning round and round in circles, pawing the ground, uncertain who to charge. Raising the sword with both hands above his head, Henri rushed the boar, but just before he struck, Renée's fifth arrow penetrated between the wild beast's eyes. It stiffened and dropped with a heavy thud.

For a moment they stood where they were, watching the beast, Henri with sword ready, Renée with arrow strung and bow pulled half taut, the hound growling with his teeth grabbing the boar's leg. Then, cautiously, Henri and Renée approached the beast from opposite sides. He nudged it with the tip of the sword. It did not move.

"Is it dead?" she asked tensely.

He did not answer but coming closer kicked it with his boot. Still no movement. "I think so," he replied. Taking his sword he plunged it deep through the chest. "If not, it is now."

She took a deep breath and collapsed to her knees. She leaned over and felt the rough, bloody bristles of the boar. Then she began to laugh, quietly at first, then more uncontrollably. She laughed and laughed until her laughter turned to sobs and tears ran down her face.

Henri squatted on his haunches on the other side and stared at her. Her eyes met his and impulsively they both leaned across the beast and hugged tightly, while she continued to shake.

When they pulled apart Henri rocked back on his heels and continued to stare at Renée. "That was excellent shooting," he said in profound amazement. He still could not believe they were alive. "I don't know that I have ever seen better. Where did you learn?"

Renée was still kneeling beside the dead beast. "A little here, a little there. When your mother despises you and your father ignores you, you learn from the servants, and a girl cannot spend all of her time in the kitchen." She answered quietly, and then aware that Henri continued to stare at her, she looked back at him and smiled.

Henri shook his head, stood up, and went back to the knight. The hound had returned and was lying beside its master. Henri leaned over to return the sword but stopped when he looked at the knight's face. "He is dead," he said somberly.

"No," Renée exclaimed, rising from her knees.

"I am afraid so," Henri said as he felt for a pulse at the wrist. "Rest in peace, my brother, rest in Christ's peace."

Standing at the feet of the fallen knight, Renée looked at him. "He was young, not much older than us. He had a fine face."

Henri nodded and then looked around the clearing. "It is getting dark. We must go."

But first Henri improvised a sled of bound branches on which they laid the boar's body, cut and quartered. This they attached to the destrier. Then Henri slung the dead knight's body over the mare, and as the darkness deepened they climbed back over the hill. Renée took the lead, walking with the mare. Henri followed with the black stallion. The hawk rode on the saddle, and the red hound, head hung low, walked at the stallion's side.

Petit pois et oignons
Trifle not with truffles—they are delicate and rare.
But mutton, duck, and pheasant, they do well to pay your fare.
And if they down the tankard slammed upon the board
Full of gold, in pockets brimmed, then bring them
A platter of steak, or goose, or roast boar,
And slap up a side of onions and green peas.

Do this my daughter, and they will be well pleased.
- *The Innkeeper's song*

It was late that night when they stopped in a small village. Still, the first thing Henri did was find the priest. He was anxious to relinquish the knight's corpse. The priest had the smell of alcohol on his breath, but when he saw the body and heard Henri's tale, he went with Henri to the town carpenter and undertaker. Henri left the body with them and then went back to an inn where Renée had waited.

The sight of the boar excited the innkeeper, and Henri was able to barter it for provisions: a dress for Renée, and five livres of silver. He suspected the keeper had gotten the best of the deal—boar meat would attract travelers—but Henri had never been good at trading. The dress he received for Renée was a simple gray surcote a couple of sizes too big, not fancy like a noblewoman's. Still it was better than the rag her dress had become.

Later, having accomplished the necessary tasks, they took a table in the corner near the fire. The hound settled itself at Henri's feet, and the hawk sat on the back of his chair. A maid brought a loaf of dark rye bread dipped in olive oil, a leg of mutton basted over the spit, and peas and onions. Renée watched Henri eagerly tackle the meal, and then her conversation returned to the hunt.

"Have you been on a lot of hunts before?"

Henri grunted and cut off another piece of meat with the knife. He was ravenous.

"How many do you think you have seen?"

He filled his mouth with mutton and shrugged. "Lots. I don't know. I couldn't count them." He tossed the first bone to the hound under the table.

"Five or ten?"

"More than that," he answered and pointed to her ignored onions on her plate. "Are you going to eat those?"

She did not answer, so he speared them with his knife. She watched him absently.

"Did you really think I did well?"

"Oh yes," he mumbled, his mouth full of food. "You were great."

"I was brave, wasn't I? Not a coward?"

Henri stopped for a moment and looked straight at her. "Truly, you did well." He swallowed and carved off another large slice of meat. "I did not realize how hungry I was. This is good, isn't it?"

"But what if I had missed?" She nibbled now on the crust of the bread. "What if I had missed?"

"You didn't miss." He gave a scrap of meat to the hawk.

"But what if I had?"

"I would rather not think about that." He put down his knife. "Let me tell you what my father told me about hunting and fighting. You can't become concerned with the what ifs? If you do, you will become obsessed with fear and lose."

Her voice dropped lower, but its intensity increased. "But Henri, that is the amazing thing. I had no fear, absolutely no fear. In fact. . . I really enjoyed it. It was a thrill, exhilarating."

Henri stopped chewing, looked at her in amazement, and then laughed. He wiped the meat juices spilling onto his chin on his sleeve. "Maiden, you are full of surprises."

She swung herself sideways so that both feet were on the bench and then wrapped her arms around her knees. "My third shot was perfect, wasn't it? Right behind the forelegs into the chest. Do you think it went into the heart?"

"Yes, I think so," Henri affirmed, though in fact he was not sure. "Beautiful shot. . . . Are you going to eat the rest of those peas?" He took her plate and set it before him.

"Are you glad I was there? I was not a coward?"

Henri laid his arms across the table still grasping the knife. "What is it, Renée? Why the questions about being a coward? If you had jumped on the horse and ridden away, no one would have blamed you. You are a woman, and no one would have expected you to join in the fight. When that boar came after me, I never expected you to join the fight. And if the boar had gored you I should have gone to my grave with that as a shame on my conscience."

"Well. . ." She paused. "My father was on a boar hunt last year at the time of the floods. He said he barely escaped with his life. I think. . . I think. . . that he was the coward that fled from your father."

Her eyes searched Henri's.

"Your father. . . Comte Sevestre. . . last spring just before the big rains?"

She nodded to his question.

He stopped, not knowing what to think. Comte Sevestre, the unknown knight who had fled when his father had needed help? It fit with what he already knew of Renée's father, a miserable creature, despicable man, likely to shirk responsibility. After all, any father who could abandon his daughter surely could flee like a coward and leave his father to battle the boar alone—though it broke all codes of chivalric conduct. With that, anger flashed through Henri. But the anger did not last; Sevestre was too pathetic, below contempt. If this were true, he was more to be pitied.

As the anger faded, however, it was replaced by a storm of great mourning, for now he could imagine the death of his father more clearly. Henri had seen the face of Comte Sevestre, and he could now imagine the final minutes of his father in new ways. There, riding on one of the beautiful steeds of Ayes was Comte Sevestre, hastening away in unmanly fear from the onslaught of the boar, leaving Sir Thommas to face the beast alone. He knew his father well enough to know that Sir Thommas had not wasted a moment in despair, even being abandoned—Henri wished he could be more like his father on that account. It was more likely that in Sir Thommas's final moments of life he would have been thinking how glad he was that Comte Sevestre had escaped. On a hunt, Sir Thommas was always jumping in, taking the most dangerous role, certain he was the best man for the task.

The other thing Henri knew was that if Sir Thommas had any last lingering moments of life, he would have thought of three things. He would have thought of Miriam, Henri's mother and the only love of his life. He would have thought of Henri, his dearly beloved son. Henri knew what his father would have told him: "Courage, my boy, the Lord will be with you." His father's last thoughts would then have turned to God. Henri could hear in his mind his father's rasping breath struggling one last time to cry out, "Jesus, have mercy on me."

Henri's lips quivered and his body shuddered.

"Can you forgive me? Henri, can you forgive me? You don't hate me because of my father, do you?" Renée asked anxiously, searchingly. She grabbed his hands. "Please don't hold my father against me. I was not a coward, was I?"

Henri, drawn back to the present, looked at Renée. "No, Renée, you were not a coward. You were brave." He added with passion, "You are not your father. You are not condemned by his failures. But if this is true, isn't it ironic that the daughter should save the son?"

"Our destinies entwine," she said as her hands slid up his forearms. "My father has tried to destroy both of our lives."

"Yet..." Henri pushed the plate away and moved closer to the fire. "Yet, I do not find myself angry with your father. I pity him. Such a miserable life he leads; how can he find any rest or peace?"

Renée glared at the fire. "I am not so merciful. I hate my father and my mother!"

Chapitre Neuf
Le Baiser du Paix

*I had not thought they should ever feel
This clean again—not on this earth—
Never guileless, never pure;
Not while vile men still roam and steal
Kisses forced from innocent lips.
But they were washed, immersed,*

And with the Host were cured,
Innocent, and with yours were sealed.
- Maiden Renée d'Ayes

Henri awoke on a straw mattress on the second floor. The sun still had not lifted over the hills to the east. He pulled his boots on and descended the stairs two at a time. The hound lifted his head as Henri passed the stables. A bell from the chapel began to ring. A lark rose into the sky and a crow called from the roof. Hearing the bells, words came to his mind. "Let your gentleness be evident to all. The Lord is near." As his steps crossed into the church he said quietly to himself, "Do not be anxious about anything, but in prayer and petition make your requests known to God, and the peace of God, which surpasses all understanding, will guard you in Christ Jesus."

He knelt as he entered, crossed himself, took a pew to the left, and then knelt again, closing his eyes in prayer. He opened his eyes to see Renée sliding into the pew beside him. She smiled, then joined him on her knees. She was wearing the dress he had bought her, and her hair had been brushed. She did not look like a woman of nobility, but at least she no longer looked like an urchin.

The priest entered and mumbled a few lines behind the lectern. Henri had seen enough priests to know this was another who could not read, and when he turned to consecrate the bread his Latin was a jumble of gibberish. This illiteracy had irritated his father. Henri was more forgiving.

The priest took the bread and passed it through the congregation. Henri had been in enough different churches to recognize the priest had initiated the kiss of peace. In the kiss of peace the host was given mouth to mouth, neighbor to neighbor. Henri was uncomfortable with the rite; many were. The Papacy and higher orders frowned on it, had tried to ban it, thought it led to immorality. And Henri, seated next to Renée, felt awkward. He glanced askance at her. What would her reaction be? At first she seemed puzzled, but after that he could not read her. The host would come to her first. What would she do?

She took it, placed it on her lips, and without a moment's hesitation leaned toward Henri. Her eyes were closed. He took the wafer as their lips met. For a moment he forgot that he was to take it from her lips. All he could do was feel her lips and think that she had offered it to him. It was a brief, but magical moment, and then it was over.

As they left, Henri, gave a sous to a blind man sitting at the gate. Outside, several of the villagers greeted them, wished them well, and asked if they had *enjoyed* the service. They smirked and winked at each other. Father Dominary, it turned out, rarely used the kiss of peace, but had thought today would be a good day for it.

"Imagine that he should use the 'kiss of peace' today?" The miller said to his wife, and then slapped his knee and laughed.

Henri blushed. Renée, however, smiled sweetly and asked, "Did he now? Did *you* enjoy it?"

"Aye, that I did." The miller nodded. "But not as much as if I had been seated next to you."

"Get on with you, you old man." His wife batted him across the back of his head with the palm of her hand. "At your age, and just coming from mass. You will have to go back in and confess again, if you do not get your hands working and your mind cleaned."

Renée laughed.

A few of the townspeople stayed around while the priest had a short funeral service over the body of the unknown knight. Henri and Renée stood side by side as the grave diggers lowered the coffin into the ground. Before departing the town, Henri left written instructions with the priest for anyone who sought news of the dead knight, telling where such a person might find Henri to retrieve the horse, armor, hound, and hawk.

Then they made their way east on the road into the hills where Cairns lay. It was another fine day, and he hoped that they could be in or near Cairns by nightfall. He settled into the saddle, trying to find a comfortable position for his left leg. The boar wound pained him today. Side by side they rode, Henri on the sixteen hand, black Frisian warhorse; the red hound hanging close behind; the hawk sitting on the front rim of the saddle. The hawk remained unnamed; the horse and hound were unimaginatively named Le Noir and La Rouge. Renée rode her mare, Fallaire.

They rode on, passing over an occasional stream. It was not much of a road, and they frequently had to ford. Here and there fields were in cultivation. On the hillside were groves of olive trees and almonds. Along the stream banks, towering plane trees rose rough and gray at the base, blanching as they ascended. Their leaves, usually the last to arrive, still had not burst open. The limbs, like giant arms reaching in odd combinations, spread majestically to the sky, where white clouds drifted. As the afternoon passed the sun seemed unseasonably hot. Henri wiped his forehead to remove the sweat. Renée, however, found the weather balmy and pleasant.

They came to several forks in the road. The choices puzzled Henri. He had been certain he would remember the way with clarity, but his mind seemed clouded, and the correct path was not clear. His leg throbbed a little more, but Henri made little of it. Too much time in the saddle. He got down and tried walking on it. The pain surprised him, but he steeled his will, determined not to let Renée see that it hurt him, and walked with barely a limp.

As the sun reached the horizon, Henri knew he must have missed the road. They would have to double back tomorrow. But they had money now and could afford a room for the night.

After seeing that the horses had been given grain and were well stabled, Henri joined Renée in the great room of the inn. The servant girl brought a breast of pheasant covered with shredded almonds, beans, a flat loaf of bread, a slab of cheese, and a bowl of stewed cabbage. Henri felt cold and sat close to the fire. He found himself surprisingly not hungry, and he gave a good portion of his food under the table to the hound. His leg hurt less if he rested it on the bench beside him.

Renée leaned across the table as she dipped the bread in a batter of garbanzo and sesame. She spoke quietly. "Tell me, Henri, stable boy," and she smiled when she said that, "are you going to marry someday?"

"Of course, someday." Henri tried to position his leg a little differently.

"What will she be like?" Renée asked.

Henri hesitated uncomfortably. "I don't know. I haven't thought much about that," Henri replied disingenuously. Truth was lately he had imagined his wife as having dark, wavy hair, green eyes, and porcelain smooth, white skin, remarkably like Renée.

"I have thought about it a lot," Renée confided. "Three years ago I went with my mother and father to the Duke of Toulouse. His court was beautiful. Everything was according to the highest standards of chivalry. Musicians attired in red preceded him when he entered a room, and the ladies of the court all wore the most fancy of wimples and hats. The knights wore black tabards and exquisitely long-pointed shoes. A great tourney was held, and each knight in the lists rode with the scarf of his lady pinned to his left shoulder. Ever since then I have thought about that. How wonderful to be a great duchess with a noble knight, a duke as my husband. He would be a champion in the tourneys, someone who could defend my honor in battle. He would be tall, with dark hair and a smile that melted hearts, but of course he would be faithful only to me."

"A duke?"

"Oh yes, well a prince would be all right," She laughed a little.

"You deserve no less," Henri replied softly.

"But you, Henri, tell me. You must have thought about it; you are of age. What would she be like?" She leaned across the table innocently laying her hand on his.

"I have no such lofty dreams," he said and moved a little closer to the fire. There seemed to be a chill in the room. "My father was a great knight, but he left me no inheritance of wealth. I don't allow myself to fantasize like you have."

"But what would she be like? Is she pretty, tall, short, does she laugh a lot or is she serious? I fear you would only like the serious ones. I told you, now you must tell me. . .Yes, you must tell me. I require it of you on your oath to serve me." They both were sitting close to the fire now, tête-à-tête. She was on the edge of her seat, leaning forward so close that her hair fell on his shoulder.

Henri looked at her and sighed. "I have never seen anyone as pretty as you."

Renée sat up slowly and took a deep breath. "Oh."

"I am sorry; I should not have said that." Henri turned back to the table, a wave of vertigo and nausea gripped him.

"No. . . . No." She stared at him for a long moment as a smile spread across her face. "That was sweet. That was very sweet." And then a tear slipped down her cheek unnoticed. "That was probably the sweetest thing anyone ever said to me."

There was a long lull in the conversation that followed as she munched on the food. A boisterous party of pilgrims entered the inn, filling the benches and sliding in beside them. Several of them were troubadours and started up songs. Some of the pilgrims got up to dance. A young merchant caught Renée's hand and led her to the center. She was nimble like a wood elf, gracefully twirling and spinning to the rhythm of the folksong. After the song finished Renée came back to the table.

"Among your many accomplishments, uncommon Henri, do you dance?" Renée asked.

"I can dance, but. . . . My leg is hurting me from the boar wound," Henri admitted.

"I am sorry. Is it bad?"

"No, it is nothing. I just need to rest it. It will be better tomorrow."

But in the morning it was not better. He woke in a sweat, and with a throbbing headache. His leg pained him now into the thigh. Only through pure grit and determination was he able to mount his horse.

"We must have missed the road to Cairns yesterday," Henri stated as they returned toward where they had already come. But he could not hide the pain as he spoke, and Renée watched him carefully.

"Let me look at your leg," she urged.

"No, it will be fine. My father's companion, Ishmael, is a Moorish physician; he practices the art in Cairn, or so he did when I left there."

"Your father was a friend of an infidel?"

"And a Jewish jeweler. They called themselves the Unholy Trinity—a Christian knight, a Jewish jeweler, and a Mohammedan physician. They accompanied my father and me when we trekked to Constantinople. He had no better friends, and Ishmael is one of the best physicians. He has studied the works of both Averroes and Maimonides. There are none like the Moorish and Jewish doctors. My wound will heal quickly in his care. I just need to find the right road. I just need to remember."

The morning, however, quickly wore on, and at each of the roads Henri simply could not remember. He found his mind more sluggish and dull.

He felt such a lethargy settling on him. Alternate episodes of heavy sweating and chills racked him. Renée watched him with consternation. Finally when they stopped to let the horses drink she insisted he take off his boots and roll up his pants. He had little strength left to object. What she saw frightened her. Swelling extended up past the knee, and a streak of redness like a line went further up the thigh. The wound itself was oozing a greenish, putrid exudate.

"If I could only get to Ishmael, it would be better," Henri repeated over and over.

The rest of that day came in only bits and pieces for Henri. Conversations in the distance, Renée's sweet voice like a nightingale encouraging him, "Hold on, Henri, hold on. We will be there soon. . .We are on the road. . . . Hold on, Henri. I can't carry you. You must hold on." Climbing a narrow mountain path, and then people thronging around him, lifting him off the saddle, and Renée saying, "This is Henri, son of Sir Thommas." The last thing he could remember were faces peering in all around him. "Hold on, boy. Hold on, Henri. Ishmael will be here shortly."

Chapitre Dix:
Dèlire

Now and then I remember when
First your sweating brow
I mopped with dampened towel,
And laid cool cloths upon your fevered
Chest, unwound the dressings weavered
On your angry festering thigh,
And sat there by the bedside
Under the window where the lark sang.
If not for worry I should have loved it most,
Sitting silent in the morning.
- Miriam of Cairns

The following days were a murky haze: drifting in and out of consciousness, sometimes delirious, sometimes almost aware, racking fevers, bone shaking chills, quiet footfalls in the hall, the squeak of the door, and then the soft hands of a young servant girl whom they called Miriam, seated beside him, patiently spooning mouthfuls of broth and encouraging him. Miriam? His mind tried to break through. Miriam? She would change the towels on his leg and replace them with warm ones; so gently she worked, and sometimes she would sing like a canary, so sweetly, in a voice familiar, and yet unknown. Then the sweep of a Moor into the room, turban wrapped and rich, flowing robes, fragrant incense, and bowls of balm applied to the wound. There was confidence in his touch, in his probing of the wound, in his hands measuring the pulse, and placed across his brow; quiet whispers, then egressing, and once more her hands tender and soft—like a rabbit's den lined with fur or the caress of a mare licking her colt—as she placed a cool towel over his head and cradled his neck to give him a sip of water. Words slipped across his mind, but the spoken word of the young girl seemed to evoke a swelling of feeling that he could not quite savvy, save that when her mouth turned to prayers his delirium came the closest to clearing. "Jesus, Lord, have mercy on him. Jesus, Savior, heal him." There was love in her voice, no mistaking it, and in her hands, and that pulled him; pulled him strong.

After nightfall on the fourth day his fever broke, and his delirium passed. He awoke and looked around the room. A full moon shone through the window. There was a chair by his bed; folded towels were neatly laid on the seat. Across the room by the door was a table. On it sat a pitcher, a basin, and several glass vials. His feather bed felt soft, but he was restless and hungry. On sitting up, however, his head swam. He sat for a couple of minutes until the spinning passed. Using the chair as a brace, he stood up. He was weak. Crossing the room he opened the door. To his right, down the corridor, issuing out from an open door, he saw the golden flickering lights of a fire dancing on the wall. Supported by the wall he shuffled his way closer.

Around the corner was a large room with several benches. On the far wall the bookcase was crammed with books. Straight ahead was a large, round, oak table. A short, gray headed man sat with his back to Henri. He was reading.

"Jehudah," Henri whispered to himself. Jehudah was the Jewish jeweler that had been Sir Thommas's friend.

The jeweler heard the whisper and looked with surprise and then a broad smile. "Henri? Praise God! You are better? Should you be out of bed?" He closed his book and laid it on a table.

"I needed to get out of my room."

"Of course you did, Of course you did. Here, have a seat." Adding under his breath, "Ishmael will kill me." He helped Henri to a seat by the fire, and pulled up a footstool.

Henri gratefully sat down. The short walk from his bed had drained him.

"Jehudah, am I in your house?" Henri looked around. "In Cairns?"

"Yes, Henri, you are in my house, and I am so pleased to have you, my friend. You were a very sick young man. It was good that Dr. Ishmael was here, rather than down in Montpelier at the medical school. No one else could have saved you, at least without amputating your leg. He is a great physician and is just beginning to get the recognition he deserves. You know, he has finally started work on that book he always meant to write. It is very good. He shows me chapters from time to time. He comes here to write. That was your good fortune. Ishmael and your servant girl, Miriam. Now there is a rare girl. Wherever did you find her? Incessantly by your side. She is a credit to the name; though I do admit it is odd, Miriam, just like your mother, and just as pretty and sweet; your mother was a beauty. But she has this your mother never had, your servant has the sweetest singing voice. In fact I told Ishmael that if you recovered, his skill could only claim partial credit, the rest would have to be the voice of an angel. You know Ishmael; good man, but proud, he bristled at the comment, until he heard her sing. But I have watched him since. I have never seen him so. . . tamed. Even Ishmael."

"Miriam? Jehudah, I have no servant girl named Miriam." Henri shook his head in bewilderment.

"You have been very sick and are still under the affects of the fever; do not let it bother you; it will return, but of course it will come back to you. It was your servant girl that brought you up the mountain trail to Cairns. She is a very attractive girl, and those types of memories will not stray long."

He stood up and stirred the fire a little. "Are you warm enough? Should I get a blanket for you?"

"No, the fire is warm enough, thank you."

The jeweler left the room and returned with a cup of wine. "Here, this will help."

Henri took a sip, and then sipped again. "How is this? It is spring, and this is unfermented. It is like fresh harvested juice of the vine."

"Ah yes, David-ben-Jonathan has rediscovered the method of our people, long forgotten, how to keep it fresh without fermentation. Isn't it delightful?"

"Quite." And Henri took a long draught. "Marvelous."

Henri pointed to the book by Jehudah's chair. "It has been a long time since I have held a book. What are you reading? "

Le verbe était Dieu
In the beginning was the Word,
And the Word was with God,
And the Word was God.
He was in the beginning with God.
- John 1:1-2 (ESV)

Jehudah paused and picked up the book carefully. He paged through it without speaking. "When I heard of your father's death I swore I would read this at least once, for his sake. Your father was a great man and a good friend. This is the New Testament."

Henri did not know what to say. His father had often suggested that

Jehudah ought to read it. "You of all people, Jehudah, you should read this," his father had said. "It is written by Jews about a Jew. Who could appreciate it like a Jew?"

"So I read it, and then I read it again." Jehudah stopped and looked meaningfully at Henri. "I am converted, Henri, and it gives me pleasure to tell you, Sir Thommas's son, I am converted. I have found joy. Your father said I would. This is a great comfort to me." Jehudah tapped on the leather bound volume. "Not only me, but several of my family have joined me in this."

"Nothing would have pleased my father more," Henri said.

"Yes, I know."

"And Ishmael?" Henri asked.

Jehudah laughed. "No, he has not changed. We no longer talk about religion. It is different without your father."

At that moment Renée entered the room. She was wrapped in a long white robe that reached to the floor.

"Jehudah, who are you talking to?" she asked, not seeing Henri at first.

Jehudah jumped out of his chair and rushed to take Renée's hands in his. "Miriam, your patient, your master Henri is up and feeling better, praise God."

"What are you talking about?" Renée asked, and then she saw Henri sitting in the chair. "Henri," she gasped with overwhelming joy and then immediately added anxiously, "You should be in your bed. Doctor Ishmael charged me with keeping you in your bed."

"Miriam? Is this Miriam?" Henri looked at Jehudah with bewilderment, and he began to make the connections.

"Of course, this is your servant girl, Miriam. As you see she is beautiful. Do not worry; with smooth skin like hers, it will not take long for you to remember."

Renée quickly interrupted before Henri could interject any other questions. "Yes, I am *your servant Miriam*, and I now intend to put you back to bed."

Henri let Renée help him out of the chair and gladly accepted her assistance as he placed one arm around her shoulders and the other around Jehudah's. His legs were weak. They walked slowly back to his room, where she laid him in bed. Then Jehudah bowed his head and left.

When he was gone Henri just looked at Renée with bewilderment. "Miriam? You, a servant girl; that should never be. You are the Maiden Renée, and no commoner. I will set this straight."

She took a washcloth and washed his face. "When I arrived in Cairns everyone recognized you as Henri, son of Sir Thommas, but I with my gray dress looked like any ordinary servant girl." She started fluffing his pillows and changing his towels. "At first I thought I would set them straight on that later, but then several things came to mind. First I remembered how you humbled yourself and became a stable boy for me, though you too are of nobility, and I thought if Henri could do this for me than I can be a servant girl to him." As he lay back into the pillows she pulled up the blanket and tucked it around him. "Second, I thought if I tell them I am your servant girl they will allow me the task of nursing you. If they thought I was nobility they would never permit me such a menial job. I knew no one would take care of you like I would. Third, I thought I am running away and no one will remember stories of a commoner, a servant girl. A runaway heiress, on the other hand. . . news like that will spread faster than fire."

Henri was speechless for a moment. "You would do this for me?"

"You did it for me."

"But, why the name Miriam?"

"It was the first name that came to mind."

"It was my mother's name," Henri said reflectively and then looked at Renée.

"Yes, so I have found out, and afterwards I remembered you told me once. I hope you don't mind." She fiddled with the blankets, pulling out the wrinkles.

Henri shook his head. He did not mind at all.

"You have been very sick. Stay in bed and rest. You need it. Tomorrow I will ask Dr. Ishmael if you can get up, then I will help you. Until then stay in bed. I don't want to have all my good nursing wasted by your stubbornness." She leaned over and stroked his forehead. "Get some sleep, Henri."

"All right," Henri agreed, "But just one more question."

"One. One question only."

Henri propped himself up on his elbows, "How did you find Cairns among all the different roads, when I couldn't?"

Renée laughed as she opened the door. "That was easy. I stopped and asked for directions."

La belle infirmière
Softly she sings crimson on the white,
Softly she brings her toils into the night,
And ever love is in her hands
As plain as crossings sands
Under the cold, cold scimitar moon

While all the world sleeps and swoons.
She sits by flickering flame
And ever so quietly
Calls, calls, calls. . .
Calls his given name.

Doctor Ishmael of Montpelier

Before the dawn, with the sky still cast in the blue darkness of night, Henri awoke as a firm hand gripped his wrist. The fingers wrapped around and stayed there. Drowsily opening his eyes, Henri looked into the face of a wiry Moor. A candle burning on the table revealed his olive complexion and outlined the groomed ribbon of a beard on the margins of his firm chin. His eyes were dark as coals, and his hair was black, salted with gray. It was Ishmael, of course. After a long counting of the pulse the Moor laid his hand on Henri's forehead.

"You say he was out of his bed last night?" Ishmael asked sharply into the darkness.

Like an angel, Renée swept forward. She wore a long white dress decorated by a red crusader's cross woven into the fabric extending from neckline to waist. Her hair in two, tight, dark braids fell to her breasts.

"Yes doctor. I found him talking to Jehudah."

Ishmael stood up and bunched his brows. "Did I not give strict orders that he was to stay in bed? How is it that you have not followed them?"

Renée folded her hands in front of her but did not answer.

Doctor Ishmael, not expecting an answer, continued with his examination, moving to the leg. He extended his hand behind him expectantly; Renée promptly filled it with a sharp blade. With deft, bold strokes he cut the bandages and then probed his fingers into the wound.

Henri grimaced.

"Hold on, my boy," Ishmael said with surprising tenderness. "I am just going to see how things are healing." His fingers probed again, and then taking the candle he looked closer at the wound. His fingers explored yet again, and then he stood up, nodding his head.

"Now let me have the balm, girl." Ishmael spoke with authority.

Renée, anticipating the request, had the clay jar filled with the precious ointment. Ishmael took the container carefully into his hands as if it were a bag of fine rubies. His hands as if by habit rubbed the glazed surface of the vase with affection.

"The good stuff," Ishmael murmured as he put two fingers into the pasty contents. "Balm of Ishmael, my best and greatest contribution to the fine world of medicine." He took the ointment and rubbed it deep in the wound and then on the surrounding surface. "No one else could have saved his leg, or even his life. I have assured my place among the notables of medicine with this."

When he had finished he handed the jar back to Renée, who carefully placed it in his satchel.

"I shall have to make another batch today." And then turning to Renée he said, "You have seen how I have done this, have you not, Miriam?"

"Yes doctor, I have."

"Good. You are a most excellent nurse, Miriam. I would that I could hire you to work for me always. You have a very winning manner, and your patient has responded well to your ministrations. He has passed through the crisis."

Renée sighed and smiled. "Thank you, Doctor Ishmael." She slipped beside Henri's bed and taking his hand squeezed it tightly with both of hers.

Gathering his materials together, Ishmael prepared to leave. "I have to leave town for a couple weeks. I have duties to attend to in Montpelier. You are to apply the balm as I have done twice a day, changing the dressing with each application. Make sure the dressings are boiled in hot water prior to each change. I will come back when I can."

Henri, who had lain in silence until this time, now stopped him. "Doctor Ishmael, must I stay in bed until your return?"

Ishmael turned. "Are you out of your delirium, then?" He pulled up a chair beside Henri, crossing his legs as he sat down. "You have been a very sick young lad, but Allah has seen fit to spare you. It is crucial, however, that you rest. You still have a long road to recovery. You must stay in bed."

"Can I at least walk a little in the house?"

"And ruin everything I have done for you, ruin all my work?" Ishmael answered abruptly. "Be grateful that you are alive and have your leg, but you must give it time to heal. My balm is good, but I am not like your Jesus. It could be much worse. Jehudah will see you well provided for, and your servant girl has a lovely voice. When you are bored she can sing to you. I swear even a Sultan would be satisfied to have such a one as your Miriam.

As moves the mountain partridge through the meads
Her tresses richly falling to her feet,
And filling with perfume the softened breeze. . .
Now you rest."

Henri sighed and turned his head to the wall. "I will do as you say."

Studying Henri for a moment, and then looking back at Miriam, Ishmael stood up. "Oh, all right, you may get up and walk in the house. I will leave detailed instructions with Miriam. You must do as she says." Then he left the room. Miriam followed close behind. When he had shut the door he gave strict orders to Miriam about what Henri could and could not do and extracted an oath from her that she would enforce these rules exactly.

When she returned she bore a tray of oatmeal, dried apples, and a cup of fresh milk.

"Breakfast is here," she said with a smile. She set down the tray on the bedside table and sat herself beside him on the bed. Taking the wooden spoon she prepared to feed him.

"I can feed myself," he said, sitting up.

"Well, of course. I have just gotten so used to having to feed you this last week."

"A week?" He arched his eyebrows in disbelief. "Have I lost a whole week? Was I that sick?"

She nodded her head as she handed him the tray.

"You were near death, Ishmael says."

Henri spooned in the oatmeal in huge, sometimes sloppy bites. Renée sat beside him, silently watching him as he ate. Taking the cup of milk, Henri lifted it to his lips. As he did he looked back at Renée. Her eyes were still fastened on him, and they were moist.

"What is it?" he asked.

"I am just so grateful to see you eating again," she said as she took a towel and wiped up some oatmeal from his chest.

"I was leaving that for a midmorning snack," Henri replied. "But why the tears, Renée?"

Renée stood up and begin to straighten his blankets. "Nothing, no reason. . . ." She stopped and forced a smile. "It's just that when I thought you were going to die, I was so lonely. You are the only person left for me." She took the empty oatmeal bowl and put it on the table.

Her blinking eyes as she wiped away the hint of a tear tore at Henri. This was uncomfortable. "Is there more oatmeal? I am still hungry," he said for a distraction.

She appreciated the opportunity to get away. "I'll get some more."

She brought it and then left the room.

When she returned, Jehudah came with her. "Now that Ishmael is allowing you to get up, I thought you might like to join us this morning in the chapel." Jehudah walked across the room and opened the curtain. The sky was overcast and a steady drizzle rolled down the window.

"Is today Sunday?"

"No, Saturday."

Henri gave Jehudah a questioning look that implied, "I thought you had become a Christian, so what are you doing still keeping the Jewish Sabbath?"

Jehudah understood. "I'll explain it when you are feeling stronger." Henri shrugged and allowed Renée and Jehudah to assist him to the attached chapel.

Midway through the service a servant entered and spoke something in Jehudah's ear. He slipped quietly from the room. Henri and Renée, seated by his side, looked back as he left the room. A few moments later Jehudah reentered and whispered quietly to Renée. She nodded vigorously. They both helped Henri down the hall and to the great room; there standing in the room, soaked through and through, were Petro and Maria.

"You have made it," Henri exclaimed. "You found us and you came."

"Of course I came. After the monastery where else had I to go? As I have told you before, you are my relic, better than any portion torn from Stephen's robe," Petro answered, but as he spoke his eyes were inquiring, "What is this? Why are you being held up? What has happened to you?"

"Jehudah, this is Petro de Lomange and his wife, Maria. He was a knight in the service of Sieur de Bixmarch. He helped us escape." Henri introduced them.

Jehudah bowed deeply. "If you are a friend of Henri's, you are welcome. But I don't think you mentioned an escape, Henri. I can see there is more to the story than I have yet heard."

"I have brought the gelding," Petro said. "Is there a stable where I may rest him?"

"Of course; my stables are behind the house. I will have my servants see to him."

"No need. I will take care of him myself, but if you would be so kind, my wife is cold from the rain."

Jehudah stepped forward. "Of course, come here closer to the fire. Have a seat and warm yourself. The road to Cairns is not an easy one."

"Nor an easy one to find," Petro replied. "I had to search for several days to find it. But all's well that ends well." He turned and bowed to Jehudah and then to the Maiden Renée. "Milady."

Jehudah did not miss that either.

The rest of that day, as the rain fell in a steady pattering on the slate roof, Henri slept off and on. He found the activity of attending the religious services and then meeting Petro and Maria had taxed his strength. Renée was in and out of the room through the day, slipping in like a shadow and working quietly or softly singing in the gray dimness. The words Henri recognized as coming from Bernard of Clairvaux:

What language shall I borrow to thank Thee, dearest friend?
For this Thy dying sorrows, Thy pity without end?
O make me Thine forever, And should I fainting be,
Lord, let me never, never out live my love to Thee.

When she took her bowl to wash the sweat off his brow he reached up and took her hand. She sat down beside him on the bed and let him hold it.

"Thank you," he said, "thank you, Renée. You have been kind, and I appreciate it."

She did not reply but stroked his hair.

A smile came to his face. "If you had known how difficult I would be, you might not have shot your arrows and saved me from the boar."

She laughed a little and stood back up. "Henri, the one thing you have never been is difficult." And then she slipped out of the room. Henri slept until late the next day.

Chapitre Onze
La Village sur le Flanc du Coteau

The streets, each one is laid in cobblestone and lime.
The houses rise one above the other on the flank.
Cooper, smith, cobbler, and each of their rank
Opening doors as the sun comes rising in the morning time,
And the lambs, bleating as toward the crest they head
Driven by the shepherdess risen early from her bed,
And all the young men stop and watch as she passes
The shepherdess from the village, on the hill she flanks.
Jehudah of Cairns.

It rained for three days, while slowly—under the careful eye and ministration of Renée—Henri's wound steadily healed, and he recovered his health. Each day he walked a little more in the house. On the third the sun broke through, and he sat outside on a bench along the main street of Cairns.

Jehudah had the largest house in Cairns. It had been in his family for several hundred years. The overall scheme was in the shape of a square with the center open for a garden. In some places second stories could be accessed via stairways inside the house; in other places they could only be reached by stone steps along the wall. By comparison with the great nobility of the times it was not palatial, but rather a sprawling of addition to addition, of stone block covered with white lime; located on the far edge of the hillside town. He lived there now with two of his sisters, one widowed, one a spinster. There were also a number of nephews and nieces who stayed there more often than not.

The town itself was nestled on the hillside, near but not quite at the crest. It was an old, unimportant town, which did its best to stay that way, unnoticed, undistinguished, out of the eye of ambitious men. It focused around two springs, the upper and lower. Of the two, the lower spring was deeper and more abundant. Around this spring were the remains of an old Roman gazebo. The upper spring was neither as deep nor as bountiful, but it had this: it was beautiful, flowing from the deep darkness of a rock cave.

One road connected Cairns to civilization, leading down from the hill to the valley. On the upper side a cattle path led over the rise and down to a secluded valley. This valley, which the people of Cairns tried their best to hide, sustained the town, and was largely the reason Cairns was mostly self-sufficient. Through the valley flowed a stream. The near side was pasture land for the sheep, goats, and dairy of the town. The far side was wooded and spread over the steeper distant hills.

It was thus as Henri basked in the morning sunshine watching the townspeople going about their daily work. A shepherd led his flock of sheep up and over the hill. A young boy pushed a red wheelbarrow of rounded cheese from house to house. Down the street, the smith stepped from his forge, wiped his sweat off his forehead, stretched, and then returned inside. Three women beat rugs on a line and traded stories. Out of sight Henri could hear the clatter of the market, and as he looked he saw, sprouting before the huts and houses, the daffodils of spring.

A small breeze tousled his hair across his eyes. His attention turned to Jehudah, who was coming from the market. He wore a gray and black leather close-jacket and had a red cloth hat. He made his way with many brief stops and greetings to people as he passed. When he saw Henri sitting on the bench in front of his lime-painted house, he tipped his hat and picked up his pace.

"Peace upon you," he said cheerfully as he drew close, stopped, removed his hat, and arched his neck back to view the sky. "Would that all mornings were like this. On a day like this I could take off to Constantinople. I could ride all day without tiring. I could soar on the wings of eagles, run and not grow weary, walk and not be faint. God is seated on His holy throne. How is it that the Psalm states it?"

Henri answered, "Great is the Lord, and most worthy of praise, in the city of our God, his holy mountain. It is beautiful in its loftiness, the joy of the whole earth."

"Yes, exactly." Jehudah sat down and threw an arm on the bench behind Henri. "I have had a very good morning, very prosperous. Good news came from multiple sources. The business is prospering."

"Have you recovered from your losses in Gascony?"

"Recovered? I suppose that depends on what the word means."

It had been on account of Jehudah and Ishmael that Sir Thommas had left Gascony. It had started when the Grand Inquisitor, passing through the Aquitaine, had commented to the Archbishop of Auch that he might be interested in spending a little time in Gascony, "And by the way, what is this I have heard about a Jewish Chancellor, and a Moor for court physician? Gascony has not become a safe haven for Jews, infidels, or heretics, has it?" He had pressed this matter so intently, and with such fervor, that the Duke had succumbed and expelled all Jews and infidels from his lands.

Sir Thommas had remonstrated with the Duke to no avail. It distressed Thommas that a Christian ruler was unmerciful to unbelievers. "If we treat them like this, how then shall we convert them?" he had argued. He illustrated his point with the Iberian Peninsula, where Jews, Moors, and Christians had tolerated each other for several hundred years. Their civilization flowered. The Duke, however, feared the inquisition; once started it became uncontrollable, and he did not want that for Gascony. Thus was born the unusual friendship of Sir Thommas, Jehudah, and Ishmael: Christian knight, Jewish jeweler, and Muslim physician.

"Our losses upon leaving Gascony were immeasurable. Many people took advantage of me and did not pay their bills. My family's fortune was stripped. Still, the trip to Constantinople reestablished family ties that had been broken for a hundred years. We have reopened trade routes, found new factors, and devised new schemes to move precious gems. This very morning I received news of a shipment docking at Brussels; we had a nice return on investments."

"And yet you live here in Cairns?" Henri looked up and down the small town with its narrow roads, chickens pecking away at the grubs in the dirt.

"And not Venice or Paris, Brussels or Rome?" Jehudah supplied the question for Henri.

Henri nodded.

"Cairns is a very unique town. It is like none that I have ever come across. It has a long history of stubborn tolerance, of independent mind-ed people. We pride ourselves on our freedom of spirit. Look, we are nothing but a village; still we have Catalans and Gypsies, Catholics and Jews, three or four families that are secretly Vaudois, some pagans, probably even a Cathar or two, and of course our good Muslim, Ishmael the Moor. Here, I do not have to wear a yellow star, for we have long held dear that God, however we see him, is big enough not to require force to obtain worship. Imagine, a God so small as that.

"Of course, there are some from time to time who do not fit. . . These we send abroad. Many of them, once they see the narrowness of the world, return as our most ardent defenders of freedom. Still, how this lit-tle town has survived is a miracle of God. Some portion of my family has lived here since before Charlemagne."

"But isn't it difficult to manage your far sprung trading from this remote location?"

"Yes it is. You asked a moment ago if I had recovered. If by this you mean have I the same wealth that I had in Gascony, then the answer is no. I shall never recover that. Maybe my family after me will, though I doubt it. But I learned a couple of lessons from Gascony. We now spread our decision-making and our wealth among a number of people and numerous cities. And I am no longer young. I have turned much over to younger ones. They still come out of respect, but I am not as involved as I once was.

"But," Jehudah said as he spread his hands towards all of Cairns, "I also learned to be more generous. I try to tie their interests to ours."

"I see," Henri replied. "In this way you will stop the relentless persecu-tion of your race."

At this Jehudah's face turned sad. "I am not so foolish as to believe that—though I, too, am now a Christian. I know that I was born a Jew, and nothing ever changes that. A great irony is it not? The one thing Rome holds against my people is the killing of a Jew, Jesus Christ. Yet this same Christian church cannot long refrain from killing another Jew, any Jew. You would think that if anyone would have mercy it would be the Church. Are they not followers of he who taught peace? Yet they persecute me and my people. Still, I have become a Christian."

"That must have been difficult."

Quand j'aurai été élevé de terre
And if he was lifted why not I?

Why should he be stricken and I not die,
When he was lifted, lifted for I.
- Jehudah of Cairns

At this Jehudah stood up and looked thoughtfully.

"It was a great struggle to me, Henri. I must admit. It was a very great struggle. When I heard the voice calling, 'Jehudah will you serve me?' I resisted and wriggled. How could I become a Christian when it was the church—whether the Pope be in Rome or Avignon—that had pasted a yellow star on my chest, had placed a pointed cap on my head, and had taken away my possessions, my position, and my respect. If not for your father, maybe even my life. How could I become a Christian?"

"So what happened?" Henri asked.

Jehudah leaned his arm against the wall next to Henri, his body sagging, as if he were reliving that same struggle. "Well, first it was your father. Don't mistake, your father was as bullheaded and zealous a Christian as I have ever met, not always tactful."

Henri remembered listening to the arguments between Sir Thommas, Jehudah, and Ishmael. Whether sitting around a table in an inn or outside squatting by a fire, they were vigorous and vociferous as they contended with one another over politics, religion, economics, science, history, food, clothing; they even disagreed about the weather.

"But he was genuine, and I knew he respected me even when our beliefs differed. That was important to me. . . after Gascony." Jehudah stopped again, changing his drift. "Gascony, the Duke was not an evil man, badly influenced, badly advised, but then what would I have done, maybe the same? I have forgiven him. The Inquisitor, however, may he rot in Hell! And he will! Well, I should. . . I have forgiven him too. . . somewhat. . . then again, maybe not." At that Jehudah looked at Henri and smirked.

"As I was saying, however, it was a great struggle to accept the Christians' Jesus. I threw up reason after reason why I should not convert; why I could not. But despite all of my philosophical objections, I kept coming back to the Jew on a cross. Though I tried to hide I could not. When I woke in the morning and looked up at the ceiling, I saw him looking at me; when I sat in the synagogue and tried to listen to the rabbi I heard him instead; and when I closed my eyes at night I heard him as if from the cross calling me. 'Jehudah, Jehudah, Jehudah. Look at me, Jehudah. Look up at me. Look at my hands, at my feet; it is for you that I am stretched. Look at my back all torn with bleeding stripes. Look at my head, thorns driven in my scalp, and soon they shall pierce me. Jehudah, if they did it to me, I who am also a Jew, why worry about what they do to you? Jehudah, I am big enough for the both of us. Come with me. Suffer with me. Follow me, Jehudah, just follow me.'"

Jehudah stopped and took a deep breath. "And so I did."

There was a long pause. Jehudah sat down beside Henri again. "I am fortunate, Henri, to have an education and money. I have had the Bible copied. By the way, I hope you don't mind, but I found your father's Bible, and have paid to have it copied. It is what I was reading. I determined that I would follow whatever the Bible said. That is why I still keep the seventh day. It is the day Jesus kept, and I find nothing in the Old or New Testament to command otherwise."

"Is that right?" Henri asked incredulously. "I will have to look into it sometime. But whatever day you worship. I am glad to have you as a Christian brother."

"But enough of that. My sister rightly says that I do tend to 'pontificate.' You get it? Pontificate?" Jehudah laughed at his choice of words. "How are you? You are looking better."

"I feel better, though still weak." Henri repositioned himself on the bench to place his left leg up. "Where did you find my father's Bible?"

"I am ashamed to admit it, but I found it in one of his trunks. I had the lock picked. I have kept his house, however, ever since then, in the best of repair, and I have put new locks on the trunks. Everything is exactly as I found it."

Henri and his father had lived in a cabin in Cairns for a couple of months. Jehudah had persuaded Sir Thommas to buy it after returning from Constantinople. It was a small thatched house on the outskirts of town, surrounded by a grove of linden trees. One of the smaller streams from the upper spring passed near the house. Sir Thommas had bought the house and then built an open stable for the horses he bought and sold.

"I would like to go there." Henri's eye brightened at the thought of going back. It was very peaceful there.

"It is a nice house." Jehudah held up both palms. "Who knows, maybe your Miriam will allow you a little walk this afternoon."

La maisonette de son père
How can this be so alone?
Mortar and stone,
How can the memories flee?
Mother and father—
How can it just be me?
- Henri at Cairns

It took some persuasion on the part of Jehudah and Henri, but when Petro fixed up a cushioned bed in the back of a wagon, Miriam relented. "But it will not be upon any of you that Ishmael will vent his anger when he hears of this."

The house was not far, but still the wagon could not make it all the way. The road became too narrow, and Henri had to get out and walk the last hundred yards. Renée took up her position by his side, laying his arm on her shoulder. Henri knew now that she was stronger than her thin figure suggested.

As he came into the meadow he looked around. The afternoon sun shone down upon the walls, a mixture of stone braced by wood and daubed with mortar. The thatched roof hung over the walls. It was in good repair. There were a few wildflowers growing along the banks of the stream that ran between the stables and the house. A wooden wheelbarrow stood on end at the far side of the house. A ladder was propped on the near wall of the stables. A pitchfork, axe, and shovel leaned against the wall inside the stable.

Jehudah pushed the key in the lock and swung open the door. Henri extricated himself from Renée and stepped in. It caught his breath away, this sudden remembrance, yet again, of his father. Henri had not been back since Thommas's death. Now, here he was, back, except without his father. Henri sagged; he could feel his legs giving way. Renée grabbed him and held him till Petro could help. They sat him on a bench by the table to the right of the fireless hearth.

"I knew he should not have come. We will have to return quickly." Renée was vexed.

"I am all right. It is passing. It's just that I miss my father, and seeing everything here exactly as we left it when we closed the door one year ago. . . ." Henri's eye surveyed the room. A quill pen lay on the desk before him. A short stack of papers, bills, and deeds of horses were neatly stacked in the center of the table. To the left was a small volume of Augustine's *City of God*. Behind him on the mantle were some vases that his father had acquired in Venice on their way back from Constantinople. Their intricate glazed flower drawings were an eternal spring, and Sir Thommas had been much taken by them. Hanging from the cross beams were kettles, clusters of spices, and wooden spoons. As he looked at this cooking apparatus, Henri understood in a new way the difficulties Sir Thommas had faced every day as a widower who must take care of a son. On the far side of the room, another table, more roughly hewn, stood with knives still stuck in the wood where they had prepared their meals. Opposite the door was a pull ladder which led up to the loft where they had slept. On either side of the windows were reed shutters, which Renée and Maria were now opening. Beside the door were two trunks: the smaller one, braced heavily in iron, was no longer or deeper than a man's forearm; the other was much bigger but not as heavily secured.

Jehudah pulled the smaller trunk to Henri and gave him the key. He turned it and pulled open the lid. The top was filled with papers. Most of them were legal documents, bills of sale, or deposits.

"I will confess yet again," Jehudah replied, as Henri sifted through the papers. "I looked through these. Your father was holding numerous loans, and several liens on land and properties. These trunks were too valuable to leave here all alone untended. In fact I had one of my nephews bring the smaller one up here this afternoon from my safe.

"Now, I mean no disrespect," Jehudah continued. "Your father was a great man. The Christian knights say he was without peer as a hunter and equal to any in the field of battle. He was more learned than any other knight I met; true and honest; and he knew horses, hounds, and hawks; but. . . as a merchant and a man of business he was abysmal; most of these are uncollectible."

Henri kept digging through the small box. He found a pair of spectacles and remembered how his father had worn them at times when he was sitting going over the bills at night. Then he found what he was looking for: the large, well worn, leather-bound New Testament. He opened it and looked at the handwritten pages, and in the margins little notes made by his father. His fingers lightly touched the pages.

"His Bible?" Renée asked softly. Henri nodded and looked up at Renée with a smile full of remembrances and deep feeling.

"Rest in peace, father," Henri mumbled as he slowly shut the volume and lay it aside. Rising from his chair, Henri limped across the room to the other trunk. Jehudah handed him the key, and he stuck it in the hole. He knew what was in this trunk. His father and he had on occasion through the years examined the contents. Still, it had been some time. He opened the lid and pulled back the covering cloth of white linen; beneath were several of the dresses from his mother, Miriam. They were carefully preserved.

"How very lovely," Maria murmured as Henri lifted out a purple velvet dress with laces to tie up the front. Several linen beige blouses and surcotes followed and then three exquisite dresses of silk of exceptional brocaded intricacy in the material. The first was red with a low waist and had gold threads interwoven throughout. The second was emerald green with a full skirt and a long train. The last one was blue, robin's egg blue, with a low décolletage across which draped a sheer mesh of sarcenet; the most exquisite of pearls wrapped across the bodice and around the neckline.

"Oh, my," Renée exclaimed, as she fingered the pearls and ran her hands over the sheer mesh. "This is the most beautiful dress I have ever seen,"

"It is yours." Henri handed it to her.

But she backed away, not taking it.

"I mean this for you, Renée," Henri offered again.

"Renée, is it?" Jehudah said and looked around the room. Seeing he was the only one surprised, he added, "I see I am the only who does not know the story."

No one paid him any attention.

Renée looked at Henri and then at the dress. "No, Henri, I cannot take this from you. It would not be proper to take it from you."

Jehudah, still in the background, and talking mostly to himself, added, "Well, of course if you wear it we can forego the servant girl story completely." And he thought to himself, "So it is Renée. Undoubtedly the same Renée that his agents had heard rumors of in the markets the last week."

Yet Renée, despite her protests, held the dress up in front of herself.

"It should fit fairly close," Maria murmured in approval, as she sized the fit. "You would not need to make any modifications. You would look beautiful in this." She helped Renée spread the material around.

Renée turned around again and again, fingering the material and tucking the dress up on this side and then that. A smile of pure feminine delight spread across her face as she turned and tilted her head down just a little in an innocent manner. It suddenly occurred to her that Henri must love her. If he was giving her this, the most exquisite dress she had ever seen, and moreover a dress of his mother's, then he must love her, and while the notion had been in the back of her mind, it had not crystallized as clearly as it did now, now that he was offering her this. For it was simply the most beautiful dress she had ever seen, and feeling the fabric slip through her hands she could not refuse.

"Thank you. . . Henri. . . . Thank you." For a moment their eyes locked in understanding.

Then Renée carefully folded up the dress. Petro and Jehudah loaded the trunks onto the wagon, and they made their way back to town.

Chapitre Douze
Le Faucon, Le Cheval, et Le Chien Courant

Have you no love, my love,
Waiting here by the door at the twilight
With your broom in your hand gripped tight,
Waiting for his hound and hawk on glove?

Have you no love, my love,
As the sun sets in the valley in a ball so bright,
Your hair let down, your form so lithe,
Waiting for him to come riding from road above.

And you a plain girl with your eyes all set
On a highborn knight, riding his destrier.
He with lips so pure and eyes most fair
Will pass you again this night, your love unmet.

Constance of Biarritz

Henri's leg healed rapidly over the next couple of weeks. When Ishmael returned, he was well pleased. Renée remained known as Miriam in the town. And with his leg healed, Henri determined to move into his father's house. Jehudah tried to persuade him not to go, but Henri was persistent. He wanted to go back home and live where his father and he had lived, if only briefly. Renée said nothing, though she always seemed to appear when the subject came up, standing silently off to one side, watching, with her big green eyes.

"What of your servant girl?" Jehudah asked, pointing to her during one of those conversations.

Henri stopped and looked at Renée in the white surcote with the large red cross emblazed on the front. She stood by the doorway to the garden.

"Jehudah, you know she is no servant girl. She is or will someday be a comtess. She must stay with you."

Thus on a sunny morning Henri mounted his black warhorse, with the hawk on his arm, and the hound following close by his side, and he rode the short distance to his house. Jehudah sent a wagonload of supplies, pots of oil, dried meats, grains, beans, dried peas, dried fruit, and Henri settled himself into the cabin of his father.

Over the next several weeks, as Henri's recovery continued, Petro and he often spent mornings honing their skills with the blade. Petro was a good swordsman and a good partner for Henri. It was quickly clear to the pockmarked knight that young Henri had immense natural talent, and that he had learned much under the hands of a master. During these morning drills the two noblemen also learned more of each other. Petro had originally come from Catalan. His great grandfather had fled the persecution of the Cathars in nearby Languedoc. Petro also confided his grief that Maria was barren. During these weeks, Henri also tried to help Jehudah straighten out the papers his father had left him, but he found his education in finance sorely lacking, and he increasingly despaired of ever getting it settled. Often, frustrated, Henri would turn to the hunt. And as Henri got stronger he spent more time working with his horse, his hound, and his hawk. It became a familiar scene in the village to see Henri ride in on Le Noir, the stallion high stepping and magnificent and the hawk perched on his left arm, while his great red hound—aptly, though unimaginatively named La Rouge—trotted by his side. Hanging by a rope behind the saddle might be a couple of doves, a duck, or a brace of conies. On one occasion he might give the birds to Jehudah and his household, but he was just as likely to stop by some small hut where a widow lived and leave the meat on her doorstep, or on a whim, seeing a small child, give it to the overjoyed boy, who would then run off to show it to his mother. And in the doorway a moment later a peasant woman would come out and express deep and passionate gratitude. Henri would smile and ride on. On many of these hunts Petro would ride with him, and sometimes Renée joined them, riding the Andalusian and practicing her archery.

On one of those particularly successful afternoon hunts, two pheasants were flushed by the hound and killed by the hawk. As the group was riding back from the valley, Henri suggested a side road leading to a rock outcropping on the ridge.

"You two go," Petro suggested. "I will take the pheasants to Jehudah's. They will be very nice for dinner tonight." And he slyly winked at Renée, for they had planned a surprise for Henri.

Trop de haute extraction
Now give way sweet dream and cherished thought;
Give way red poppies, they are sped
Like frail shades and swirling winds;
It washes away, washes far away.
All the beauty in woman's form I sought
I found in you, but they are led
Too high aloft for such a friend
As I. The wind and the rain wash away.
- Sir Henri at Cairns

Henri and Renée steered to the right and rode three hundred feet before dismounting. After wrapping the reins of their steeds around a gnarled pine limb, Henri led Renée up to a granite rock above them. They scaled the face, with Henri's encouragement—Renée feared heights. On the top they looked first to the west and the town of Cairns;

the people were as small inkblots in the streets. Then they looked towards the western horizon where the sun was descending through scattered clouds. A gust of wind caught Renée's hair. She brushed it down and glanced at Henri. He was watching her. She smiled and faced the valley.

At the cliff's edge Henri sat and dangled his feet. "I often came up here with my father, and I have come many times since returning," he said as she sat down close beside him.

"It is peaceful," she responded.

"Listen," he said reverentially.

They sat side by side and listened. From the valley they could hear the tinkling of bells, sheep, goat, and cattle, each one a little different, their harmonies playing and echoing from the distance. Renée's hand brushed Henri's. He clasped it.

"It's lovely," she murmured.

"Isn't it?" Henri said.

For several more minutes they sat like that, each one silent, not wanting to destroy this perfect moment, hand in hand, serenaded by the summer breeze, the bells of the valley, and the occasional flat caw of the crow.

Finally she sighed, "I have never been so happy in my entire life."

Henri snapped a pine needle and held it to his nose and then offered it to Renée. She smelled and smiled, then swung around, crossing her legs in front of her. She faced him. "Do you remember when we were in the inn, and I told you about what type of person I would like to marry?"

Henri remembered. He marveled at the sparkle of her green eyes, as she held back her hair from across her face.

"You said I was the prettiest girl you had ever seen. Did you really mean that?" Renée asked with a trace of disbelief in her voice, almost as if she wanted him to repeat it.

"Undoubtedly," Henri responded, now turning in to face her.

She looked at him and sighed. "That was very sweet," she said. "I have thought about that a lot."

He looked at her for a moment and then rose to his feet. "We should go."

"Go? It is so peaceful and beautiful here. I don't want to go yet."

"No, we need to go."

Renée was puzzled. Why the sudden change? She took his hand as he helped her to her feet, and she pondered his words as they descended the rock. On the trail he walked in front of her. She watched him, his obvious muscular frame beneath the gray surcoat and a sword at his side, taking firm strides with almost no limp in the large, black, supple boots.

As they came to the horses and he handed her the reins of her horse, she asked, "What is it Henri? What did I say?"

Standing with his hand patting the large neck of his black stallion, Henri looked over at Renée. She was so slender, so lovely; her lips were red and parted, her head cocked slightly to the left.

"You are beautiful, Renée, and I mean that, but I was wrong to say that to you. I was out of place. It could never come to anything."

"What could come to nothing?" she asked, though she understood the meaning.

"You. . . me. You and I. I have been foolish." He spoke as he checked the cinch on her saddle and then lifted her onto the horse.

"I don't understand," she persisted as she took the reins in her hand. A wave of sadness was beginning to wash over her.

Henri swung into the saddle, and then they sat side by side on horseback as he spoke.

"I love you, Renée. I think I loved you from the first moment I saw you, but you are to be a comtess, a woman whose station is above mine. You are too high for me. You are too beautiful, too sweet, too noble. You are right to have set your desires on becoming a duchess, though I swear you deserve to be a princess, or a queen, and that I could never provide. It is true I am not a stable boy, and that is a curse. As a stable boy I could at least stay in your employment. I could ride with you when you have married your great lord, but now that you know I am a nobleman of no account how can this continue? I am just climbing a cliff of delusions; at some point I must fall, fall in despair. That is why I left to live in my father's house, to be away from you."

"You love me? Is this true?" Renée asked incredulously.

"Of course it is true. You know it is true. How could I help but fall in love with you? You're beautiful, kind, courageous, funny, and you have got grit. Tell me you did not know I was in love with you."

"Well. . . I knew you liked me, but I am not like you, Henri. You have known love from your mother and father. You have known it, and you recognize it. Me? I have never had anyone love me."

Henri paused, "Then hear this now, Maiden Renée d'Ayes. I, Henri son of Sir Thommas the Hunter, I love you." He stopped, looked at her, then shook his head sadly. "But it can come to nothing. I am not worthy." He was about to spur his horse until she held him back.

"Henri, I could never find anyone half as worthy as you, my uncommon stable boy."

Then they rode back into the village.

La fille en bleu

She, who with such beauty blessed
Could well adorn the highest

Courts with grace and winsomeness,

Enters with youth and sweetness

Like the partridge and the dove,
So cooing soft. The light above

Falling off her sloping shoulders,
Slender as the day is past.

Now comes the night, the princess
Enters and all are smitten.
- Doctor Ishmael

Later that night, as Henri sat in Jehudah's house smelling the aroma of savory meats basting in the kitchen, his appetite increased by bounds. Jehudah sat at his desk with quill pen adding a column of numbers with his nephew Simeon-ben-Adar, who was standing by his side. He had been trying to explain how Simeon had straightened out Henri's papers. If prudently managed there would be enough to support a small household, but try as he might, Henri could not follow the numbers.

A disturbance at the back door startled them and they jumped to their feet. At the back entrance Petro stood panting heavily. He caught his breath and then quickly pulled a curtain and glanced out. "I don't think they saw me."

"Who?" Jehudah questioned.

Petro looked at Henri. "Two of Bixmarch's men. They were in the town square. I saw them as they were putting their horses into the stables. One of them glanced my way, but I don't think they saw me. I slipped into the alley and ran here. Make sure that Maiden Renée does not leave the house until they are gone."

Jehudah looked at Henri. "Bixmarch, isn't he the maiden's uncle?"

And when Henri nodded, Jehudah gave instructions to his nephew. "He will go to the inn. The keeper is clever. He will ply the two knights with ale and get their tongues loosened. We shall know by tomorrow what brings them here, but now it is time to eat." With that Jehudah led them into the dining hall. There was a larger than usual party at the long, rectangular table. Many of Jehudah's family and several of the more prominent townspeople were there. At the far end Doctor Ishmael sat engrossed in a book, oblivious of all others.

"Henri, you take the seat at the head of the table." Jehudah ushered Henri to the seat of distinction.

"No, no, this is your seat," Henri started to protest.

Jehudah insisted as Henri began backing away.

"Me, why?"

"Because tonight the festival is in your honor," Jehudah replied. "I believe today is your birthday, is it not?"

"My birthday? This is for me?" Henri looked around in genuine puzzlement.

At that Petro clapped Henri across the back. "Happy Birthday, my good friend."

Reluctantly Henri took the seat. The servers were bringing out the dishes: basted pheasant brushed with olive oil and surrounded by cut almonds, pike from stocked ponds in the valley, leeks and cabbage, long loaves of bread with thick crusts, beans, cherry tarts, and a tankard of fine wine. He looked around for Renée and Maria. They were not in the room. He wondered if his words this afternoon had destroyed their friendship. Was she even at this time holed up in her room? Had she realized how right he was? Would she now begin breaking off contact with him?

His commiserations, however, did not have much time to pile upon each other. For at that moment she entered wearing the blue dress he had given her, and it molded perfectly to her youthful curves. The pearls along the neckline shone against her white skin, and a choker of diamonds sparkled around her neck. The left side of the dress was pinned up to show supple leather boots and peacock blue silk stockings on her calf. Her eyelashes and brows were penciled darkly and a cerulean tint lay on the lids. Her lips were lined full with vermillion red. Her brunette hair was French braided and topped with a glistening tiara, set prominently with a large sapphire. Mostly he noted, however, her smile like a minx, as if she were saying, "If you thought I was beautiful before, just look at me now."

"Mother of God," Petro exclaimed. "Is this the same Maiden Renée? My, O my!" He rose from his chair, as did all the other men at the table, spontaneously, instantly, as if driven by an ancient instinct preserved from the beginning of time.

Even Ishmael, looking up from his book, rose in astonishment. "Is this the servant girl, Miriam? I think not. I think this is Scheherazade. Oh, the Prophet would have liked this one!"

She approached the table slowly, holding her dress up a little with her left hand. Henri stood witless as she came to the chair. His eyes had not left her since she had entered, and it very well might have been that he had not breathed since then, either.

"Happy Birthday, Henri," she breathed. "Do you like the dress you gave me? It's nice, isn't it? It fits well."

Henri stood dumfounded. Renée looked back at Henri and smiled. His silence was better than any words. She stood for a moment at her chair, and seeing he was not going to move she looked at the chair and then at him. He did not catch her meaning. She was more direct. "The chair, Henri. Would you help me with the chair?"

In a flash he jumped to pull it back for her.

As she sat down words finally came. "You look marvelous, Renée."

"Well, it is your birthday," she said with just a lift of an eyebrow, as if that was all the explanation he should need. "Maria helped me a great deal, and I am afraid I don't have any other gifts for you."

Sitting across the table, Ishmael commented, "What more could a man want on his birthday than a beautiful damsel?"

The feast proceeded, and for a period of time Bixmarch's men were forgotten. The food was eaten, and gifts were presented. Petro brought Henri a sword. "This was the sword of my uncle. It is a good blade."

Henri examined it. It was superior to the sword he had been using, better balanced. He stood up and took a few cuts through the air. "Thank you, Petro and Maria," he said as he sheathed it.

Ishmael brought out a small but beautifully illustrated volume of the Old Testament. "On this we agree. May Allah bless you and keep you in health, my friend."

Jehudah then brought out a ring of blue sapphire. Henri looked at it closely; in the reflection of the candlelight he could see the glistening of a cross in the midst of the stone. "I will cherish this and our friendship," he said as he slipped it on his finger.

After that Jehudah called for the musicians. The table was pushed against the wall to clear the way for dancing. But the music and dance were Jewish, and Henri and Renée, much as they liked watching the nephews and nieces, were not adventurous enough to join. Instead, as the night wore on, they migrated farther and farther from the music. In their promenade they ended up in the garden beside the rock pool. They sat upon a stone bench facing each other. The moon rose over the slate roof, reflecting off the still pool. Three carefully spaced cypress trees sealed them off from inquisitive eyes.

Henri turned to the pool and began to recite:

"The rising moon, the firmament it loves;
The waving cypress seeks its native groves;
The fountains are still, the waters are clear;
But I shall never find love as blue, as dear
As this I see, as this I feel in the springtime,
In the springtime of our love."

"That's beautiful. Who said that?" Renée asked.

"I did," Henri answered.

Renée laughed gently. "Yes, I know Henri, but who wrote it?"

"No one," Henri replied. "It just came to me now as I was sitting looking at the garden and. . . you."

Renée blushed unseen. "You thought of that just now, while we were sitting here? You truly are an uncommon stable boy." She stroked his face with the back of her hand. He covered her hand with his, and held it against his face.

"You're beautiful, Renée."

"Thank you," she whispered.

He circled his arm around her waist and drew her to him. "I just want to hold you forever."

"I'm not resisting."

And with the moonlight glowing off the pool he drew her lips to his; she shut her eyes, and they kissed.

Chapitre Treize
Stratégie

Your strategy I fear too much;
What is gained, but what is lost?
What is a maiden thrown among such
Ravenous wolves? What is the cost?
- Maiden Renée d'Ayes

Early the following morning, Simeon-ben-Adar arrived at Henri's house with a message. Henri was to come as soon as possible. The tavern keeper had gleaned important information last night. He would be at Jehudah's. Henri dressed, pulled on his boots, strapped his new sword around his breeches, and walked quickly down the streets to Jehudah's house. The sun was shining on the first buds of the rose vine growing up the rock wall surrounding Jehudah's house. Henri knocked and the door was opened by Hadassah, one of Jehudah's nieces, a girl of about ten, with pretty auburn highlights in her dark hair.

"Ishmael and my uncle are in the library," she said.

Henri tussled her hair playfully, thanked her, and left his sword hanging on the post.

Inside the library, Petro, Ishmael, Jehudah, Simeon-ben-Adar, and a stranger were seated around a large oak table. The sun shining from an outside window gave good light and the windows were open, resulting in a pleasant warmth.

"Peace to you, Henri. Have you eaten?" Jehudah greeted him cheerfully.

"No, not yet."

"Hadassah, can you bring him some of that bread and cheese we had this morning and a large bowl of hot oatmeal? Be sure to put extra honey on it," Jehudah directed his niece.

She nodded and ran off to the kitchen.

Henri took a seat and looked at the stranger. He was an older man, gray haired, and rather stout. He surmised that the stranger was the innkeeper. He then looked expectantly at Jehudah. "So, what did you find out?"

"You shall hear in a couple minutes, but we will wait for the Maiden Renée. This concerns her most."

They had not long to wait before Renée entered. She had her hair tied up in a kerchief and wore a simple gray sleeveless surcote over a close fitting beige linen undercote. Slung low around her hips she wore a leather kirtle with the tongue hanging nearly to the knees. She looked tired. She smiled briefly at Henri but did not say anything as she settled into her seat.

When Hadassah brought Henri the bread, he offered some to Renée. She declined.

"Well, everyone is here," Jehudah announced. "First off, I would like to introduce Pierre. Pierre is the keeper of the White Hart Inn. He is a friend of mine in whom I have great trust. Like Balaam of old he could get even a donkey to talk." Then, turning up his palm towards Pierre, he gave him the floor.

Before beginning, Pierre nodded at each of those gathered around the table. "As usual Jehudah is very generous, and as to getting a donkey to speak, I should hardly agree. For me a donkey will not even walk. Nevertheless, as for these two fellows last night, they hardly tried my expertise. They spilled everything they knew before the second tankard of ale." Turning to Jehudah he shrugged. "I had hoped I would have to bring out expensive wine to charge to your account. Alas, it was the cheapest I had. This will not cost you much."

Jehudah laughed appreciatively.

"Anyway, here is the long and the short of it. The two are horseman under a certain Sieur de Bixmarch, who recently has been trying to become the new Comte d'Ayes. Apparently his marriage proposal was rudely rebuffed by the heiress d'Ayes, a waif of a damsel—nothing compared to her curvaceous mother.'" And the innkeeper drew a well endowed hourglass in the air but then, remembering Renée's presence, apologized profusely.

Renée waved it off. She had heard remarks like these all her life and had grown immune to them.

Recovering from his faux pas, the keeper continued. "His soldiers have been searching this region and thought they might have stumbled onto something when they heard of a knight and a woman coming this way a few weeks ago. I believe I was successful in distracting their attention away from Cairns. In any event, they left early this morning, pressing on farther to the south to search toward Languedoc."

Ishmael, looking at Renée, remarked, "Your Sieur de Bixmarch is very persistent."

Renée shuddered, remembering again the repulsiveness of his kiss on her lips, such a contrast to the sweetness of Henri's last night, and instinctively she drew her chair closer to him, as if being close to Henri could keep her safe even from memories.

"So then, we are safe?" Henri half questioned, half stated.

"For the present," Jehudah nodded, "But. . ." He stopped and looked at Pierre. "You are welcome to stay, friend, but if you have other things to attend to, we are going to spend a good deal of time discussing matters this morning."

"Indeed, Jehudah," Pierre rose from the table. "I would love to stay. It would be fascinating, but as you have correctly pointed out there are a lot of things I need to do before the day is done." He nodded to each in the room and apologized to Renée again as he departed.

As he left, Jehudah stood up and took down a map from one of the shelves. He spread it over the table. "This is France. Here is Ayes, in the southwest. To the north is the powerful Duc d'Aquitaine, controlled by the English and their free-city of Bordeaux; to the east the Duc de Toulouse, to the south Gascony and Navarre. As you can see, Ayes is at the cross sections where these come together. Though it is not a big city, it does line the Gerond river; thus its strategic value. It has passed from hand to hand through the centuries. Only recently, due to the anarchy of these last couple of decades, has it been overlooked."

Jehudah paused and Doctor Ishmael spoke. "You must remember, Henri and Maiden Miriam." He persisted in calling her that, though he too now knew her real name. "Jehudah-ben-Ibrahim was once the chancellor for the Duc de Gascogne. When he speaks of politic and intrigues, it is from experience. He will not say it, but I will: the Duc de Gascogne never has had anyone who understood finance and the politics of finance as does Jehudah. What he is saying is that, while it is true Ayes was ignored under the later years of Comte Raymond and during the time of Comte Sevestre, it will not stay this way. It appears that Sieur de Bixmarch and your mother, the Comtess, realize they have to move now, quickly."

Renée stood up and pointed off to the southeast corner of France. "Do not forget Avignon. The church is greedy, too."

Jehudah nodded. "Very insightful. You paid attention to your lectures. Now, will they all descend on Ayes? That is unlikely. Especially if a siege is required. Most of the powers have competing interests and more compelling problems. Still, that brings us to the crux of the problem: what should Maiden Renée do? Should we be looking for ways for her to return to Ayes as the Comtess or not? Should she remain in exile, in hiding? The Abbé proposed sending her to a convent; however, our fair damsel will have no part of that." At that Jehudah arched an eyebrow to look at Renée.

Renée shook her head vigorously. "I will not spend the rest of my days in a convent."

"All right," Jehudah continued, "option one, the convent, has been rejected. The second option would be for her to stay in Cairns under an alias. She came as the servant girl Mirriam and few in the town suspect otherwise at present. But this solution has problems, best illustrated by last night. The maiden has grave limitations as a servant girl, with all due respect; she is entirely too pretty. Now, Cairns has been known to hide fugitives in the past, but a Comtess of Renée's beauty is beyond even these reclusive people's ability to keep quiet. Furthermore it would be neither just nor fair to ask the Maiden to spend the rest of her days hidden away as a servant girl. That being the case, Cairns cannot protect her. Cairns has no army to guard her, and when her secret leaks out to the surrounding countryside. . . well." Jehudah characteristically spread his hands palms up. "Therefore we are drawn back to the map. What powers can be called upon."

"What of the people of Ayes; any options there?"

Renée shook her head sadly. "Some might join me if I had an army, but I have no strongman with a band of knights to lead."

"Indeed, you can muster only two knights, Sir Petro de Lomange and Henri." Jehudah tapped the map.

"And I am not a true knight, have never been dubbed," Henri added.

"She could flee to the Moors in Granada," Dr. Ishmael suggested. "She would be safe there."

"Relatively. But as a servant girl or comtess? As a servant girl, what type of life would she expect, a Christian servant girl among the followers of Mohammed? No, dear doctor, that would not do. And as a comtess she is impoverished, without resources. Thus, she must find refuge in one of the powers that impact on Ayes; that is to say in Aquitaine, Toulouse, or Gascony."

"Not Aquitaine," Petro objected. "It is still controlled by the English. A more bloodthirsty and dishonorable people cannot be found."

"She would be better treated among the Moors," Ishmael agreed.

Petro nodded.

"So it is between Toulouse and Gascony."

Henri spoke up. "I know you and Ishmael were mistreated in Gascony, but the Duke would support her cause."

"Exactly my thoughts, Henri," Jehudah agreed. "What do you think, Maiden Renée?"

Renée looked around the room, coming lastly to Henri, and settled her eyes on him. She understood more than Henri what would be the harvest of his suggestion. She, being a woman, knew the way of men and power. If she went to Gascony seeking protection from the Duke, he would undoubtedly pluck all the benefits he could. He would want her to marry a son and thus put Ayes in his dominion. Henri had no inkling, but she saw it clearly. She saw it as plain as a pikestaff. One followed the other like thunder following lightening. And she did not want that. She wanted Henri.

"No, no, I don't know, let me think," she cried, jumped to her feet, and fled the room.

Her abrupt departure startled the room.

"What was that?" Doctor Ishmael asked.

"Who can understand a woman?" Petro murmured.

"Indeed." Jehudah nodded. "The Proverbs say:

> *'There are three things that are too amazing for me,*
> *four that I do not understand:*
> *the way of an eagle in the sky,*
> *the way of a snake on a rock,*
> *the way of a ship on the high seas,*
> *and the way of a maiden.'"*

Henri sat silently for a minute and then rose and looked closely at the map. "Was I wrong to bring her here? I thought surely Cairns could hide her." His finger traced the map idly, running from Paris to the north, through Brittany, Aquitaine, and then ending with a tap on Gascony.

Jehudah stood and placed a hand on Henri's shoulders. "Your father trained you well. She is your charge. Do what is right by her. You must convince her to go to Gascony."

La belle servante
A sparkling-eyed maiden is she,
And as gentle in her walk as free.
She sings with the morning lark,
All gold and scent,
A maiden of a jinni;
My daughter you have made your mark.
- Doctor Ishmael of Montpelier

One month passed. Renée buried her identity deeper. She assumed the role of servant girl Miriam more and more. Sometimes she worked in the kitchen for Jehudah, sometimes as nurse for Ishmael, though mostly she cleaned and cooked for Henri. Henri protested, but she insisted. She enjoyed keeping the little stone house clean and preparing meals for the two of them. Petro and Henri continued their swordplay, and Henri trained the horse, dog, and hawk daily. Periodically Henri tried to discuss the future, but she was clever at diverting the topic. No matter what Henri tried, he got no further.

Early one morning as the sun rose over the crest of the mountain, Renée made her way along the path toward Henri's cabin. She knocked once and then opened the door. Henri was kneeling by the table, his hand resting on the volume of the Torah that Ishmael had given him. He looked up when she entered and smiled.

"I am sorry, I did not mean to interrupt," she said.

"No, come in, Renée," he said, rising from his knees.

"Miriam," she corrected him. "I am Miriam. How often do I need to tell you?"

"Sorry, but it is difficult. You know I like the name Miriam. How could I not, since it was my mother's name? Still, Renée." He said the name slowly, letting it linger on the lips. "You will always be Renée. I love that name."

"Well, get used to it," she said in a tone that let Henri know she was in no mood to discuss it further. She drew the curtains open. "It will be lovely today. What are your plans, master?"

Henri grimaced at the word, but he knew better than to return to that conversation. "Well, I planned to go hunting in the valley." Henri looked at Renée, trying to gauge her reaction. Since the council she had nearly given up riding or hunting as too much like nobility, something unfitting for her role as servant Miriam.

"Oh." She stopped short and looked out the window at the sun, at the blue skies, and let the morning breeze catch her hair. Henri could see she longed to ride. "I hope your falcon brings us back a gadwall like last time. It was very tasty," she said, taking a broom and sweeping vigorously. And then she stopped and looked at Henri, her head cocked a little to the side, and the hint of a smile flashed by, quickly replaced by another vigorous burst of sweeping.

"The poppies were just blooming in the valley yesterday," Henri said as he closed the Old Testament and put it on a shelf. "Just a wash of red flowers in the meadow by the stream, and the hay is so lush. Fallaire would enjoy the. . . ."

Renée interrupted, "No, do not tempt me, Henri. I must give up the hunt and riding."

Henri sat down on a three-legged stool and pulled on a new pair of boots he had bought from the cobbler just a week ago. "Come with me one last time, Renée. If you persist on being a servant girl, so be it, but today is beautiful. The flowers are blooming. The trees are in leaf, and the birds are calling. You ride your white mare, and I will ride my black stallion, and I will be your knight and you be my lady. Come with me, Renée."

When he finished pulling on the boot he stood up and put his hand out for hers. She took his hand and sighed. "All right, today, one last time." A large smile brightened her face. "I do so love to ride and hunt."

An hour later, Henri on the right, Renée on the left, they rode over the crest of the hill and down into the valley. The black stallion was full of energy, smooth-combed mane, broad muscular chest, head held upright, he pranced with Henri on his back. Henri was dressed all in black, the same as his steed: black trousers, black leather belt around his waist, black linen sleeveless shirt, and black leather tabard. His sword hung in front of the saddle, while on his left arm the falcon perched on a leather glove. To his left Renée rode the white mare. She wore a cream sleeveless surcoat over a tight fitting undercote. She had her hair in two braids falling on her back, and behind the saddle her bow and quiver. Down the path they rode into the meadows and passed field upon field of poppies in full bloom, fields and fields of red. The red hound followed closely, chasing off now and again to stir up a rabbit.

As they came over a ridge Henri dismounted. There was a marsh just ahead. Renée slid off her horse, brushed down her dress, and grabbed her bow. Henri started to take the hood off the falcon.

"I just love watching the falcon hunt," Renée said. "It is a work of art. But I have often wondered why men started the sport. It takes such patience to train the hawk. Train it to fly and then return to your arm, when it could just fly away. Have you ever thought about it? Why did they take such time when they could do the same thing with bow and arrow?"

Henri laughed.

"What are you laughing at?" Renée asked.

"You, but I mean no harm." Henri could not help but laugh again.

"What did I say that was so funny?" Renée smiled politely. She had not meant to be funny.

"Well, it's just that you. . . have you ever tried to shoot a duck in the air? It is very difficult. There are few who are that good."

"You mean most hunters cannot shoot a duck or pigeon in the air?"

"Yes, that is exactly what I mean. A good bowhunter will aim carefully at a still object, but it is difficult to shoot any animal while it is moving, especially a duck or pigeon." Henri suppressed his laughter. "My father was a great hunter, and I have hunted with him and many other great hunters. There were only one or two who had any skill at that."

"I have done it," Renée replied matter-of-factly.

Henri stopped and looked at her incredulously.

"You don't believe me, do you?" she said.

"No, no, I don't think you are lying, and maybe you hit one once. I don't know."

Renée glared at Henri. "You don't believe me." She pulled an arrow from her quiver and notched it in the bow. "Put the hood back on the hawk. The next bird your hound stirs up is mine. . . just keep him working close to me."

Henri hesitated and then put the hood back on the hawk. "You don't have to prove yourself to me, Renée. I know you are a good shot. Remember, you saved my life in the boar hunt."

"But you think I was lucky," Renée said heatedly. "Grateful, you are not." And then seeing Henri still standing there she added, "Put the hawk on the saddle, get your dog, and I will show you."

"Renée," Henri protested.

But she was marching towards the marsh. Henri placed the hawk on the saddle, whistled for the hound, and ran to catch up to Renée. As they neared the marsh Henri whistled the dog closer, and Renée and Henri crouched behind the cattails. Suddenly a flurry of wings arose right in front of them. Renée jumped to her feet, stretched the bow, and shot. It was a very good shot, but not quite good enough; the arrow caught feathers but did no damage to the bird.

Wisdom would have been best served by silence. It had been a remarkable shot. Henri had rarely seen its match, a combination of dexterity and hand and eye skills honed to track and release quickly at a startled bird. But Henri felt a little vindication; he after all was the hunter. Hunting was what he knew best, from horse, to hawk, to hound; he knew how to track, how to trap, and how to finish the hunt. She was good, which pleased him; still he was the hunter. Thus as he spoke, he sounded a little condescending. "That was really good."

She shot him a severe glance.

"No, I mean it, it was really good. Not many could have made that shot. I don't think. . . ."

His words were quieted by a second flurry of wings. A duck rose rapidly from the water. Almost faster than he could follow, Henri watched Renée notch a second arrow and let it fly. This one caught the duck in the neck and it dropped.

"I could have shot for the breast, but you would have thought it was just luck." Renée smirked with satisfaction. Henri stood blinking in disbelief.

"Would you mind sending your dog out to retrieve it? I would call La Rouge myself, but I don't know the whistles," Renée added.

"That was amazing!" Henri repeated.

"Thank you. It was a decent shot. I'm satisfied, but would you mind sending the dog."

"I've never seen its like."

Renée smiled and pointed to the hound.

"You are a very uncommon servant girl, Renée."

"Thank you, Henri, but I would like to eat the duck, and I don't swim well. Would you mind sending the hound to fetch it?"

"Of course. Right." Henri gave the command. La Rouge plunged into the pond. Henri continued to stare at her.

"Don't be too discouraged, Henri; falcon hunting still has its beauty. Besides which you can read and I can't. I will always need you, Henri," she replied, feeling generous as she gave him a hug with her free left arm.

Henri picked up the duck after the hound dropped it at his feet and then stepped back to avoid the hound's shaking off the water. He looked back at Renée. She was smiling, still very pleased with her shot, and it seemed much more appropriate to be looking at her as the Maiden Renée, rather than as a servant girl. He hung the bird on his saddle.

From there they rode up the stream and dismounted to let the horses drink and graze. Standing side by side on the sandy soil, where the path forded the creek, plane trees towering above them, holding the reins of their horses, Henri looked at Renée again, and as he looked he saw how wrong it was for her to be a servant girl. She was nobility; anything else was robbery.

Renée stooped to scoop some water in her hand. Henri restrained her. "We need not quench our thirst here in the shallow stream, for there is a great fountain just above. We may freely drink there, if we will walk a little higher on the path."

Au wasserfall cristal

Now rise and kiss me, Sir, for Sir have you become,
Here beneath the cypress in the rainbow spray.
The waters may dampen our eyes, but we have not yet
Wet our lips, nor yet embraced like maiden and her knight,
And so new a kiss shall be mine that though you seek it,
You shall not find another kiss like this, I swear.
- Maiden Renée d'Ayes

Henri took the reins of the horses, lashed them around a couple of trees, and then led the fair maiden along the trail. Soon they came to a small waterfall splashing onto a large rock and filling a deep, clear pool.

"The water is good," Renée said while wiping her wet hands on her skirt after taking her fill.

"The best water on earth," Henri agreed. "Sometimes I imagine it as the rock from which Moses struck, and waters flowed, the pure waters of life, with Christ as fountain."

Renée nodded, sat down on the rock, and looked. The sun shone down on her white skin and glimmered off her dark, lustrous hair. She wrapped her arms around her legs. Blackbirds flew across the pond. Above it was a mackerel sky; cedar trees lined the lower end.

Henri leaned back against the wall of the rock next to the falls and looked at Renée. Presently, she turned and looked at him. Seeing him watching her, she smiled and patted the rock beside her. "This is so beautiful. I could stay here forever."

But Henri did not sit. He sighed and hopped off the rock. Picking up a flat pebble, he skipped it across the waters and then threw another, hitting the trunk of a cedar tree across the pond. His actions, however, were not the idling, languid movements of contentment; rather, they were the measured release of frustration.

Renée noted it. "What's wrong, Henri?"

Henri turned towards her. She was so pretty, her eyes sparkling like the fountains. "Can I speak plainly?"

"If you must."

"It's just that you cannot stay here," he said emphatically.

"Of course, I know that. We will have to go back to the village soon."

"That's not what I mean."

Renée sighed and turned her back on Henri. "I know what you mean," she replied. "You think it is wrong for me to be the servant girl Miriam. You and all the rest. You think that since I am the heir of Ayes, it is beneath me to take up servant girl robes. But tell me this, Henri, did not Christ himself take the robes of a servant when washing the disciples' feet?" She looked over her shoulder at Henri before continuing. "So then, if it was not too low for Christ, how can it be too low for me? Oh Henri, I know you want the best for me. I know you have not a single selfish bone, but you don't understand. You, who were dearly loved all your life, take this for granted, but I do not. Here, I have peace; I have the beauty of nature surrounding me, the sun shining, the welcome breezes, birds singing. I have friends: Jehudah and his sisters, Petro and Maria, Ishmael, and. . ." She paused for a moment before speaking quietly. "Besides, I have someone who loves me. What more could I want? What more could I need?"

Henri picked up another rock, his fingers habitually stretching around it. He then tossed it up and down a couple of times. "But, Renée," he protested.

She stopped him with a finger to her pursed lips. "Shhh, Henri. I know what you are going to say; I should go to Gascony, and seek help."

Henri nodded. "Yes. I lived there. The Duke liked me. He would protect you, and I think he would help you as well."

"O, Henri," she said, sadly shaking her head, "I dearly love you, but you are so naive. Don't you understand?"

Henri shook his head vigorously. "No, I don't understand. Renée, you are meant to be a comtess. You were born for it. You have high nobility written through your every movement; your walk, graceful like the hind, your voice like the nightingale, your beauty like Esther's, and not just your pretty face and figure, but deep inside you. You are beautiful through and through."

Renée laughed. "Henri, you are so sweet, and it suffices me if I am your princess. If you will be a knight faithful to me, I am satisfied."

"But it is not safe here," Henri blurted. "I cannot protect you; we cannot protect you here in Cairns."

"And Gascony is safe?"

"Yes, Gascony is safe. Sieur de Bixmarch will not rest until he has you and Ayes. You know this. The Duke, however, can protect you."

She stood up and took Henri's hands in hers. "No, Henri, Gascony is not safe. You have grown up in a life of sheltered purity; you do not understand the way of men and power."

"Then tell me," Henri said, a little insulted. "You tell me I am naive, and I do not understand. All I want is to protect you. All I want is the best for you. I have lived in Gascony, and the Duke is a good Christian man. What is wrong with Gascony?"

"I am sorry; I did not mean to offend you." She dropped his hands and dropped her head. "All right, I will tell you. If I go to Gascony the Duke may protect me as you say, and he may very well try to restore me to my city, but at what cost? The price will be me. The loss will be you. The Duke will only protect me if he can marry me to one of his sons."

"You would be the Comtess d'Ayes, with the Duc de Gascogne as your protector. What a glorious destiny!" Henri exclaimed.

"But. . . ." Renée turned her eyes up to Henri, and they glistened. "Didn't you hear me? I would rather be with you."

He saw the tears and leaned against the trunk of a pine tree. "Do you mean. . . ?" He halted again. "Do you really mean. . . ?" It seemed unfathomable that someone as lovely as Renée would rather be with him, an impoverished nobleman's son, when she could be a comtess or duchess. He was undeserving.

She nodded slightly without turning her eyes from him.

"You would?" he asked hesitantly.

She nodded again. "I would," she said softly, but passionately. "I would."

"You would rather have me than the son of a duke?"

"I would rather be your servant than marry anyone else, even a prince," she said and bit her lip.

"Oh. . . Oh, my." Henri could feel his knees buckling. He always got weak in the legs when he got emotional. "Renée, Renée." He could not contain his emotions, and his voice broke. "I would do anything. . . anything to deserve you."

She dropped down on her knees and hugged him. "It is I who does not deserve you. You who are so pure and noble. You have already done great things in my sight. "

"But I have not even been knighted. I have nothing to give you."

"Well then, I shall knight you," she declared positively as she rose to her feet. "Give me your sword, Henri, son of Sir Thommas the Hunter."

"Sir Thommas de Bretagne, son of Duc de Montfort de Bretagne," Henri corrected her as he handed her his sword. If he was going to be knighted, she should get his lineage right.

She raised her eyebrows in question. "Your father was the son of the Duc de Bretagne?"

"Yes, but disowned when he married my mother. She was the illegitimate daughter of the Archbishop of Brest."

"You never cease to amaze me, Henri, uncommon stable boy. But now kneel."

Henri knelt in the pine needles beside the fountain. The splash of the spray from the waters cast a cool thin mist. Above, the noon sun bore down in its early summer warmth. Renée stood above him in her cream dress against the background of dark green, her hair braided over her shoulders. She took the sword in her two hands. She was not used to wielding the sword.

"Do you promise to serve me and voluntarily accept me as your liege?" Renée asked.

"I do," he said.

"Then I hereby knight you to serve as a good Christian, watching and protecting the poor and rich alike, being careful to give alms as God blesses you, defending the Holy Christian faith with sword, if need be. Take up the sword, and may God grant you a life of honor, that you might be proud in thought, in word, and in deed. Indeed, may no weapon forged against you prevail." She then tapped both of his shoulders and on the top of his head. "And now, rise Sir Henri, son of Sir Thommas de Bretagne and of Maiden Miriam the beautiful. Rise." And as an afterthought she added, "Rise and kiss your liege lord."

Chapitre Quatorze
De Peur de la Flèche

You do well to pay the pain of arrow
Caught in flesh, of barbs and blood
For kisses forced and not bestowed.
O lush revenge, its merits would
Now for fear of notched string fly,
And pense again your fair niece's reply.
- Maiden Renée d'Ayes

Soon afterwards they mounted their horses and rode the trail out of the valley toward the village. Halfway up the hillside they saw Sir Petro de Lomange riding frantically toward them, raising a cloud of dust along the path. They pulled their horses to a halt. He drew up his horse sharply.

"Bixmarch is tearing up Cairns. He is there with fifty mounted cavalry and one hundred spearmen. He is searching for you, Renée. He says he has positive proof that you are there and will not leave until you come with him, dead or alive. You must leave immediately."

"But what of my things? I must go back to the house," Renée protested in alarm.

"I have packed what we will need. It is waiting in the woods," Petro assured her.

"On the east road?" Henri looked at Petro. There was a narrow path known only to the people of Cairns, used when secrecy was important. Petro nodded.

Renée continued to protest, "But I must go back. I need to get something."

"It's too dangerous," Sir Petro de Lomange insisted. "Besides, I have everything you will need."

"Please, there is one thing I must have."

Sir Petro de Lomange smiled at her. "The blue dress? Maria was sure you would want it. I packed it."

"You have that?" Renée sounded both pleased and embarrassed.

"Will you ride with us, Sir Petro de Lomange?" Henri asked.

"Yes, I will stay with you. Maria will stay in Jehudah's house until I call for her."

"And where will we go?"

Petro looked at the damsel. "Jehudah and Ishmael think. . . ." he said, and then hesitated.

Henri nodded, "And so do I."

Renée resigned. "So be it. I shall go to Gascony."

At the top of the hill they bore away from the town and behind some boulders, working their way into the forest near Henri's cabin. As they came to the stream that passed by Henri's house, they met Simeon. He was holding the reins of one horse and two mules loaded with supplies. Henri quickly dismounted and started looking through the saddlebags. Simeon told him of all the things he had packed: money, knives, helmets and armor, pots, a change of clothes, food. Henri nodded appreciatively but kept searching through the saddle bags.

"Did I forget something?"

"No, you have done well; everything is here, except. . . ." Henri closed up the last saddlebag. "One thing." Turning to Sir Petro de Lomange, he said, "I must ride to the house. I will not leave without my Father's New Testament and Ishmael's Old Testament."

"Of course," Simeon slapped his palm across his forehead. "You would want that."

"I'll be right back. It is not far from here to my house," Henri said, quickly mounting the black stallion.

"Be quick. We will wait here."

"It should not take me more than a few minutes. Hold the hound and hawk here until I return," Henri called over his shoulder.

He galloped up the narrow path, dodging in and around the trees, and was shortly at his cabin. He pulled up by the house and hopped off. He did not see the horses tied up by the stables on the far side of cabin.

Inside, all was havoc. The chairs were scattered and broken. The table had been split in half by an axe. The trunks had been smashed and his mother's dresses, ripped by the sword, were strewn across the floor. Jars of clay were shattered against the stone hearth. The straw mattress had been gutted. He searched frantically through the disorder and found his Old Testament. The binding had been partially torn, and several pages ripped out were lying on the floor. How could anyone do this? He stashed the loose pages in the back of the book, and then found his father's New Testament. It was untouched. Henri grabbed it and held it tightly to his chest. He stood up and glanced once more around at the chaos of the room.

As he came out the door he looked first to the stables. Now he saw the horses. The soldiers who had torn up his cabin were still nearby. He turned to run to his horse, but drew up short.

Sieur de Bixmarch held Le Noir by the bridle.

"So we meet again, stable boy," Sieur de Bixmarch growled. "Was your cabin cleaned to your satisfaction? Now, if you will just hold still one moment, I will finish the job by ripping out your bowels." With that he drew his sword, stepped forward, and swung at Henri.

Henri jumped back, unsheathed his sword, and turned aside Bixmarch's blade in one fluid motion. Sieur de Bixmarch stopped and gave Henri a puzzled look.

"Tell me this, stable boy: how is it you handle a weapon?"

Henri assumed a guarded, defensive position. "I am no common stable boy. I am Sir Henri de Bretagne, a sworn defender of the Maiden Renée. May God grant justice on the side of he who is right."

Bixmarch advanced with a combination of thrusts and slashes. Parrying the strokes, Henri backed toward the stables.

"Divine help? You will need more than divine help," Sieur de Bixmarch sneered. "An extra blade beats a prayer every time."

Bixmarch continued his relentless assault even as he spoke, but the more he thrust, hacked, and cut, the more Henri realized how much he had learned first under his father, and lately with Sir Petro de Lomange. His footwork came naturally; his sword flew into correct position. Most of the practice with Sir Petro de Lomange had been with sword and shield, but his father had spent most of the last couple of years teaching him to defend with sword alone. He could hear his father's advice in his mind: "You may not always have a shield with you. Sometimes all you will have will be your sword, but don't be afraid. The shield is often just a crutch. A good blade, properly wielded, in a skilled hand is superior."

Furthermore, Sieur de Bixmarch had primitive technique. He was strong and bold, but he practically announced every stroke. Henri warded them away with little effort as he continued to retreat toward the stables, toward the horses tied to the posts. With a flick of his sword, Henri cut the horses loose and spooked them off.

Frustrated, Bixmarch charged again and hacked hard with his sword. By itself it was an easy stroke to defend, but when the swords clashed a flaw in Henri's sword caused it to splinter a foot from the hilt. Both Henri and Bixmarch stopped and looked first at Henri's now worthless sword and then at each other. They were now standing in the doorway of the stables. Henri had little room to maneuver.

"Well, well," Bixmarch said derisively. "It comes to this, a sword against a prayer. But pagan as I am—or so they say—still you fought well, and thus if you wish I will grant you the opportunity to take your death on your knees."

Henri glanced around him and saw no escape. He bent slowly to kneel, as three of Bixmarch's men entered from the opposite end.

Bixmarch saw them. "Do you remember Henri, the stable boy? He fought well. He would have made a good knight, but. . . well; his blade was inferior and broke." Then turning towards Henri, Bixmarch raised his sword. "Have you said your prayers?"

"Drop your sword!" a feminine voice yelled. Henri glanced and saw the Maiden Renée sighting down the shaft of a notched arrow, bowstring drawn taught. Never had he been so glad to see her; never had he appreciated the power of a bow so keenly.

"You would do best to heed her," Henri advised.

"A woman!" Bixmarch smirked and cocked his sword. Henri's head would soon roll.

The twang of the string sounded a split second before Bixmarch's howl. Renée's first arrow had skewered Sieur de Bixmarch's right hand. The sword clanged to the ground as he dropped to his knees and grabbed his hand in agony. Henri swept up the sword and jumped to his feet. The other three knights rushed him.

"Stop or your lord is a dead man," Renée warned as she notched the second arrow. They stopped and looked for directions from Bixmarch. He held up his left arm to halt them. Henri cautiously slipped past Sieur de Bixmarch and then warily backed towards Renée.

Bixmarch slowly rose to his feet and leaned against the pole of the stable, watching them. Henri whistled for his horse, and it trotted up beside them. The three men-of-war stood their ground, watching for the signal to charge, but Renée kept her bow drawn. Henri climbed into the saddle and prepared to take up Renée behind him. She glanced at Henri and the horse and back at Bixmarch and his warriors. She started to relax her hold on the bow, then changed her mind stretched it taut and released. The arrow penetrated Bixmarch through the fat of his buttocks, and he howled.

"Remember me, uncle. Remember me when you sit down and when you rise up. Remember me when you lie and when you walk on the roads. Do not forget me, uncle."

Chapitre Quinze:
La Route à Gascony

The road before us again upon my white mare—
The birch, the elm, the maple and white oak.
We stop beneath a spreading walnut tree and drink
From the water currents and babbling brooks;
Eat a plum and listen in silence shared
To the bunting, the finch, the woodpecker in the tree—
O that that this peace would not end here.
- Maiden Renée d'Ayes

Through the many contortions of the narrow path, by boulders, over streams, through woods, around switchbacks, the foursome hurried down and away. At intervals they halted and listened, but they heard no footsteps, no galloping horses; all they heard was the cawing of the crow, the shuffling hooves of their mounts, and the wind blowing amidst the pines. They passed the last hidden turn. Before them was the highway leading southwest to Gascony. Simeon-ben-Adar pulled his horse to a halt. He went out onto the road. He looked carefully in both directions before returning.

"The road is empty. I will leave you here. Henri, you know the way to Gascony?"

Henri dismounted and checked the road for himself. Then he nodded to Simeon. "Yes, I know the road."

Petro and Renée joined the twosome. While Henri helped Renée slide off the horse, Petro unhooked the mules from Simeon's horse and lashed them in tandem behind his. As Petro worked he asked, "What happened at the cabin?"

Henri gave a brief summary, though when it came to the part of the sword breaking he was intentionally vague. He did not want to offend or embarrass Sir Petro de Lomange, since it had, after all, been a present. Sir Petro de Lomange, however, was not easily deceived. For one thing, he knew his uncle's sword well and readily saw that the hilt in Henri's scabbard was different.

Sir Petro de Lomange pointed to the sword at Henri's side as he spoke. "How is it then you have a different sword? Where is my uncle's sword? It was a fine sword, and should not have been discarded."

Henri gave a questioning look at Renée, as if to ask, "Should I tell him?"

She answered for him, "The sword broke, Sir Petro de Lomange, splintered at the hilt, leaving Henri at Bixmarch's mercy."

"It is not true! Is it?" Deep disgrace registered across his pocked face. "My good friend, Sir Henri, please, forgive me. I did not know. I had always been told it was a sword from Toledo—they are the greatest of sword smiths. I am so ashamed."

Henri grabbed Sir Petro de Lomange by the shoulder. "Even the best of swords may have hidden faults. The right hit at the wrong place. You know this. Be assured I do not hold you responsible. It has not even crossed my mind. If I did not mention it at first, it was only to spare you embarrassment."

Sir Petro de Lomange hung his head. "It is a blot on my family, and I am sorry. I shall endeavor to prove our valor and worth in the future." He turned away and finished his work and then mounted his horse without saying a further word.

After watching Sir Petro de Lomange for a moment, Simeon, speaking in a lower voice, asked, "So what did happen? Your sword broke, and you were at the mercy of Bixmarch, and yet here you are without a mark on you, and you have his sword. That suggests a story worth hearing."

"Indeed, it does," Henri replied as he gave Renée another grateful smile. "Behold my savior, the master archer, Maiden Renée." He gestured to Renée and then told Simeon of her timely arrival and matchless accuracy.

When he finished, Simeon looked at the maiden with new respect. She tried to maintain a facade of humility, but her satisfaction showed.

"But. . ." Simeon paused looking back at Sir Henri. "You had the sword, and the opportunity; he has proved himself to be your enemy, and yet you did not strike him dead with his own sword. Why?"

That was the question in all of their minds. To Simeon-ben-Adar it seemed the most logical. Sieur de Bixmarch was the cause of the current trials, and the easiest answer would have been to dispatch him to his eternal destiny, especially when the opportunity had been presented, as it were, on a silver platter. For Petro it was the logical conclusion to a perilous swordfight. If the fight was to the death—Bixmarch, clearly had intended it that way—then the victorious knight had justification for the coup de grace. Besides, that would have allowed Petro to be reunited with Maria. Renée would have agreed with each of the others, and added her own intense personal revulsion. Bixmarch had defiled her with a kiss, not to mention the unnamed viler ambitions. Twice now Henri had opportunity to kill Sieur de Bixmarch but had not.

Now looking at Henri, head tilted to the side and her hands resting on her hips, she posed the question again. "Yes, Henri, why didn't you thrust him through? A knight's duty is to protect his liege lord from her enemies, you know."

He looked at the three of them. They stood awaiting his response. He did not like disappointing any of them, the least of all Renée. What they said made sense. No one would have faulted him; no one would have accused him of breaking chivalry's code had he struck down Bixmarch, struck him down with very same sword that had only moments before been posed above Henri's own head. He had momentarily considered it, but he had quickly dismissed the thought.

He spoke first to Petro. "How could I? Where is the honor in striking a defenseless man? How can I face myself if I strike down a man when he is weaponless?"

Petro nodded in quiet agreement. "Your actions are of the highest honor. No one can fault you. . .though given the same circumstances, I think I would be wiping blood off my blade."

Simeon nodded at Petro and protested to Henri, "But he would have killed you. Do you doubt that?"

"No, you are right, but then Sieur de Bixmarch would do many things I would not, and he shall answer for it." Henri then looked at Renée. "For you I wish I could have done otherwise, and I swear I thought about striking him, for all he has done to you, and may do to you yet. But. . . but when I stood there sword in hand, it came upon me forcibly, 'I would have mercy upon him who does not deserve it, as God has mercy upon me, who does not deserve it.' And I just could not strike him. I am deeply sorry, my liege. I am sorry Renée. I know I have disappointed you. But if the opportunity was presented again, I am not sure I could do differently."

Renée stepped forward and embraced Henri. "I know, Henri. I know. I think I have the lucky misfortune to have the most noble of all knights."

Petro was moved, and speaking softly aside to Simeon-ben-Adar he said, "I think someday he will be a saint, St. Henri."

"Could be." Simeon nodded. "But I hope not."

Petro gave Simeon a questioning look.

"Saints die young," Simeon answered.

Simeon gave his farewells and returned to Cairns. The two knights and the maiden took the road to Gascony. They stopped each evening at an inn, and rising before the dawn each day they rode hard. By the evening of the third day they had but a short ride to Auch and the courts of Gascony.

They stopped again at an inn, a large one. It was packed. The dining hall was filled with priests, guildsmen, and merchants from the cities of Toulouse and from Auch, and they all seemed to want to speak to a priest sitting silently in the corner. He wore a black robe with a dark maroon mantle around the neck. His hair was shaved both above his ears and on the crown of his head, leaving a small ribbon of hair. Despite all the feasting and commotion around him, he ate nothing, nor spoke, but continued in an attitude of prayer. This prayer, however, was interrupted regularly as the officials of first one city then the other presented their proposals to him.

Henri, Petro, and Renée watched while they ate their supper and then found mattresses to fall asleep on.

La Danse Macabre
Dance if dance you must, then dance upon my tomb;
Lift your feet and shout your curses, shout them loud—
You must raise the dead, for I sleep quite restfully.
So jig a jig, and jog a jog—your tunes are always of gloom—
But they shall not disturb me in my white shroud
As I wait, still slumbering, still sleeping, still blissfully
Awaiting another sound, another call of trumpets blasting
And earth splitting, tombs cracking, heaven coming.
So dance then, if dance you must, for I shall see him soon.
- Sir Thommas de Bretagne

The road to Auch was congested the following morning. The three travelers found themselves near the end of a great procession. Soldiers of Gascony lined the sides of the road in full armament: mail habergeons, pikes in their right hand planted firmly by their leather boots, shields on their left arm, each shield painted gold with three black chevronels and three silver fleurs-de-lis on a blue canton, and over their mail armor they wore blue, black and silver surcoats. In front of them, at regular intervals were various liveried members of the guilds: the weavers in dark olive green, the cobblers in brown, the wheelwrights in tan, the coopers in gray, and the tanners in beige. At the gates stood the mayor, town councilmen, and the richest of the merchants. Behind and all along the great throngs of people pressed to watch, to see.

At first the three were included in the great procession, but it soon broke down behind the obvious object of the people's veneration at the front. But none of the three could see what important nobility was being feted so richly.

As they rode through the gates, however, Henri turned in his saddle and smiled. He remembered it well. Little had changed. The bridge, the massive oak gate, the iron portcullis, even the sergeant of the gate he remembered. There, next to the gate, was the duty guard barracks where his father had often stopped to chat after a hunt. Behind the barracks rested a small shack where lived the widow Isidora. Sir Thommas had rarely failed to bring her a portion from the hunts. Her husband had been one of his best houndsmen, only to die of rabies. It had been gruesome, but Sir Thommas had remembered the widow afterwards. Henri wondered how she had gotten on since they had departed. On an impulse he gave five sous to a young boy, instructing him to deliver it to the widow.

The press of the crowd pushed them along until they were finally in the great square. Behind the square the castle rose up in its formidable stone strength. It made the castle of Ayes dim in comparison. There was a large stage set up in the square, and all the crowd was eagerly watching. There was a tremendous expectation developing. Sir Petro de Lomange, the Maiden Renée, and Sir Henri remained in the saddle. The red hound took shelter beneath the black stallion. By this time they had learned that the festival was in honor of Jean de Vienne, a popular preacher of the age.

Then there he was on the raised platform, dressed in a long white gown. He stood and said nothing. He stretched out his arms, assuming the position of the cross. The crowd hushed. Some of the women began to weep. At first it was just a muffled moan from the crowd, but the longer he stood, head turned toward heaven, arms outstretched, unflagging, the more earnest grew the wailing as if to participate with the preacher. Shouts rang out from both men and women, "Savior, have mercy on me!"

He continued to stand, still, silent. The sun in its noon heat beat down on his tonsured head.

"Mary, blessed mother, remember the agonies of your son!" one shouted.

"Father Jean, plead for us. What must we do? Tell us, how shall we live?" A young nun cried out, "Will you not speak to us?"

Still he stood, his arms raised, unflagging, and the wailing continued to increase, building, strengthening, until it was a chaotic orchestra of shrieks and piercing cries.

Then suddenly Father Jean collapsed and curled up into a small, shrunken ball. The crowd gasped; had he been overcome? Had God stricken him down as he had His own Son? But no, he was slowly rising, though all curled up, his arms clenched to his chest, his head now covered with a white hood. All the wailing stopped. Silence. He continued his ponderous rise. Deliberately, cautiously he rose, until when nearly full upright, his arms sprang out once more to assume the position of the cross, except now his white robe was stained deep crimson on his wrists, on his feet, on his head, and on his side. A large swash of crimson on his left side kept expanding. Many of the crowd fainted.

Renée, sitting next to Henri, grabbed his arm with shock. "O Henri, he has the stigmata!"

But rather than being overcome by these wounds, Father Jean now strode to the front of the platform.

"Children of Auch, it is the hour of our Lord's passion. Our Lord bore your wicked sins, you unrepentants, and he has granted me the rare privilege of feeling his pain every day. I feel the thorns on my head, the stripes on my back, and the nails through my wrists, even the spear through my side, but in contrast to Our Lord, I do not die—rather a great strengthening comes upon me. And I feel the hunger of our Lord.

"These three days while I waited upon the Lord, deciding whether to come here to Auch, or instead to go to Toulouse, I have fasted. I have not partaken of food. I wanted, when I came here and saw you today, I wanted to feel an even greater oneness with our Lord's hunger. You know his hunger is great beyond measure; it is insatiable. He hungers for each of us. No matter what he eats he cannot become satiated. He is greedy, and his hunger is beyond our fathom. He desires to eat each one of you, to eat all of you. It does not matter if you are poor or rich. It does not matter if you are here on this square, or. . ."

And at this Jean swung around and pointed to the castle walls where many of the noble lords and ladies were watching. He pointed to them. "Do not think, you the rich of the world—you great men and ladies with your gold bracelets, your silk purses, your sarcenet dresses—do not think he cannot see beneath, see even beneath your corsets. O, you are the so called fine of this world. Our Lord must eat you, too. He must devour your fingers, your arms, your breasts, he must devour even to the marrow of your bones."

Then sweeping his arm out to the crowd, his voice broke with a great agony "Do not begrudge him this. If we could see the greedy lust which Christ has for our bliss you would not be able to stop flying into his mouth. For you see, if we are consumed by Christ, then we shall develop a hunger for him. For this reason Christ himself gave up his own body for glorious hot blood in our nature. Just as the Easter lamb was well cooked and roasted between two fires of wood or coal, so our Lord was tied on the spit of the cross on Good Friday, and he was slowly roasted, cooked in order to save us. He was roasted."

At this he paused and looked back up at the nobles watching from the wall. "Do you understand what this means? Do you understand? No, of course you do not, or you would be on your knees weeping. But of course it means that he has seen the fires of hell, has felt the fires of hell."

Henri had heard a similar preacher with his father when he was about eleven. His father had been agitated for several weeks afterward and had talked incessantly to Henri about how the preacher had been blaspheming. Henri had taken the lessons to heart and listened without the hysteria sweeping the rest of the crowd, including Petro and Renée. Petro had sweat dropping from his forehead, and his hands were gripped in white fists. Renée was watching with wide-eyed fascination.

The preacher had not stopped. "Now I ask you young people with your glowing muscles and smooth tight skin, have you ever considered, have you ever looked at your parents, your grandparents, and seen how your skin must wrinkle? No, you have not. You are like all other youth, thinking that for you time will be surmounted; you will be the first to never grow old, but consider this, consider what will happen when you die. Have you dug up the body of those who have died? Have you exhumed the dead? Have you seen how the worms eat away at the eyes? How they multiply in the bowels, becoming a writhing ball like serpents eating away at the flesh? This is the destiny for this body of yours. This pretty body. O vanity, how wretched you are, for it shall decompose, a stench as the flesh rots off the bone. But even this is better than the fate of your souls."

He paced across the stage like a caged lion. "Do you forget? Do you not remember? Have you never considered? Hell fire is coming! O do not think about it. Do not consider it; live your lives in sheltered innocence; do not pay attention to what can be done now; for if you do you will see the agonies of a never-consuming hell. Remember this, wicked people of Auch: once you are assigned to hell, the agonies you shall experience will be like none you have ever known. Have you had pain on this earth? Good. It is but a dim mirror of the torture of hell. And it shall never end. Never. Just as you think there can be no greater agony, God himself shall reprimand the devil, and he shall stoke the fires ever hotter. Therefore do not dally with the Lord. Bring your gifts and silver to him today, and maybe he shall have mercy on you.

"Men, women, children of Auch, we are so quick to forget, and that is why I want for you to have these woodcuts." At this a colleague handed up to Father Jean a woodcut. It was dans macabre, that is, a picture of three skeletons and a devil chasing three young men. "I want you to put this in your houses so that you can always remember."

And with that he stopped and then dramatically disappeared from the stage.

The crowd gasped and then began to press toward the booths where they were selling the woodcuts.

"I have to have one of those," Renée pleaded with Henri. "Will you get one for me?"

"I'll get it for you," Petro volunteered. "Maria surely will want one for our house. I will buy two." Petro slipped out of the saddle and began to make his way through the crowd to the stands.

Noting how quiet Henri was, Renée asked, "Don't you want one of the pictures? Doesn't it scare you to your very bones, death and hell? He was magnificent. Truly *he* is a saint."

Henri then glanced at Renée, and she could see he was becoming greatly agitated. "O, Renée, I feel so defiled and so disturbed. When I see this I feel this inner unrest. It is like everything I hold most precious has been cast into the dirt and trampled. This Jean," and saying the name Henri spat on the ground, "this Jean de Vienne is no saint in my eyes. I do not know whether he is just mad, or whether he is a charlatan, but I do know he has taken the cross and the passion of Our Lord and brought it to shame."

Renée was confused. "What do you mean? Should we not reflect on the cross? Does not God hunger for us? And what of hell? Surely we must do everything we can on this earth to avoid that."

"Yes, yes, Maiden Renée," Henri replied softly but passionately. "There is nothing more valuable, nothing came at a higher cost than the cross, and it is a topic we should meditate on, but he has made a mockery of it. Rather than like Christ drawing all men up to it, he has cast it to the ground. And as for the hungering, yes our Lord does hunger for us, but this man has taken the whole idea of God's great and boundless love and made it vulgar. Rather than elevating the minds of men and women, this Jean has brought them even lower, like throwing pearls to swine for them to trample on. And as for his disgusting images of the bodies decomposing, indeed it may be true, but he looks at only one side of the picture, the seamier side. I do not see it that way at all."

"Well, tell me," Renée urged. "Please tell me. His description of death horrifies me."

"Death is not all bad, Renée, not to the Christian." Seeing Renée's intense interest, Henri continued, "We were made from the dust, and we shall return to it. But we do not need to fear, as do the pagans, for we know that we shall be raised immortal at the resurrection, and in the meantime those who die in Christ will rest in the grave. And if our bodies decompose, then out of that ground will sprout the lilies of the field. Even the greatest of enemies, death, has no victory to those who are one in Christ."

Henri stopped, turned in his saddle, and looked at all the people with latent energy pressing forward to get their woodcuttings. "But these people. . ." Henri's voice trailed off.

Renée briefly looked at the crowds, but she did not want to be distracted. What Henri said was comforting, and new, like nothing she had heard before. "What then of hell? Tell me there is no eternal burning hell, and I shall love you forever."

He looked back at Renée with a half smile. "No, Renée, there is a hell."

She sighed, and he could see the same tension and anxiety returning to her face.

"But," Henri added, and she leaned closer to him, "But this Jean has gotten it all wrong. He tells only the dark side, and then leaves us there. He wants to leave us in terror. It sells better."

"Shhh, Henri," Renée cautioned as he raised his voice. "Be careful. The people love him, and even I could not defend you, should they turn on you. But don't stop talking. I am listening. Truly I am."

"Where was I?"

"You were telling me the good side of hell?" Renée suggested.

"Yes, the good side of hell." Henri chuckled at the way she phrased it. "Well first, Renée, hell is eternal but not never-ending. God is a consuming fire, and his fire will reduce everything to ashes. The unrepentant sinner will one day be thrown into the lake of fire and consumed. But the good news is that our redemption from hell has been assured. The fear of hell is not for the Christian, but for the pagan. Jean was right when he said that Christ has suffered hell for us. That was the whole point of the cross. Jesus' death has redeemed us from death and brought us to eternal life. And see. . ." Again Henri stopped, biting his lip.

"What Henri?"

"What he missed, this Jean, what he completely omitted was the love of God, the overpowering, all consuming, everlasting love of God. There is death. There is hell. But, most of all there is the love of God. Death and hell may frighten someone into buying a woodcut, but it is only love that redeems. It is only love that will change. It is only love, which is truly never-ending. Are there tears? They will be wiped away. Is there fear? It shall be comforted. Is there death? It will end. Even sin will be done away with; there shall be a new earth, and then we shall be with Christ forever."

Renée stared at Henri for several moments before saying softly, "Thank you, Henri. Thank you; you have brought me more comfort than I ever thought I could have known. Now I truly am beginning to understand you. But why don't we hear this? It is so beautiful. Why doesn't the church teach this?"

"It's there, Renée, in bits and pieces. If you keep your ears listening, and your eyes open you will find it. The priest at Anwar-de-la-Bay, he understood this."

"You learned this from him?" she asked.

He shook his head. "No, it was from my father."

She nodded. "You had a very special father. I would have liked him."

"Yes, you would have, and he would have liked you."

Renée smiled.

Chapitre Seize
Élevez Vous Portails Antiques

Lift up your heads, O ye gates; and be ye lifted up,
Ye everlasting doors; and the King of glory shall come in.
Who is this King of glory?
The LORD strong and mighty, the LORD mighty in battle.

Lift up your heads, O ye gates; even lift them up, ye everlasting doors;
And the King of glory shall come in.
Who is this King of glory?
The LORD of hosts, he is the King of glory.
- Psalms 24:7-10 (KJV)

When Petro returned, they entered the river of people jostling in the streets. They guided their way up the hill to the castle. The gates were open and the traffic of farmers pushing carts, milkmaids balancing jugs, and woodcutters leading burros laden with brush flowed freely back and forth. Three soldiers in their silver, blue, and black uniforms watched the flow. It was more form than substance; the city was presently at peace—a rare commodity in the tumultuous 14th century. The lieutenant stood beside the arched stone gate. Two knights sat on short three-legged stools engaged in a game of dice beneath the shade of a locust tree.

While the traffic of farmers and peasants passed through the gates without second notice, Henri, Petro, and Renée were different; Henri and Petro were armed. They were stopped.

"Halt. State your business," the lieutenant said, as two guards crossed their pikes before the horses. The knights glanced up from their game, and seeing the three were noble, rose.

Henri spoke for the party. "I am Sir Henri, son of Sir Thommas the Hunter de Bretagne. I am in the service of the Maiden Renée d'Ayes. . ."

He was interrupted by the lieutenant. "Little Henri? Are you really Sir Thommas's Little Henri? My, you have grown." Turning to the knights he called, "It's Little Henri."

"Henri?" The first knight asked.

"Surely you remember Sir Thommas's boy." And the second knight slapped his companion's helmet with the palm of his hand. "Don't be dense. It's Little Henri, remember, always trailing right behind his father, just like that hound trailing him now." The knight pointed to the red hound. "Fact is, it was just like that, Henri always with a dog." Then turning to Henri he added, "Where you been, boy? Where you been hiding?"

By this time Henri had dismounted, and the second knight clapped both of Henri's shoulders in friendship. There was a small pause and a shift in mood. "We heard about your father. Sorry. He was a good one. Won't be another hunter like him soon. He's been missed here, and make no mistake about that." Then the knight glanced at Petro and Renée, who were still on horseback. "They ride with you?"

Henri nodded. The knight looked back at Renée and winked at Henri as he muttered under his breath, "She's a pretty one."

Henri smiled.

The lieutenant had been standing to the side during the interview. Now he whispered to one of the guards, and the guard ran into the gate-house and up the stone staircase. A moment later two heralds stepped out onto the wall above the gate. Raising their horns they blasted a fanfare.

"In honor of your father's passing," the lieutenant explained. "He was a great knight."

The fanfare brought the milling throng inside the gates to a halt for a moment as they looked at the gate, wondering what important person had entered.

The second knight asked, "What brings you to Auch?"

"A private matter, at least until I have spoken with the Duke," Henri answered.

"Private affairs," And he glanced again at Renée. "I hope they are good ones."

"I wish they were," Henri replied.

"Mmm, well, private matters they will remain. Welcome back, Little Henri. You will want to stable your horses. Do you know the way?" he joked, knowing Henri had grown up in and around the stables.

Henri laughed. "Yes, I think I can find them." He swung back into the saddle. As they rode, many of the servants, tradesmen, and working women gathered in clusters and nodded when Henri lifted his hand in recognition. Renée noticed.

Parcelle de vert terrain
Green earth, brown earth, what does it matter?
Blood's been spilt, bones are shattered.
Between the bailey and the list
Limps a knight with broken wrist,
But 'twas in fun, but 'twas in gest.
Remember this, my son, he who lives
Is he who does it best.
- Sir Thommas the Hunter

Before coming to the stables, they passed the drilling yards. A larger than usual company gathered on the hard packed ground: closest to Henri and Renée stood a cluster of young nobles; to the left a band of knights leaned against the bailey's stone wall; near the castle's back wall twenty men-of-war faced the yards; while on the right, by the stalls, the stable hands had broken away from their grooming to watch the sparring in the yard's center. Two knights clashed sword against shield on the green. Not a fight of anger, just practice, but otherwise intense.

Henri wondered what the interest was. Sparring and practice on the greens occurred every day. Why was this different? Petro slipped from his horse ahead of Henri and edged himself into the circle. After Henri helped Renée dismount, he slid in beside Petro and looked to the field of combat. Immediately, he knew the attraction. The knight with the red and black dragon on shield and jupon was a champion. His strokes were rapid and powerful; his moves were fluid and effortless. His opponent, a Gascon of the Duke's retinue, strove valiantly but was taking a battering.

The knights along the bailey wall called out encouragements. "Watch your head. Aaaagh. Oooh, that hurt. Watch it; he's going to. . . . Oooh, that one must have hurt, too. Keep your shield up. No, not that high. He got you in the legs. You're done for." They mixed their comments with laughs and groans. The dragon knight then combined a couple of broad strokes with a rush and knocked the other knight off his feet. He placed his mailed foot on the chest of his opponent and placed the blunted point at his neck.

"Well, that was quick," one of the young noblemen pronounced before turning towards Henri.

Henri instantly recognized Christophe, the Duke's second son. Beside Christophe stood his two younger brothers, Picard and Quercy. All three had dark, fine hair and curved noses. All three were a little heavy: chunky, though not truly fat. Today, all three were dressed in lavender ermine-trimmed coats that stretched to their knees. Beneath the coats they wore dark blue hose down to their shoes. The shoes themselves were of the finest silk and leather, the latest fashion from the courts of Burgundy, with long, curling, pointed toes.

"So, what was the fuss at the gate all about?" Christophe said as he inspected Henri with assumed indifference. He had always been the leader of his younger brothers, and they had always been a pack, running together.

But his indifference was interrupted by the cries of joy from three accompanying maidens. "Henri!" they screamed, running to greet him.

Petro took the reins from Renée and handed them to the hostlers. Renée looked over her shoulder as the young ladies hugged Henri and petted his hair.

"Hello, Henri," Christophe stuck out his hand to Henri.

"Hello, Christophe," Henri responded, as he stepped free. Both spoke in measured tones. They had never been close, though not from want of effort on Henri's part. Christophe had been, after all, the focal point of the young nobility's social life. He had a witty tongue and was at the center of any sport or amusement in the castle. Unfortunately, Christophe and his brothers had always felt compelled to compete with Henri at everything: at horseback, at swordplay, at reading, at writing. And whenever they did, the competition had been one-sided. Henri always won. Henri was a little older, naturally more gifted, and definitely more industrious. Still, they did have one thing Henri did not have:

station. Christophe and his brothers, Picard and Quercy, were the three younger sons of the Duc de Gascogne.

Christophe gave Renée a cursory glance and then turned away. "Will you be staying long?" he asked as he began to walk toward the bailey.

"I have come to ask the Duke's protection for Maiden Renée." Henri walked beside him, and as he did he could not help but notice how much taller and broader of shoulder he had become as compared to Christophe. That reminded him of how his father had looked next to the Duke.

"My father and older brother are not here at present," Christophe replied. "I expect their return in a matter of days. You, of course, are welcome to stay."

At that, Christophe veered from the bailey over to where the dragon-knight was pouring water from a clay jug over his head.

"That was a masterful display, Sir Galahad," Christophe said.

"Galahad? A rather hard name to live up to," Henri commented.

The dragon-knight dropped the jug and wiped his mouth with the back of his hand. He stared sharply at Henri.

"Sir Galahad has been fighting the Moors in Iberia. He is considered one of the greatest of living swordsmen." Christophe introduced Henri, and then as a second thought he said to Sir Galahad, "Henri is descended from the line of Sir Lancelot, or so it is said."

Sir Galahad gave Henri a second look. "Do you wield the sword?"

"Some," Sir Henri answered.

Sir Galahad grunted and walked away.

"He has been teaching me and my brothers," Christophe said.

Quercy, who had been trailing Henri and Christophe, challenged Henri, "I bet I could beat you in a passage of arms."

Henri just smiled at Quercy. He was four years younger than Henri, still a boy.

"I am serious. I can beat you."

Henri looked from Christophe to Quercy. Were they serious?

"He is very quick," Christophe defended his brother, "and Galahad has taught him well."

"All right, if you wish I will spar you sometime."

Quercy nodded appreciatively, paused, and then baited him, "How about now?"

"With those shoes?" Henri pointed to Quercy's awkward and pointed shoes.

"I can change."

"Fine. Change. I'll be here," Henri replied. The brothers had not changed a wit, Henri thought as he shed his tunic and went to put on a coat of plates.

Picard, overhearing the challenge, passed on the news, and the crowd, which had been dispersing, now gathered again.

Sir Petro de Lomange and Maiden Renée joined Henri. Sir Petro de Lomange shook his head in disapproval. "This is not good," he said. "There is no way you can win."

"What are you talking about?" Henri asked. "Sir Galahad could not have taught him that much. He's just a boy." Henri continued to dress, fastening plate armor cuisses to his thighs and greaves to his shins. A page handed him the poleyns for his knees. These were standard issue. Henri adjusted them as best he could. "

"Exactly," Sir Petro de Lomange answered. "No matter how you fare, you lose. If you are too rough on him, they will criticize you because he is just a boy. If he is quick he could score a couple of touches, and then it does not matter what you do, you have lost. No, this is not good."

"Well, it's done, now," Henri replied. "I have accepted his challenge." Still he understood Petro's concern. He took the bascinet and fitted it over the padded arming cap.

A few minutes later Henri stood in the center of the drill yard facing off Quercy. They shook hands and then stepped back. Henri drew his sword and looked around. In a far corner the dragon-knight pretended indifference, but in fact he was watching intently. On the wall the guards had turned to watch again. The knights by the bailey wall had pushed off from the wall and had closed in to form a large circle. Henri looked over at Renée. She was biting the ends of her long hair, and at the sight of her, Henri felt fear, not for his personal safety, but fear of embarrassment. He realized even more how right Petro had been. This was an absurdity. Any loss would be through the castle before he sheathed his sword. Any embarrassment he suffered at Quercy's hand would be compounded on Renée. And what if Galahad had really trained Quercy well? What if Quercy had some tricks Henri had never seen before?

Quercy approached. He had the cocky self-confidence common to a privileged adolescent. After all, he had trained these last six months under the great Sir Galahad and had proved himself very quick. He had even beaten some of the lesser knights, and Henri had been away from the castle for three years. What could he have learned? What knight could have trained him like Sir Galahad had trained Quercy?

Quercy struck first. Henri easily caught it with his shield. He struck again, and again Henri caught it with his shield. Now that the battle had joined, Henri's fears fell away, displaced. It was just like fighting with Sieur de Bixmarch. Although the boy tried a number of feints, Henri foresaw them. Henri's defenses were tight and effortless, almost languid. After letting him take the offensive for several rounds, Henri followed one of Quercy's strokes with a backhand broadside. It caught the young nobleman flatfooted, and the force took him off his feet and left him breathless on the ground, and that was that.

Sir Armignan de Languedoc, one of the more respected knights in the castle, pushed himself off the wall. "So he took a boy. I wonder what he can do with a man." His comrades encouraged him as he approached Henri.

Le vétéran

Long have been the days in saddle borne;
Sharp has been the blade that I have worn;
Red has been the color of fields fresh tilled;
Red has been the color of blood I've spilled.
I am the veteran; I walk alone.

Many are the battles I've waged from dawn to night;
Many are the foes fallen to left and right;
Many are the scars on my arm, and face, and side;
Few are the friends still alive;
Still I stand; still I ride;
I am the veteran; I walk alone.
- Anonymous

"Little Henri, before you give up the sword, let's you and I have a round." As he approached he twirled his sword over his wrist several times. The knight was in his prime, and though not quite as tall as Henri, he weighed more.

Henri turned his arms out as if to say "as you wish." Having started with Quercy, a mere boy, he could not turn down a real competition, not if he wanted to achieve his objective for Renée.

They shook hands and then took several steps back. They crossed their swords in tribute. Again Henri took a defensive pose, blocking the slashes with the buckler on his left arm, neatly sidestepping the lunges, and parrying the thrusts.

Armignan's warrior mates surrounding the spar at first called encouragements and then, seeing Henri block all of his attacks, began to jeer, "C'mon, Armignan, take him. He's barely old enough to shave. He's making a mockery of you."

The three sons of the Duke watched. Quercy, who had been embarrassed, started feeling better. The older, more experienced Armignan was having the same difficulties. The young maidens of the castle watched. They remembered Henri as a boy, but now here he was doing well against one of the better knights. He could wield the blade. He could make the steel sing. Renée watched. Henri was her knight, and by St. Denis he could fight. He could fight like an ermine, a weasel, or a wolf. He was almost hypnotic in his battle dance. Kneeling on one knee, Sir Galahad watched and noticed the same.

Armignan became frustrated after several minutes of inability to penetrate Henri's tight defenses. "Do you mock me? You block my thrusts, but you do not reply. You defend, but you do not attack, is that because you have no skill in the attack?"

Henri stepped back and looked at Sir Armignan. "Pardon me. I did not mean to mock you. I have not had opportunity to spar with many partners recently, and I wanted to see how you would fight. But you ask for some offense. That is well. It is time."

Ever since the fight with Sieur de Bixmarch he had been remembering some of his father's last lessons, lessons after they had returned from the Orient, lessons his father said he, Sir Thommas, had learned from the Hospitalers. His father would have Henri put down the shield and defend without it. "You don't need the shield to defend, Henri. A good coat of plates is adequate defense. Rid yourself of it. You can parry the attacks with the sword. It is all in the eyes, in the feet, in the wrists, and without the shield your offense becomes quicker and more deadly. It's a dance, Henri. Remember that. It is a dance. A dance with death, to be sure, but still a dance. Don't be afraid to dance." With that Henri flung his shield several feet to the side and pointed his sword along his extended arm.

"What is he doing?" Sir Petro de Lomange gasped. The knights stopped their jeering. The Duke's sons glanced at Sir Galahad as if to see what their master thought of this tactic. He had risen to his feet and now took his place surrounding the courtyard. It was unheard of to throw off the shield. True, at times in real battle, the shield took such a battering that it was tossed aside, useless, but not voluntarily.

At that Armignan slashed hard to Henri's left. The natural response would have been to block it with the shield. Instead Henri blocked it with the blade and then, unencumbered by the shield, spun around Armignan and hacked at the shield. Armignan blocked the first one, but was not quick enough to block the second slash into his side. With quick, precise foot movements, Henri continued to cut, thrust, and lunge, catching Armignan again and again off balance, out of position. First right, then left, now high, then low. It was a dazzling display of sword fighting like the legendary mongoose of the orient on the hunt of the cobra. It was a style of bladesmanship that had little been seen in the west.

Armignan valiantly and gamely took his beating before collapsing to his knees with exhaustion. "Have mercy, Little Henri, have mercy."

Henri stepped back with a smile and licked his lip; it was bleeding.

"Bravo," the soldiers on the wall called out. "Bravo."

Armignan rose from his knees with a groan. "I sparred with your father. He was a great hunter, but with the sword I could hold my own against him. You are the best I have ever fought."

At that Sir Galahad turned and walked away, the three sons of the

Duke joining him.

Unable to restrain herself any further, Renée ran forward and hugged Sir Henri. "You were marvelous, simply marvelous. I have never seen anything like it."

"I have," Henri replied.

"Really, have you?"

"Sure, except it was in archery, and it was when I badly needed a good archer."

"You're sweet," she said, and kissed him on the cheek.

"Help me out of this armor and I'll show you around the castle."

Chapitre Dix-Sept
Promenade sur la Muraille

We walked among the hoardings along the allure,
Crenel and merlon, stepped over the machicoulis,
And looked through the embrasures of the bretèche,
Down from the wall to the valley where ran the Gers.
We passed the castle gate with flanking towers,
Drawbridges, stepped over the trap door, bypassed
Portcullis, black iron drawn tall, and guards all chevronel.
Then past the chapel to the gardens and flowers,
With the sun setting orange horizon in our view,
As the day flamed forward spokes in its final power,
And sat we then, sat we side by side in the dusk hour.
- Sir Henri in Gascony

They climbed the stairs to the outer walls and looked out over the cultivated fields that lay beyond Auch. A light breeze blew her hair across her eyes. She swept it back and gazed upon the green of early summer, verdant and reassuring. Late afternoon and the golden glow mirrored off the Gers River. Small streams lined by the willow, the plane, and the beech tree wound their way to join the river.

They wandered back through the maze of passages, cool stone, musty odor, archer slits in the walls every twenty yards. Henri showed Renée the Duke's private chapel, an exquisite gothic miniature, complete with small angel and goblin sculptures; lit in warm red and blue from the blush of the stained glass windows. Candles, white candles, hundreds of lit candles burning on the sacrament table. Renée slipped to the front of the quiet chapel and knelt down. Henri followed behind her. Her lips moved without sound. After a few moments Henri rose and went to the side table. He opened the Bible. He read in silence while Renée prayed; her lips moving but not speaking. Eventually she rose.

"It is a beautiful chapel," she commented as they left.

Henri took her hand. "It is that."

They looked in at the grand court. The walls were hung with rich tapestries: scenes of knights on the hunt, hind, wolves, bear; scenes of beautiful ladies walking through ornate gardens in splendor; scenes of the battle of Roland, of Charlemagne, of Arthur. Renée stood at the doorway and looked down the long marble passage. At the far end sat the duke's and duchess's thrones.

They passed by way of a balcony that overlooked an inner courtyard pool. In the middle of the pool a statue of a great stone stallion reared and kicked at the air. Cypress trees lined the outside of the courtyard. Renée stopped and leaned on the balustrade.

"I can see why you liked this place, Henri. It is so peaceful."

"At times," Henri replied. "Sometimes, however. . . the bickering and court politics can ruin it all."

She stood up. "And that is why your father left. . . still, this is what I always dreamed of. I always wanted to be mistress of a castle like this."

"As well you should."

Again he took her hand, and they continued.

"Down that hall are the private chambers of the Duke and his family." Henri pointed to the left.

"What is the Duke like?" she asked.

"Duke Henri? He is wise and considerate. I always liked him."

"Henri? His name is Henri?" She was surprised.

"Yes, I was named after him. He is my godfather. His oldest son is also Henri. That is why they call me Little Henri. My mother and father were so grateful for his kindness."

"It must have been hard for your father to leave," Renée said.

"Yes, it was, and I am not sure the Duke ever really understood why my father felt he had to defend the Jews and Mohammedans."

They were walking again and had passed through a doorway to an outside walk that overlooked the gardens. A maze of boxwood hedges lined the paths dividing beds of flowers, violets, poppies, and lilies; myrtle and holly trees provided shade in separate plantings, and by a stone wall was the duchess's prized collection of climbing roses. From their vantage they could see the wall formed the shape of a cross.

Henri slowed behind Renée. Her questions about his father, especially surrounded by all these remembrances, choked him up. He felt forlorn. His father had been such a close friend.

Henri pointed to a door on the far side.

"That leads to the grand hall. We will eat there this evening."

"So if the food gets bad, or the company too difficult, you can slip out to the peace of the garden. That is a nice touch." Renée laughed a little.

"Yes, it is."

By now they had passed to the back wall of the castle. A tower rose in front and above them. Henri pushed the door open and held it for Renée. She went in front of him, her dress sweeping along the narrow winding staircase. It was quiet in the tower, except the sounds of their breathing as they climbed round and round. With no inner railing, the deepening draft worried Renée; she latched onto Henri's hand. Higher and higher they ascended until they reached the pinnacle. Henri shoved open the trap door and held it for Renée.

They climbed out onto a small platform surrounded by a crenellated wall. The sun was just setting, and they could see for miles and miles.

"In the evenings I would come and sit and watch the stars." Henri drew in a deep breath.

"It is nice," Renée returned.

"Isn't it grand?"

Renée, however, had not forgotten the narrow, winding staircase, and the thought of going down them in the dark oppressed her.

Henri took a seat on the outer wall, facing the setting sun. "Come. Sit beside me." He patted the stone beside him.

Renée looked at him and then back at the trap door. She could see that Henri really wanted to be with her. She steeled herself and resolved to be courageous. Nevertheless, she could not help but remember the tunnel leading away from the monastery, the fight in the stables, the fight with the boar, the fight with Bixmarch in Cairns. With all the dangers they had overcome, it seemed presumptuous to go down the staircase in the dark. Still, she had come to know Henri well, and she could read his face like a priest could read a mass.

She smoothed her skirt and sat down beside him. He put his arm around her shoulder and drew her close. They sat that way in silence for some time, and then, cradling her face in his hands, he turned it to him. It felt soft, and in the twilight's last rays she was even prettier, more lustrous, like an angel.

"I *am* happy," he said. She shut her eyes as he kissed her, but with her eyes shut all she could see was the deep darkness of the staircase, plunging, bottomless, a yawning abyss, a measureless crevasse, a hollow shafted well, and to her it was like the castle, the court of Gascony; seemingly sturdy, with stone steps, and hard walls, beautiful fountains and flowers, lilies, violets, roses. But roses have thorns, and in the center of the castle, like the center of the tower, was the pit. This she feared.

Chapitre Dix-Huit
Trois Belles Femmes

Now heigh! Now Ho! Now hail a toast
To the memory of beautiful women;
To the delight of form and dress,

To the softness of loving caress—
This of all God's gifts is best—
To the honor of beautiful women.
But of them there are three foremost
Three women who stand above all others;
Three of whom you cannot compare;
Three of whom all history has listed best;
Three of whom make meager all the rest;
So raise your cup and down it fast
Dispute these names you will not dare
For they are three: mother, wife, and daughter.
-   Sir Tistol of Hartville

That evening in the dining hall Henri was seated in a chair at the far end of the head table. Between the stone pillars of the hall four other tables were set in two rows. The hall was lit by candles dangling from brass chandeliers. Directly across and on either side of him sat Constance, Armanda, and Charlotte; three young friends he had known from childhood. The table was set as he remembered: with white linen of Egyptian cotton, silver pitchers, pewter mugs, and burnished bronze trays; the trays were stacked with pears, figs, and apples.

Servants weaved through the tables bringing platters of meat and sweet tarts. Henri reached out, grabbed a bone from one of the trays, and stuck it under the table where his hound lay. He petted him a few times. It reassured him to have La Rouge near, especially since Renée's seat was separated from his own. He saw Petro taking a seat at a table of knights-bachelor.

Armanda and Charlotte were pressing Henri to tell of his adventures since leaving three years ago. He told them of Venice, Athens, and Constantinople and savored their attention; still, his glance often strayed down the table to where Renée was seated between Christophe and Picard. They were plying her with questions. He wished he could have been beside her. How they had been separated he still had not quite figured out; it almost seemed planned. They had entered together, but from the moment they had entered Christophe and Picard had taken her by the arm, engaged her in conversation, and seated her between them. While Christophe and Picard were drawing Renée away, Armanda and Charlotte positioned Henri opposite Constance and between them.

"Henri, your dueling was splendid. I have never seen anyone fight that style before. Wherever did you learn it?" Armanda asked. Armanda was the daughter of the Baron of Plaisance, two cities to the west of Auch. She had a lovely olive complexion and dark brown eyes.

"My father learned it on our trip to Constantinople."

Armanda placed her hand on Henri's arm. "Constantinople, is it as exotic as they say? Is it lovely?"

On the other side of Armanda, Charlotte interrupted, "I had an uncle who has been to Constantinople. He bought me an exquisite crystal figurine."

Armanda's hand still lay on Henri's arm. He reached for an apple and dislodged it.

"I would love to go to Constantinople. Maybe you would take me there, Henri," Charlotte asked with a flirtatious smile.

Henri had known Charlotte the best. Her father was a cousin of the Duke's and was a respected knight of the castle. Charlotte had sandy hair and soft gray eyes. She had the fullest figure and the lowest cut neckline.

"Constantinople is a long trip, a dangerous trip, not a trip for pleasure."

"I would not be scared if you were with me, protecting me." She rested her arm around Henri's shoulders.

Constance objected, "Charlotte, will you never stop? Henri's gone for three years and within a half hour you have your arm around him. Have you neither pride nor modesty?" Constance was the youngest of the three girls.

"O, be quiet, Constance. It's Henri. I have known him since we were in diapers." Charlotte laughed off Constance's criticism.

"That's right, Constance," Armanda added, "it's Henri." She stopped and, leaning back, looked up at Henri. "Except, well, it's not the same Henri we knew." She squeezed his biceps a couple of times.

Charlotte, following Armanda's lead, squeezed Henri's other arm. "Oooh, they are so large," she cooed. "I think we need a new name for Henri. I don't think we can call him Little Henri anymore."

Henri shrugged off both girls' hands. "I see you two have not changed."

"No, they haven't," Constance agreed.

Charlotte feigned a hurt expression and flounced in her chair. "Haven't I changed, Henri? Not even a little?"

"O, Charlotte, stop it!" Constance exclaimed in disgust.

Armanda laughed.

Henri grimaced and looked down the table toward Renée. Christophe had kept her in conversation throughout the whole meal, while Picard, sitting beside her, had spent most of the meal just looking at her. Henri did not like Picard's intent stare. He did not like it at all. At that moment Renée leaned forward reaching for her pewter mug, and as she did she looked toward Henri. Their eyes met for the briefest of moments.

Le Récit de Christophe
I may not a clever student of Paris be;
I have not studied in yonder university;

I have not the gender of scholars; still
I sense in his measured récit
A foul odor of fetid deceit.
- Constance de Biarritz

With a nod from Christophe the doors to the dining hall opened; a troop of gymnasts entered doing cartwheels and back flips. They bounced off each other and ran up and down the tables. With a boost, one acrobat leaped to the chandeliers and did a couple of flips before landing in the arms of her band.

After they had started, Christophe left Renée's side and ambled up behind Henri. He swung in a chair. "She says you have sworn fealty to her," Christophe said. His words were simple, but the tone suggested more than a simple statement. There was also questioning, and even annoyance, as if he were asking how Henri, the son of Sir Thommas, could pledge loyalty to anyone other than the Duc de Gascogne.

"It is true," Henri replied.

"Why would you do that? She has little to offer," Christophe replied.

Henri turned and stared at Christophe. "My service to her is on the basis of what I can do for her, not what she can do for me."

"Very noble, I am sure," Christophe replied. Christophe stroked his chin and smiled at the acrobats. "They are good, don't you think?"

Henri nodded, but he knew Christophe, and that was not why he had come to sit with Henri.

"So her uncle is Sieur de Bixmarch."

"She told you that?" Henri was a little surprised that she had given out her story so quickly, and a little putout—it had taken him several days to get that story.

"Well, actually, Sir Petro de Lomange and I had a long conversation this afternoon." Christophe had always been good at prying out information; a skill that would suit him well, as he was slated for the church.

"Yes, Sieur de Bixmarch is her uncle." Henri had planned to wait until Duke Henri returned before telling the story and asking for protection, or if not the Duke, at least the oldest son, Comte d'Auch. Henri had always gotten on much better with them than with Christophe. Having the same name had created a bond.

"And her father is Comte Sevestre?" Christophe continued. "So ironic, so bizarre, don't you think? I mean that you of all people should be her rescuer and hero, don't you think?"

Christophe obviously knew something Henri did not.

"I am not sure I follow you." Henri turned his chair away from the gymnasts.

Christophe studied Henri. "Surely, you know."

"What?"

"How your father died." Henri did not like Christophe's tone of sympathy. It rang like tin.

Henri sat back in his chair. "I found him. He was killed by a boar."

Christophe pulled his chair closer. "But you do know how he died, right?"

Henri found Christophe's interest in telling the story unsettling, and he remembered his conversations with Renée. "From studying the tracks I gathered my father had not been alone, and Renée thinks her father, Sevestre, might have been there. Do you know more?"

"Oh, indeed I do, indeed I do. But. . ." At that Sir Christophe placed his hand on Henri's shoulder in a gesture of compassion. "You may not want to know, that is, not if you wish to continue as her faithful knight." Then looking back down to where Renée sat, he murmured, "She is a lovely young thing, very sensual lips. Picard and I are both struck by her beauty."

Henri tried to ignore the last comment, wanting to find out what Christophe knew about his father. "What do you know?"

"Well, it's just that two merchants of Auch happened to be in an inn and overheard. . ." Christophe stopped and looked back to the entertainers. They had brought in some acrobatic dogs, little white dogs bouncing across the floor on their back legs. Henri heard Renée's laugh. She was entranced by the dogs, and the gymnasts, seeing her interest, had signaled one of the dogs to jump into her lap, and it was now licking Renée's face.

"Aren't they darling," she cried out.

Henri returned his attention to Christophe. "Tell me."

"Are you sure?" Christophe's compassion had been replaced by a charm as oily as his complexion. "All right, I will tell you. And tomorrow if you want to know more, one of the servants can take you to the merchants. You and the damsel were right, her father was there. Comte Sevestre was hunting boar. While separated from his companions, the boar charged him. Sevestre wound the horn, and your father must have heard." Christophe dropped a meaningful pause. He had always taken pride in his careful enunciation and derived pleasure from the timbre of his baritone-rich voice. He liked words, especially when he spoke them, and when listening to him one could not avoid thinking that much of the reason he was speaking was to hear himself.

He continued, "Your father was the first to arrive. Apparently, he diverted the boar's attention and quickly finished off the beast with a well placed lunge. Comte Sevestre's hunting companions did not come for nearly an hour. When they finally arrived they found Sir Thommas and the Comte had nearly quartered the boar and had it strapped behind the horses, the biggest share on Sir Thommas's horse."

"That would have been Brilliance, my father's great stallion," Henri interjected.

Christophe continued, "When they were near completion, however, a second boar rushed them from the brush."

"The mate?"

"It charged Comte Sevestre and whether it was accidental or intentional is uncertain, but one of Sevestre's companions knocked down Renée's father with his horse. The boar, seeing the downed man, turned for him, would have quickly gored him, except your father stepped in. . . again. Your father always had an overabundance of the hero in him. But, well, this had happened so suddenly that your father did not have his sword, and the boar gored him, mowed him down, bowled him over. Comte Sevestre called for help from his companions, but they rode away. They left the two knights on the ground."

"The cowards!" Henri exclaimed. "What type of man would do something like that?"

Christophe stopped and waited for Henri to finish. "Your father grappled and hung close to the boar, allowing Sevestre to stumble to his horse. That night at the inn the Comte insisted that he had tried to help but was unable to. When it was over, he rode away. That night at the inn he accused his companions, but they laughed at him."

Comte Sevestre had tried to help, Henri thought. He had wanted to help, but had been too weak, too impotent. It fit.

"The last piece to this puzzle," Christophe added. "Comte Sevestre's hunting companions? Sieur de Bixmarch and Sir Reginald."

Henri's mouth dropped. "Bixmarch and Sir Reginald? Sir Reginald is Bixmarch's most trusted lieutenant. Why would they be hunting with Sevestre? It's almost as if they were hoping he would die in a hunting accident. Why?"

"Don't be dense, Henri. Bixmarch wanted to kill him for the same reason that he would commit incest with his niece: power, Henri, power. Power drives people. Everything is justified in the attainment of it. Surely you know that."

"O, Henri, I am so sorry," Constance said, taking Henri's hand in both of hers.

Henri looked at Constance. In her eyes were sympathy and compassion.

Sonnez la cloche

Now ring the bells in their granite steeples,
Call masons, wheelwrights, bakers, peoples
Of every trade and age, now while the sun is barely peeking
Over ridge and tower, wall and keep, its morning rays reaching
Skyward to fill the darkness with its fury of burning light.
Let harmonies of sonorous bells come sending cover to night

And waking praise from every lip and throat
As we gather, listening to fading bell note.
- Sir Henri in Gascony

The following morning, before daybreak, Henri stretched and rose from his featherbed. The rooster's crow parted the predawn stillness as Henri pulled on his boots, raced down the castle stairs three at a time, and half walked, half jogged across the courtyard. He heard the hounds baying, and an instant later Rouge came loping up to him. Through the castle gates, across the bridge, and into the awakening city he walked at a clip; every little side street, each alley, he knew. He entered the square. The cathedral in the dim morning towered, radiating quiet strength from its granite columns, the majesty of the tower rising above the porch. He had wanted to be here before the bells began tolling. He took a seat on the stonewall surrounding the plaza fountain. He pulled his coat a little closer and waited.

"Teach me thy way, O LORD, and lead me in a plain path, because of mine enemies," he began to recite, the words of the Psalmist moving his lips, but barely uttering the words. "Deliver me not over unto the will of mine enemies. *I had fainted*, unless I had believed to see the goodness of the LORD in the land of the living. Wait on the LORD: be of good courage, and he shall strengthen thine heart: wait, I say, on the LORD."

Then the great bells in the belfry began to swing, and melodious tones flowed out over the city. Henri leaned back, leaned back, and reveled in the resounding music. He appreciated the richness of the bass and the clarity of the treble. He celebrated in their interplay off the castle walls and echoed back across the still city. It was a wonder to him, this so familiar music. Gooseflesh rose on his skin. It was like flying through the courts of heaven with angels ringing bells from the towering alabaster walls of the New Jerusalem, calling, summoning the saved to worship, to take a knee, to fall prostrate before the Almighty. In his mind's eye he saw the great multitude gathering, streaming along the streets of gold, in joy. Suddenly in his view he saw his father standing ahead of him, looking back over his shoulder with his hand held out for Henri, beckoning him. Standing beside his father was the figure of a woman. Try as he might, however, Henri could not picture her face, could not see the face of his mother. For a moment this brought shearing pain, but it passed, replaced by an unimaginable brightness, the Shekinah glory, and Henri could only conceive of one possible response. He fell to his knees.

The bells faded. Henri opened his eyes and looked around. He was still seated on the fountain wall. The glimmering dawn cast its first rays on the building facades as a small stream of worshipers climbed the porch stairs. To his left, he noted a slight figure sitting, watching him. It was Constance. He smiled at her.

She lit beside him. "You seemed so far away, lost in a dream; I did not want to bother you."

"I love the bells," Henri said.

"So do I." Her face beamed with joy like sacred incense, an aroma of innocence and kindness.

As they climbed the steps Henri asked, "Do you come often to day-break mass?"

"I thought you might be here," she replied. "When I was a girl tugging at my mother's dress, I often watched you with your father."

Henri had no such memories, but she would have been quite young then. He looked at her and laughed. She was graceful, self-conscious, and pretty, a sprite of a thing with tawny hair neatly tied back with a white ribbon. Her gaze stayed on him; that she liked him was obvious and pleasant; she was not a coquette like Armanda and Charlotte.

Henri ordered his hound to sit, then entered the cathedral with the other worshipers. After mass, when they reemerged, Henri headed toward the stables.

"Where are you going this early in the morning?" Constance asked.

Henri was at the main stable. Several stable boys were already at their work, tossing hay into the stalls. He noted the sun skimming above the castle walls.

"I thought I would take a quick ride before everyone else got up."

"Do you mind if I come? I ride well enough or. . . would I be a bother?"

Henri looked at her and smiled. "Of course, you can. You're no bother, Constance."

He intended to ride out to the grave of his mother, a small cemetery outside the walls. No consecrated site for his mother, no piece of holy land for her burial. She had never reconciled with the church; she had never forgiven her archbishop of a father, had never forgotten that she was one of the church's bastard children. She had made peace with God, but not with the church; maybe she would have if she had not died so young. His father had made his peace, albeit an uneasy one.

But as for Constance, she was easy company, quiet, undemanding.

His stallion nickered and moved restlessly when Henri approached.

"What a beauty," Constance murmured, reaching out to pat the massive shoulder of Le Noir.

"He is, isn't he?" Henri knew his way around the stables. The older stable boys remembered him well. He grabbed his saddle and threw it over the large broad back of his charger.

One of the other hands saddled an Arabian roan for Constance.

They rode side by side through the castle gates, returning the guard's greetings as they passed. Trotting along the main thoroughfare they watched potters winding up the metal mesh in front of their stores, blacksmiths already hard at work pounding out their burning iron wares—their apprentices sweating at the bellows—and merchants setting up their displays.

The sun cast early shadows, yellow-green on the dew covered fields as they rode out through the town gates and down the main road. Henri spurred his horse to a canter. He glanced back at Constance. She rode well enough, not effortlessly like Renée, but well enough.

It was not far, barely a mile from the town walls before they turned off on a side road leading to a grove of poplars. A little stream coursed through the middle. Henri slid from the saddle, letting the reins fall. He unlatched the cemetery gate and entered. It had been three years since he had been here, though as often as he had come with his father he could never have forgotten the way. Her plot was on a small knoll with a fine view of the pastoral countryside. He remembered sitting on the wild grass looking and listening as his father talked. He dropped to a knee and laid his hand on the ground. It was odd and empty to kneel here at the grave without his father. He wanted to sit and talk to his father about many things, but mostly about Renée.

Constance came up behind him. She had gathered a spray of white wildflowers. She stooped and laid them on the gravestone. Henri was glad she had come. She was a decent girl, though he wished it had been Renée.

"My mother told me she was the most beautiful woman she ever saw," Constance said quietly.

"Your mother knew my mother?" Henri looked up in surprise.

Constance nodded. "They were friends during the years your mother lived here, before she died."

"You know how she died?" he asked.

"Smallpox is what my mother said."

"Yes, it was the pox, when I was young."

"Before I was born," Constance added, "but my mother once said it was probably better she died. She thought it would have been a tragedy for a woman of her beauty to live the rest of her life so badly disfigured."

"Maybe so," Henri agreed as he stood up. "Sometime I would like to see and talk to your mother."

Looking down at the grave one last time, he turned, walked out the gate, and mounted his charger. He would ride back to the castle and find Renée, though he felt guilty for spending so little time at his mother's grave.

Sous le platane

Under a plain plane tree we sat upon the grass and watched the rooks call

From their rookeries on corking white limbs while the clouds came by, all

Sailing on the hot summer wind, when the sun was full and the tree was tall.

We sat in the shade, traced our fingers in the dust and drank from the well.
I drank from the cup after you, put my lips where yours had been, and drank until
I met your eyes. In the shade of the plane tree I drank, drank, drank my fill.
- Constance de Biarritz

Back at the castle, he went to Renée's room. The door was shut; he knocked; no answer. He slipped down the steps to the great hall and asked a servant if she had seen the Maiden Renée. No, she had not, but she had seen a gathering of the young nobility riding out the east gate early this morning, the Duke's three sons with a company of knights and a number of noble ladies. She might have been with them.

Back down to the stables he went. Constance lingered there.

"You're looking for the Maiden, aren't you?" she asked.

"I am her knight," Henri replied.

She smiled. "The hunt master said they rode east this morning. They took several servants, a couple pack horses. They were going to make a little pilgrimage to St. Roland dans Le Montaigne and have a picnic. They didn't tell you?"

Henri stopped and looked at her. "No. . . . No, I was not told."

"They did not tell me either, but that does not surprise me. Christophe does not like me," Constance said.

"What of Sir Petro de Lomange?"

At that, Sir Petro de Lomange strode up behind them "What about me?"

Henri explained the situation.

"No, I was not told," Sir Petro de Lomange responded.

Odd no one had told them, and why would Renée have consented to go without him? He remembered the hunger in Picard's stare last night. It was disquieting.

Henri knew the little church, St. Rolands dans Le Montaigne. It was a couple of hours ride east. The two knights ordered their horses saddled. Seeing Constance standing off to the side, watching, Henri asked her to join them. She eagerly agreed.

A few minutes later they had passed the city walls and were riding along the dusty roads. Under the rising summer sun, the three rode silently. As they entered a small village, Petro halted to ask a farmer if a party of noblemen had come that way earlier. The farmer shook his head. "No, milords, we have had no lords nor ladies this morning."

"This is the way to St. Rolands?" Petro asked, wondering if Henri had taken a wrong path.

"That it is, just a few miles further down the road."

Henri and Petro exchanged looks. Where was Renée? Where were the Duke's sons?

"Well, we are almost there; we might as well ride on," Sir Petro de Lomange said.

They approached the chapel from the west. Its central tower stood in the shade of a massive plane tree. At the front its porch was recessed, and above, an octagonal stained glass window was set in the shape of the rose. There was a small sculpture in front of the church depicting the legendary Sir Roland leaning on his elbows and dying as he looked towards heaven. But what attracted the attention of Henri and Petro were the horses. For a moment they thought it must be Christophe and his brothers and Renée, but that thought quickly passed. There were too many horses, just shy of fifty.

They dismounted before entering the surrounding gardens. Henri helped Constance down. When he turned around, three knights had come out of the chapel and had stopped to look at him. The knight on the right was the most richly clothed, wearing a black silk tunic with a silver fleur de lis on a blue emblem over the heart. He had long brown hair, wavy, and—rather unusually for a nobleman at that time—a dark, well-trimmed beard. Henri recognized him. It was the Duc de Gascogne's first son, Henri the second, Comte Henri d'Auch, or, as he was more commonly called, Comte d'Auch. He was ten years older than Henri and had not paid much attention to Little Henri when they had lived together. Henri remembered him as being diligent and fair.

"On. . . on pilgrimage?" Henri II greeted them without recognition. He had always had a stutter, of which he was keenly aware, but he assumed such a serious demeanor that it was never mocked. He was apt to be sparse with words.

"We are, indeed," Henri replied. Constance hung behind him a little to his right.

"I have ju. . . just returned from Avignon. A swill of cor. . . corruption. It is good to breathe pure Gascony air again. I am Comte d'Auch, son of Duc Henri de Gascogne, and you. . . you are?"

"Yes, I know you well," Henri answered.

Comte d'Auch eyed Henri closely. "Do. . . do I know you? I hope we are at peace? You are not English, are you?"

"We are at peace," Henri replied. "I, too, am named Henri, after your father."

At that the Comte d'Auch smiled and looked at his companions for the answer to the riddle. Suddenly it dawned on him, "Do not tell me that you. . . you are Little Henri? We received a message from Christophe earlier this morning that you had. . . had arrived, and that you had brought a damsel with you. My father changed his plans and was to arrive at the castle this evening to see you, but. . . but first we wanted to stop by here." Comte d'Auch nodded toward the chapel. "He is inside."

Surveying Henri from top to bottom, Comte d'Auch nodded approvingly. "You have grown into a goodly knight. I remember you. . . you as a boy constantly in tow behind your father." And having mentioned his father, Comte Henri's tone dropped. "I was sorry to hear of your fa. . . father. He was an honest and chivalrous nobleman."

"Thank you," Henri replied, and then quickly deflected the conversation. "May I present Sir Petro de Lomange, a fellow knight?"

The comte nodded at Sir Petro de Lomange, and then turned his gaze toward Constance. "And this is the Maiden. . . ?" He could not remember the name of the damsel that was to have accompanied Little Henri.

"No, no, this is not the maiden Renée; this is Constance, daughter of the Comte de Biarritz."

"This is Constance?" The Comte's face displayed surprise and pleasure. "I. . . I. . . I have been away at Avi. . . Avignon too long. If it does not offend you may. . . may I say you have become very fair."

"Thank you, milord. You are most kind," Constance replied.

There was a pause in the conversation. Henri looked at Constance; she had dropped her eyes; the blush on her cheeks made her even prettier as she stood, hands folded in front of her pink surcote over the silver silk close dress. She had a slight but pleasantly curved figure.

"But where then is the Maiden Renée?" Comte d'Auch asked as they moved toward the shade of the plane tree and took a seat on a stone wall beside the cemetery. But before giving Henri time to explain, he spoke to Constance again. "And how is your father. He. . .he is well I hope?"

"Tolerably, milord. Though he does suffer from the gout on occasion."

"Does he? I am sorry for that. Have you been here at the castle long?" Comte d'Auch questioned.

Constance took a seat on one of the stone benches before the wall. "Nearly six months."

"Really, that long! Have I been at Avignon that long?" he said more to himself than out loud. "Well, it was successful." Turning to Little Henri he said, "What a bed of deceit and chicanery, still I was able to obtain a ca. . . canon position for my brother Christophe there at Avignon. He will be delighted. He wants to be in the thick of it. To thrive there one must be ambitious, callous, and absolutely without conscience. Christophe should do well."

Constance remonstrated, "Christophe is not that bad."

"You said Christophe does not like you," Henri reminded Constance of her earlier comment.

"Christophe does not like you?" Comte d'Auch replied with amazement. "No wo. . .wonder I find myself attracted to you."

"Milord, you embarrass me."

"My apologies, maiden," the Comte said and then turned to Little Henri again. "Where did. . . did you say the maiden was?"

Chapitre Dix-Neuf
Les Trois Henri

Come sit between me, three,
And see if we cannot agree
That life is best upon the wall
When three strong men, brave and tall,
Gather heads and gather words
Gather thoughts beneath the woods.
And I shall sit, soft and small,
And watch these men who in common all
Are christened by the name Henri.
- Constance de Biarritz

Before he could answer, however, Duke Henri came out the chapel door. He stopped on the porch and covered his eyes from the glare of the sun. He took his felt hat and covered his wavy brown hair. Behind him followed a large retinue of other nobles and officials. They were all dressed in variations of the black, silver, and blue colors of Gascony. His valet handed him a cane before he started down the step. The Duke, favoring his right leg, descended the steps. The Duke was broad at the girth, but although he walked with a limp, he still gave the impression of a man with energy and vigor. His chamberlain handed him a large cup of water from the bubbling spring to the far side of the chapel.

"Still the best water. Did you have some?" The Duke's voice was deep, gravelly, and unusually loud, accustomed as he was to giving orders that needed to be heard and obeyed. Then the Duke saw Henri's black charger. "Whose horse is this? What a fine animal." He petted the neck of Le Noir and searched around the yards. Comte d'Auch approached his father while Little Henri stayed back by the wall.

The Duke's voice boomed, "So there you are. You missed mass."

"The priest was drunk," Comte d'Auch replied. "You. . . you know my opinions on drunken priests."

"The church has resolved that issue; the sacrament of mass does not depend on the worthiness of the priest."

"And I say it is blasphemy," Comte d'Auch retorted.

The Duke put up his hand for silence. "Leave it; we will not discuss it, but tell me whose is this excellent stallion." And at that the Duke saw Little Henri, Petro , and Constance by the cemetery.

Henri had wondered what this moment would be like, seeing the Duke again. He felt a little like a schoolboy who was too old but who was forced to return to the classroom because he needed further education. Then again, he was like a young warrior returning, eager to be approved by his master; or a hurting child returning home and wanting the welcome of a favorite uncle. But he was returning with fear—the leaving had been bitter. He steeled his resolve, remembering that he came not on his own behalf, but on Renée's. He was her protector, despite his youth.

"Little Henri?" the Duke asked. "Is that you, my boy?" There was nothing but joy in his voice. "I should have known by the beast it would be you. You always picked the best horse in the stables. You must be doing well to have a steed like this. Of what line is it?"

"Your Grace," Henri bowed as he approached. "I discovered the horse beside his fallen knight, a victim of a boar attack. I think it is Frisian."

"A boar attack." The Duke's face turned grave. "Like your father; I mourned when I heard of his death."

Comte d'Auch added, "We. . . we lowered the banners to half mast for a week upon learning the news."

The Duke continued, "I have not had a huntsman like him, no one who could handle the horses, the hounds, the hawks. No one knew the forests, could manage the servants like him. I have had others, yes, I have had others. My current houndsman knows dogs, but is churlish, and the dogs don't like him. The horse master is competent, but knows only the local strains and is not good at breeding. The master of the mews lost more than half of my hawks. The truth is, I find hunting so frustrating that I only go when I must entertain a peer, and then I am often embarrassed. But what I miss most is the friendship of your father. He was the most honest man I knew—and probably shall ever know— and so well read; hunting with him was a great delight."

Then seeing the hound seated at Henri's side, the Duke smiled. Henri reached over and petted La Rouge's big head.

"So where is this Maiden Renée that Christophe told us about?" The Duke looked all around him, nodding first at Sir Petro de Lomange and then at Constance.

Comte d'Auch stepped forward and introduced Sir Petro de Lomange and then started to introduce Constance but was cut short by the Duke. "I may be getting old, my son, but I still can remember the names of the pretty young maidens who frequent the court. It is as always a pleasure to see you, Constance." The Duke did notice, however, the way his son's eyes lingered on her.

"Where is this Maiden Renée? I am very anxious to meet her. Christophe said she was very charming and in fact has quite taken Picard's heart. If it had been Quercy, I would not be surprised; he is constantly falling in love. If it had been Christophe, I would have feared for the young woman."

"Just like a ch. . . churchman," Comte d'Auch said cynically.

The Duke continued, ignoring the comment, ". . . But Picard, he has always been quieter. I have worried about him more than the others. What shall become of Picard? And I wonder if this Renée is the answer. You shall have to tell me more of the story, Little Henri. Here we shall sit on these benches, the three Henries, and have ourselves a little chat." At that the Duke limped over to the benches back in the shade of the plane tree and sat down. He motioned for Little Henri to sit beside him, and his son to sit opposite him. Then seeing Constance still standing, he added, "Constance, you must not stand while the men sit. Come have a seat beside my son."

Henri sat down beside the Duke, but he was deeply disturbed. Picard had fallen for Renée, and the Duke was clearly pleased with that. Renée had been right after all. She had predicted castle politics would break up their romance if they came here. What was he to do? He knew neither what to do nor say.

"Now tell me, where is the Maiden Renée, and what is her story?"

Henri gave the story starting from the beginning: how she had come to Anwar, how her mother had tried to marry her to her uncle, Sieur de Bixmarch; how Renée had run away with Henri and they had fled to Ayes; how her father, Comte Sevestre, had refused to see them at the monastery, and then how Sieur de Bixmarch had attacked them—with special mention of how Sir Petro de Lomange had been such help; how Henri and Renée had then gone to Cairns and met Jehudah and Ishmael again; and finally, how Sieur de Bixmarch had tracked them down and fought with Henri again. Throughout the narration Henri had avoided any mention of his love for Renée. He wanted to talk to her first and get her suggestions on what would be best. Now more than ever, he realized how much better prepared she was to deal with the games of men and power.

When Henri finished, the Duke looked at his son and gravely nodded. Then to Henri he said, "That is quite an adventure. But why didn't you come here first? Why, when your father died, did you not come? You worked as a stable boy? You, the son of Sir Thommas de Bretagne, working as a common stable boy? The only Latin-reading stable boy in all of France I would wager. Why did you not come to Gascony?"

Henri paused. "I don't know. When my father died I was at a great loss. I was very confused for a long time. And I would have been afraid to come."

"Afraid? Nonsense! How could you be afraid? I am your godfather. I have always been fond and proud of you. Why would you be afraid?"

"Well, when my father left, you told him if he left to never come back,"

Henri replied tentatively.

The Duke rose to his feet and, supported by his cane, began pacing, "Ah yes, yes, I suppose I did. But you must understand, Henri, that it was a difficult time. A very difficult time. Do you think I wanted to expel the Jews and Ishmael? No, I did not. Why would I want to do that? Jehudah was the best treasurer I ever had. My castle finances have never been the same. I miss him greatly, but the times were delicate. The archbishop warned me that if I did not banish all the infidels, the Grand Inquisitor would come to Gascony and that would have been a greater tragedy to all of my people. You are too young to know the havoc the Inquisitor will unearth if he sets up a court of inquisition. The archbishop and I felt the only way to avoid this was to appease him from a distance, and it worked."

The Duke tapped his cane emphatically on the bench to punctuate each point. "Your father is an honest man, as I have said, but he refused to compromise. He took his position with a Jew and a Moor. That infuriated me, and I did tell him not to come back, but it was not because I did not love him, even then, as a brother. How I missed him! You, Henri, are welcome in the castle."

He laid his hand on Henri's head. "So you met Jehudah and Ishmael. I tell you I would like to see Ishmael again. He had a balm for my hip that I could surely use, and tell me how is Jehudah?"

"Jehudah has become a Christian."

"Jehudah!"

"Yes, though," Henri paused before finishing, "he is not very Catholic."

Instantly the Duke's hand rose. "Stop, stop, I want to hear no more, and whatever you do, do not say any of this to Christophe."

Puzzled, Henri looked to Comte d'Auch for an answer. The Comte replied, "My. . . my brother, Christophe, is a true anti-Semite. He hates Jews. He believes they are con. . . conspiring to take over all the treasures of the Christian world, and he doubts that a Jew can tru. . . truly become a Christian. He believes a converted Jew is just. . . is just a Jewish spy infiltrating Christendom in order to attain more power. If . . . if you want to hear someone rant for an hour, just start him on that line of conversation."

The Duke returned and sat down. "So what is it you want of me?"

"I am the Maiden Renée's knight, and I wish only for her safety." Henri said. "If, however, it is possible, I would very much like to establish her as Comtess at Ayes."

"Safety and protection I give you, and more than that, I would gladly appoint you as hunt master, but to establish the damsel as Comtess d'Ayes probably means war, and war costs money, and that is hard to raise, especially without Jehudah, but we shall see." Turning now to his oldest son he asked, "What is your advice?"

The Comte looked at Henri and Petro and then back to his father. "Le. . . let me complete the final details of my mission to Avignon wi. . . with the archbishop, then I shall take a party of knights. I shall go see the Comte Syl. . . Sevestre and the Abbé, and this Sieur de Bixmarch. This may be an answer for the Picard question."

Le chiot
Squiggling;
Small nose black;
Fur so white, soft.
Red tongue friendly;
Body twisting
Like. . . . Like?
Like a puppy.
- Maiden Renée d'Ayes

Back in Auch at the stables, Henri sat on a bench waiting with Constance. The afternoon sun was beginning to decline when the Duke's sons, Renée, and the party of nobility rode into the courtyard. Henri quickly went to Renée's white mare and assisted her out of the saddle. She let her arms linger around his neck, as if to feel his reality.

"Where were you?" she asked looking queerly at Constance.

"Where was I? Where were you? I was at St. Roland's chapel, where they said you were going."

Christophe, now off his steed, joined the conversation as he pinned the gray mantle around his neck. "Henri, you missed a wonderful day. We had a great time. Where were you?"

Henri arched his brows in puzzlement. "I was at St. Roland's chapel where the servant said you were going."

"What!" Christophe exclaimed, "No one told you? We went to the gypsy camp in the mountains north of here. I told the courier to be sure he told everyone. Did he fail to tell you? That must be because you are new here. I should have specifically mentioned your name. My apologies."

"The servant said you went to St. Roland's." Henri did not trust Christophe.

"Oh, that. Well, truth is we had planned on going there but changed our minds."

Renée positioned herself just behind Henri's left shoulder as the other nobility began to gather around laughing and talking.

"I hope you do not think I intentionally forgot you," Christophe said, irritated at Henri's doubtful expression.

"You told me Henri had gone on ahead," Renée accused Christophe. Then to Henri, she repeated, "They told me that you would meet us there."

Quercy joined them. He stooped over and curled the tip of his shoe a little more.

Christophe, speaking to Quercy, said, "Henri was not told that we were going to the gypsy camp, can you believe that?"

The younger son was interested at the moment only in getting his shoes curled just right and grunted an unintelligible comment.

Renée slipped her arm in Henri's and then impulsively gave Henri a quick kiss on his shoulder.

Christophe, looking around, saw Picard. "Picard, Henri thinks we purposely did not tell him."

"Really? Ridiculous, of course. Why would we do that?" Picard brushed it aside, looking only at Renée. He held a small white puppy in his hands. "Here is your puppy, my fair one."

Renée cuddled the little puppy in her arms. "Thank you," she said. To Henri, she asked, "Isn't she beautiful? Picard bought her for me from the gypsies. It is the same breed the acrobats had last night."

Picard had now stepped between Henri and Renée and was petting the puppy. Renée nestled the wiggling, chubby, furry little thing under her chin and laughed as it licked at her face.

"What do you think I should name it?" Renée asked Henri.

Picard, however, was first to answer. "How about Rose? It is, after all, the pet of one whose beauty is matched only by the rose."

Renée blushed and did not reply but looked past Picard at Henri.

"Have you seen a dog like this before?" Christophe asked Henri. Henri recognized this as the setup it was meant to be. Henri, son of Thommas the Master Hunter, was supposed to be the expert on dogs, but no one had seen dogs like this before.

"No, Christophe, I don't know what type it is; please tell me."

"It is a Bichon. They come from the Canary Islands, just off the coast of Africa."

"I know where the Canary Islands are," Henri snapped.

Christophe stopped abruptly and gave Henri a sharp stare. Picard, meanwhile, was guiding Renée away to feed the puppy. Henri watched them as the rest of the party left Christophe and Henri standing by themselves. Christophe placed his hand on Henri's shoulder.

"We had a great time. There was a palm reader; we all had our fortunes told. Quercy is soon to become a great knight and champion of the tournaments. I am to become prominent in the church, and she thought she even saw red cloth for me, a cardinal. Picard is soon to marry a beautiful young woman, dark hair, complexion like a peach, a woman of high nobility." Christophe raised his eyebrows in an all-knowing expression.

Henri turned back toward Christophe. "And what of Renée? What was her future?"

Christophe shrugged. "She chose not to have her palm read."

Good for her, Henri thought.

"I do believe Picard is quite struck with your liege," Christophe said with a nod as they both now watched as Picard and Renée went indoors, Picard still doting on the puppy. Christophe, whose hand had stayed on Henri's shoulder all this time, now gripped tighter. "A loyal knight would not interfere." He let the words sink in for a moment, and then in parting, he added, "Just so you know, we will be eating in the great hall tonight."

"What?" Henri asked.

"I just wanted you to know where we would be tonight, so you couldn't blame me if you weren't there," Christophe said curtly, straightened his belt, wiped his nose twice on his sleeve, and then walked across the courtyard all the time looking all around, nodding at the other knights and whistling a gypsy tune.

La couleur d'amour
The damsels of the court most fair
Exclaim that I am a chevalier extraordinaire.
They marvel at my wit and my panache.
They cannot resist kissing me on my moustache,
And when it is the colors of green I wear—
Blue I shall never wear—
They are all taken with my debonair;
For I am a knight, a chevalier extraordinaire.
- A satire by Maiden Renée d'Ayes

That night, as Henri entered the hall, the main table on the dais was empty, waiting to be filled by the duke and duchess and probably Comte Henri. Looking down the hall's columns he saw Renée stuck in the middle between Picard and Quercy. He groaned. They did not let up. The table was located behind two columns and near a window that looked out on the gardens. Armanda, Charlotte, Constance, and Sir Galahad were also at this table. Christophe sat at the head with two empty chairs on either side of him. Seeing Henri he quickly got up.

"Please do come and join us." His tone was exaggerated.

Henri took the chair Christophe designated to the right. Renée smiled at him as he sat. She was wearing the blue gown he had given her, and she looked stunning, but he wondered why she would wear it tonight. Picard had his arm on the back of her chair. She sat on the front half. Picard was dressed entirely in green: green felt hat, cape, tunic, hose, and though they couldn't be seen, Henri was sure the shoes would be green as well. It was an unsubtle hint, for green was well known as the color of love. The nobility wore green to declare their love. Renée was watching Henri. She had seen how he had looked at Picard. She reached down and fingered her dress while looking at him. And suddenly it hit him why she was wearing blue. As green was known as the color of love by all of 14th century France, so too did blue have a recognized meaning: faithfulness.

He smiled and prepared himself for Christophe. At that moment, however, Christophe stood up and guided in another guest to sit across the table from Henri. It was the preacher they had heard on the day they entered Auch, Jean de Vienne.

The entrance of the Duke signaled the beginning of dinner. At first the conversation centered on uncontroversial matters: how the crops would fair with the recent rains; whether the preacher had adequate quarters and whether the populace was responding well to his sermons and woodcuts; where he planned to go next—hoping of course that he would not need to leave too soon.

"I learned today that I am soon to be given an appointment at Avignon." Christophe gestured with a leg of chicken in his hands, and then wiped his greasy hand on his tunic.

The preacher slammed his tankard. "Avignon! I preached there. No results. A bed of snakes and politics. Never have I seen a city so numb to the gospel; unconcerned over the condition of their eternal souls; no fear of the damnations of hell. And the cardinals, they refused to allow my woodcuts. They would not admit it, but I knew it was because the woodcuts would cut into the sale of their indulgences. Still. . . I envy you. I admit it. I envy you. Frankly, between us I am weary of travel and would like an opportunity to have influence on the church from the inside."

"Really?" Christophe put down the chicken to grab a loaf of bread. "My initial position will be as canon, but there was intimation that I would soon get a bishopric, and I would need a loyal chaplain should that happen."

"I would be your man," the itinerant preacher said vigorously. "I confess I am ambitious, and between the two of us, we could rise high."

Christophe studied the preacher intently and then extended his hand. "As I rise, so will you."

"With St. Christopher as my witness, you will not regret it." Then they both tipped their tankards in toast.

Having accomplished that strategic alliance, Christophe looked around the table with satisfaction. Henri and Sir Galahad, seated next to him, were silent.

"Sir Galahad, what did you think of Sir Henri's little bout yesterday? Have you seen that style of fighting before?"

Sir Galahad did not look up from his meat as he spoke. "I have. I saw it in the orient fighting the Saracen, and in Spain it is commonly used by infidels."

"By infidels!" Christophe exclaimed.

The conversations at the other end of the table quieted.

"Tell me, Sir Henri, did you learn it from infidels?" Christophe asked with feigned innocence.

Henri finished his glass of wine before answering. "My father taught me."

"But where did your father learn it?" Quercy took up the line of questioning, pressing it forward from his seat across the table.

Henri did not answer. It was obvious to him any defense he made would be little credited.

"Tell me, Sir Galahad," Christophe asked, "you are a true knight errant. Have you ever had a close friendship with an infidel?"

Galahad kept eating his meat and muttered, "I protect the Holy Church. I kill infidels."

"What do you think, Father Jean? Should we make friends of infidels?"

Picard, hearing the conversation for the first time, tried to get Christophe to lower his voice, nodding in the direction of their father the Duke.

"Let him hear. He knows my opinion." He repeated the question to the preacher. "What do you think? Should we make friends of infidels, and what of the rich Jew? Should these be our companions?"

"Well, milord, I have thought about this, and I have begun to form opinions, but I would be anxious to hear your thoughts." The preacher equivocated, not wanting to strike out too far.

"What of you, Henri? What is your opinion?"

"You know very well that my father traveled in the companionship of Jehudah ben Ibrahim the Jeweler, and Ishmael of Grenada, the Physician, a Jew and a Mohammedan. These have been my father's friends and mine also. You only ask the question to start an argument."

Christophe, turning from Henri, addressed Jean. "You see, three years ago my father expelled all the infidels from Gascony."

"As well he should have," Jean said, nodding.

Christophe continued, "Henri's father, a knight under my father, however, abandoned his loyal oath to my father in order to take up with the Jew and heathen, and so I was wondering what others thought about that."

At that moment Christophe felt a familiar hand on his shoulder. He did not need to look to know the hand of his father. "That topic is not to be discussed. I forbid it." The duke looked up and down the table and then, clapping his hands, called for a jongleur. When the entertainer had set up his seat in the middle of the hall, Duke Henri gave Christophe another reprimanding glance, and then to Henri he added, "We had a really interesting singer here a month ago. You would have enjoyed him. He sang several songs in Breton and was hoping to find news of your father. He had been sent by Duc de Montfort himself. I wonder what became of him? I imagine you would like to hear some Breton songs. You know that language, don't you?"

"Yes, your Grace. My parents spoke it when I was young; my father felt it important that I know it well," Henri replied.

The minstrel sang several small ballads and then launched a particular favorite of the Duke's: the Chanson of Roland.

As he was nearing the end, Christophe said, "That is a particular favorite of our family, as we are related to Roland."

"In fact," Picard continued with enthusiasm to the preacher, though his words were really intended for Renée, "we can trace our ancestry to Charlemagne as well. Eleanor of Guienne was my father's great-great-grandmother, and we are third cousins from King Charles."

The preacher responded, "Your noble blood is very obvious. I noted it instantly on entering Auch. It is very distinctive."

Turning to Renée, Picard added, "I don't believe we have a drop of common blood."

She smiled and said nothing.

He continued, "Well, in a way it is nothing to be proud of. I mean, after all, it is just the fate of destiny, of God's hand, that I am born into such purity of noble blood. Still, having been born noble, it is something that I must jealously guard, and could never sully. Which, however. . . ." Now turning to Henri, he continued, "Which leaves me at a total loss as to how you could ever—even in the circumstances you were in—how you could even consider working as a common stable boy. Didn't that offend your very sensibilities?"

Sir Galahad, without stopping his eating, sneered at Henri. "A friend of infidels; and a stable boy—you are a disgrace to your line." With that he left the table and joined a table of older knights.

"I guess he made his point," Quercy laughed. "Say Henri, if you finish early, could you throw a little straw down for my horse?" Most everyone at the table laughed.

Henri laid down his cloth napkin and went out the door to the garden.

As the troubadour had now finished, Picard stood up and began to recite a poem:

> *When Renée draws her mantle round her face,*
> *Sweeter than all else she is to see,*
> *That hence unto the hills there lives not he*
> *Whose whole soul would not love her for her grace,*
> *Then seems she like a daughter of some race*
> *That holds high rule in France or Germany.*

Henri wandered in the garden. The night was warm, the air close. The aroma of summer hung near: the smell of newly harvested hay, the smell of barbecued meats, the smell of the stables and the fertilized gardens. It was a familiar incense to him, recalling childhood memories. At times heavy clouds obscured the nearly full moon, turning the garden into darkness, but, as the clouds passed on, the return of the moonshine seemed magical. From out the open windows he heard the music start again as several minstrels now struck familiar dance tunes. Through the window he watched the tables being shoved to the side and dancing beginning in the center. He stood in the shadows and watched as young and older knights rose and paired off with the maidens and ladies of the castle. Quercy, Galahad, Armignan, Charlotte, Constance, Armanda, and there now Picard was drawing Renée to the center. Henri turned away, moving farther into the garden. Past the bed of foxglove, through the meandering hedge, on some stepping stones that made a path through a lilly-covered pond, until he came to a bench in the center of the garden. A stone wall rose behind the bench. As he sat, the thorn of a rosebush pricked his arm. It drew blood. Clouds briefly covered the garden in darkness again. When the moon shone again, he looked at the bush and leaned over to smell one of the flowers. The fragrance was delightful. It was a white bud of perfection, purity, and the promise of beauty.

He heard the soft rustle of her dress and then felt the touch of her hand on his—Renée. He stood, picked the rose, and handed it to her.

She held it to her nose.

Chanson du rossignol
The magpie and the golden thrush,
The skylark and the nightingale
Warble a thrilling note

Then take to air

Across the moon,
Their flight graceful
Amidst the garden,
Rise above the wall
And fly so free.
Ever beauty shall not fail
While sings the nightingale.
- Sir Henri

Henri spoke. "Do you remember when you first told me the story of your uncle and the wickedness he desired to burden you with? Remember I told you of a rose planted in a bed of manure; planted in filth, but blossoming chaste?"

Renée nodded. "How could I forget? You'll never know what that meant to me."

"This is that rose."

She smiled as if suddenly seeing a relic of the Virgin Mother for the first time and smelled the fragrance of the rose again.

For a moment they stood there in the silence of the moon-glow looking at each other. His face was newly shaven, his smile true. His cotton shirt had sleeves cut high on the arm for freer action. A gray tabard buttoned down the front and was bound around the waist by a leather sword belt. Fastened around his neck, a long, gray cloak reached to his knees. His pants were tucked into calf-length leather boots. Renée, standing but a rose petal away from him, wore her blue dress with the deep sleeves, and a silver filigreed belt hung low on her slender hips. Black lashes shadowed her oval eyes, and a narrow ribbon of silver thread bound her braided hair.

A cloud moved across the moon. Renée saw the silhouette of Picard at the door of the hall peering into the garden's darkness. She slipped her arm in Henri's and drew him quickly behind the wall. They waited in suspenseful stillness, Renée's hand grasping Henri's arm. Then Henri, climbing a few steps on the stone wall, peered toward the door.

Dropping quietly back to the ground, he whispered, "He's still there."

Renée leaned around the wall and looked too. "He's coming," she said urgently. "Where can we hide?"

Henri took her hand and led her noiselessly through a maze of bushes to a dark corner, far from the dining hall. A little breeze started to blow. Renée sat down on a hidden stone bench behind a cherry tree and crossed her legs. Henri stood back. Neither of them spoke; they just looked at each other and listened. A nightingale was singing from a nearby bush. They listened to its melodious songs, its modulated whistles, buzzes, and flutelike trills. Their dark sanctuary was shattered by the shuffling footstep of Picard and the quiet calling of her name.

"He will not go away until he finds me. His unrelenting persistence is so annoying. Its like trying to get all the strands of a spider web out of your hair."

"You're worth searching for," Henri replied.

She didn't answer, but she twisted around to see if she could see Picard.

He was getting closer.

"There is a back gate," Henri suggested and pulled on her hand.

Renée gathered her skirt with her right hand. Tiptoeing, they crossed a large open area to the wrought iron gate. Henri unlatched the gate and gently pushed. It squeaked a little. He ushered Renée out and slid the latch back into position. They stepped behind the wall, exhaled in relief, looked at each other, and smiled.

She leaned against the wall, resting on her hands. "Me and my stable boy on the run again."

The breeze became gustier. Henri looked to the sky. The clouds now hid the moon.

"I smell rain," Henri said and looked around. There were a few torches on the wall where the watch paced their guard. Elsewhere it was darkness. Henri took Renée's hand and led her under the cover of the large oak tree standing in the middle of the grounds. If it rained the oak would give shelter.

Not much later the rain did come, slowly at first, a drizzle on the leaves of the old tree. They slid down side by side with their backs to the large trunk and listened. They heard the guards grumbling from the wall. They heard the music from the hall more distantly. The darkness and the rain seemed to separate them and envelop them in a world so close and yet so distant, a world all their own.

The winds blew stronger and the showers began coming in gusts. Their oak tree shelter began dripping.

"We are going to need to make a run for the stables," Henri advised.

Renée gathered up her skirt, slipped off her shoes, and then challenged, "Race you."

Henri laughed, remembering well their run in the monastery.

"Go," she said, and took off across the courtyard. Despite the disadvantages of her dress she still beat him, but in the few seconds they ran they both were drenched.

"You win," Henri acknowledged as he ducked under shelter of the stables. "Again." Facing her, he leaned his arms on her shoulders and caught his breath. "You're soaking wet." He unfastened his cloak, put it around her shoulders, and then left his arm there. She pulled the cloak around her and nestled in close. They stood for a few moments watching the water fall in sheets off the stable, listening to the wind and the pounding rain.

Henri felt a furry head nuzzle against his leg. "Hello, Rouge." He leaned over to pat his hound. The dog often slept beside Le Noir in the stables.

Renée knelt down and hugged the hound as the dog wiggled. "You have a new sister now, Rouge, and I hope you like her. You must be good friends."

"What will you name your puppy?" Henri asked.

Still petting the dog, Renée shrugged. "Rose would have been a good name until Picard suggested it. But now I think I will name it Le Blanche."

"You don't like Picard?" Henri asked.

"He's not as egotistical as Christophe, nor as brash as Quercy, but he's swarmy."

"Swarmy?"

"Yes, you know, like a swarm of flies always buzzing in front of your eyes, always trying to light on your skin. He won't leave me alone, and you know I don't think he really cares. His attentions seem forced and false."

They heard nickering from the far end of the stables, and Renée led the way to see her mare. The mare was waiting for them, her head leaning over the gate waiting to be petted. Henri and Renée stopped, stroked her forehead, and combed their fingers through her mane. Henri scooped a cupful of grain and gave it to her.

In the next stable Le Noir swung his head restlessly, rolling up his lips and baring his teeth while they petted the mare.

"I had them stabled next to each other," Henri said.

"You don't like to be separated, do you?" Renée said to the stallion as she reached over to pat his heavy neck. "You will watch over her, won't you?" And then, patting the mare with the other hand, she added, "Try not to beat him too often at races. It will make him feel bad."

Henri patted his stallion and grumbled, "My advice is to never race. If she wins you will never live it down."

Renée laughed and turned back towards the stable door. Thunder rolled across the castle grounds. The rain came down in gusty waves. She sat down on a wooden bench opposite their horses. Henri stood over her, leaning on his right arm.

"Here, sit beside me." She slid over as far as she could, but when Henri sat down, he could only get one leg on the bench. He sat for a moment and then stood again. At that she got up and gently pushed him onto the bench.

"I should not sit while you stand," Henri protested.

"Shhh," she whispered. After straightening her dress, she sat down on his lap, slid her arms around his neck, and buried her head on his shoulder. Henri pulled her close. They sat in silence for a long time listening to the rain, Rouge lying at their feet.

"Why can't it always be this way?" Renée asked softly without lifting her head from his shoulder. "We have three horses, two dogs, and each other. What else could we want?"

"Nothing," Henri replied and pulled her closer for an unmeasured time.

The rain finally slackened, leaving only a steady dripping from the roof.

"We should probably go back," Henri said. "They will start worrying, and rumors may start."

"Let them rumor all they want. It will not be far from the truth," Renée said. Nevertheless, she rose, brushed off her dress, and, after unclasping his mantle, handed it back to Henri. The clouds were now flying away, and the moon shone clear. Walking slightly ahead of him, her wet hair glimmered in the moonlight. The braids had loosened, and knowing he was watching, she pulled her braids out, letting her hair flow long and free.

Henri opened the gate to the garden. They looked to the dining hall. It was dark and abandoned. It must have rained longer than they thought. Guiding their way carefully through the chairs and tables in the night shadows, they made their way to the halls. Cressets burned at spaced intervals, providing just enough light to guide them up the stairs toward the living quarters.

Qui nous séparera de l'amour du Christ
We like sheep. We may die.
Bolts of lightning upon tree and limb strike,
Thrown down from angry skies—
A rest remains among the storm.

We like doves. We fly high.
Let roll the peals of thunder above the peaks,
Among the barren heaths—
There remains a rest for you and I.

We like colts. We run by.
Come heaven's pale horsemen, red, white, or black,
Dealing bow and sword and famine—
There is a table of rest where we may dine.

We like babes. We may cry.
Bowls of incense plagued, the sun like sackcloth,
The moon dished blood red—
Still in blessed time there remains a rest.

A rest made unbreakable in love.
- Sir Thommas de Bretagne

They passed the chapel and stopped to look in. The warmth and flicker of the candles beckoned. Meandering slowly through the chapel, they looked at the frescoes painted on the walls and then at the sacramental table.

Renée, reverently fingering the intricate carvings of the table, spoke. "He has been good to us, hasn't he? Hasn't he, Henri?"

"God has been good," Henri answered, as usual drawn to the Bible chained to the lectern. He turned the pages slowly and then, following a passage with his finger, added, "Listen to this." He read in Latin and then translated for Renée:

"Who shall separate us from the love of Christ? Shall trouble or hardship—like you had with your mother or the death of my father—or persecution or famine—we did go rather hungry there for a while—or nakedness—well we haven't had that, though you did cut your one dress pretty short, and you do have nice legs. . . ."

"Henri!" she reprimanded him, smiling, a little embarrassed that he would allude to her legs here in the chapel.

He smiled and kept reading. "Or danger or sword—yes, definitely we have had that." And then he quit reading, closed his eyes, and began reciting from memory. "For I am convinced that neither death nor life, neither angels nor demons, neither the present nor the future, nor any powers, neither height nor depth, nor anything else in all creation, will be able to separate us from the love of God that is in Christ Jesus our Lord."

When he opened his eyes Renée was standing by him, her eyes glistening. "Is that what it says?"

Henri nodded.

"Show me."

Henri took her hand and pointed her finger to the words as he repeated them again.

"Would you teach me to read? I want to read this for myself. It is so beautiful."

Chapitre Vingt
Avoir le Bosse de Cheval

When in search of horses, led by men
I travel up both river and mount'n roads,
Like the summer hath my departure been,
Unending days of weary toiling loads,
Of lifting hooves, stroking manes, sizing steeds;
When rather I'd be lying by your side,
Rest my head upon your young bosom. Breathe
Softly, love; we have all the day, alive,
To lie beneath the lemon tree, gather
Garlands, and weave them in your fragrant hair.
Count the clouds that drift—as if it mattered
Which way the wind chose to blow them and where.
But alas, those thoughts are but dreams of mine
When day's passed and on my bed I recline.
- Sir Henri (Sonnet XXIII)

The following morning the Duc de Gascogne summoned Henri and requested Henri help his seneschal in purchasing horses. In his chambers, speaking privately to Henri, hand on his shoulder, he appealed, "You seem to have your father's gift of sizing up a good horse. It'll be your decision, and yours alone, which horse to buy. If you say yes, my man will buy them."

Henri was honored and accepted; that afternoon, in the company of a mounted escort, he rode south toward the Pyrenees. Over the following days the company rode along the Gers River through Castelnau Magnoac; they crossed the Baise and Arros rivers, went through the pass east of Tarbes, and passed through Lourdes. They traversed the Pyrenees as far as Gedre in the shadow of Mount Perdido and the peak of Vignemale. Following the west branch of the Garonne, they made their way back through Arreau, Montrejeau, and as far as Cazeres before turning north toward Auch. The trip itself would not have taken the month it did, except that the seneschal told Henri they were to purchase fifty horses, and Henri was very selective. Thus, for the next month they toured the riverine towns and manors and rode the mountain roads visiting forlorn farms. On an exceptional day they might find three worthy horses, on many a day none. Henri's meticulous exams frustrated the seneschal.

"What was wrong with the sorrel?" he complained one afternoon, deep in the Pyrenees, after having inspected fifteen horses at a manor, none of them satisfying Henri. "He was a good sixteen hands, and not over eight years of age. He had spirit. I would have been proud to have bought that one."

Henri looked at the seneschal with bewilderment. "The sorrel? You liked the sorrel?"

"Yes, what was wrong with him? A fine gelding. At this rate, it shall be winter before we find fifty horses."

"The sorrel?" Henri asked again. "Did you look at him. . . Did you look at him well? He was calf-kneed, with a broken back pastern." Henri shook his head. "Under the stress of the Duke's stables he would be lame within a year. He might be fine as a young farm girl's pet, but he is not at all suited for Gascony."

"What then of the bald chestnut?"

"Toe-in, paddling gait; not exaggerated, but clearly there. You must watch them very closely from the rear as they walk."

"And the black?"

"Post-legged."

"Well, I still like that bay we saw yesterday."

"Yes, she had nice conformation, but when I rode her she had no heart. Still, we *could* have bought her. She *might* have turned out all right."

The seneschal huffed and rode on in silence. But over the following weeks under Henri's continued careful inspections they added one here, two there. When they had ten horses they sent a captain and guard to take the small herd to Auch. When the captain returned he brought the Duke's effusive praise, praise directed both at Henri and the seneschal.

"Whenever I buy a horse he always faults it: too old, too swayed, too small, too mean. It is always something. You must have the eye," the seneschal acknowledged, and their relationship warmed. Still, it was nearly a month before they returned to the castle, and Henri missed Renée.

Trompeur poursuite
Down, down the flanking times of earth's biting soil
He rides his dread pursuit, on dread horse, and dread wing;
He rides in fury with dread name, and dread death he brings.

Up, up from Dante's fabled circled burning hell
He tromps his iron boot, clanks his iron sword. Iron shield
Will not halt his foul steed until his mission of death he wields.

Beware, then, O sinner, man, and stray not from the fold;
Stray not far from mother church, lest in sinister chase
Your name the blots of heaven's angelic penmarks erase.
- Abbé Odile of St. Stephen's (Taken from *The Fall of Man*)

It was not until he returned, however, that he discovered Renée was gone. On the same afternoon Henri had left on the horse-buying quest, the maiden Renée had gone to Biarritz. A company of knights led by Sir Picard had escorted Constance and many of the young maidens of Gascony to Constance's father, the Comte de Biarritz, and his castle by the sea. They were still there. In fact, they were not expected for at least another month. The shore was lovely this time of year. To top it all, when Henri went searching for Sir Petro de Lomange, he learned that the knight had left two weeks previous, returning to Cairns. Their little trio was broken.

Feeling the emptiness, Henri went down to the stables and sat down on the bench, remembering Renée and waiting out the rain. Rouge laid his big head across Henri's lap. Henri rubbed his ears. From across the tiltyard Henri heard the boisterous voice of Christophe approaching.

"Here he is, indeed," Christophe called over his shoulders.

A moment later Sir Quercy, Sir Galahad, and four other knights strode into the stables.

"Hey, stable boy, want to saddle me up a horse?" Quercy jibed to the guffaws of his companions.

Henri glared at Quercy.

"It's the chestnut down on the end," Quercy continued.

"Very amusing," Henri retorted.

"Knock it off, Quercy," Christophe intervened, and then said to Henri, "It's just a jest, Henri, but we were wondering if you would like to ride on a hunt with us. We were thinking of going hawking, thought you might enjoy coming along. Your bird would probably like to air his wings a little."

Henri perked up. "Thank you, yes, I will come."

They rode two abreast as they left the castle into the surrounding hills. At the front were Christophe and Quercy, their silver capes sweeping behind them, sitting erect with peregrine falcons on their leather guards. In the second row came Henri and Sir Galahad, both with goshawks on their arms. Behind them rode the chief falconer and four other knights. Running alongside were several of the houndsmen with dogs under leash.

They turned off the main road to enter a field and descended to a marsh surrounded by reeds and cattails. Loosening the hoods of their birds, the four knights readied them as the dogs began to rustle through, searching for fowl. Christophe released his falcon first. It took to a great height, and when a dog stirred a partridge, it swooped and killed the bird.

"Well done, Christophe," Henri complimented him. "A fine bird."

"Thank you, though a goose would have been more meat," Christophe said as he inspected the bird brought to him by one of the boys. Then he gave Quercy a quick, sly smile. "We shall see who kills the best bird today."

Sir Galahad loosed his bird next at a small duck rising from the water. But the goshawk on the stoop only grazed the bird, and the duck fled to cover away from danger. Sir Galahad cursed as the hawk returned to his arm. Disturbed, the bird started to fly away before the chief falconer intervened.

"You go next, Henri," Quercy invited.

Henri unstrapped the leather jesses that tied his hawk to his arm, and took off the hood. With reassuring soft words to his raptor he held his arm ready for the next game bird the dogs flushed. It was a quail rising from the tall grass. Flinging his arm, Henri sent the bird on the hunt. A moment after he released, he observed Quercy pitching his falcon. Henri knew the game. Quercy's falcon was to hunt his hawk. It would not be a fair match. The goshawk did not know he was being chased; even if he had, he could not have match the speed and size of the peregrine.

Christophe and Quercy smiled at each other. Then, seeing Henri's betrayed look, Christophe added, "It's just a game, Henri. Don't take it so hard. It will be great sport."

Henri stood in the stirrups and gave a piercing whistle. The goshawk instantly gave up the chase and turned towards Henri; seeing the falcon rapidly closing, the smaller, more agile goshawk swerved. The falcon caught only a wing, and the goshawk dropped to the ground. With a second whistle and hand motion, Henri signaled his hound. The hound's presence scared off the falcon. Henri set the spurs to Le Noir and galloped up to the goshawk's fluttering form. Leaping from the saddle he gathered the bird gently in his hands. The wing was broken. Wrapping it in cloth, he soothed it with gentle words. As he walked back to the two ducal sons he asked bitterly, "Are you satisfied? What else do you want from me?"

"Well done, Henri. I have never seen a hawk or hound so well trained." Christophe spread his arms as he spoke. "But since you ask, we would like to see you fight Sir Galahad. You see, Quercy did not like being embarrassed when you fought him." Christophe now changed his tone to one truly vexed. "You do not know your place, Henri. A knight of inferior rank should not beat a Duke's son. It is not done; it is not chivalrous."

Quercy looked to Sir Galahad, who, after handing off his hawk to the falconer, had dismounted and was strapping his sword to his side. "Quercy is my student, and when you beat him you insult me, his teacher. I take his place as a champion."

Seeing two pages bringing Henri a coat of mail and a helmet, Henri understood this had all been planned. Away from the confines of the castle and the oversight of the Duke, they could play their mean games. Sir Galahad was a good fifteen years older than Henri, much more experienced. And though Henri was taller, Galahad, being older, was more solid. This would not be a combat Henri would have chosen, but he could not refuse.

He pulled the mail coat over his linen shirt, fastened the greaves to his legs, and placed the leather mittens over his arms. He took the sword handed to him and examined it closely. A little unbalanced, nothing spectacular, not of the caliber of Sir Galahad's Toledo-forged blade.

"Are you ready?" Sir Galahad asked as he drew his sword with fanfare.

Henri pulled on his helmet. The knights formed a perimeter for the fight.

Sir Galahad extended his hand toward Henri. Henri took it as Sir Galahad glowered at him. "I have never been beaten, and frankly, I would rather not waste my time on someone as inexperienced as you. But you did have the gall to pitch me into this."

At that Sir Galahad jerked Henri over his extended leg. The move, so ignoble, caught Henri totally by surprise. He tripped and fell on his face. Galahad kicked him hard in the flank and rested the tip of his sword against the back of Henri's neck.

The whole thing, the disingenuous handshake and the trip, had caught Henri completely off his guard. He had never seen such dishonor, such lack of chivalry. But now his face was in the dirt, and he had been beaten.

"Next time get me a man to fight," Galahad said as he kicked Henri again and sheathed his sword.

"F. . . Foul! F. . . Foul!"

Christophe, Quercy, and Sir Galahad looked over their shoulders to see Comte d'Auch galloping onto the field from the road above. Behind him rode Sir Picard and the maiden Renée.

Henri rose and dusted himself off. He was even more humiliated that Renée had seen his disgrace.

"I ha. . . have never seen anything as cheap. Sir. . . Sir Galahad, you. . . you. . . ."

"Just spit it out!" Sir Galahad snapped. "Speak plainly; enough of your maimed speech."

The three younger ducal sons gasped at Galahad's audacity.

Comte d'Auch pulled his horse to a halt at Sir Galahad's feet. Now, speaking very slowly and deliberately, Comte d'Auch continued, "That was the worst display of dishonor I. . . I have seen." Try as he might, the stuttering came back. "You. . . you are to be ashamed for that foul trick. You have taken the coward's way."

"You call me a coward! No one has ever called me a coward, whether he be king, duke, or comte. I demand justice from you."

Christophe and Quercy had now placed themselves between Sir Galahad and Comte d'Auch and were pulling him away. "You cannot fight with my brother. If you fight my brother, you will have to fight all of us."

Galahad stepped away from their restraining arms. "That would be easy enough. I have fought infidels five times as good as any of you. Draw your swords and we will battle, Sir Galahad against the four sons of Gascony. May God help you, for you shall surely need it."

Sir Henri glanced at Renée. She was as beautiful as ever, seated sidesaddle on her white mare, holding her puppy in her arms. Her gown was a new one of blue and pink Venetian cloth embroidered with velvet hearts. Her hair was bound by a tiara with a large blue sapphire in the middle. Clearly Picard had been showering her with gifts. Their eyes met and she smiled.

He swept the dirt from his shoulders and stretched his neck and shoulders a couple of times before sliding past the ducal brothers as they faced Sir Galahad.

Now speaking to Comte d'Auch, he offered, "This duel was started between Sir Galahad and me. If it pleases milord, I offer myself as your substitute. I have matters to settle."

Voici l'homme
I stand now in your stead—
Though there is one I have not mentioned who for you has bled—

> *My sword is strong of steel—*
> *His, still sheathed, was stronger still—*
> *And all our shame of love did fill.*
> *Behold the man on yonder hill,*
> *Whose blood stained stones and on Friday dead.*
> -   *Sir Henri*

Comte d'Auch hesitated. "You are too. . . too young, Henri, and you are our guest. It . . . it would neither be generous nor prudent."

"I am man enough," Henri countered. "My father taught me the blade and how to wield it against such as him."

Comte d'Auch looked at Picard, Christophe, and Quercy for advice. Picard and Quercy nodded. Christophe added, "He is good, brother. He is very good, though against Galahad, well, still he has offered, better him than us. . . ."

"Trust me," Henri said. "Though. . . if you have a better sword than this. . . ." He held up his mediocre sword. "I would appreciate it."

Comte d'Auch dismounted and pulled his sword from its scabbard in front of the saddle. "This is. . . is a fine Toledo sword, no word has ever been spoken against it. It has been in the family for five. . . five generations. You may borrow it." Before handing it over, Comte d'Auch raised it to his mouth and kissed the cross-engraved hilt.

"I offer to go one on four, and you send me a boy instead." Sir Galahad took a swig of wine from a wineskin, swirled it around in his mouth, and then spat it on the ground.

They approached with their swords drawn. They did not touch their blades as custom dictated, but warily began circling, just out of range, swords pointed halfway to the ground. Henri turned his mind toward battle. Fencing at this level required highly focused concentration; one must always be wary, always ready for defense or attack. It required technical skills of footwork, and the proper handling of the blade, lightly held, but not so lightly that it could be bound and drawn from the hand. It required a soft eye that could all at once watch the blade, the arm, the feet, and the eyes of the opponent. It required courage and an ability to use fear productively.

Sir Galahad took the initiative, combining a couple of feints and then a deadly lunge. Henri recognized the feints and sidestepped the lunge. On his second flurry, Galahad slashed from the right, caught Henri's blade, and then whipped back to slice into Henri's jupon. The mail blunted the blade at Henri's left flank. Henri did not feel the ooze of blood trickling from the wound. When Galahad stepped in for his next attack, Henri anticipated it well, and Galahad barely got his blade up in time to turn Henri's sword to the broadside as it hit into Galahad's leading shoulder.

Galahad leaped back and watched Henri for a few moments. On his next flurry he had completely changed his footwork, and the feint caught Henri leaning in. Henri took most of the blow of the sword on the leather brace of his left arm. That one he felt. It would need stitches. Later.

The champion was craftier, faster, and stronger than anyone Henri had ever faced. Still everyone had a weakness—his father had drilled that into him—he just needed to discover it. Galahad came at him again, letting Henri parry a couple of obvious swings and then trying to thrust at Henri's shoulder too high for Henri to parry. Henri caught it with the guard of the sword, but the blade still sliced the skin. He winced and stepped back. Galahad gave up the initiative for the moment and let Henri throw a couple of easily parried strokes.

What was his weakness? Henri knew it was there. He could feel it but could not quite grasp it. It was something in his lunges, which he had been taught, taught to see, taught to take advantage of.

Galahad, taking a breather, now came back like a wildcat in a dizzying, blinding speed of slicing blade, intending to finish off this duel now. Suddenly Henri saw it. The arm was too extended, and the defenses could be penetrated if he could trespass the blade. Catching a sidecut with his arm flexed tight, Henri spun in and caught Galahad with the butt of the sword on the back flank. Galahad reflexively doubled for just a moment. It was all Henri needed. He struck Galahad with the butt on the helmet, and then stepping back blasted the champion across the chest. The armor stopped the blade, but the impact made Galahad stumble backwards. Henri doubled back, hitting Galahad on the arm just above the sword. The blade tumbled free as Galahad grimaced, grabbing his right arm with his left hand. Henri flicked the blade up into his left hand and stood now watching Galahad angrily dropping to his knee.

Henri handed the sword back to Comte d'Auch. "Thank you for the blade." The next moment Renée was hugging him.

"Gently, gently," he said, now feeling the wound in his side.

Tête-à-tête
It's no go, Constance, it's no, it's not;
It's never mind the others,
Though their beauty is well shown.
It's none but one, and she is there
Riding among the maidens, white-lily fair.
- Sir Henri

They mounted a few minutes later and started back for the castle. Christophe and Quercy were at the front, uneasy with the events of the day. They had never expected their brother Comte d'Auch to return with such spectacularly unfortunate timing. It had certainly dampened the day's enjoyment. And now how were they to relate to Sir Galahad? He had been so valuable to them. Could they continue to favor him when he had threatened to fight their brother?

Behind them rode Henri and Renée, and on the other side Picard. The fact that Henri and Renée spoke only to each other, Picard disregarded. He would not go away, nor would he stop from interrupting the conversation to recall events from the time at the coast. Behind them, separately, rode Sir Galahad, morose and bruised. And then came the other knights of the castle as well as the young ladies, including Constance, who had returned with Picard and Renée. At the back rode the Comte d'Auch.

A houndsman got Henri's attention and told him the Comte d'Auch wished to speak to him.

Reluctantly Henri pulled his horse aside and waited for the Comte d'Auch. He could not help but notice how Picard reached over to pat Renée's hand.

When Henri was beside the Comte and the distance between them was sufficient to avoid being overheard, Comte d'Auch started the conversation. "I ha. . . have just returned to Auch. I came back with Pi. . . Picard, Renée and Constance, and her father the Comte de Biarritz. It is on her. . . her account that I wanted to speak to you. Earlier this summer when we first met she was with you. . . you, and I wanted to be sure you had no romantic understanding with her."

"With Constance?" Henri asked, shaking his head. "No, I have none with her."

Comte d'Auch sighed with relief. "Good, because I. . . I have thought that I should discuss with her father, well, you know?"

"With Constance?" Henri smiled. "That would be wonderful." Pointing to Renée in the staggered column ahead he said, "She's the one I love."

Comte d'Auch screwed his eyebrows in puzzlement for a moment, and then let his shoulders sink. "Renée? You? And does she feel the same way?"

"Yes."

"O my, O my!" Comte d'Auch hung his head and shook it several more times. "By the saints I wish you had mentioned that before. . . before I went to see Sieur de Bixmarch, Comte Sevestre, and. . . ."

"I thought it was obvious; surely your brother Sir Picard knows?"

"I. . . I assure you I had not the least knowledge of it. I knew you were devoted to her, but I thought it was only because you were her knight. Why. . . why did you not mention it before I had audience with. . . with King Charles?"

Henri was too alarmed to question him further. What did it mean? Comte d'Auch had been to see the King. Why would the King be interested in their little details? They rode silently for a little while, before Comte d'Auch said once again. "I. . . I wish I had known." Then he spurred his horse to ride alone at the front of the column.

Dans le mews

The gyrfalcon has stricken my hawk this day,
Has caught him by the wing in fury flayed,
Opened the flesh, hanging purple and pale,
When in false-hearted hunt he caught him in stall.
And I gather bird in my hands—he so small—
Bring him to the mews—his eye grown dim—
Tender stroke his feathers to comfort him;
Plaster balm upon wing and wound;
Sing a song his heart to soothe.
-   Sir Henri at Gascony

Back at the castle Henri took his little goshawk to the mews where the falconer began mixing a poultice from the stock of herbs. It was doubtful the bird would fly again; still he must relieve its pain and protect it from infection.

"Master, certes it is that I knew nothing of this!" the falconer said as he handed Henri the pestal of balm. Henri did not answer but touched the cloth into the poultice. "All that I know of falcons I learned from your father," the falconer said as he held the bird down while Henri carefully touched the balm to the wing and then bound the wing to the body with soft linen. "They were always a polluted sort, those sons of the Duke; that is, save the Comte—he's always been a decent sort—but the other three, like rancid meat they are. Can you imagine anything viler than to fly your falcon at a friend's? They know nothing of these fine birds. They cannot understand, can they?"

Henri finished the wrap and then laid his hand on the bird's noble head. "No, they have no love for any of God's creatures. What a sorrowful existence they must lead, a meaningless sounding of brass and tinkling of cymbal, signifying nothing. I feel sorry for them. I truly do."

"You have not changed, Henri. You were always the kindest and gentlest of boys. If my boys become like you I shall be grateful."

"Thank you, Joseph. Watch out for the bird." Henri handed the hawk to the falconer as Rouge lifted his nose to sniff at the bird. Then, turning to leave, Henri said to his dog, "Come on, boy; now I need to get my wounds dressed."

The hound looked up at Henri, sniffed the bird again, and then lay down beside the box where the bird was placed. Henri smiled. "All right fellow, you stay here and keep watch."

Chapitre Vingt et Un
Comme Agneaux Innocence

Come like an innocent lamb to the slaughter.
Come like orphan lamb, no guard from mother or from father.
Come one, come all, come strike me with your rods,
For I am downtrodden, quaking in the sods.
- Maiden Renée d'Ayes

While Henri was taking care of his hawk, horse, and wounds, the Duke had summoned the maiden Renée to his antechamber. A guard opened the door for her and pointed to a seat before an oak table. She took the seat and folded her hands tightly in her lap. She had an idea this was about Picard. He had been anything but subtle on their tour to Biarritz. As she entered he was the only one who noted her. The Duke stood before a window overlooking the city. Comte d'Auch stood beside him talking quietly. Quercy sat by a fireless hearth, his back to Renée, whittling shavings into the grating. At the table Christophe read a parchment with intense curiosity. His finger traced across the page and tapped on the document when a point caught his attention. From time to time he shook his head, and a smile flickered across his face. Still, it was Picard that made her uneasy. He had a smile like she had not seen on him before, an all-knowing, sickeningly sweet smile.

When Christophe had finished reading the document, he exhaled and exclaimed, "Sacré bleu, the hunt is up is it not? You shall have your ever tender goose, Picard."

Picard interrupted his brother and gestured at Renée, sitting quietly in front of them. Christophe started and then regained his composure.

"Father, brother," Christophe rose from the chair and tapped on Comte Henri's shoulder, "our guest, the demure maiden, is here."

The Duke and Comte d'Auch stopped their intense conversation and looked at Renée.

"Indeed, indeed," the Duke said as he took the seat at the table. "Welcome back to Auch. I hope your trip was pleasant. How did you like Biarritz?"

"The Comte and Comtess were very hospitable, your Grace."

"Good, good, that is very good," the Duke said while obviously thinking of something else. He repositioned the parchment before him. "Do you read?" he asked, picking up the parchment as if to hand it to Renée.

Renée shook her head, wishing she did. What did this piece of paper have to do with her?

The Duke paused, rubbed his hands together for a moment, rose from his chair, and then came around to the other side of the table. He sat on the edge of the desk closer to Renée. For a moment he struggled, trying to find the conversation starter. "Picard has told me about the trip and some of the enjoyable times you two had together: dancing, picnics, evening strolls, trips to the beach, riding horses together. I hope you found my son a good companion."

Uncertain how to answer this, she said nothing.

"It must be apparent to you by now that my son Picard is very fond of you, maiden."

The Duke paused and looked at Renée for a response. She did not answer immediately. It was obvious where this was headed. Picard had not been subtle about his intentions, and it had been only with constant vigilance that Renée had kept him from passing the boundaries of propriety. In this she had much to thank Constance, who unfailingly appeared when Picard had isolated her. She did not trust him within hand's reach.

"Yes, your Grace, your son has been very attentive, but it is only fair to say that my heart has been given to another."

The Duke shoved off the desk and began to pace in front of the desk, glancing at her as he spoke. "Yes, yes, that is known, and Henri is a good boy."

Christophe interrupted harshly, "You see, maiden, what my father is trying to say is that things have changed. Your little romance with the stable boy is now over. The King orders it so."

The King? What did that mean? What did the King have to do with her? Renée did not like the vindictiveness in Christophe's voice. She felt cornered in this room five to one; the Duke and his four sons all converging on her. Quercy still whittled with a satisfied smile. Christophe stood behind the desk glaring at her, daring her. Comte d'Auch had left the window and was drawing closer. Picard stood behind her by the door. She looked back at him. He seemed very smug. The Duke was harder to read.

He raised his hand and shut off Christophe.

"It is true. King Charles has weighed in on this. This letter decrees that my son Picard is to wed you."

Renée exhaled and slumped. She had never expected this from the King. She should have trusted her instincts in Cairns and stayed away from Gascony. She only knew that she wanted to be with Henri, that she loved him and him only.

While the Duke took his seat, Comte d'Auch apologized, "Renée, I did . . . did not know that Henri and you were in love. I did not know. I swear."

"So what if you had known?" Christophe said. "Surely, you would have still negotiated for your brother's benefit, rather than. . . Henri. I hope I can give you at least that much credit, that much family loyalty, my brother. You would have not sacrificed Picard because of the maiden's previously misplaced affections, would you? Affections come and go; love is just the passing of wind, a fart. Very lovely at the passing, but hardly worth a second thought. But blood—family blood—that is something."

Comte d'Auch shook his head in disgust. "And you are to be a canon. I . . . I am ashamed I had a part in that."

"Be quiet, Christophe." the Duke held up his hand as Christophe prepared to continue the argument. Turning back to Renée, the Duke said, "When my son Comte d'Auch left here, what was it, about five or six weeks ago?"

"Six weeks."

"Six weeks. He rode first to Ayes, but before he arrived he learned that Bixmarch had taken an oath of fealty to King Edward of England."

Renée gasped and covered her mouth with her hand.

"Yes, that is exactly right, my dear maiden. As you can well under-stand, that changes the picture entirely. Suddenly your little city of Ayes has come to the attention of nations. And while Ayes may not be much by itself, in the hands of the English it suddenly becomes a nice little strategic fortress along the Garonne. You are too young to remember when Gascony was also an English ally, and how we suffered under the Black Prince, but I assure you I am not. I was the one who led the rebellion against the nefarious English. Thus my son, when he heard of Bixmarch's treacherous actions, went instead to King Charles, who was in Orleans at the time. And well, here it is." At that the Duke read from the decree stripping the title from Comte Sevestre, making the maiden Renée the ward of the court, and then offering her in marriage to Picard, son of Duke Henri of Gascony.

At that Picard came around and knelt before Renée. "My fair maiden, I have accepted the decree of the King. I shall take you as my wife, and the lands of Ayes. I shall be the Comte d'Ayes and hold it for King Charles."

This was a proposal? It seemed rather like a summons.

"But we cannot marry!"

"Why should you not marry?" Christophe pounced on the statement like a weasel on a duckling. "We are not closely related, such as the despicable Bixmarch, and I have seen you often taking mass, so I know you are a believer. There is only one other reason. You are a virgin, aren't you?"

Comte d'Auch groaned. He hated to watch his brother launch into the attack. He felt sorry for Renée. A future sister-in-law should not have to be inquisitioned at the moment of her proposal. Though, in fact, being born a woman of rank with an estate to pass to her husband almost guaranteed that she would be bartered like a valuable horse. Still, he did not like it, and his heart went out to Renée.

Renée recoiled from his attack. "No. . .Yes,"

"Which is it, no or yes?" Christophe demanded before the Duke pulled him away. Picard had gotten up from his knees by this time and was waiting by the end of the table for her answer.

The Duke was not as malicious in his question, but there was clearly still an urgency. This matter was important, and there was no polite way to approach the question. "Are you a virgin?"

She blushed. "Yes, I am a virgin. That is not what I meant. I am a virgin, though I have had to slap a couple of men to stay one, one of them being your sweet Picard."

The Duke shot Picard an angry, censuring look and shook his head, but he was obviously relieved by her answer. "Then what is it, my daughter—I hope it does not bother if I call you that—why can you not marry?"

"I am betrothed."

"In truth."

She nodded.

The Duke glanced back at Comte d'Auch in question, and then back to Renée. "To Henri?"

She nodded again.

The Duke was taken aback a moment. This made the problem more complex. He turned and walked away. Christophe approached again, but Comte d'Auch laid a firm hand on his shoulder and turned him away.

"Henri never told me this. Why have you not mentioned it?"

"It was not before a priest, but a private troth."

Christophe quickly responded, "If it was not before a priest it is null, and can be swept aside."

Clearly the Duke and his sons were much relieved. "I understand your reluctance, but I assure you, you will discover Picard a good lord for you. Furthermore, I have already set orders in place to mount a siege on Ayes. We mean to put it to siege, and you may rightfully return to your home. Picard will lead the siege and prove his worth to you. Now what do you say?"

Renée looked around in confusion. What was she to do? What could she do? How could she avoid obeying the King's orders? "Before I agree I would like to talk to Henri."

There was silence in the room as the five Gascons looked at each other. After a moment Comte d'Auch ushered her to the door. A guard was there, and Comte d'Auch ordered him to escort her to her rooms. As she passed along the corridor she saw Constance sitting in the hallways beneath an open window. Constance looked at her and smiled.

When she was out of the room, Christophe was the first to speak. "She cannot speak to the stable boy. Do not let her."

"Why, what harm will there be in that?" Comte d'Auch countered.

"Plenty: an opportunity for mischief. They are both very stubborn-minded people. The best way to deal with this is to keep them separated. Put her in the tower and lock it."

The Duke looked to Picard. "And what of you, my son? Will you still follow the King's request, now that you know she loves another? What do you want?"

Picard looked to his brothers Quercy, Comte d'Auch, and then to Christophe before answering, "I would be Comte d'Ayes. I care not where her heart lies."

"Callous; a definite want of true courtly love." The Duke rose and reluctantly nodded to Christophe. "All right, take her to the tower, but make sure she is well treated."

"Of course, father." Christophe sounded offended. Before he left he pulled Picard aside and whispered a few words in his ear. Picard smiled and nodded.

The Duke, nervously rubbing his hands, approached the window, and looked out at the afternoon sky; high, cirrus striped clouds like a colt's-tail spread across the dry blueness. "Well, I guess we should call Henri. And what will we do with him? I wish there was some other way. I do feel sorry for him, and for the sake of his father I wish I could do something different."

"But it was either him or me," Picard retorted.

"And he is twice the man you will ever be. He has integrity, honesty, and a truly noble heart," the Duke responded. Then, seeing Picard's crestfallen countenance, he added, "Do not take it too hard, son; you are at least better than your brother Christophe. Though you are peevish, sullen, and ungrateful, at least you are not completely corrupt."

Ignoring the Duke's exchange with Picard, Comte d'Auch suggested, "I can take Henri with me when I solicit the Duke of Toulouse's help."

"That would be good."

Et le décret du Roi
Above the knight there is lord,
Above the lord there is king,
Above the king there is LORD.
May all his servants obedience bring.
- Paul of Brest, Archbishop de Bretagne

A few minutes later Henri entered the room. His arm was wrapped at his side. He was obviously tired, but when offered the chair he refused, he remained standing. His sword hung at his side. Christophe still had not returned. The Duke stepped away from the window and took a seat behind the desk. He motioned again to the chair; this time Henri sat.

"How are your wounds?" the Duke asked.

"Superficial, mostly wrapping; not more than five stitches."

"Good." The Duke smiled warmly. "My eldest, the Comte, has told me how you stood in place of my sons against Galahad's challenge. You are as brave as your father, and if the story I heard is right, you are a better swordsman than him. He was a great hunter, and a wonderful companion, but not an expert swordsman; good, but not excellent. From the sounds of it, however, you are, or at least will be. To beat Sir Galahad so handily is no mean feat. I want you to know that I appreciate what you have done for my family."

Henri was touched. "Thank you, milord."

From across the room, Comte d'Auch asked, "And. . . and how is your goshawk?"

Henri shot a bitter glance at Quercy. "The wing is broken."

The Duke looked curiously at Quercy, Picard, and Comte d'Auch in succession before looking back at Henri. "What's this? What happened to your hawk? It was a fine bird."

There was a heavy pause. Quercy dropped his head and turned his attention even more to his whittling. Comte d'Auch, seeing Quercy intended to remain silent, briefly recounted Christophe's and Quercy's malicious attack on Henri's hawk.

When he finished the Duke was livid. He rose from his chair, grabbed Quercy by the neck, and threw him out of the room. "Get out. Get out of my sight, and tell Christophe not to come back, either. Go with him to Avignon."

The Duke slammed the door and walked heavily across the rush-matted floor. He looked around the room in silence and shook his head repeatedly. "You were not involved in this, Picard, were you?"

"I just arrived this morning. I knew nothing of it. "

Sitting back down, Duke Henri could hardly bear to look at Henri. "I apologize for my sons. They will bring me down in disgrace. How could I have so failed in raising them? They invite you on a hunt to attack your bird. I am truly embarrassed. And it certainly makes what I called you to discuss more difficult, much more difficult."

"What is done is done," Henri said, though he surmised the Duke had not heard the whole story, how they had set up not only the hunt, but also the first fight with Sir Galahad. But it was over, and he had no wish to mention it.

"Yes, it is, but they will repay you. I assure you." Then, patting the document in front of him, the Duke groaned. "Still, there is this. I believe my Henri told you he saw King Charles. It happened like this. After our visit at St Roland's chapel he rode to Ayes. He planned to talk with Bixmarch, but before he arrived he discovered that Sieur de Bixmarch, as he titles himself, had sworn fealty to the King of England. Well, that changed everything. Comte Henri then tried to visit Comte Sevestre—I knew Comte Sevestre at one time. We met on hunts, though it has been several years now."

"Did he talk to you?" Henri asked Comte d'Auch as the Duke paused.

The Comte shook his head. "I. . . I saw him. Sitting and rocking in the corner of a room, head in his hands. He has gone mad."

The Duke resumed the narrative. "The Abbé had already gone to Avignon with his legates and lawyers; they are trying to possess Ayes for their monastery. Thus Comte d'Auch rode to Orleans to the Royal Court. The Court had already heard of Bixmarch's treasons and his plans of usurping Ayes. They were also aware of the Abbé's plans and were thus delighted Gascony would aid the Court and reclaim Ayes for France."

Now leaning forward in his chair, the Duke looked Henri directly in the eyes. "Henri, I am aware you have developed attachments to the maiden. That is to say, I understand you are fond of her. But you see, the King has decreed that Picard is to wed Renée. This ties Gascony and Ayes and strengthens the fabric of our defenses. It would be dangerous to Gascony with a hostile Ayes perched so near. Besides, it is a good position for Picard, a good match for Renée, and good for the Kingdom. So what do you say to this?"

Henri stared blankly back at the Duke. A sudden pang of emptiness gnawed his guts. How could he give up Renée? This last six weeks without her had been miserable, and now he was being asked to give her up forever. He remembered her premonitions back at Cairn. He had not foreseen it then, but she had. He had thought that they could just cling to their love in the face of all circumstances, but he had not thought of this, the King.

"Does she know?" Henri looked around at Comte d'Auch, the Duke, and then reluctantly at Picard. Picard's smile twisted inside him like a poignard, ripping his bowels.

"Yes," the Duke said. "We talked to her first."

"And what did she say?"

The Duke took in a deep breath as he glanced at Comte d'Auch, obviously hoping for aid.

Comte d'Auch spoke quietly. "Henri, the maiden is very fond of you."

Picard, who had not spoken to this point, now interrupted, "That may be true, but she sat in that very chair here before us. Not but a few minutes ago, sitting as I said before all of us, and her very words were, 'I agree.' Did she not say before all of us, 'I agree?" Picard searched his father and brother to confirm his statement.

The Duke fidgeted in his chair.

"She said that?" Henri asked, sinking, but realizing the inevitableness. "May I?" He asked pointing to the decree.

The Duke willingly handed it to Henri. Henri carefully read through the letter, noting with a mixture of awe and resignation the King's seal.

"Can I talk with her?" Henri asked.

"We do not think it would be best. This came as a very deep shock to her. And we have taken means to see that you do not see each other again."

Henri handed back the decree. "You have put her in the tower?" He could feel himself growing weak. Suddenly being cut off again from everything, so very alone, he did not feel like a warrior knight, but like a young boy without family. He struggled valiantly to keep his voice from cracking. "I am not to see her ever again."

"Well, it does not need to be that long, but at least until Ayes has been retaken and Picard and she are wed," the Duke said, trying to encourage Henri. "You understand how difficult this is for all of us. When I sent Henri to Ayes, we did not know that you were so fond of the maiden, nor she of you. It is very awkward. But this," the Duke had now rolled the decree and tapped it on the desk, "it is the King's decree. I dare not disobey, and it will be good for Picard, for Ayes, and in time for Renée. You are young. Your fortune is before you."

Henri rose abruptly. "Is that all then?"

The Duke rose with him. "Yes. . .You will cooperate then?"

"I will not storm the tower, if that is what you mean, but the heart, how can you control the heart? Will I continue to love her? More than. . . ." He struggled to keep his emotions tight, and left the rest unsaid. The chamberlain shut the door behind Henri, and the Duke sank into his chair with a sigh.

"That turned out pretty well," Picard said pleasantly.

Both of the Gascon Henris stared at him in disgust.

L'abîme s'appellent

Deep from my human sorrow
In my solitude with no tomorrow
My joy of life is stricken, as if I lie beneath the gallow;

Your company from me withdrawn—
I who have no other to belong—
Then shall I weep from evening until the breaking of the dawn.

Then anger burns like kilns of fire,
Bellows flail to stoke it higher,
And I shall tread unfazed like fabled salamandrine pyre.

I shall not rest nor weary be—
O Lord my rightness thou shalt see—
I shall not rest until in love and justice you are restored to me.
- Sir Henri

As Henri walked back along the halls, he passed Constance still sitting at the window seat. She stood up when he came by.

"I heard everything." She pointed to the open window and softly took his hand.

Henri looked at her and began to weep. She led him to the chapel where they sat down on a shadowed back bench. The chapel was empty. He buried his head in his hands. She rubbed his back without saying a word.

When the initial grief began to pass, Henri looked at Constance and remembered Comte Henri's comments about her. "Comte d'Auch is planning to make a proposal to your father for you. He is not like his brothers; he is a good man. You will be happy with him."

Constance smiled and nodded. "Yes, I was aware something might be in the works. He will be a good husband." She stopped and looked directly into Henri's eyes, her hand still resting on his back. "But if you want, I will marry you."

"Oh, Constance, you are such an angel of mercy. I shall always cherish you, and your gift just now is priceless. I see there is still love on the earth, even for me." Henri took her hands in his, and bringing them to his lips, kissed them. "But I cannot. You know my heart. Fond as I am of you."

"I know." Constance smiled. "I did not think you would, and I shall be happy with the second Henri, if I cannot have the first. . . but. . . since they will not allow you, maybe I can take a message to Renée for you."

"Would you? O thank you." He kissed her hand and then went to the front of the chapel. He paged through the Bible until he came to the Psalms. "Memorize this," he said.

"How deep I am sunk in despair,
  Moaning in my distress,
    but I will wait. . .,
    I will hope. . .,
    in God, my deliverer.
  Deep calls to deep,
    at the waterfalls.
  All the whitecaps, all the billows of the bay
    Swamped us.
  Waves of sorrow arch over me
    like being drowned.
  But his love will not fail.
  Lord you are near.
  Your presence by day,
    and at night the nightingales song
  shall be my memory and my prayer."

Then taking off the blue sapphire ring from his finger, he gave it to Constance. "Take this to her. Tell her it is the color of my heart."

Chapitre Vingt deux:
Silenceiux

Like the cat,
Stealth and silence,
Now my defense.
- Sir Henri

Two mornings later, in the predawn, while the city was just beginning to reawaken—dim silhouettes of stone buildings rising shadowless along the streets—Henri rode Le Noir at the rear of Comte d'Auch's troop of knights. His charger's heavy shoes clattered against the cobblestone. Though early, the blacksmiths were already well at work welding and repairing armor for the upcoming campaign. The evening before, the Comte de Mont de Marsan and the Baron de Roquefort had arrived, each attended by their knights-errant and bachelor, and another dispatch had been sent out to summon the rest of the Duke's comtes, barons, lords, his knights, all that owed martial fealty to Gascony.

Henri passed through the central square before the cathedral's granite facade. The bells were silent. They would not ring for another hour. One more time he looked over his shoulder to the castle and tower. Had Renée slept well? How was she? Had she been at the window this morning? Had she seen him ride away, ride through the gates of the castle?

He reached over and patted Le Noir's neck as they trotted past the square and into a narrow street. An early rising washer-woman dumped a chamber pot's dross out the window. It barely missed a knight three horses ahead of him. The knight turned his head upward and spat out a long line of curses. Henri smiled, but it fled fast. When, where, if ever would he see Renée again? And under what circumstances? Would he ever be able to sit beside her and look into her eyes? Would they ever ride side by side on horseback? Would they ever hunt together again? Would they ever listen to the nightingale's song or laugh at the cuckoo? Would he ever kiss her again, hold her close around her slender waist and kiss her?

They were traveling to hasten the Duke of Toulouse's aid for the siege of Ayes. As they passed through the city gates, wagons with supplies were already lining up. When all of the Duke's army had mobilized, they would set out for Ayes, Picard in command of the Gascony contingent. As husband-to-be, it was his duty and honor to free Ayes from the soiled English sword. They expected over one hundred knights, five hundred infantry, and three trebuchet. With that they could begin the battle while awaiting reinforcements from Toulouse.

The Comte rode at the front of the ten-man party. Henri rode at the rear. The Comte had signaled that Henri could ride beside him up front if he wished, but Henri did not wish. He rode with this party because the objective was to reclaim Ayes for Renée, and he was Renée's knight. He had no wish to converse with any family member of the Duc de Gascogne, not even Comte d'Auch. To his mind they were all implicated, some maybe less than others, and the Comte would have been on the lesser column, but they were all still one family, and they had conspired to deprive him of Renée.

À regret
To sorrow I pay my regrets;
It is a mistress most severe.
To sorrow I offer my eyes moist and wet.
O dame sans merci, I swear to revere
You if only you will let
This be my last tear.
- Paul of Brest, Archbishop de Bretagne

They arrived in Toulouse that evening and spent the next week in the castle of Toulouse and surrounding lands helping the Duke gather his forces. The first messenger from Auch came at the end of the week. They were stopped at a well, watering their horses and munching on some bread and cheese they had bought at a nearby village. Henri was sitting on the wall of the well sipping from the ladle when the messenger rode up, looked at Henri, and then found the Comte.

Swinging off his horse, the messenger slapped a sealed letter into the Comte's hand. The Comte scanned it, walked to where Henri sat, and handed it to him without a word. Henri read the following:

Greetings, Comte d'Auch, my brother,

Greetings from your devoted brother, the future Comte d'Ayes.
I pray that you are having success in your trip. We embarked from Auch yesterday. Not all the knights have yet arrived, but daily they are joining us. I now have under my command seventy-seven knights and three hundred and forty-six men of war. The supply train is well laden, and we are off to war.

This morning in a private ceremony I have taken the maiden for my wife. She was reluctant, wishing to wait until Ayes had fallen. I think she hoped Little Henri would rescue her at the last moment, but I insisted and I think quite rightly. She will soon enough know my devotion. You might as well tell Henri.
We shall soon meet to destroy the English.

Onward to battle in the name of justice and honor.
- Picard

When he was finished reading, he handed it back to the Comte without a word. Then, taking the reins of his horse, he swung fiercely into the saddle. Rouge rose from where he lay beside the horse's side.

Comte d'Auch stood watching him for a minute. They had not said more than twenty words in the space of a week. Now, walking over to Henri's horse, he spoke softly, "If. . . If it means anything to you, I. . . I think you would have made her a better husband, and I. . . I am sorry."

Henri looked at him with disdain. "Your family has not changed since my father left three years ago. There is nothing you would not do for power."

Taken aback, the Comte was silent for a moment. "That's not quite fair. I had nothing to do with your father, and I. . . I was not the one who wanted Renée put in the tower. I have been on your side."

"I am sorry, but I don't believe you."

"You. . . you don't believe me?"

"It's pretty straightforward. You were there in the room when Renée was consigned to the tower. Did you fight for her? I don't think so. Nor did you come to my aid when I wanted to see her," Henri said without looking at the Comte.

The Comte shook his head. "You. . . you do not understand because you are not landed. If you were, you. . . you would understand conflicting interests. Sometimes the best thing may not be straightforward, though others wish it were."

"In other words, it is a lie."

"This is so un. . . unlike you Henri. What has gotten into you?"

"I don't know, maybe it has something to do with Renée's forced marriage," Henri snapped.

"You. . . you just don't understand." The Comte tried again. "Ayes is no longer a small, unimportant river town; it. . . it is a pawn between France and England. As nobles we must put aside our personal interest's for the greater interest of the Crown."

"Lovely thought. Very moving. But it would be more convincing if your family ever sacrificed for the greater weal, ever did anything that did not advance your own affairs."

"And you. . . you are different?"

"I don't know about me, but I know my father was different. He stood up for the Jew and the infidel when they were mistreated."

The Comte stopped. "But what did it get him?"

"Honor and a right standing before God."

"You. . . you mean poverty, heresy, and a lonely death."

Henri, still sitting astride his horse, shook the reins. "I have nothing further to say. I am here as Renée's knight. I have no further allegiance to Gascony."

Comte d'Auch turned away, then stopped. "Well. . . whether you believe it or not I. . . I. . . I am, I am truly sorry about all of this." He kicked a stone angrily with his boot. "I. . . I am sorry about you and Renée, and I. . . I find Picard's words and actions very low, very mean. I. . . I am sorry, Henri. I am truly sorry."

Henri watched as the Comte walked away, shoulder slumped. True sorrow, Henri could never ignore. "I believe you."

Without turning the Comte raised his hand slightly to acknowledge that he heard.

They mounted and rode.

Le drapeaux dans le champ
Oh the joy to ride over rise and hill and see in the grassy field
The waving of banner and flag as the sun's setting rays yield
A marshalling of all heralding, motto, and chivalry:
The iron cross, the spread-eagle, the regal fleur-de-lis;
Their devices, their achievements, above canvas top on pole arise.
The coat of arms, the noble's crest, above the encampment flies.
O what glory when on great horse you descend, sheathe the sword you wield,
Take rest among the tents in the martial field.
- Duc de Montfort de Bretagne

Toward evening they stopped on a knoll and looked down on the banners and tents of an encamped army. In a clearing, surrounded by beech trees, was a large red and white striped tent. From the top a flag flew, a Scandinavian black cross on a white field, and in the upper left canton was a black iron cross. A chill coursed down Henri's spine. He recognized the banner as that of the Duc de Bretagne. Was one of his uncles there in that tent, or maybe even his grandfather? He was not sure how to react. His father had been sent away from Brittany never to come back, and indeed he had died without ever returning. Now in front of him flew the heraldry of his ancestry, a lineage that he had only acknowledged in theory, never viscerally.

Comte d'Auch prodded his horse, and the troop started down the road toward the camp. Henri, however, halted. It had been a bleak day already, and he was not up to facing the uncertainty of estranged family. He was in no mood for being slighted, shunned, or rejected. Tonight he would rather grieve his loss of Renée alone. He scanned the countryside. To the west a brook passed through a field of high grasses where his horse could pasture. He had a stash of dried meat in his saddlebag. It would suffice for his supper. Thus he turned off the path and guided his charger into the meadow.

Sliding off his mount, he hung a loop of rope around a hickory tree, then tied Le Noir to the lead. After unsaddling, he began brushing his horse. He dug through the bags and found some hardtack. He tore off a hunk and gave it to his hound. He had just begun dangling his feet in the cool waters when he heard hoof beats behind him. He jumped to his feet and grabbed sword and scabbard.

It was Comte d'Auch and another knight, older, with a flush of white hair, straight black eyebrows, black moustache, and a strong chin. Despite his age, the second knight showed no decline in vigor. He rode well, tall and proud, on a beautiful chestnut gelding. He wore a dark maroon tabard lined with ermine above olive-colored chausses. They approached and dismounted.

Comte d'Auch was off first. He called out, "Why did you leave us?"

The older knight now was even with Comte d'Auch. He stood a head taller.

Comte d'Auch continued, "Henri, this is the Duc de Bretagne."

Henri had already known that; the eyes, the chin, even the walk were all a powerful remembrance of his father. This was his grandfather. The Duke approached to within ten feet and stopped. The two stared at each other without a word.

Comte d'Auch looked from one back to the other, puzzled. "Duc de Montfort, this is Sir Henri, son of Sir Thommas."

"Yes, he looks like his father, stubborn," the Duke remarked. "Well, boy, will you not give your grandfather a kiss in Christian peace?" The Duke held out his arms.

Henri paused a moment and then came forward to his grandfather's embrace. "My father is dead, you know."

"So I have been told," the Duke replied and looked for a place to sit. There was a log a few feet away. After unclasping his black mantle and laying it over his horse's saddle, he sat down. "All my boys are dead. Etienne died of the bloody flux five years ago. Richard, my oldest, died pierced by an English archer. And lately I heard of Thommas, gored by a boar. All my sons are dead." At that he pulled off his boot and shook it out. "Let us look at you, though," he continued.

The Duke scanned Henri from top to bottom. "The head is good; there is a spark of intelligence in those eyes. The body is good and strong and tall, taller than your uncles were, more like your father and. . . grandfather. You stand straight, which shows character, and your eyes do not waver—honesty. Your father raised you well, I can see, though. . . ." And the Duke shook his head disgustedly.

"What?" Henri involuntarily exclaimed. What was it that his grandfather did not approve of?

Turning to Comte d'Auch he said, "Is this how your family allows a son of Brittany to be attired? His coat and tabard, his armor is all fit for a common, petty nobleman, not a progeny of Brittany and of dukes. Have you really done so badly by my grandson as this?"

Comte d'Auch, now seeing Henri through the eyes of high nobility, realized how shabbily Henri was attired. His coat was threadbare, his braises had runs in them. His armor was chain mail, not plate, and his sword was standard issue. He stammered an apology, feeling embarrassed not only by the clothing, but by the knowledge of how poorly they had treated Sir Henri.

The Duke turned his head and spotted Henri's horse. "Well now, that is a fine warhorse, a fine one, indeed. Comte, if you had any doing in getting him this horse, than I withdraw my complaints." The Duke pulled his boot back on, got up, and patted Le Noir on the croup.

"I found him in the forest this spring," Henri explained. "He was standing beside his fallen master." The Duke's compliment of Le Noir lessened Henri's reserve.

"Found him? Wasn't that a lucky day, though of course not for his previous master." The Duke crossed himself, gave the Comte a glance as if to tell him that the points in the plus column of Gascony had just been removed. "This is obviously your warhorse, but where is your riding horse and your squire?" The Duke again scanned the meadow. "Ah, I see. None. Tell me, Comte, do you really treat all high nobility so poorly?"

Comte d'Auch dipped his head, accepting the blame, but then softly added, "And what of Brittany? Why do the sons of Brittany dwell in Gascony?"

"Forsooth, in that you have scored the mark," the Duke answered sadly. "You have struck your blade in the weakest point of my armor and wounded me. Why, indeed, do the sons of Brittany dwell in Gascony? In truth, there are no sons in Brittany, no sons, no grandsons, not even granddaughters remain in Brittany. There is only Henri, son of my Thommas. Thommas, so much like me: headstrong and yet so faithful to love." Turning now to Henri he spoke in reverent tones, "Your mother was a rare beauty, an angel. It was no surprise that your father was so stricken by her. . . . Still. . . ." His voice resumed his usual authority as he said, "A nobleman must put aside much in loyalty to family and the crown. Your father would not yield, and I cut him off." The Duke sighed and patted Le Noir one more time.

"Oh, don't think I had no regrets. Thommas, though not the firstborn, outpaced his brothers: sharp-witted, he could put the churchmen on their heels." The Duke smiled, reminiscing. "Oh, the way he wound them around so that they ended up denying what they had started off to prove. It was great fun, better than any court jester. And the Paris scholars, the young university lawyers; he never met one he could not debate to a draw. It was a good time in my life. He was not only smart, but he was the best in the saddle, the best on the hunt. He had a way of making everyone around him a better hunter. And he was the most faithful, and the kindest. I missed him greatly. . . but to defy his father so blatantly—to marry a bastard. He should have just taken her for a mistress. If he loved her that much, he could have had her as a mistress. Everybody does that. I have had five mistresses myself. I told him that; I tried to reason with him, but he would not hear of it." The Duke stopped and sighed deep and weary. "That is past. Thommas is dead, and you are here. Tell me, are you well trained in the saddle and in arms?"

"He is that," Comte d'Auch vouched for Little Henri. "I saw him spar and best Sir Galahad, quite handily."

"Sir Galahad? Sir Galahad of Catalonia, the champion against the infidels in Spain? I have heard of him. He is reputed to be quite the swordsman." The Duke looked at Henri with admiration and then clapped him on the back. "Well done. And tell me, were you taught letters?"

"I can read and write in Latin," Henri answered.

The Duke nodded and then cautiously asked, "What of Breton, do you know any of the language of your people?"

Henri shifted to Breton as he answered, "It is my mother tongue. I think in Breton."

At that his grandfather truly smiled. "Thommas did well by you." The Duke paused before asking, "What did he tell you about me?"

"He said you were a hard man and unforgiving."

"So he went to his death hating me," the old nobleman said mournfully.

Henri watched his grandfather a moment before adding, "No, he did not hate you. He had forgiven you, but I think he always hoped that you would one day forgive him."

"Forgive him? For what? It was I who was wrong. He was faithful in love; where is the sin in that?"

Faithful in love. That struck Henri to the quick, and before he knew it he was weeping. Tears were streaming down his face as he thought of Renée, his love, and of how she had been forced into marriage against her will. Tears, too, were called forth as he remembered his father and thought how Sir Thommas would have loved to have heard Duc de Montfort's apology. And those tears were fed still more when he considered that, after a year with no family, he suddenly had a grandfather.

Duc de Montfort pulled him into his arms and embraced him. "Yes, I should have forgiven him a long time ago. Come with me, Henri. Let us go back to my tent. I have no heir, and I need you."

Nouveau complet et un jeu

Just a game my friend, no reason to fret.
Just a game gentle lord, I'll take your rook yet.
Why worry over matters little? Pawns must fall
To protect the queen. A little gambit or a stall
All in time, the game is led, the pieces set.
- The Grand Inquisitor, Christophe of Gascony

Back at the camp the Duke commissioned his steward to attire Henri properly. Soon tailors were measuring Henri, armorers were bringing in different pieces of plate mail and trying them on. The stable hands were searching for a suitable riding horse for Henri, so that his warhorse could be saved for battle. Heralds were painting the device of Brittany on his shield and sewing them onto his tabard and cape. Cobblers were working with the tanners to make him a fine pair of boots.

After the initial measuring had been done and the craftsman had left to finish their work, Henri sat down to dinner with his grandfather, Comte d'Auch, and Comte Petain, the Duc de Toulouse's brother. The meal was generous if not varied, loaves of bread, beans, and beef. After the meal, Duc de Montfort pulled his stool up beside an open chess set, which was set on an upright short log. "Do you play, Comte Petain?"

"Indeed, I do. I make much of the game of chess, the strategy of battle." Comte Petain had a broad, red face, and small mouth. His hair was thinned on top, and his belly hung over his leather belt. He planted himself on a chair. It squeaked and groaned.

"Good, good. We shall sit here and play while Comte d'Auch fills us in on the details of Ayes again. What is the situation?"

Planking down a chair, Comte d'Auch sat backwards in it, his legs straddling the upright back. He then proceeded to tell them when his brother Picard had left Auch, how many knights and men he had with him, and of Picard's strategy to besiege Ayes until help arrived. They discussed the particulars of Bixmarch's changing to the English and what the English response was likely to be. Comte d'Auch thought the response would be muted. Because the English were so engaged to the north, there could be little reinforcement spared for Ayes.

"Well, enough," Duc de Montfort noted as he replaced Comte Petain's bishop with his King's knight. "But tell me more of this Sieur de Bixmarch. Of what relation is he to the Comte d'Ayes? I knew Comte Raymond well, and I met his son Comte Sevestre once. He had a most enchanting wife."

"That. . . that would be Lady Elaine," Comte d'Auch offered, glancing across the table to Henri. This could get rather delicate, and he wondered how Henri would respond. "Sieur de Bixmarch is Lady Elaine's brother."

"And what are his claims to Ayes? What are his noble lines?" Duc de Montfort asked, noting with satisfaction that Comte Petain had missed the opportunity to pin his knight.

Comte d'Auch faltered. "I. . . I am not quite sure on that score. Henri do. . . do you know?"

Henri replied matter-of-factly, "He has none. He was born the son of a tanner."

That startled Comte d'Auch. He had not known that; he had assumed Bixmarch was of noble lines if he held the title, and the realization struck him like a bolt from a crossbow that if Bixmarch was the son of a tanner, then Elaine was also a commoner, and thus Renée was not of pure noble blood. Comte d'Auch inwardly revolted at the thought, and he knew his brother Picard would have been shocked to realize that he had just sullied the line of Gascony.

"Really!" Duc de Montfort exclaimed. "Son of a tanner, and now self-titled Comte d'Ayes, and the English have credited his claim. Truly, they care only for lands. I believe they would make an alliance with the infidel if it suited their plans."

"So we are to aid your brother Pi. . . Pi. . . ?" Duc de Montfort could not remember Comte Henri's brother's name.

"Picard," Comte d'Auch supplied the name.

"And he is to marry Renée, daughter of Comte Sevestre and this commoner Lady Elaine, beautiful though she was. I suppose this Renée is a voluptuous vixen like her mother."

Comte d'Auch glanced again at Henri. "She. . . She is pretty, though I would not call her voluptuous, but then," at that he laid the flat of his hand toward Henri, "I would defer any comments on Renée to Henri."

"Really, you know this Renée?" But before Henri could answer, Comte Petain castled his King. At that Duc de Montfort took the rook's pawn with his queen and placed Comte Petain in checkmate. "Play again?"

Comte Petain rose in disgust, staring at the table. "Let Comte d'Auch take a hand at it."

Comte d'Auch gladly sat down at the table opposite Duc de Montfort.

"So tell me about this Renée?" Duc de Montfort asked Henri again as he set up the chess board.

"With your leave, I would excuse myself in this matter." Henri stood up and walked to the edge of the tent where the flap was lifted up. The last glimmers of the day were fading in a pink cloud. The heat of the summer still hung close, though cool breezes came occasionally through the green beech leaves.

"You must understand," Comte d'Auch explained, "that he was in love with Renée." He moved his king's pawn to e4.

"In love with Renée the heiress of Ayes. What's wrong with that? Sure she is a commoner, but I have lost one son because I was stubborn in matters of the heart. Henri here is now my only heir, and if he loves this Renée, then what is to stop them getting married?" Duc de Montfort answered the game with king's pawn to e5.

Henri heard the conversation and turned to listen as Comte d'Auch handed Montfort the letter. Montfort looked at it and then handed it to Henri, who was now back by his side. "Read this to me, my eyesight is not what it once was."

Henri gave it back angrily to Comte d'Auch. "You read it. I have not the heart."

The Duke looked anxiously at the two of them. Comte Petain, feeling the tension, gathered closer. Comte d'Auch moved his queen pawn to d4 and then picked up the letter. When he finished he handed the letter back to Montfort.

Duc de Montfort looked at the board and then at Comte d'Auch. "So the maiden must be Renée, who 'reluctantly' marries Picard. 'Reluctantly' he says, but I think that is better written as against her will. And this Renée, if I understand correctly, was in love with my Henri, the heir of Brittany, but Gascony has sent him away and then married her against her will to your brother." He looked back to the chessboard. "And now you offer queen's gambit, in which you sacrifice the poor pawn. In this case the pawn is my Henri. Do I see it right?"

Comte d'Auch nodded. "I can offer excuses for my behavior, but in the end the facts are as you state."

At that the Duke crushed his fist onto the board sending the chessmen flying. "And then you have the gall to come and ask Brittany for help?"

Comte d'Auch sat back and watched the Duke rise to his feet.

"We ride back to Brittany. Gascony can ride alone. Henri will come with me."

"Duc de Montfort," Henri pleaded, "I am the maiden's sole knight. I must ride to help her, treachery or not."

Duc de Montfort stopped and looked aghast at Henri. "You will ride with them even though they have tricked you out of your love and lands of Ayes?"

Henri nodded.

"You are truly Thommas's son. So be it. I will ride with you." Duc de Montfort paused for a long time. He stared out at the evening, and then back at Henri before sitting back down. "Gascony does not deserve this, but my grandson was lost and now is found, I will not leave him again."

Pourquois les démarches des coupables réussissent-elles

Why do the wicked prosper in their wicked ways
While virtuous men pass meek and mildly away?
Their sad friends with sad breath do say,
"He is interned now and in dust may stay."

Why do the wicked in gold and finery strut
While honest men with rags and copper must
Find their dwelling in shacks of sticks and mud
Until at last in weariness their eyes are shut?

Why do the wicked find so sweet success
While godly men and women pure and chaste
Are driven like swine in swill, brine, and mess?
Why is this? I do not know, I confess.
- Sir Henri

The army progressed slowly, delayed by the oxen-pulled wagons and the foot soldiers, held up by breaking and setting up camp every day, and detained by three days of rain and rutted, muddy roads. On a good day they only traveled seven or eight miles a day. Henri rode beside his grandfather, hardly able to contain his impatience. He wanted to put the spurs to the young buckskin palfrey he now rode. He wanted to gallop to the north and west. He wanted to be back at Renée's side.

Then again, the thought of being at Renée's side was painful, for she was no longer his Renée—though her heart had undoubtedly been true—she was now Picard's bride. Still, he wanted to complete the task, restore her to Ayes. That was his mission, his quest, and when that was finished he would ask her to release him. Then he could let his heart mend. Maybe he would travel again to Venice and Constantinople.

With each day the tailors and cobblers added to his wardrobe: a cream linen tunic, soft to his skin, not scratchy like the flax shirt he had been wearing; a jupon coat of white Florence cloth; and elegant black leather riding boots reaching nearly to the knee. The armorers also added piece by piece: to the mail habergeon was added a plate armor breastplate; his gauntlets were bell shaped; his bascinet helmet was fitted with a snout shaped visor; and his legs were covered completely with plate armor cuisses and greaves. They also caparisoned Le Noir with the banners of Brittany. Viewed from the left, the black Scandinavian cross on a white field, with the iron cross in the upper left canton; from the right the white field was covered with black ermine spots, reflecting the legend of the ermine who preferred to die rather than cross a pool and soil his white coat, thus the motto of Brittany: 'Rather to die, than to be soiled.' They had not, however, produced an adequate sword that met either the Duc de Bretagne or Henri's standards, and they assured him that they were still working on his mantle.

On the third day, in the midst of a downpour, another courier arrived. He stopped first beside Comte d'Auch. The Comte took the letter, and finding cover under a large walnut tree opened the seal.

Greetings brother,

> We surprised Bixmarch and a contingent of his knights on the road running south from Ayes. We cut off his retreat and engaged them. Sir Galahad and I have taken Bixmarch prisoner. We sent our terms to Lady Elaine and expect to hear from her within the day.
>
> The battle of Ayes may be over before you arrive.
>
> - Picard

The Comte gave it first to Duc de Montfort, who then gave it to Henri.

"Well, well, this may indeed shorten our march," Duc de Montfort remarked. "What a stroke of fortune. This Bixmarch indeed fights as a commoner, so quickly defeated. Shall we continue then?"

Comte Petain, who had the least invested in the outcome of the battle, and who was providing the wagons and foot soldiers, suggested, "We should at least halt until we hear further. There is no need to continue traveling in this inclement weather if the battle is already over."

This they did, setting up camp, while Comte d'Auch sent the courier back for further information.

As Henri waited with the others, ate, slept, and walked in the nearby hills, he felt a salting of satisfaction that Bixmarch had been captured and that Renée would soon resume her home in Ayes. For the most part, however, he found, try as he might, that he was mostly filled with jealousy and remorse. He resented Picard so easily capturing Bixmarch, and this without even Henri's aid. He grieved that Picard—who had been deceitful, duplicitous, and dishonorable—should succeed. It was neither fair nor just. Why in the name of God should the wicked prosper while he who had been so faithful had lost his true love?

When they had not heard anything within another three days, Comte Petain de Toulouse struck camp, heading back for home. Comte d'Auch, Sir Henri, Duc de Montfort, and the iron cross knights of Brittany mounted and rode forward.

Then they had a succession of three messengers within the space of a morning. The first messenger was not an official courier of Gascony, but a young squire. He arrived just as the knights were mounting to resume their ride. Galloping up the road, he waved his arms wildly to catch the attention of Comte d'Auch. Comte d'Auch, about to step into the saddle, handed off the reins to his squire and turned to greet the messenger. The messenger pulled Comte d'Auch aside to speak privately. They stopped in the midst of a field of barley that reached to their thighs. Henri, already in the saddle, watched as the messenger spoke with agitated gestures. Comte d'Auch nodded dispassionately at first, and then suddenly dropped his jaw in disbelief. For several minutes more Comte d'Auch interrogated the messenger with increasing distress, and then he waved the messenger off and walked farther into the field and sank to his knees, his hands braced on his thighs. Henri dropped out of the saddle and cautiously walked out to the Comte. Duc de Montfort waited beside his steward. Seeing Little Henri approaching, Comte Henri rose and signaled for Duc de Montfort to join them. The morning sun was above the tree tops and rising. The barley field was still wet with dew as the three noblemen stood on the land.

Looking at Little Henri and then at the Duke, Comte d'Auch began, "Brace yourself Henri; this is distressing news. It galls me to have to repeat it."

Henri glanced at his grandfather and then clenched his fist. It had something to do with Renée, and it must be very bad.

"Have you seen Renée's mother, Lady Elaine?" Comte d'Auch questioned.

Henri nodded.

"Is she beautiful?"

Again Henri nodded. He thought he might be beginning to understand. "That she is. Many men would say ravishingly so, and from what her daughter has told me she is a polished seductress, like Aphrodite."

Comte d'Auch continued, "Indeed, she must be, because after my brother captured Bixmarch, Lady Elaine arranged a parley with Picard. They opened the gates of Ayes and she met them in the castle. Well. . . ." His voice trailed off.

"What?" Duc de Montfort exclaimed. "What type of a man is your brother, this Picard? You do not mean to say that he has taken up with the mother of his bride? The bride whom he married against her will?"

"Aye, that I do. She seduced him," Comte d'Auch said, and then shuddered. "I never was close to my brothers. I always found them base and lacking discipline, but I would have never thought they could sink to this level."

Henri turned away, swallowing hard. He had been grieved knowing of Renée's forced marriage, but at least he had comforted himself with the thought she was returning to her inheritance and allying herself to the house of Gascony. But this, this tortured him. His heart went out to her. To be shamed like this by her husband! What infamy!

"And what of the maiden?" The Duke asked, glaring hard at Comte d'Auch.

Comte d'Auch finished the story. "My brother, Picard, has taken the title of Comte d'Ayes, and the Lady Elaine is confining Renée to a convent in Bavaria."

"Then I must be away," Henri called out as he ran for his horse.

Following him a few feet behind, the Duke signaled for his knights to mount. Rapidly the knights resumed their seats in the saddle.

While awaiting the other knights forming their lines, the Duke swung his steed beside Henri's. "You loved her much, then?" he asked.

Henri hesitated before turning to look at Duc de Montfort, his grandfather. Now as he did, he was reminded again of his father: the eyes, the chin, even the voice. "Gladly will I ride into the fires of hell for her sake." After he spoke he kept staring and wondering at the resemblance. Was his grandfather quite like his father?

"Indeed?" the Duke responded with one packed word. "You and your father." The Duke reflected a moment. "I treated him wrong. I was stubborn and chased him away, and then, then I was too proud to search for him. . . until it was too late." The Duke spoke matter-of-factly as one who, while acknowledging his wrong, would not wallow in despair. He reached over and patted his horse's neck before adding, "I had a love like yours once."

Henri waited for the Duke to continue, as his horse flicked its tail at the flies, but the Duke was content to leave it there.

Finally Henri asked, "So what happened?"

"She was the daughter of a no account knight, and I was to be the Duc de Bretagne. My father insisted I marry your grandmother, the daughter of the King of Navarre. I did as I was told."

"And the damsel?"

"The Second Coming."

"The Second Coming? I don't understand."

"The return of the plague was called the Second Coming. She nursed her father, mother, and brothers. They died. Then she died; those were bitter years in Brittany."

"So I have heard," Henri replied.

As the column started up, Henri fell in beside his grandfather. His mind was now occupied with newly arisen thoughts of Renée and her plight. Where was she? How was she handling this? Was she being strong? And he thought also of the unexpected humanness of his grandfather. His father had rarely mentioned Duc de Montfort, and Henri had imagined him sterner and harder.

After they had ridden only three miles, the second messenger of the morning arrived. He rode as hard and furious as the first. Again he signaled to the Comte d'Auch as he brought his galloping steed to a skidding halt on the damp roads.

"What news?" Comte d' Auch asked.

"The pox!" The messenger exclaimed.

"What!"

"The pox in Ayes! It started in the castle. Many have been struck."

A deep silence stunned them all. Smallpox, like the plague and leprosy, aroused primal fear.

In alarm Henri asked, "What of the maiden, the damsel Renée?"

"The Lady Elaine was one of the first stricken, but of the maiden I am uncertain. No. . ." The courier stopped and rubbed his chin. "I believe I overheard someone say that she was complaining of fever and headache." Then, turning to Comte d'Auch, he added, "There is great panic in the army; most have fled."

Ashen faced, Comte d'Auch shook his head. "And. . . and what of the others? What of Bixmarch and. . . my brother, Picard?" Despite his knowledge of all of Picard's failings, there was still concern in the Comte's voice as he mentioned his brother's name.

"They have isolated themselves in the keep."

"When did this start and how far away are we from Ayes?" Henri asked.

The messenger answered, "Two days ride."

"You do not mean to continue?" asked the Duke and Comte simultaneously.

"I should have never left her, and I swear I shall not do it again, not while I breathe." Henri sat up in his saddle and looked around him. He looked forwards and back. The hidden path to Cairns was along this road. He must find Ishmael. Ishmael was the only physician he could entrust with Renée's fate.

"Do not be a fool, Henri. There is nothing you can do." The Duke pulled his horse in front of Henri's. "If you must do something, go to a monastery; say a prayer to Mary; light a candle. She is in God's hands."

Henri looked past the Duke to the road beyond, and then back at his squire. "Take my war horse to the Inn of the Cock's Crow at Laplume. It is just outside of Ayes. Stay there. I will find you in two days."

Comte d'Auch now joined the Duke in restraining Henri. "Your grandfather is right, Henri. Come, I will ride with you on pilgrimage. We will go to St. Sernin. It is a great cathedral. We will offer prayers for Renée."

Henri shook his head. "I am going to find the Moorish physician, Ishmael. He will know what to do for the pox."

"That is absurd!" the Duke exclaimed. "No doctor, however great, whether he be Christian, Jew, or Moor, can treat the pox." Upset at Henri's obstinacy, the Duke continued, "If you ride to Ayes, you do it alone. I cannot peril my knights in that folly, nor can I endanger myself. I am the Duc de Bretagne, and I . . . O, it is fruitless. I see you are as stubborn as your father. I found you and thought that now I would have an heir, but now I see it is as Penelope's web, useless."

"I am sorry, milord, grandfather," Henri apologized. "I am sorry, but I must go."

He put the spurs to his horse and started his horse to a gallop but was stopped before he had gone three hundred yards by the third of the three messengers racing along the path to the battalion of knights. Henri wheeled his horse and came back to the group to hear the message.

Comte d'Auch, now sitting on a rock beside the road, head in his hands, barely looked up as the messenger pulled to a halt.

"Ayes is burnt to the ground, cinder and coals. Lords Picard and Bixmarch set it afire and then fled with Sir Galahad."

Chapitre Vingt trois
Cherchait pour le Docteur

Always have I been for you searching
Never may I be content
Other than on your road searching
While life I am lent.
- Sir Henri

Henri did not stay to listen to more. He swung the reins around and galloped toward Cairns. He found the little path between the rocks and guided his horse up the winding trail, back and forth along the switchbacks, through the narrow rock boulders, over the streams, into the forest, finally emerging at the top. He rode down beside his empty house—past the barns where he had last fought Bixmarch, where Renée had saved his life with a well placed arrow—thinking that if he had slain Bixmarch, then this would not have occurred. Along the main street he rode, drawing notice with his rich black jupon emblazed with ermine spots and the ironcross.

"Henri?" several of the villagers whispered and pointed.

He ignored them and rode to Ishmael's house. The gate was bolted and the windows were boarded. He had not even considered that Ishmael might not be home. Had he gone back to Montpelier? That was over one hundred miles away. It would take too long to go get him and bring him back. Henri's plan had consisted only of one central idea: getting Ishmael from Cairns to Ayes as fast as he could. Panic began to crash upon him like three demons from the deepest hell.

"Oh, God, no!" he whispered as he shoved the gate. "O God, please!"

"Henri," a familiar voice called to him with great joy.

Turning, Henri saw Jehudah trotting across the street to meet him. He was beaming. "Hadassah said she saw you. You look fine. O, look at this the heraldry of Brittany. Has your destiny really changed that much? Come, come, we are just sitting down to meal. You must tell me all about it."

Henri shook off Jehudah's arm and held his hand up to quiet Jehudah. "I am in terrible need. It is the maiden Renée. I must find Ishmael. Has he gone to Montpelier? Renée has the pox!"

"Renée! Ishmael. Ishmael? No, no, Ishmael is not gone. He is even now breaking bread with me."

"Ishmael is here? He is with you? O glory, glory," Henri burst out as Jehudah and he ran across the street. They met Jehudah's nephew, Simeon-ben-Adar, at the door. Henri rushed into the house while Jehudah paused a moment to instruct Simeon. Turning into the dining room, there was an outcry of joy as they saw Henri. The first to greet him was Maria, quickly followed by Sir Petro de Lomange. Both hugged him tightly.

"Come sit down and eat." Maria motioned to a chair. "Where is Renée?"

From the doorway the young girl Hadassah stood transfixed and radiant.

"No, I cannot halt for a moment," Henri said, looking at Ishmael. The physician had observed Henri come to the door, but seeing the great commotion everybody else was making, and being absorbed in his book, and wanting to finish his bowl of stew, he had remained seated. Now, however, he placed a marker in his book and looked up at Henri.

"Doctor, it is Renée. They fear it is the pox."

"The beautiful maiden Miriam?" Ishmael persisted in calling her the name she had used as his nurse. "And where is she?"

"In Ayes."

"Ayes, is it. Tell me, what are her symptoms?" Ishmael rose from his seat abruptly.

"They say she has fever and headache."

"They say? You do not know?" Ishmael asked sharply.

"I was not with her."

"You were not with her? Are you not her knight? And yet you were not at her side? How is this?"

Ashamed, Henri said nothing.

Walking briskly through the halls, Ishmael glanced over his shoulder at Henri, as if to express wonder at how Henri could have ever left her side. "Well, we shall do what we can. You are fortunate that I am here. I only arrived this morning from Montpelier."

"I am coming with you, Henri," Sir Petro de Lomange said as he caught up to them. "As you see, I have had the pox. It can harm me no more."

Ishmael gave his servants instructions. "I shall need all the red cloth I have, and the curtain room. Pack the mules with my balms and oint-ments, and here take this book, pack it. I will not have time to search my library for other books to read. Well, so be it. The maiden Miriam is worth a few days wasted without writing or reading, and time is slipping away."

As they exited from the house, they found Jehudah in the midst of the loading. He carefully placed loaves of bread in the saddle bags of a mule and slung wine skins across the neck.

While they waited, with bustling servants all around them, Ishmael stood back against the archway of ivy and silently watched Henri. His eyes surveyed him from head to foot, taking in all the refinements of his tunic, lined with ermine, the fine boots, the finely woven baldric and scabbard. They stopped at Henri's sword, and he frowned.

"I see your condition has changed. Your fortunes seem to have improved, but you still have an inferior sword." Ishmael walked to the side of his horse and pulled out a magnificent eastern sword. It was a two-handed long sword, polished and glistening. As he offered it to Henri he said with pride. "This is Damascus made. There is no finer."

Henri took it with wonder, letting his fingers glide along the edge, so very sharp.

"It was tested in the rivers of Damascus. A blade must be able to cut a leaf flowing downstream to pass," Ishmael explained.

Henri studied the blade against the light, seeing the characteristic interplay of steel and iron that made the Damascus swords so coveted, strong and not brittle. They were forged on fires hotter than anywhere else in the world—the very secret of the fires was jealously guarded— forged in the night so the smith could watch the colors of the weapon, knowing just when to cool and when to fire again. There was nothing like it. The hilt was plated with gold and caught the sun in blinding brilliance.

"I cannot take this from you. It is too great a gift. I have not the money to pay for it." Henri reluctantly offered it back.

"Of course you cannot pay for it; it is priceless. The Caliph of Grenada gave it to my father. But if you will protect the maiden more carefully in the future, it shall be payment enough. She too is priceless."

Henri looked at Ishmael. He had not realized how much Ishmael had valued Miriam. "That I can do," he promised.

After a hard night of travel they arrived in LaPlume and stopped at the sign of the Cock's Crow. The inn stood along the main road, built of logs, with a covered front porch. Beyond the inn, over a bridge, the wheel of a watermill steadily revolved. There were two large cottonwood trees in front of the inn, and a large flock of blackbirds roosted in the branches. They nervously fluttered from tree to tree, making a racket, and then as one descended to the stream banks and fed on the mill's discarded seed.

As Henri stepped down from the stirrup of his palfrey, he saw Le Noir in the stables and Rouge, tail wagging, running to him. Henri knelt on one knee and hugged the large hairy hound. Behind Henri, Ishmael handed off his reins to the lackey and entered the inn. Sir Petro de Lomange, hanging back, looked to the north.

"There is still smoke over Ayes," he said as he tightened his sword belt and pulled up his braises.

"Yes, I have noticed."

Petro watched Henri for a minute as Henri looked at the fine line of smoke in the distance. "She will be fine," Petro said, trying to be reassuring.

Henri did not answer.

A moment later Henri's squire ran out of the barn. "Milord, welcome. You see your warhorse is here and in good condition."

"But the other horses, where are they? Where is the Duc de Montfort and the iron cross knights of Brittany? Where is Comte d'Auch?" Henri pointed to the empty stalls.

"They heard a message this morning that Lords Bixmarch, Picard, and Galahad with their brigand band had attacked a convoy of merchants on the road east of here. They went to intercept."

Henri nodded and then entered the inn. Rather than one great room, as was common, this inn had many rooms, until it seemed you were burrowing deep into the hill upon which it was built. The matron, a buxom woman with graying hair, met them with a toothless smile. She led them back to where Ishmael sat before a table.

"So where is this Comte d'Auch and the Duc de Bretagne? The inn is empty," Ishmael said as they entered.

Henri relayed the squire's news.

"I see," Ishmael responded.

"Shall we await their return?" Petro asked.

"No, we must move on. I must find Renée," Henri added urgently.

The matron, still standing at the door, protested, raising her hands before her face. "Good sir, you cannot mean the Maiden Renée. Not Ayes. The pox is there!"

Ishmael rose and placed a restraining hand on Henri's shoulders. "I know how much the maiden means to you, Henri, but Ayes is no place for you. What good will it do if I with my balms and ointments heal Renée only to have you succumb? You can go no farther. Petro and I are immune to the pox. We will find Renée."

"How can I stand it? How can I bear it? I must come with you." Henri pushed aside Ishmael's arms and rose. "I am going to Ayes; you will not stop me."

"Henri, listen to Ishmael," Petro said, adding his voice of reason as Henri started striding through the maze of rooms toward the door, getting lost and finding himself in a dead end room.

Ishmael stood at the door. He wore a dark blue—almost purple—silk jacket and held a velvet hat in hand. "Henri, if you go, I will return to Cairns. I will not be party to suicide."

"You wouldn't do that?" Henri questioned, but he knew that Ishmael was not one to joke, nor bluff.

"We shall find her, Henri." Petro took Henri's right hand in both of his. "We will find her if we have to turn up every stone in the castle."

"All right. . . find her. I leave her in your hands." Henri sat slowly on the edge of the bench, and then rose just as suddenly. "Go! Be quick! Save her and be gentle with her."

Ishmael looked at Petro. "Shall we be off?"

L'angoisse d'amour
The pain I feel! Oh gloom at fall of night!
Distress most real that binds my grief in her!
Cloth bands wound tight around her form, my friend.
I languish; despair has come to master me.
- Sir Henri

Petro nodded and they walked briskly, following the matron to the exit. Henri followed them to the door and stepped out into the hot, blue summer. He managed only a weak nod as Petro turned in the saddle and waved roundly as they galloped away. Off to the north Henri watched the smoke ascending. He ambled mindlessly to a stone bench in the shade of a cottonwood and sank to a seat. Through habit he began scratching Rouge behind the ears.

He stayed on the bench through noon. The matron brought him bread, a jar of wine, and a leg of roasted chicken. After eating he scrambled down the bank and paced up and back along the creek side. He tossed stones in the water and watched a white duck leading her ducklings across the stream. He climbed back up to the bridge and sat down on another bench, but he could not sit long. One more time he arose and entered the stalls. Searching through his saddle bags, he found the Old Testament Ishmael had given him. He opened it to the Psalms, but try as he might, he could not concentrate enough to read. Walking down the main street in the late afternoon, he entered the chapel through the wrought iron gate. He stopped for a moment at the statue of St. Catherine, patron saint of the unmarried. Then he sighed, remembering that Renée was now married, and passed into the chapel. Candles were lit in the front. Searching through his pocket, he found ten pence. He gave them to the priest to light a candle. His father had never felt candles were of any value. "Prayers do not need to be bought, Henri. If they could be, the rich would live and the poor would die. But Jesus came for both poor and rich." Henri, however, was not thinking theologically today. He knelt down at the back.

"God, into your hands I place Renée. Watch her. And be with Ishmael. And Petro. May they be quick. May they arrive in time."

Time passed while he stayed on his knees. Words had stopped, and he knelt appreciating the quietness and the coolness of the chapel, a sense of peace settling within him. Whatever happened he must push on. He had been through much—loss of a mother, loss of a father. Faith had seen him through. He would continue to lean on faith. But the pain of losing Renée seemed. . . now. . . well, it was more than he could bear. His shoulders began to shake quietly. No sounds escaped his lips; no tears came, as his hands gripped tighter on the bench in front of him. The priest came and knelt beside him but said nothing.

His quietness was interrupted by the sound of hoof beats. He rose weakly from his knees and, holding his hand over his eyes as he return- ed in the daylight, looked out on the main road. The knights of Brittany in their black and white jupons and mantles trotted up the road. The banner bearer rode at the head beside the Duc de Bretagne. Henri stepped out into the street. Seeing him, Duc de Montfort raised his hand, signaling the halt.

"Greetings, Henri. How is it with you?"

"The Lord keeps me, Lord Montfort. And you?"

"Mmmm," Montfort said as he slid off his horse. "Well, frankly, I am tired and wroth."

"So you did not find Picard, then?" Henri asked

At that moment Comte d' Auch joined them. "No. . . . No we did not find them. My brother an outlaw. He brings shame to Gascony, to my father." Seeing Henri alone, he continued, "Do you. . . you come alone? Where is Dr. Ishmael?"

Henri swung his head in the direction of Ayes.

"And you are here?" Comte d'Auch asked.

"Ishmael would not let me go, because of the pox. He went with Sir Petro de Lomange. They have both had the pox."

The Comte d'Auch and Duc de Montfort nodded, understanding. Then, turning back to the banner bearer, Duc de Montfort ordered the Iron Cross Knights dismissed. The troop rode on to the stables, handed over their horses, and went into the inn. Henri, Montfort, and Henri d'Auch walked slowly side by side along the dirt road.

The dinner at the Inn of the Cock's Crow was spread out in the several rooms. The matron, seeing a very full house with well paying customers, had brought in all of her sons and daughters, brothers, sisters, nieces, nephews, and even the older grandchildren to help with the work. She spread a good though not rich board. Quantities made up for delicacy.

As darkness deepened, Henri made his way through the doorway, off the porch, and back out onto the street. He wandered to the bridge and sat down on the bench. Rouge lay at his feet as always. Noise from the inn began to fade as the night passed. The few lights in the nearby houses one by one were extinguished. There would be no moon tonight, just the stars through the trees. Beneath him the rippling sounds of water passing over the rocks; behind him the steady whirl of the mill- wheel. From the distance he heard the song of a whippoorwill, and then it faded and stopped. The door of the inn opened. Light spread across the street. In the doorway stood Duc de Montfort. Henri knew he was looking for him, but he was not sure he wanted to be found. The door shut, and Duc de Montfort went back inside. The Milky Way slid slowly across the sky. Henri laid his head down on the bench, his eyes open and watching. An owl hooted from the distance. Coolness spread over him. He rolled onto his side and fell asleep. He was awoken by Rouge growling in the darkness. Henri rubbed his eyes. Light was just beginning to creep into the sky from the east. There were hoof beats, slow plodding hoof beats. He sat up and looked to the north across the bridge. He could see nothing. He rose and, with Rouge walking close by his side, crossed the bridge. It was Petro. Sagging in the saddle.

"Did you find her?"

Petro sat upright and peered into the predawn gloom. "Henri? At this hour? You should be in bed. At this hour all men should be in bed."

"Did you find her?"

Petro did not answer.

"Where is Ishmael?" Henri asked, seeing Ishmael was not with him.

Petro did not answer.

Henri took hold of the bridle of Petro's horse. "Petro, where is Ishmael? And what of Renée? Did you find her?"

Petro groaned as he swung out of the saddle. "Henri, I am tired. I am very tired. I have not slept in two nights. Ishmael stopped a mile back."

Henri walked beside Petro for a moment, watching him. His friend was indeed very tired.

"But what of Renée? You must tell me, and then I will let you sleep."

Petro sighed deeply and reaching the stone bench sank heavily onto it. "Yes, we found her, though it was difficult. It is not far from here to Ayes, and we were there early in the morning, but it is very awful. The city has been devastated by fire, and it still smolders in many places. Even the castle has suffered much damage. And the people, most are homeless. A few were wounded in the battle, some have suffered burns, and many. . . many have been taken by the pox. The healthy and sur-vivors have fled, leaving only the infirm."

"But what of Renée?" Henri pressed. Petro was intentionally avoiding that subject. "Is she. . . dead?"

Petro got up slowly and started again for the inn. "We found her in the cook's house. She is not dead."

Henri waited for more. It did not come.

"Petro, she has the pox? Is it bad?"

"Ishmael and I brought her on a suspended bed between our horses. He set up a tent in a field a mile from here. He is the doctor; ask him."

"Is she really that bad?"

Petro groaned and looked at Henri with profound grief. "It would have been better if she had died. The pox is everywhere. It is awful. God have mercy."

At that Henri stopped as Petro lumbered on ahead mechanically and disappeared in the inn. Henri sank onto the bench.

Un sévère case
I am bound by oath and would be ever loath to break faith.
Ancient forbearers of my trade, I in your stead now stand.
Stable the scapel; stable the hand; let me not abandon—
No matter how severe the case, nor the risk to my flesh—
Those by whom I am called the name physician.
- Doctor Ishmael de Bretagne

When Henri woke in the morning he was lying on a mattress on the second floor of the inn. The sun was beating down on his face. The room was growing hot and stifling, though the window was open. Flies were buzzing off the walls. He rolled off the mat and sat for a moment trying to gather his thoughts. In the corner on another mattress, Petro was still sleeping. Looking out the window, he figured it must be a little before noon. From outside the window he heard voices talking from the ground. He recognized the Moorish accent of Ishmael and the stuttering of Comte Henri d'Auch, but he could not make out the conversation. Groggily he rose from his mattress, and taking the pitcher of water on the cabinet, poured it into a basin. He washed his face and hands; then, sitting on a three legged stool, he pulled on his boots before descending the rough hewn stairs and exiting to the covered porch.

Ishmael was standing on the edge of the porch, with one leg on the top step and the other perched on a chair. His beard, usually neatly trimmed, was scruffy from three days of growth. His fine blue silk coat was grimy and soiled with sweat, soot, and grit. To the left, five knights of the iron cross lounged on benches in the porch shade, their feet propped on the rail. To the right, Henri d'Auch leaned against the wall as he drained a pitcher of water.

"You are up," Ishmael said tersely.

Henri shut the door behind him. In the morning he was uncertain if he wanted to hear the news from Ishmael. He looked both right and left and then slowly settled himself on the step of the porch.

"So," he asked tentatively, "how bad is she?"

Ishmael studied him without answering, climbed the stairs, and entered the inn. Henri followed him. Ishmael sat down at one of the tables and called for food. Ishmael motioned for Henri to have a seat. "Eat with me, and then we will talk. My day will be long, and I will not likely get another good meal today, maybe not even tomorrow."

Reluctantly Henri sat down beside Ishmael and ate. He tried to restart the conversation while they were both eating, but Ishmael ignored him and continued to eat. Finally, when they were finished, Ishmael went back out to the stables and mounted his steed. Henri's squire had his palfrey saddled and ready.

When they were riding across the bridge, past the watermill, Ishmael finally spoke. "The University of Montpelier teaches that the pox should be treated with red cloth wrapped around the patient's entire body surrounded by a tent of scarlet hangings. I have used this method with indifferent success in the past. With Renée I have added an inner layer of whale oil ointment, mixed with cinnamon, aloe, and myrrh, spread over her entire body. She has a maid in attendance. I have trained this woman in the wrapping process. I am most anxious and curious to see if this will be more efficacious. I will make notes of the process. She will indeed be a great trial for this method, as she has a very severe case."

"A very severe case?" Henri latched onto these last words.

"O, indeed, a very severe case," Ishmael repeated, and then with empathy he added, "Maiden Miriam is in grave danger. I doubt there is anyone except myself who would have even taken on this case. She runs a high fever and has shaking chills. She is weak, emaciated, parched and. . . totally covered with the pox." Ishmael paused, and there was a hitch in his voice as he concluded, "She will be a beauty no more."

Henri swallowed hard.

Ishmael, without looking, sensed Henri's reaction.

After that Ishmael talked of the multitude of wounded and ill patients at Ayes. He recounted what he had already done to establish wards where the less ill ministered to the critical, and he listed the countless needs that would hinder the recovery of Ayes: lack of food, no protection from brigands, a need to rebuild the city, impending anarchy.

About a mile north of Laplume, Ishmael guided his horse off the path to a flat field. At the edge of a plum orchard, in the middle of the field, stood a red tent sheltered by a massive oak. Before the entrance four knights of Brittany sat in the shade and rolled the dice in a game of backgammon. Seeing Henri, they nodded and continued their game. But when Henri made as if to enter the tent Ishmael restrained him and the knights rose simultaneously.

"She is quarantined, Henri," Ishmael instructed. "No one may enter except me and the maid who attends her."

Henri knew it was fruitless to argue with Ishmael. "Will you tell her that I am here?"

"Yes, yes, that I will do," Ishmael said as he entered.

Ishmael was in the tent for what seemed a long time. "Now, will you ride with me to Ayes?"

"To Ayes. Yesterday you refused me. Today you wish me to come."

"Just to the hill overlooking it. You should see it."

"No, not today. I want to stay here beside her tent."

Ishmael studied Henri closely. "You will not try to enter while I am gone? She is very contagious. Do I have your word?"

"Yes, doctor, I promise."

"Well. . . ." Ishmael hesitated and then stepped into the stirrup. "These knights are sworn to keep her under strict quarantine." Along the road Sir Petro de Lomange pulled his horse off into the field. Ishmael noticed him, gave Henri another stern glance, and then joined Sir Petro de Lomange.

Henri stood for a few minutes in the shade and then sat down with his back against one of the plum trees. Rouge came over and licked his face.

Quelque chose d'emprunt, quelque chose bleu, quelque chose aigu

Aigu, sharp I have borrowed that from you,
And if it is closer you wish to come,
Then it will be blood, yours, even if it's blue.
You doubt? Then by all means come,
And yours will run upon this satin of white;

Yours will flow until there is none.
I mean not to be touched by you this night.
- Lady Renée d'Ayes

A few minutes after Ishmael had left, a peasant woman poked her head out of the tent and, seeing Henri, closed the curtain behind her. She came to where Henri was seated. "Will you walk with me, milord?"

Henri rose, feeling certain that she had a message from Renée.

"How is she?" Henri asked as he worriedly rubbed his hands. "Does she know I am here? Does she have a message for me?"

The woman—a middle-aged woman in simple garb, who was neither pretty nor homely—alternately shook, then nodded, then shook her head again. "Yes, I believe she knows you are here, but she is too weak to give you a message; however, she did give me a message the morning after her marriage. I was instructed to give it to you and to you alone. "

The woman looked behind her at the knights who were watching them with curiosity. The woman's voice dropped lower and softer. "She said this, 'Tell Henri, for whom does the rose bloom? It blooms only for thee.'"

Henri bit his lower lip as he looked away. How he loved her.

"Oh, but there is more," the woman whispered. "She did not tell me to say this, but I will tell you anyhow. On the night that Picard. . . that. . . that spawn of the devil, on the wedding day, on the marriage night, I was in the next room, just a tapestry between us. I overheard the night's activities."

"No, no." Henri tried to stop the woman. "I do not want to know this. I am satisfied that her heart remained true."

"Oh, but you will want to know this." The woman smiled with a sense of satisfaction and redemption.

They stopped in the field while the sun beat down on them. The maid said confidentially, "When Picard came to her to take her as a man does a woman, she refused him. When he tried to force himself on her, she pulled a dagger from her boot and told him if he so much as touched her she would cut out his heart." The woman laughed as a lioness might after bringing down the gazelle. "She is a brave one, that maiden is."

"She pulled a blade on Picard?"

"Aye, that she did. He was no more her lawful husband than I am a queen. At the wedding, when they asked her if she would take him for her husband, she replied, 'I will not.' But Picard just proceeded as if she had agreed."

"So what did Picard do? What did he do when she pulled a knife?" Henri asked.

"What could he do? He is not brave like her. He does not have a heart like hers. He slept on the floor."

"And you are sure of this?" Henri asked.

"I heard it all, though it was all done in whispers. And the next morning, when I gathered the sheets from the bed, I looked at the mistress. She gave me this strange look, as though wondering what I had heard. I said only that tapestries sometimes whisper wonderful things in the night. She smiled wanly, a little fearfully, and that is when she told me that if something were to happen to her, I must tell you that the rose blooms only for thee."

The maid stopped then, looked back at the scarlet tent, and sighed. "Such a brave heart, such a beautiful young girl, to be struck down, devastated by this. Where is justice? Where is God?"

"No," Henri replied. "Do not accuse God. No, please do not do this."

The woman stopped and looked at Henri in amazement. "Well, who knows the end from the beginning? We shall see."

In the late afternoon Henri mounted his horse and started slowly riding back toward the Inn of the Cock's Crow. Looking over his shoulder, he saw smoke still winding to the sky, and on an impulse he reversed directions and headed toward Ayes. Tapping his steed's flanks, he set it to a trot and then a canter.

He rode to a hill overlooking Ayes. Dropping from the saddle, he gazed upon the smoldering fires of the city. What he first noticed was the paucity of life. Only a rare person dragged wearily through the streets. It was so very different from the last time he had been here, for now the whole west side of the town had been ravaged. And the south side where the artisans worked had suffered heavy damage. To the east the castle still stood, though smoke billowed from the keep. Only the north side of the town, near the cathedral, was relatively unscathed.

Turning his eye from the city, he looked along the river valley. Refugee camps dotted the banks of the river. How were they surviving? What could be done for them? How did one rebuild a city devastated by war, fire, and disease? In this he had no training. The very prospect of co-ordinating such a large project was daunting. One would need to muster, encourage, organize, and plan, plan, plan. Still he worried about all these people, homeless, hungry, and defenseless. They were ripe for bandits, which led him to think about Lords Bixmarch, Picard, and Galahad. What an odd threesome, and yet somehow they were indeed very much alike, without mercy, without justice, without faith—in truth without God.

His eye then noticed an erect figure walking outside the gates and mounting an Arabian. Even from the distance Henri recognized Ishmael. Henri swung in the saddle and started to go to meet Ishmael when a motion in the bush to the left caught his attention. As he guided his horse to the side of the road, Henri saw a young toddler running away. The child fell over a bush and then continued to run down the hill whimpering. The toddler had just disappeared behind a big rock when a hand snatched him. Carefully guiding his horse off the road, and ducking beneath some of the lower branches, Henri navigated toward the big rock. Holding the reins with his left hand, he laid his right hand lightly on the gold hilt of his sword.

Near the rock he stopped for a moment. He could hear whispers. "He is coming."

"Should we make a run for it?"

"How did you let Jean get away in the first place?"

They were the whispers of children.

Henri nudged his horse forward, and from his saddle he looked down upon six children. Six ragged, dirty, thin children. The oldest was a young lad of no more than thirteen, of slight build and coal black hair. The next was a young girl, obviously the boy's sister, though her hair was auburn, unkempt, and uncombed. She held a young baby in her arms. Then there were two twin boys about seven years of age. Finally there was the toddler hiding behind the girl's flax brown skirt.

The young lad brandished a large stick. "Stay away, sir. Do not attempt to harm us, or I will have to fight you." At that the twins picked up their sticks and formed a line beside their brother.

"Do you challenge me?" Henri said drawing his sword. The very sight of these children raising their sticks as a defense amused him.

"No, it is not a challenge." The lad stepped forward pushing his brothers behind him. "But we are not as defenseless as you may think. My father is also a great knight and will be back shortly."

As Henri advanced slowly the children began to retreat en masse, staying tightly bundled.

"A great knight, is he? This is even better. I shall take you as you my prisoner, and he will have to ransom you." With that Henri swung his sword and cut off the lad's stick at the hilt.

The lad looked at his stick with dismay and then at Henri.

"It appears your blade is defective. Too bad. I think you could have put up a good fight. Now must I kill you, or will you beg mercy?" Henri chuckled.

The two twins rushed him with flailing sticks. With a flourish Henri cut their sticks just as he had their brother's. Instead of being dismayed, however, they latched onto his legs and tried to bite through his boots. Henri could not contain himself any longer and broke out laughing. The twins kept a tight clasp on his ankles.

Through all of this the girl watched intently; she watched as Henri cut off her brother's stick without harming him; she watched as the twins tried to bite him, and she watched Henri begin to laugh. "William, Thommas, leave him alone." She called to the twins. Then to Henri she said, tentatively, "I think, good Sir, that you are not an evil man, nor do you mean to hold us as prisoners, which in truth is good as we have no one to pay a ransom. Our father was a stonemason, a good man, but he died last week fighting the fires in Ayes. A beam fell on him; crushed him. Our mother died of the pox day before yesterday."

"I'm sorry," Henri replied, as he pulled the twins off his legs and handed them back to her. "Then you are orphans?"

The oldest boy threw down the remains of his stick as he nodded sadly. "Indeed, we are, and very hungry. Mind you, it is not me that I care about, but the babe and Jean." He pointed to the infant in his sister's arms and the toddler.

"We're hungry, too," the twins added, sensing the danger had passed.

Henri stopped and thought for a moment. He had no food in his saddle and giving them money would do no good. They would be robbed. In a way, this small challenge was a relief. The project of restoring Ayes was beyond Henri, but he could get food for six children.

"And if I give you food, what will you give me?"

The girl shook her head slowly. "We have nothing, good sir. We have nothing to give."

"Will you promise your loyalty to me, Sir Henri, and serve me whenever I have need?"

"Gladly," both the lad and girl said at once.

"Then come with me." Henri lifted the girl into the saddle and handed her the baby. He put the toddler on behind the girl and told him to hang on tight. Then taking the reins, Henri led them back up to the road and back toward the Cock's Crow.

They had gone only a little ways before Sir Petro de Lomange and three knights met them. Sir Petro de Lomange looked at the little band of ragamuffins, then at Sir Henri, and smiled. "What have we here?"

"Their father died in the fire one week ago. Their mother day before yesterday."

Petro looked at the oldest boy. "You are a good looking lad. What is your name?"

"I am Petro."

Sir Petro de Lomange clapped the boy on the back. "It is a good name. Well, come on Henri, let us get these tired and hungry children back to the inn," Petro said as he swung the boy behind him on his horse.

Chapitre Vingt quatre
Prière Dans la Nuit

*Do not leave me so
All alone.
Resist and fight
Death's pale and cold stone.
Hold against the grave;
Struggle, my love.
Be brave.
- Sir Henri de Bretagne*

In the middle of the night Henri arose and slipped out of the inn. He walked the mile up the road to Renée's tent. Two soldiers squatted a-round the fire, talking quietly. Henri had promised he would not go in the tent while Ishmael was gone, but he had said nothing about visiting her when Ishmael returned. Sneaking in the shadows to the back of the tent, he slid underneath the siding. In the masked light of the fire he could make out Renée's cot in the center. Her maidservant slept on a mattress at the front.

Carefully Henri crawled to Renée's side. He knew this was foolish. He could catch the pox. Then again, what if Renée should die? What would he care then? It was too much to ask him not to visit. He had to be at her side. She would have done as much for him. She had. She had nursed him by his side day and night when he had been delirious and sick with St. Anthony's fire.

He reached for her hand. The cloth binding surprised him momentarily until he remembered Ishmael's total-body, red cloth wrapping. Her hand moved away when he touched it. She groaned and rolled on her side, trying to find comfort from the blistering pain of the pox, but there was no position of comfort to be found. He reached to stroke her hair, only to find her head bound as well. Slowly he laid his hand on her forehead, and stroked down her cheek. Still asleep, she instinctively moved towards his stroke. With one hand on her hand and the other on her forehead, kneeling by her bedside, he turned his heart to prayer.

He stayed by her side for an hour before crawling back out of the tent and returning to the inn. He slid back onto his mattress and pulled the blanket over him.

For the next couple weeks the routine remained: Ishmael, rising at sunrise, would first stop at Renée's tent, examine her, and then ride on to Ayes, where he made his rounds of the sick and wounded. Returning after dark, he jotted notes in his journal by lamplight before retiring to bed, slept soundly, and then rose to do it again in the morning. On most mornings, Sir Petro de Lomange and Henri rose with him. Petro rode on to the city of Ayes, where with a cadre of peasants immune to the pox he organized the cleanup of the charred city; pulling down the buildings that were beyond repair, salvaging lumber where they could, piling the corpses onto wagons, and burying them outside the city. He appointed constables and assigned guard duty for the gates. And on his return to the inn, he checked on the children, almost always having something special for them.

"That Petro is a smart lad," he told Henri. "And Isabeau is a very good little maid."

Rising with Ishmael and Petro, Henri went first to the chapel, then to Renée's tent to talk to the maidservant. How was she? Had she slept well? Was she eating? Did she need anything? The maid always answered that she was improving, though Henri knew she was saying it because it was what he wanted to hear. Then he would ride to the refugee camps and find someone to help. After the first couple days, Henri d'Auch joined him regularly. The Comte d'Auch proved adept at rallying the people.

Finally, in the middle of the night, while the others slept, Henri would return to Renée's tent, slide under the siding, and kneel by her side. They never spoke, but after the first two nights she usually awoke when he came in and blindly stretched her hands out for him.

Montfort, Duc de Bretagne, had left for Brittany on the first day. He promised to return as soon as he could, and he left several knights.

Ste. Stephen's
Come walk with me, and I shall show you the greatness of my works.
For it is I who have made all this, this mortar and stone,
This cloister and wall, that library, that great granite basilica.
I have drawn, I have labored long into the black night.
I have done this all . . .I have done it with my labor, all alone
Have risen with the new moon, while other men would swoon.
Come walk with me, and I shall show you the greatness of my works.
May they live on through all posterity.

- Anonymous monk of St. Stephen's

In the third week a peddler disrupted their routine, arriving at dawn at the Cock's Crow Inn, his arm badly cut and blood caked on his leggings. The matron tried to show him out of the inn—not wanting to disturb her noble and well paying customers—but when he said he had just come from the monastery, he was quickly surrounded by Ishmael, Henri, Petro, and Comte d'Auch.

"You received these wounds at the monastery?" Dr. Ishmael asked as he pulled catgut suture out of his medical bag. "The wound is deep. I shall have to sew it."

"What. . . what happened?" Henri d'Auch asked.

"Lords Bixmarch, Galahad, and Picard with their free company sacked the monastery early this morning before sunrise."

"Burned to the ground?" Petro asked in surprise.

"No. They robbed the monastery of its gold, its books, its reliquaries, its vestments. They stole the horses, pillaged, and set the scaffolding of the cathedral on fire. The cathedral, unstable without the scaffolding, has collapsed, but they did not raze the monastery. As a condition for their leaving they required indulgences for their sins and a promise to say prayers for their souls," the peddler answered as Ishmael put his needle into the skin and tied his first surgical knot. Ishmael worked quickly.

"Rob. . . robbing a church," Comte d'Auch said in dismay and disgust. "My brother!"

"So they have left?" Petro asked.

The peddler grimaced as Ishmael threaded the needle into the wound again. "They had not left when I escaped this morning, but I think they were soon to leave."

"They. . . they had not left yet?" Comte d'Auch replied with fervor. "To arms! To horse! We ride within the half hour."

The inn set to with a great bustle. Stable boys and squires readied the warhorses. Knights pulled on their mail habergeons, fastened on the greaves, threw the helmets to their squire, buckled their sword belts, gulped down the last swallow of ale, and grabbed a loaf of bread to eat on their travel. The knights from Auch with their black chevronels and silver fleurs-de-lis rode at the front with Henri d'Auch. The iron cross knights of Brittany rode with Sir Henri, Ishmael, and Sir Petro de Lomange. They rode an alternate route that branched to the east a half mile north of the bridge. They rode at a brisk trot three abreast, intending to regroup at the monastery. If either of the parties met with the free company, they would sound the horn and collapse on them from the front and rear.

When they met two hours later in sight of the monastery, neither party had encountered the bandit lords. Henri pulled up on the reins of Le Noir as he looked at the monastery. The walls were manned with guards. Monks were scurrying all around the yards in disorder. Smoke was rising from over the cathedral. The dome had collapsed over the transept. The years of work that Abbé Odile had devoted to its construction had been wasted.

"They. . . they should have done that be. . . be. . . before it was too late," Comte d'Auch said as his party joined with Sir Petro de Lomange and Sir Henri where the two paths merged from the woods.

"Done what?" Petro asked.

"Had. . . had the walls manned," D'Auch replied. "They guard the chick. . . chicken house after the fox has already been in and out."

"Well, let us go down and visit," Henri urged.

"You. . . you go," the Comte said. "I will search for Picard."

"Good," Henri answered.

Henri' d'Auch assigned the captain of the Brittany knights to search to the north while he and his Gascony knights searched to the east. Meanwhile, Henri, Ishmael, and Petro rode to the monastery.

At the gate, Brother Matthew met them. His robes were soiled with sweat and soot. He was tired and troubled.

"We have heard of the raid and have come to help," Henri called from the saddle to Brother Matthew, who was standing on the wall above the closed gate.

"You are too late. The bandits have come and gone. They have robbed and pillaged, destroyed and burned. They have taken our gold, our books, our food, and our peace. They have in one night of havoc undone years of our labor."

"We seek information, for these bandits are our sworn enemies. They have done similar things to us," Henri answered.

"And who are you?" Brother Matthew looked at the threesome with numb expression.

"I am Sir Henri de Bretagne, heir to Duc de Montfort, but you may remember me better as Henri, the stable boy of the maiden Renée, whom you guided through secret tunnels this spring escaping this same Bixmarch."

Brother Matthew looked closer at Henri and then ordered the gates open. When the oak gates swung wide, Brother Matthew was standing to the left. "Things have changed much for you then!" he said to Henri, noting the powerful build of his warhorse and the gold hilted sword in the scabbard.

"Not so very much," Henri replied. "My mistress is still in grave danger, as she was when last we met."

"Indeed, I have heard of Renée's illness from her mother. Lady Elaine is in her recovery and staying with us."

Henri wondered at the presence of a woman in the monastery, but he said nothing. She was here. He had never really spoken with her and wondered if he would today.

"And who are these that accompany you?" Brother Matthew asked, looking pointedly at Ishmael.

"This is Sir Petro de Lomange, a knight of good faith, and Dr. Ishmael of Grenada, the greatest of all physicians."

"Sir Petro de Lomange can enter, but not the infidel," Brother Matthew commanded his guards.

"We have come to your aid. Are there not some who will need his attention?" Henri argued.

"We were despoiled by bandits in the night; should we then during the day turn aside from the paths of Christ? No, we will not willingly allow a pagan within our walls."

Ishmael stayed Henri from continuing the defense in his behalf. He smiled as he surveyed the courtyard. Spying a statue of the Madonna and child in front of what remained of the cathedral, and replicas of St. Christopher and St. Jude near the library, he pointed to them and said, "You call me infidel, but tell me, what is the second commandment of Moses? Did he not forbid the building of graven images? And when the people pressed Aaron to make a golden calf, didn't he melt it to the ground? Yet here you have graven images. Tell me righteous monk, do you say prayers to Mary and the saints? You call me pagan, but judge between us who is it that has many Gods? You call me unbeliever, because I follow the Koran, but you do not follow your own Bible. You pray to graven images, keep an unknown day holy, eat swine, and get drunk on wine; all explicitly forbidden in The Book. You are the heathen. Nevertheless, I came to help. If you do not allow it, then I shall kneel outside the gate. It is time for my prayers."

With that Ishmael dismounted, spread his prayer rug, and began the ceremonial washing of hands and forehead before prayers.

Turning over his reins to a stable boy, Henri hesitated a moment as he looked at Ishmael. Ishmael paid no attention to him. With Sir Petro de Lomange beside him, Henri then followed Brother Matthew back through the column-covered porches, through the libraries where he had been last spring. The quiet order of last spring had been replaced by bustling chaos like ants that have had their dirt homes kicked open. There were now no monks sitting quietly illuminating their manuscripts, nor did the kitchen spill its succulent aromas.

They came to the Abbé's office. The door was wide open. Brother Matthew entered. Some monks hurried to and fro, others stood immobile against the wall fixed in shock. Several had arms, legs, or heads bandaged and splinted. The Abbé stood behind what remained of his desk—it had been hewn in half by a war-axe. A door to an adjacent room stood ajar. Through it, Henri could see Comte Sevestre pacing re-lentlessly back and forth, swaying to the left and right, and holding his head in his hands.

Seeing Henri, the Abbé stopped and looked to Brother Matthew for an explanation.

"This is Sir Henri de Bretagne, heir to the Duc de Montfort, and his knight Sir Petro de Lomange. There was also a Moorish physician who I refused entrance to, a said Dr. Ishmael of Grenada."

"Dr. Ishmael of Grenada? I have heard of him. His reputation at Montpelier is growing," the Abbé remarked.

"Do you wish me to call for him?" Brother Matthew asked.

The Abbé waved him off. "No, you did right. It has come to me that our misfortune is the judgment of God for our sin. We allowed a woman to enter our gates. The Lady Elaine, like Achan of the Bible, is the cause of our tragedy. . . ." Cutting off his discourse, the Abbé followed Henri's gaze to Comte Sevestre. But then he resumed, "We must get rid of her; this morning. She must be thrown out of the monastery."

"But, good Father," Brother Matthew protested, "she is still recovering. She has little strength, and where would she go? It is one thing to keep women from entering the monastery, but how can we turn her out in her condition? Our superiors will hear of this; it will certainly be spread even to the Pope. We must have Christian pity."

"Pity? It is a pity we ever let her enter in the first place. Woman has always been the folly of man. No, we must put her out today, put her out this morning, put her out now!" The Abbé spat on the ground. "Throw her out! It is better that one should perish, than that all should die." Then, seeing Brother Matthew's horror, he turned to Henri and Petro. "She needs a doctor. What better thing than to put this whore with the infidel Dr. Ishmael? Yes, indeed. Turn her out with Dr. Ishmael. He can restore her to health. Even the Pope must approve of that."

"A Christian to be treated by an unbeliever, and a Moor at that! Father, you cannot be serious," Brother Mathew remonstrated.

The Abbé quickly replied, "Quite serious." But seeing that Brother Matthew still had hesitations, he motioned to another subordinate to carry out his wishes. Looking back at Henri and catching him again watching Sevestre, he motioned dismissively to Henri. "You wish to talk to the Comte. Go ahead, but be warned, he is quite entirely mad."

Le Fou
I am the madman. I am the fool.
I rave, I pace,
I drool.
I long to face
Down the devil in my mind,

But I have lost all touch with the sublime,
And now I simply stand and walk;
Gather wool, my mind is blocked
From the small talk
That marks the great man,
The social being. The company
Of friends is barred me.
I cannot, nor will I; all muddled are my thoughts;
I am the lunatic, the daff, the rabid.
I. . . I. . . can speak lucid
No longer.
I am the madman. I am the fool.
- Comte Sevestre d'Ayes

Henri cautiously crossed the room. He did indeed want to speak to Comte Sevestre; Sevestre, after all, was Renée's father, and Henri was filled with curious ambivalence. How could Sevestre as Renée's father not adore his only daughter? Renée had so many fine qualities: she was intelligent, brave, charming, loyal, kind. Henri could go on and on listing the things he liked about her. But Sevestre had abandoned all responsibility, and consequently his daughter had suffered. On account of the Comte's spineless actions, Renée had been forced to pass through the darkness of the pit.

Stepping in the path of Comte Sevestre's pacing, Henri came face to face with the madman. Comte Sevestre stopped. His hands fell by his side as he stood looking vacantly past Henri.

Henri was not sure what to say for a moment. What do you say to a lunatic? "I have come from Renée, your daughter."

Comte Sevestre's eyes fixed on Henri.

Henri continued, "She has contracted the pox, and may not live." Henri stopped and looked at Petro for advice. The Abbé was standing beside Petro, watching.

Comte Sevestre's eyes shifted from Henri to the Abbé and back to Henri, but he said nothing.

"She is very sick. Your daughter Renée is very sick. Would you come to her?" The Comte walked past Henri as if he were not there and began his pacing again. His hands reached to his head and covered his ears. Henri stood where he was, still in the path. When the Comte turned around, he stopped in front of Henri, looking at him as if he did not remember the events that had occurred only moments before.

Henri reached out and grasped the Comte by both shoulders to stop him forcefully. "Your daughter, Renée, is sick. You are her father. Don't you care? Don't you understand?"

The Comte did not resist Henri's grasp. He just looked woodenly ahead.

"It is futile," the Abbé commented. "He no longer hears anything but strange voices."

Henri nodded and released his grip. The Comte resumed his pacing. Henri shook his head sadly and started to leave the room, but then he turned around and arrested the Comte's pace one more time, placing his arm across the Comte's path.

The Comte stopped and looked at Henri with the same stupid stare.

"I am Henri. I love your daughter, Renée, and I will take care of her for you."

The Comte's expression did not change, but he did not resume his pacing, and a tear trickled from his eye. Impulsively, Henri embraced the madman and then left.

Back at the gate, Ishmael was examining Lady Elaine. She was covered in a white hooded silk dress. Her back was to Henri and Petro. When she heard their footsteps she pulled a veil across her face. She lay on a mattress that had been placed on the grass beside the road.

Ishmael stopped his exam and looked up at Henri. "They threw her out. Women and infidels are below the mercies of the Christian," he said scornfully.

"He is no true Christian," Henri answered. "Christ said to care for the sick and to go to the heathen."

"Yes, yes I know," Ishmael interrupted. "Be assured that I do not measure Christianity by the likes of them. Your father was a Christian." Then, nodding to Lady Elaine, he continued, "You know the Lady Elaine, of course."

"As a matter of fact we have not met," Henri answered.

Lady Elaine turned to see who Ishmael was talking to. She covered all but her eyes. But even there Henri saw that she was heavily scarred. He shuddered to imagine how the rest of her looked, she who had been such a beauty.

"I am Sir Henri, the most devoted knight in service of your lovely daughter Renée."

Elaine started, clearly surprised. She rose with some difficulty from her mattress and spat angrily, "You! A common stable-boy, calling yourself a knight. You are the cause of all my trials. You are the one to blame. You have stepped between a mother and her daughter. You are a fiend incarnate." She jumped to grab him, but collapsed weakly back onto her mattress and began coughing up blood.

Henri shook his head sadly. "A father that is mad and a mother like you—Renée deserved better. I will see that she has it in the future."

When the coughing stopped, Elaine spoke again. "Dr. Ishmael has already told me that my daughter may in fact die and was severely affected by the pox and will be, like me, scarred. Any beauty she had will be gone, and you, like all other men, will abandon her. A woman without beauty is of less value than your hound beside you."

"No, I have sworn to stay with her."

"Even worse: self-righteous pity. You are young and handsome. Many women will want to be with you. If my daughter lives she will wish herself dead." Lady Elaine laughed cynically and then began coughing again.

Henri did not answer. Ishmael signaled for Henri to step away, and whispered, "We cannot bring her near Maid Miriam. I do not trust her. If she did not outright try to kill the maiden, her harpy tongue would destroy any progress I have made."

"She is indeed a wicked woman," Petro agreed.

"Have them take her to the Inn of the Sunrise tonight. Tomorrow they can take her by litter to the convent at St. Sylvestre," Henri said.

Petro enlisted four of the lay monks around the monastery, promised them two sous each, and carried her to the inn. Ishmael delivered to the innkeeper exact directions as to how they were to treat her. The innkeeper needed some convincing that she was indeed no longer contagious. It was difficult, but a few extra sous poured into his leather money purse finally persuaded him. With that concluded, the threesome sat down at a table to eat. The innkeeper brought out barley cakes, fried eggs, trout, and bacon.

Pushing the bacon aside, Ishmael muttered, "Swine eating pagans."

Petro laughed and took an extra share. Henri left his uneaten.

Un combat equitable
Wheezing wolves and lean crows, what has come over you?
Is there not justice left upon the earth that I might rise and slay
This favored of the wench, the blade to rip, and to lay
Apart his belly, all drying under a summer wind blue?
- Sieur de Bixmarch of Anwar

Their meal was interrupted by loud arguing outside. Leaning back, Henri looked through the window to see the disturbance. Instantly he jumped to his feet and drew his sword. Startled, Petro stumbled over the bench as he tried to follow Henri's lead. Before he could fully recover, the door burst open and Bixmarch entered like a wolf entering a sheep pen. Behind him in a wedge followed Galahad and Picard. They were arguing vociferously about the spoils of the night. Outside, ten of their highwaymen were tying their horses to the stable posts.

"Innkeeper!" Bixmarch bellowed. "Victuals! Wine! Load the fires. . . ." He stopped suddenly as he spied Henri, Petro, and Ishmael. "What do we have here?" His left hand moved to his sword.

Henri noticed the stump of Bixmarch's right arm, amputated below the elbow.

Observing Henri's gaze, Bixmarch held it up. "This is your doing, yours and Renée's."

Henri could only surmise that Renée's arrow to the wrist must have led to infection.

Bixmarch dropped his arm. "It has not turned out well, has it?" There was a hint of regret in his voice. "I am not the Comte d'Ayes, nor, indeed, is there much to be the comte of in that devastated city. Elaine's plans have truly recoiled upon her, my beautiful sister. I even feel a little sorrow for Renée. She is, after all, my niece. . . . But the die is cast, is it not?"

Picard pushed past Bixmarch, stopped, and glared. "Well, Henri, this is a surprise indeed." The innkeeper backed away. "It has been some time. You undoubtedly have heard that I have married and deflowered your little flower." Picard elbowed Galahad in the ribs as he chuckled to himself. "Deflowered the flower, get it?"

Galahad grunted, but did not find it quite as amusing.

"That's not what I heard," Henri answered. "I heard that the maiden would not agree to the marriage, and when you forced it anyway she pulled a knife on you and kept you away all night."

"Ridiculous!" Picard exclaimed, but his reply lacked confidence. Clearly the truth had caught him off guard. "Don't be ridiculous. It's a lie. She lies."

Bixmarch and Galahad smirked at Picard. They had not heard this story.

"I didn't hear it from Renée," Henri answered calmly. "The maid in the next room behind the tapestry heard it all."

At this, everyone in the room laughed, even the innkeeper, though he tried to suppress it. Picard angrily drew his sword.

"Put it away." Henri waved it off. "What type of fight would it be for me to take on a swordsman who cannot even best a woman with a knife?"

That provoked Picard, and he flew at Henri with his sword blazing. Henri parried the attack and knocked Picard up against the stone hearth. Picard staggered to his knees, catching his fall with his arms. Warily Henri backed away as Picard rose to his feet, rubbing his ribs.

"You must understand, Sir Picard, that I am Renée's loyal servant, and as the Lord is with me justice will be served."

Picard slid against the wall back toward Galahad and Bixmarch.

"So it is three against three," Bixmarch said. "Of course, I am handicapped by having to fight left-handed, but don't let that fool you; I am handy with the left." With that Bixmarch gave an agile flourish of the sword to demonstrate his proficiency. "We are also handicapped by having a knight who cannot even fight off a slight little lass." With that he looked at Picard and shook his head disdainfully. "But then we do have Galahad. He might count for two or three. You, on the other hand, have two good swordsmen and a Moorish physician, and I suspect he can handle his scimitar well enough; most of those Mohammedans can. All in all, it should be a pretty fair fight. Wouldn't you say?"

Bixmarch raised his eyebrow as if to ask for confirmation of his assessment. Indeed Henri thought the advantage was on their side. He had beaten Galahad and could do so again. Petro could take on Bixmarch, and Ishmael could at least hold off Picard until either he or Petro could help him.

Reading his reactions, Bixmarch continued, "Three on three, quite fair. . . . Unfortunately I have ten more knights outside. Thirteen on three. It is unfair, I admit, but then I am not feeling in a fair mood." He thrust his stump at Henri again.

Backing slowly to the door, Bixmarch opened it and called to the others in his company. One by one they filed in and took up positions around the room, cornering Henri, Petro, and Ishmael toward the far corner away from the windows. Henri and Petro recognized several of the knights from Anwar.

"Well now, let's see what justice we can find this morning," Bixmarch muttered. "I lost a hand. Doesn't the Bible, of which you are so fond, doesn't it say a hand for a hand? Still, that just doesn't seem quite enough for me. I think today it will be a head for a hand. You see, Henri, you have become a very great bother to me, and. . . ." Bixmarch drew his sword and began advancing.

But at that moment they heard the winding of a horn. Galahad looked out the window toward the alarm.

"It is Comte d'Auch. He leads thirty knights. They are on the hill by the monastery and coming this way."

Bixmarch hurried to the window and cursed as he saw the heavy cavalry of Auch and Brittany galloping toward the inn. He glanced back at Henri, wondering if they would have the time to dispatch Henri and still escape.

Galahad, understanding his thoughts, clarified the question. "They will be here in less than five minutes. We must leave immediately."

Bixmarch cursed again as they rushed out the door, mounted their horses, and fled.

Henri and Petro joined Henri d'Auch when the mounted warriors arrived. They chased Bixmarch and his compatriots until they came to a narrowing where the road ran through two towering boulders on either side of the road.

Pulling up, Comte d'Auch studied the road. "I. . . I don't like it. It is perfect for an ambush."

"I quite agree," Petro added.

Reluctantly they turned back.

Chapitre Vingt Cinq
Fillette, je te le dis, Reveille-toi

Talitha koum
- Jesus of Nazareth

A week passed. Ishmael, rising from his prayer rug, called to Henri as he came back from morning mass. Henri joined Ishmael under the cottonwood trees. Clouds were floating overhead. "I will be unwrapping Renée this morning." Ishmael stopped and looked carefully at Henri.

Henri nodded. "Is she past the crisis?"

"She will live," Ishmael answered.

Henri sighed in relief.

"Do not be too relieved yet. We have not seen what the pox has done to her."

"But if she will live, then I am satisfied. God is good," Henri answered with fervor.

"Allah is good, of course, but. . ." Ishmael shook his finger in admonition at Henri. "But we shall see. The pox can disfigure so badly that she may wish herself dead. When you see her, all your love may vanish in a moment. I have seen it many times. Even the most devoted have in one moment gone from passionate love to total repugnance. Good men, great men even."

"Not I, Ishmael, not I. I shall love her always."

Ishmael raised an eyebrow in question. "Do not be so sure, Henri. Even your father found it difficult to be with your mother when she was scarred with the pox. It was fortunate for her that she was delirious and died. It would have been an even greater tragedy had she lived to see her true love draw ineluctably away. She died not knowing the effect the scarring was having on his love."

That made its mark on Henri. If even his father could be so changed, then maybe he did not know himself as he thought, and he began to doubt.

"Can I come?" Henri asked.

Ishmael studied Henri for a moment. "I don't know if that is wise. I think it would be best if I saw her first, and then I could prepare you."

"Please," Henri pleaded.

Ishmael rubbed his neatly shaved beard for a moment before answering, "You may come to the tent and wait outside. After we have unwrapped I will make my decision."

They rode together across the bridge, past the watermill, and side by side on the dry dusty road. Rouge followed close on the heel of Henri's horse. They did not speak. At the tents Ishmael gathered his medical bag, his scissors, several vials filled with balms, ointments, and herbs.

He   handed to the maid a satchel filled with bandages and cloth. Then they went inside.

Henri slid down against the trunk of the oak tree and pulled his knees up close. Rouge found a patch of grass four feet away and lay down, occasionally opening his eyes to watch Henri and the soldiers who were standing outside the tent. A turtledove cooed in the branches above Henri. A hawk sailed over the meadow, gliding on the thermals. Henri glanced at them and then back at the opening flap of the tent. He could not hear Ishmael's quiet voice, but he could hear the maid.

"Scissors? Let's see, oh, here they are. Are these the ones you want? No. Oh, well, well here we go, how about these? Now, now lass, hold real still while he cuts. I do hope that she is. . . . Yes, yes of course, I agree, we should be quiet. Now you be real quiet, maiden. . . . Just hold still."

And then there was silence in the tent. Henri rose and began pacing in front of the tent flap, getting as close as he could, trying to overhear Ishmael's voice, but all he heard was the maid's occasional gasps, "Oh my, oh my. Yes. . . yes, I shall be quiet. Hold still my dear. . . . No, no, dear, keep your hands down. We will get to the hands in just a moment, but he wants to cut away at the legs first."

Then another silence, dead silence, for what seemed like an hour.

Finally Ishmael slid out of the tent. Henri watched the physician as he walked to his horse and took a flask of water from the saddle. Ishmael drank it slowly and started walking away from the tent, past the oak tree near the shrubs that surrounded the meadow. Henri followed, fearing the worst.

When they were a hundred yards from the tent, Ishmael turned and said, "I unraveled her legs up to above the knees, some on the hands and arms, a little on the abdomen, and a small portion of the face." Ishmael took another swallow from the flask and offered it to Henri. Henri declined.

"And?" Henri prompted.

Ishmael shook his head. "She is covered with scale."

Henri waited for more, but that was all Ishmael said.

"So what then?"

"The maid will rebind her in the cloth," Ishmael said quietly, and then uncharacteristically slammed his fist into his palm. "The treatment has been a failure. She will be scarred. I am not even sure if she will be able to see."

With that Ishmael returned to his horse, drew out his notebook, quill and ink, and kneeling on one knee began writing his observations of the case. For a moment Henri watched Ishmael writing beneath the shade of the oak tree, and then he went to the front of the tent, slowly parted the flaps, and looked in. The maid was still wrapping the legs. Henri saw the sloughing scale of her leg, like that of a dead fish. At first a rush of nausea struck at him, but he steeled himself, and his second impulse was of an overwhelming sorrow for Renée. She did not deserve this. Why should life be so unfair? Why should she who had been neglected by father, despised by mother, forced into marriage, jilted by adultery, why should she be now so permanently scarred? Why should she who had been so beautiful lose it all and become an oddity, a freak? And suddenly Henri knew he could love no other. It was clearer than the most expensive crystal goblets ever set at King Charles's table, clearer than an artesian spring, sharper than the blade in his scabbard; he had no doubt; he was Renée's knight and would always be so.

The maid looked back to see him as she finished wrapping the bottom of her feet. She shook her head and clucked sadly as she slipped outside. Henri moved to Renée's bedside and knelt down.

"It is me, Renée. It is I, Henri."

She was crying. He took her hand and said nothing. The wrapping a-round her head prohibited her from speaking. There was only a small slit through which they fed her and gave her sips of water and slits around her nose. The sheet that usually covered her had not been replaced. She lay on the cot wrapped in the red cloth. She had lost weight with the illness, weight which she could not spare. Now she was just a gaunt bundle of skin and bones, and it was not even decent skin at that. She took her hand and tried to pull away the cloth around her mouth.

"What is it? What is it Renée?"

She tried now to pull the cloth from her eyes, but it was bound too tight, and she was too weak. She became frustrated and began shaking in her sobs. Henri looked around and found Ishmael's medical bag. He found the scissors and cut the cloth beneath her chin. She worked with him and loosened it more. Now she could speak.

"Henri, help me, loosen it around my eyes. I want to see you."

Henri was not sure that was a good idea. Ishmael had said that she might not be able to see, and if they confirmed that now, it would make her despair worse. Still, she was insistent, so he took the scissors and carefully cut away on the temples so that he could part it away from her eyes.

"Get it off, Henri. I want to see you."

Henri pulled away for a moment, overcome by the sadness of it. For her eyes were crusted together.

"Henri, get it off."

"It is off, Renée," he said softly.

She was quiet then, as she processed what that meant. The cloth was away, but she could not see. "I cannot see," she said with resignation, and then a few moments later asked, "Am I . . . ugly. . .? Henri?"

"Not to me." he said as he took her hand again.

She held his hand in silence for a moment before she spoke again. "I was faithful to you Henri. Really, I was."

"I know; your maid told me," Henri said as tears began to flow down his cheeks. Leaning forward, he lifted her light body into his arms and hugged her. She put her arms around his neck.

"Henri, my Henri," she cried. "My very Henri." She squeezed hard for a few seconds and then relaxed. Henri laid her back down on the bed. "You have been faithful too, but I release you now. I release you, Sir Henri de Bretagne. I release you from your vow. You must live. Live for the both of us. I will go away, and I will pray for you."

Putting his hand across her lips, he hushed her. "I shall not leave you, not now, not tomorrow, not ever."

"No, Henri, you are free. I cannot keep you. I have been cursed by God, like Job, and you cannot stay with me."

Holding her face in his hands, Henri stopped her again. "But I shall stay, and if you will have me I will be your husband, and you will be my bride."

That quieted Renée, and then she began to sob.

Ishmael, at the entrance to the tent, marched forward angrily. "What have you said to upset her like this? Henri, you are heartless and cruel. I cannot believe you are the son of Sir Thommas. Why have you cut off her covering over her eyes? Get out!"

Controlling her sobbing, Renée interrupted, "No, Ishmael. It is not from despair, but because of happiness that I cry. Sir Henri has asked me to marry him, even though I am scarred by the pox."

Ishmael stopped and looked at Henri. "Is this true?"

Henri nodded as he rose to his feet, backing toward the tent flaps. At that Ishmael rushed forward and embraced Henri, vigorously kissing him repeatedly on both cheeks. "Allah bless you, God bless you, may even your Jesus bless you. To see her like this and still love her. You are a good man. Oh, this makes me happy."

The maid, hearing the conversation, ran back inside and hugged Henri, Ishmael, and then Renée.

Parting the tent, Henri whistled for Le Noir. He wanted to ride. The horse trotted up to him with La Rouge by his side, and Henri leaped into the saddle. Giving the horse a nudge, they trotted across the field and onto the road. Without forethought Henri turned left toward Ayes. The ride seemed to go quickly, as Henri was wrapped deep in thought. Now that they were to be married, he wanted to proceed directly, no delays, no further waiting. But what must be done? They must be married in Brittany, not because it mattered to Henri, but because it would matter to his grandfather. Henri would have to ride ahead and make preparations while Renée recovered further. He would see to the details. It must be a grand wedding. Then again, maybe it should be a simple wedding.

What would be best? On the one hand he wanted to demonstrate that he was truly proud of her and truly loved her, whether she was scarred or not, and a large wedding in a great cathedral would show that. On the other hand, Renée might prefer something smaller; she might not want the crowds gawking to see if she was as scarred as they had heard, and he knew those type of rumors could not be denied. Well, he would ride ahead and search out the great cathedrals and the smaller chapels. Then she could decide when she was well enough to travel.

A little after midday, Henri came to the hill overlooking Ayes. All the fires were now gone. By the bank of the river Henri saw Petro directing a large party of workers. They were cutting trees to rebuild the city.

Henri dismounted and, leading his horse, walked down to Petro. The pox-scarred knight was in the thick of the work, helping to hoist a large log onto a wagon with rope and pulley. Many a nobleman would have directed it all from horseback—that is, if they even came to the site at all. Not Petro; he pulled off his tabard and worked with just a linen shirt like one of the men.

Seeing Henri, Petro, without relaxing his grip on the rope, turned his head and called, "Good day to you, Sir Henri. Careful, keep it tight. Pull more from the rear. Now slide it forward. Everyone, on my mark we will let it down on the wagon. Be careful. I have seen a man lose a hand doing this, and we do not want to give Dr. Ishmael more work today." Looking back over his shoulder, Petro smiled broadly. "Now."

The log swung onto the wagon and sank heavily; the wheels moved a little, and the horses pranced nervously while the handlers steadied them.

"You are making good progress." Henri nodded toward the construction underway in the city.

Petro let the lax ropes drop and rubbed his hands. "Indeed, we are. We have to rebuild Renée's domain. These men d'Ayes are hard workers and quite skillful."

"Unfortunately, we have too much experience at rebuilding," said a passing citizen of the city.

"But what of Renée; how is she?" Petro spoke again.

"Dr. Ishmael took off some of the wrappings today."

"Yes, he told me last night he would do it today."

"She will be scarred," Henri said quietly.

Petro sighed and then spoke. "Me, I am a man. My skin is scarred, but what is that to a man? But for her, and she was so beautiful." Petro spoke now several yards away from the workers, who were passing the ropes to load a second trunk on the wagon. Farther up the river the sound of axe could be heard. Along the bush, Henri's red hound was sniffing and searching, tracking the many smells. "What will you do now?"

"I have proposed to her," Henri replied.

Petro stopped and looked at Henri. "It is not that bad, the scarring? She is still beautiful?"

"The scarring is widespread, scales all over, but she is still beautiful—to me."

Still staring at Henri, Petro said nothing for a moment.

"I will need to ride to Brittany and make arrangements for the wedding. I was hoping that I could entrust you to bring her when she is ready to travel."

"You are serious. You would marry her even though she is scarred by the pox?" Petro searched Henri's eyes as he spoke.

Henri nodded. At that a large smile crossed Petro's face, and he clapped Henri hard on the shoulder. "You are good, Henri. You are very good. I said that my scarring does not matter to me, but the truth is, even though I am a man, I am constantly aware of my scarring. I can see it in everyone's eyes. Even Maria when she does not think I am aware, I can see her shrink from it. But I never saw it in you, still. . ." And he stopped again. He gave Henri a quizzical look. "Isn't she already married to Picard?"

"But she never consented. Surely that is not a valid marriage; the church could not confirm it. It must be annulled."

Petro shrugged his shoulders. "You can never know what the church will do. If she truly did not assent, then yes, you are right. But the church can be unreasonable at times."

"Then I will go to Brittany. I shall find my grandfather. Surely he can help. Then I will make arrangements. Will you bring her when she is well?"

"But of course. You will not travel alone will you? Take some of the Brittany knights with you."

Le Rouge began barking by a small bush. Henri whistled for him and continued with his conversation. "I shall travel with my squire and two knights. I will leave the rest to protect the maiden."

"Then you will leave shortly."

"Tomorrow morning," Henri said as he whistled again for Rouge, who kept looking back at Henri and barking. Henri wondered what he had found. Leaving Petro to return to his work, Henri walked across the field to where Rouge stood. Parting the branches of the small bush, Henri saw nothing, but Rouge would not leave, so Henri pulled the branches aside again and searched even closer. Then he saw it, a small bundle of fur lying on the ground. He reached down and picked up Renée's little puppy, La Blanche. It was alive and breathing, but just barely.

"The poor little thing is starving," Henri said as he wrapped it in a blanket and patted Rouge on the head. "Good boy, this will make Renée much happier. With a little food he will make it. We can bring it to her this evening. Come on fellow; let's go take it to her now."

Chapitre Vingt Six
Bretagne

From Ouessant, who sees his own blood, the seal and storm petrel,
To Rennes, where merge the rivers Vilaine and Ille,
From St Malo, Welsh missionary and harbor of corsairs,
To Vannes of the Place des Lices and tournament fairs,
Long have we lived among our dolmen at Carnac.
O Bretagne, may we never forget
We would rather die than soiled be;
Independent may we live free.
- Sir Henri

It took Henri and his companions two weeks to arrive at Nantes, where he had heard his grandfather, Duc de Montfort, was residing. On reaching Nantes, however, they discovered that the Duc de Bretagne had traveled to western Brittany. Henri followed, traveling through Vannes, Hennebont, and then on to the small town of Le Conquet on the far western coast.

On a rocky cliff with the wind blowing, Henri found his grandfather. He was standing among a troop of knights and advisors. By their robes Henri instantly understood that many of the coterie were distinguished clergy.

As he approached up the hill on horseback, his grandfather turned and faced him, puzzled for a moment, and then a broad smile crossed his face. Henri dismounted and welcomed the Duke's embrace.

"You? All the way from Ayes? I planned on returning in a couple days, but I got delayed. There are some difficulties. There are always difficulties. This time it is pirates along the coast. We have uprooted several bands, but the leader has escaped to Lampaul." At that the Duke pointed across the sea. "You may not be able to see it today, but there is an island out there, the Ile D'Ouessant. He has taken refuge there. I cannot capture him and he knows it. But you here, all the way from Ayes? What is it?"

Henri hesitated. What would his grandfather say? And it came to him that his father had once been in this same position, seeking the Duke's blessing on a marriage. Henri told of what had happened in Ayes since the Duke's absence, his visit with Comte Sevestre, the Lady Elaine, the battle with Bixmarch, and of Renée.

"She is heavily scarred then?" the Duke said, shaking his head. "And you still want to marry her? Now that you are the heir of Brittany—which reminds me we need to talk about that a little later—there are many beautiful young ladies with more to offer than this Renée. The King of Navarre has a beautiful daughter, so does the Duc d'Anjou. Or we might strike an alliance with England that would put some fear in King Charles's heart—lately he has been taking Brittany a little too much for granted, but we are not like the rest of France—we are Bretons."

"No, I have pledged to Renée. She has my heart."

The Duke nodded his head equivocally. "Still, have you thought about this? If she were to marry you she could not hide, and people have rough tongues. They may not mock her to her face, but their actions? She would be the butt of jokes by both the noble and the common. Would it not be more merciful for you to put her away, in the company of compassionate sisters?" At that the Duke turned suddenly away, as if remembering something.

"I am set on this, Your Grace," Henri answered. "I will be husband to her, that is, if it can be arranged. But there is a complication: Picard. He married her, but it was against her will. She never assented; certainly the church will annul it."

The Duke went into the cluster of officials who were involved in intense conversation. Taking the sleeve of a churchman, the Duke drew him out. He was an older man, in his seventies, with white hair around his bald pate and a thin face, but despite his age he was still elegant.

Le chagrin me ronge les yeux
I had thought the drought of passing years
Would have dried the corroding sorrow of my tears.
I had leaned on glory and fame, power and name
To render faint all images with times wane,
But found they grow sharper in my mind.

Then at least let mind with age grow dim,
Muddled with babbled thoughts like flotsam
And jetsam. Forgetful, let it erase
The memories of my babbling child; let it efface
My sin, my disregard, to which I paid no mind.

But no, with age has mounted my ascending grief
As I remember how I disavowed her I made conceive,
And how my pettiness, my self-advancing baseness
Deprived her of name, filled her days with shame and distress—
I still see her cherub face clear in my mind.

No man awaiting the grave ever regrets
Time with lover and child spent.
- Paul of Brest, Archbishop de Bretagne

"Archbishop, this is Sir Henri, son of Sir Thommas and Mirriam."

The Archbishop drew close. "Well met, Henri." But there was a quiver in his voice that caught Henri by surprise.

"Henri, this is Paul of Brest, Archbishop and Cardinal. Archbishop de Bretagne."

Henri shook his hand. He resembled someone. Henri just could not place the connection immediately.

"I am quite certain I have not met you before. I would have remembered meeting the Archbishop de Bretagne, but. . . ." Henri stopped and stared at the man.

"Indeed," the Archbishop answered, seeing Henri beginning to put it together.

Henri withdrew his hand and recoiled two steps.

"Fair enough," the Archbishop said quietly. "Fair enough. It is just."

"But, then you are . . .," Henri paused.

"Indeed, I too am your grandfather. Your mother's father, and I doubt you have heard much good of me." Still watching Henri, the old Archbishop sat down on a rock. Henri backed up another couple of steps, but he did not let his gaze fall from the Archbishop's face. "I did not treat your mother well, and I have come to regret that immensely. Immensely. My daughter deserved better. She was a great beauty, but then so was her mother, and I did little to make life easier on either of them. I saw her only maybe a dozen times." The Archbishop stopped as his voice trailed off.

"Paul of Brest, Archbishop de Bretagne," Henri said quietly.

"I have heard that Miriam died when you were young. Tell me, did she die in the church? Had she forgiven me?"

"No," Henri answered honestly. "No, she never reconciled with the church. But she did believe in Christ."

"What good is it to believe if you are not in the body? What good will that do her? I had always soothed myself with the hope that she had reconciled herself, and that maybe having borne my neglect, the trials I laid at her feet, she would fly straight to heaven. Now I must go to my grave with even this on my conscience." The Archbishop rose to his feet. "If it means anything to you, she was my only child, and her mother was my last indiscretion. I did learn, and I swear I have wept bitter tears in recent years as I finally realized what I had done."

"God is merciful," Henri answered.

A little startled by the comment—it was usually his role to deliver the pious comment—the Archbishop stopped and then nodded quietly. "He is indeed. Henri, you are Miriam's son; will you forgive me?"

Though the question was delivered quietly, Henri could see that the Archbishop was sincere and that this request meant much to the great man of the church.

"If my mother was alive she would have forgiven you had you asked. But she is not alive; she died unloved by her father. What can I say? What will my words mean? They cannot speak for another. I cannot forgive you for her sake; I am not God. But if you wish, I will forgive you as her son."

"Thank you," the Archbishop said.

At that the Duke motioned to Henri. Henri looked, at first not understanding as the Duke motioned his head toward the Archbishop, but then Henri nodded and stepped over and embraced his grandfather. At first the Archbishop was surprised, but then he put his arms around Henri and held him tightly, and again Henri could feel a quiver in the old man's frame.

"Well, now that you have met we can discuss again what Henri has come to ask me. Paul, as my spiritual advisor, I could use your advice on this." The Duke then summarized Henri's story for the Archbishop, ending with Henri's marriage request.

"That is no problem, Montfort. The church's teaching on this is very clear. No one can be married against their will. The marriage will be annulled. And as to her 'condition,' of course he marries her. Should we not learn something, the two of us, in our old age? I will marry them myself. Brest has a wonderful cathedral. Where is this Renée?"

"She has not come yet," Montfort explained. "She is to recover before coming, and of course Brest has a delightful cathedral, but why not the Mount in Peril of the Sea?"

"Mont Saint-Michel?" the Archbishop asked. "Why not, indeed? But, Henri, if we have a little time before she comes, then you must ride with me. I wish you to come with me to Morgat."

"Morgat?" The Duke exclaimed. "Why would Henri want to go to that little town?"

"Alix," The Archbishop replied. "She lives in Morgat."

"Alix? My grandmother, my mother's mother, she is still alive?"

"She is, and she will be overjoyed to see you. She will remind you much of your mother. This too will ease my conscience. You are young, Henri, and may not understand, but when you get old like I am and all you face is death, you start taking the judgment much more seriously. The church sells indulgences, which ease the conscience of the simple man, but I am not easy in mine. Come with me. Bring joy to Alix. I would make up for a life too much focused on the politics of the church and too little focused on feeding the poor and doing good."

"I will go with you, your Grace," Henri replied.

Chapitre Vingt Sept
Mont Saint-Michel

The cock has crowed; I will now go.
To war! To war!
I am St. Michel the archangel,
Sent of God.
Now build me a place
Upon this rock,
This granite, this ascent
From the peril of the sea,
That I might ever live
Above the tides.
Let them wash sands.
I still stand in divine majesty.
- Abbé of Mont St-Michel

Six weeks passed, and with them summer gave way to autumn. Oak leaves turned gold and yellow before fading russet in small drifts driven by the winds. Wheat fields were ripe for the harvest, now filled with rows of men, long scythes slashing through the grain. Wagons lined up before the mill were loaded with bags of flour and then driven away.

Five days ago Sir Petro de Lomange had arrived in Rennes. Leading an escort company of Brittany knights, they had carried Renée by litter. In the company had also been Ishmael, Henri d'Auch, and Simeon, Jehudah's nephew.

Henri had been to see Renée every day, but Ishmael allowed only short visits. She had taken to wearing delicately woven veils of Florentine silk, and when she walked she rested on the arm of her maid. Still, despite her handicaps, she seemed to have recovered all the inner enthusiasm she once had had. She had projects and adventures in mind, and more than once Henri had to remind her gently that perhaps they might have to slow down, at least for a time. Each time it came as a surprise to her, and she would recover and agree with him. Henri, however, marveled at her, because she refused to allow a word of regret to pass her lips. She was full of optimism. On leaving, Henri would at first be filled with her optimism, but then as he had time to process his thoughts he would become saddened. Why did one such as she have to be so limited? Why had the pox been so severe, handicapping her? He tried to talk about it with Ishmael and had been cut short.

"She lives. Isn't that miracle enough for you?"

If he brought it up with Petro, he gave cryptic comments, such as, "A well groomed head wears the helmet badly." What that was supposed to mean? Henri did not know.

Only once he had tentatively asked Renée to lift the veil. Her alarm at his suggestion had stymied any further suggestions along that line. After leaving, the maid had hurried after him and tried to explain.

"She is hoping that you will not be offended, but she really wants you to remember her as she was before the pox, at least until after the wedding. Please, good knight, humor her on this. It is important to her, and she has had such a difficult time. Do not press her on this."

"But, of course, if she feels that way about it." And Henri did not bring up the subject again.

After her arrival, both of his grandfathers had taken him aside and questioned him. Did he really want to still go through with this? No one would think the less of him if he should back out, considering the circumstances. He was unwavering, however, and they did not revisit the subject.

Yesterday they had traveled to Mont Saint-Michel; had crossed the expanse, the strand of white sand separating the steep mass of rock—soaring three hundred feet above the horizon—had ridden in a column from the shores of Brittany to the ancient Benedictine abbey church built on the summit of the rock. Henri had never seen it before and was struck as so many had been before him. It was a cathedral of dreams, like a pyramid of the seas. This ancient church had been first built in the eighth century by St. Aubert and then successively added to by the later Abbots Maynard, Hildebert, Jourdain, and Robert de Torigny, under the encouragement of the Dukes of Normandy and Brittany. They had come across on dry land, for the tides were not high, and the moon was neither new nor full. Their troop of horses had passed carts and caravans of pack horses bringing supplies to the abbey. Henri had ridden in silence, restrained by the quiet strength of the church, its triumphal arch, the solid support of the heavy columns. How could anyone see it and not be drawn to God? As they passed through the city gates, they turned the horses over to stable hands. Henri dismounted and looked up, to the central tower supported by the four great piers, up its steep roof to a slender spire, at the top of which—five hundred feet above the sea—stood a statue of St. Michel. And then they had climbed to the monastery.

Alix de Morgat, his grandmother, had come, and in the afternoon had sought a private interview with Renée. On leaving the room she found Henri.

"She is beautiful, Henri, beautiful. Beautiful where it really counts."

Chant d'amour
Come babbling, my little one
My cherub, my precious son,
Come toddling to my knee.

Tall and strong, my darling child,
You grow fast, like cherry wild,

Come sprinting now to me.

Turn now your face toward she
My son, your bride, your beauty,
Turn love, all love to she.
-    *Miriam de Bretagne (a lullaby)*

But that was yesterday. Today they would wed; the wedding would start in less than an hour. Already merchants, guildsman, lawyers, and freemen, the more prosperous commoners, had taken their allotted places to the rear and sides of the church. Now the nobility were passing up through the chatelet and taking their places. Knights, barons and baronesses, comtes and comtesses, they came from Brittany, Picardy, Normandy, Gascony, and other regions of France. They came also from Navarre, Catalonia, and Flanders. There was a baron from Ireland—Montfort's cousin—and a chieftain from the highlands of Scotland. There was even an earl from England—for Montfort had long striven to keep a delicate balance in his allegiance between France and England, giving Brittany independence above most other provinces of France. Then there were the clerics, the canons and friars, priests and prelates, monks and nuns, Abbés and abbesses, the bishops and the Archbishop.

Waiting outside, standing at the edge of the granite platform, Henri looked down the two hundred and thirty five feet to the sands below and then out to the expanse of the sea. The sea was beautiful under the shining sun. He could see the tide was beginning to recede. The wind tussled his hair. He brushed it back, then turned and passed through the cloister. He let his hands touch the slender columns and looked at the exquisite carvings along the molding. There was something serious about the Mont that he liked, as if simple faith was all that was needed. That was comforting.

His path led him into the refectory, a large hall supporting an unbroken line of arches from which windows softly diffused their light upon the room. Henri had never seen anything like it. With good reason they called this west wing the 'Marvel.' He stopped and looked out through the stained glass windows. What a mysterious beauty.

His quietness was broken by Sir Petro de Lomange sliding up beside him. "It is a grand day," Petro said with a wide knowing smile, and then laughed seeing Henri's nervous face.

At that moment Henri d'Auch, with Constance beside him, came up from the Guest's Hall into the refectory. Seeing Henri across the room, Constance waved and then left Henri d'Auch, coming towards Henri.

"Have you been standing in the wind?" she asked. "Your hair is a mess." Taking her brush, she turned him around. "Would you really have entered like this?" She gave a disapproving look at Sir Petro de Lomange and then began grooming his hair. "That's better." She stepped back and looked, and then walked around him, tucking his white stockings into the black leather boots, tugging on his blue and white tunic, rearranging his sword, straightening the black mantle. "It always amazes me how much time a woman puts in to make herself beautiful, and the man walks through the door, runs his hands through his hair, and feels like he has done all that he needs. Do you know Renée has been awake since four this morning brushing her hair, styling it, putting on her makeup, eye-liner, lipstick, blush? All the ladies of the court have been working with her and she is beauti. . . ." Constance suddenly stopped and looked wide-eyed at Henri and then turned and quickly left.

Henri stared at her in bafflement; all the ladies of the court working with Renée, in her disfigured state, full of scars and blind. Why would they do that? Why bother with makeup? Would not that be almost a mockery? He did not understand.

From the nave they could hear the monastery choir begin singing. They crossed over and into the cathedral.

First came six little girls in white dresses, dancing and spreading rose petals in abundance. Behind them followed ten young pages wearing an array of colors: red, green, yellow, blue, or purple. Each of them bore a gift. The first two carried a chest brimming over coins, and as they walked they dipped their hands in and sent them scattering among the commoners. The next two followed with another chest filled with silver. They did the same. The next two carried a box of crafted daggers which they handed out to knights along the path. The next two brought forward necklaces which they handed to the ladies. Then followed a page carrying a sword, and the last page entered bearing the cross before him. Afterwards the pages, twenty knights of Brittany, their iron crosses embossed on their white tunics, spaced themselves along the central corridor. Behind them twenty ladies-in-waiting, all dressed in blue, took a position, each beside a knight.

There was a pause; then the trumpets blared. Henri looked. She entered. She was leaning on the arm of his grandfather, so petite as compared to the great pillars of the nave. She wore white silk with an embroidered silver stomacher. Her train was of long shimmering satin and borne by four young maidens. On her head she wore a wimple with a veil. White muslin covered her face.

Henri was beset with conflicting emotions. On the one hand was his love and a yearning to be with her. On the other hand was this: seeing her walk down the aisle, in front of all these people, leaning on the arm of his grandfather, blind, with a muslin veil covering her marred face. It should have been different. Was he doing the right thing, or was he just exposing her to ridicule? Should he have let her retire to a convent? Was he being selfish? And there was sorrow. Amidst his joy, there was sorrow: sorrow that her mother and father had cared so little; sorrow that her beauty had faded so soon; sorrow that he could not share this with his father.

The Duke had now brought her to Henri, and he beamed as he handed her over. His smile, though genuine, seemed odd to Henri. Henri took Renée's gloved hand. It felt good as she touched his, and they grasped tightly, then they turned to face the Archbishop.

Like all grooms, Henri heard not a word of the ceremony. He noted only the feel of her hand and the warmth of her arm as it lay through his; the quiet breathing of her chest as she stood beside him. How amazing that he should now be wedding this young woman—was it only last spring, on a morning, with the sun rising over the bay, they had fled on horseback? And yet she knew him, knew him in ways that even his father had not, and she, Renée, was to be his bride.

Taking the ring, the archbishop joined them together and pronounced them man and wife.

"You may now kiss the bride."

Henri had anticipated this; he had planned it carefully. He knew all would be watching him, watching for some momentary loathing, some innate repulsion as he viewed her scarred face. The whole gawking public was waiting. They were waiting to see how marred her features were. Would she be some freak, like the gargoyles on cathedral walls? They were also waiting to see his reaction. How awful it would be to ruin her wedding day, with a momentary lapse of unwilling abhorrence when he first lifted the veil. So he had planned it. He would turn her away from the public, lift the veil, shut his eyes, and kiss her.

He did as he planned, lifted the veil, and, eyes shut, laid his lips gently on hers, but unexpectedly he found her flinging her arms around his neck, and instead of a private quick kiss, she was passionate. Surprised, he opened his eyes. She was not blind. She was looking at him, and her eyes were unscarred. He drew back and looked at her. Her face was unscarred and beautiful. Stunned, he stared at her for a moment. She smiled broadly. He then looked at Petro and the Duke. They grinned and nodded. He saw Constance, and she was biting her lip in joy as tears ran down her face. Overcome by emotion, Henri felt his legs weakening. Renée tried to hold him, but could not. He slumped to his knees and sobbed. Renée dropped down beside him and hugged him.

"Henri, are you all right?" Renée asked.

The Archbishop stepped back and laughed. The commoners in the back were clamoring, trying to discover what had happened. When the word passed back to them a great laughter and murmur swept through the cathedral.

Ishmael by this time was standing beside the Duke and Petro, who were standing over Henri. "It is my greatest triumph! My therapy has been a success. The red cloth of Montpelier is good, but it is the combination of my special balms and the emollient baths in the scaling stage that have accomplished this. Look at her. She is radiant, a woman in the prime of her beauty, not a hint of scar. Well, her maid says she still has some scarring on her belly and thighs, but it is minimal." Raising his hands together Ishmael gushed, "I am just so pleased, so proud of my work. This is satisfaction, and for her, too. There is none like her. She is as a daughter to me. May Allah be praised. . .that is to say—" Ishmael caught himself as he looked at the Archbishop and around at the cathedral. "May God be praised."

Through his tears Henri looked at Renée. "Why didn't you tell me?"

"I wanted to surprise you." Renée smiled, and then looking at the commotion all around them and at Henri still kneeling weakly on his knees, added, "I think I did."

"Renée, you were beautiful before, on the inside, but now. . . ." Henri could not finish.

"Yes, I know," she said, laughing. "I'm gorgeous."

At that Henri laughed and hugged her. Feeling a little stronger he rose up and lifted Renée with him.

The Archbishop stepped forward. The bailiff pounded the mace several times on the granite floor, trying to quiet the crowd. "Lords and ladies, peers of the realm, knights, squires, and all citizens, brothers and sisters in Christ, I present to you this morning Sir Henri de Bretagne, sole heir to Montfort, Duc de Bretagne. I present to you Sir Henri and the beautiful—" He had to pause as there was an outbreak of whistles and cheers as he pointed to her. "The beautiful Lady Renée, husband and wife. May God bless them and keep them. May he turn his face toward them and be gracious to them. May he look upon them with favor and give them peace."

And then there was again a loud hurrah and disruptive cheer. The bailiff looked to the Archbishop to see if he should bring them back to order. The Archbishop smiled and shrugged. It was an unusual wedding, not the solemn ceremonial service he was accustomed to, but he rather liked it. For a moment he stood on the dais watching the commotion, and then he stepped down into the fray and clapped Duc de Montfort hard on the back. "I think he was surprised, don't you?"

The Duke laughed and looked back over at the young couple accepting the spontaneous congratulations, handshakes, embraces, and backslapping for Henri, kisses for Renée. "That could have been my Thommas and your Miriam, though, you know."

The Archbishop nodded. "Yes, I was thinking the very same thing. It could have been. We were both fools, the two of us."

Periront par l'epee

Shall defy
Hallowed rules,
All conventions I deny;
Let them lie,
Let them lie.

Desire for power have
I ever longed for in all my ways, would
Exchange them for anything. With this sharp

Blade of mine I hurl scorn on all who stand in my way,
You, them, they.

The man who will resist my sword
Has not been born.
Ever shall I resist;

Swagger, stagger, I will not desist,
Whether he be noble, lord, or little god
Only power to me exists
Rule I will
Die I'll not.
- Abbess Elaine de Morvan

Following the wedding, before the evening feast, the Duke led a large party of the nobles across the sands to the mainland for a little falcon hunt. Renée, however, was still recovering her strength, and Ishmael recommended she rest. Henri stayed with her.

In her chamber Renée quickly fell asleep. Henri lay down beside her for a while and then got up. He left a message with Renée's maid that he was going to explore the cathedral. Not long after he left, Renée awoke. Rubbing her eyes, Renée raised up on her elbows. She looked around for Henri. She had had a terrible dream, but she could not remember any of the details; still she felt this pressing disquiet.

"Where is Henri?" She asked her maid.

"He went for a walk in the cathedral."

She arose and went to the window. The sky was overcast. She looked out over the sea in the far distance. Something was wrong. Something was terribly wrong. She gripped the curtains with her hands as she stood before the window.

"My lady what is it?"

"I fear for Henri; something is amiss."

Renée leaned forward on the stone and looked out the window. There was a break in the clouds where the sun shone through. Like an arrow shaft of light it struck a part of the beach obscured by the walls of the town; the light breaking through like that reminded her of the day last spring when she had first approached Anwar-by-the-Bay. She remember-ed how apprehensive she had been that day; she remembered her concerns regarding her mother; she remembered the fear of meeting her uncle. How right she had been to be afraid. She remembered the child-ren lined up along the road, so hopeless; she remembered her prayer, a prayer so concerned for her own safety. What was it she had said? "Jesu, Jesu, Jesu Christus, I am in trouble, in danger. Jesu, help me." Yes, that was it, and then the light had broken through the clouds, on the stables, on Henri. A light just like now.

Her maid came tentatively to the window. "Henri? Something is wrong with Henri? Is that what you think?"

"Yes, Dete, it is. I cannot explain it, but I have this foreboding. I wish he were here with me."

At that the maid became very agitated. "My lady, forgive me. I should have said something, but I was uncertain. It seemed so improbable, and I didn't wish to disturb you. . . ."

"What?"

"At the wedding, standing among the commoners I saw. . . I thought I saw. . . it was only for a moment."

"What did you see?"

"My lady, I should have said something, please forgive me."

"Yes, you said this, but what did you see?" Renée had now turned from the window and was gripping her maid by both shoulders. "Tell me."

"Well, I saw, or at least I thought I saw, but like I said it was only for a second, not more, but I thought among the commoners there was one who looked much like. . . Picard."

"Oh, my God!" Renée blanched and grew faint. "Are you certain?"

"No, my lady, not at all, or I would have said something; it is just that when you said you were worried about Henri, well, I have been worried about him too. I have felt it all this afternoon."

Renée twirled and looked out the window again. The clouds had closed and the light shining on the beach had passed. She clasped her hands to her bosom and prayed, "Jesu, Jesu, Jesu Christus be with Henri. Jesu keep him safe."

And then she ran out of her room. Her maid followed. "My lady, you are in no condition. You should rest."

The maid could not run nearly as fast as Renée and was quickly left behind.

After leaving Renée, Henri had wandered back through the cathedral. It was empty and quiet. He admired the moulded gothic columns of the choir, the interlacing circles of the triforium, and above that the magnificent windows. He had passed through the Guest's Hall where the servants were setting up for the evening's feast. They bowed as he passed. Stopping, he admired the tapestries along the wall, then slipped down and looked into the almshouse where pilgrims rested. From there he had gone down the abbot's staircase to the gardens. Sitting there for a few minutes, he reflected on the goodness of God, and then he looked out over the ocean. The tide was still receding, and the beach sands beckoned him. Finding a path, he scrambled down the rocks, one hand reaching out for the support of the rock, the other holding back his sword. Along the beach he looked back up at the great cathedral. What magnificence. He felt small. Skirting some large boulders, he wandered toward the northwest end of the massive rock island. He had so much to be thankful for, so much for which to praise God.

He took a seat on a rock and gazed out at the sea. Some clouds were gathering. It was early in the afternoon.

From behind him he heard the sound of hoof beats on the sand. As he looked over his shoulder, he saw the capes of three knights galloping toward him. At first it surprised him. He had thought everybody had gone on the hunt with the Duke, but as they approached his stomach turned. He recognized their banners: the wolf of Bixmarch, the dragon of Galahad, and the gold and black chevronels of Gascony: Picard. They were almost on him.

Henri quickly surveyed all around him. He started running toward the cathedral and the granite hill it was built upon, but they swerved in and cut him off.

"Well, if it is not Little Henri," Picard said to Sir Galahad. "How did we find him here all alone? And look, Bixmarch, he is not wearing his habergeon."

"Fancy that!" Bixmarch replied. "What a chance coincidence. If I did not know better I would have thought that we had been watching these last two weeks for this, but to imagine it so aptly falling in our lap, and on his wedding day even. It must be providence, predestined, fore-ordained."

They were dressed in mail, swords sheathed on their horses, shields on their arms, crossbows slung over their backs.

Henri looked around again at the granite rock, at the beach behind him, even at the ocean. Which was the best avenue of escape? Could he climb? Could he run? Could he swim? He broke for the sea.

Picard grabbed his crossbow, notched a bolt, and cocked it. "Run if you want to, Little Henri. But I will kill you."

Bixmarch put his arm across Picard's arm and took the bow. "No, this is mine." He spurred his horse and drew near Henri. With the tide out, the water line was far away. Pulling his horse to a halt he raised his crossbow. Henri glanced over his shoulder just as Bixmarch released the trigger. The quarrel buried into his left calf. He stumbled and fell, clutching his leg.

"Go ahead run some more," Bixmarch said as Henri pulled himself to his feet. "Run, swim, fly if you can. I have more bolts to shoot, and I have time. Besides, it is fair. You have been struck in your leg, as I was shot in mine. Think of it as my wedding gift to you, a remembrance of your whore's arrow in my thigh at the stables. I will always have a limp, and now you will too. . . though it is likely you will not have to limp so very long." He chuckled at that, before continuing, "Mind you, we do not wish to kill you with the crossbow. We are not men of arrows, but of blades. We wish to duel you with swords. You see our honor has been sullied, and we mean to satisfy it. Here. Now."

Henri looked at the three of them as he braced his leg with his left hand. They took up positions all around him: Sir Galahad behind, Bixmarch before, and Picard cutting off his access to the cliffs. Henri slowly drew his sword and thought of Renée. How unjust that the day of her greatest joy should turn to tragedy.

"Good, I see you accept our offer," Bixmarch said as he dismounted. Picard followed suit and then Galahad, each of them lashing their horses to a large driftwood log.

Henri eyed the horses; maybe that could be his escape.

Seeing Henri's glance, Bixmarch laughed. "Forget it, Henri. We will not let you near the horses."

Henri nodded. "So will it be one on one, or all three at once?"

Picard grimaced. "Henri, you do us no justice. What type of honor would we have if we were to fight you one on one? The three of us are like brothers. If I were to slay you how could I answer to Sir Galahad, or Sieur de Bixmarch? Where would be their sense of honor?"

Bixmarch laughed loudly. Galahad said nothing.

Henri asked, "Does it mean nothing to you that you would break a woman's heart, killing me on her wedding day? Have you no fear of the judgment? Appoint another day. I will meet you then. You have my word of honor."

"It is precisely on account of Renée that I am here," Picard exclaimed angrily. "How dare you wed my wife? Holy, do you think you are more holy than I? Do you consider yourself pure? You know she is my lawful wedded wife. Marrying her as you did is mortal sin. You speak of the judgment; I am here to administer judgment."

"Quite right, Picard," Bixmarch said as the three of them drew in a semicircle around him. "It is because of this Renée that we are here. I liked you as a stable-boy, Henri. I treated you well, but you had to inter-fere. Now you are heir to Brittany. Amazing. Frankly, I am jealous. I admit it. I am a jealous man. I don't like being jealous, so I will have to kill you. The thought of you being Duc de Bretagne wedded to Renée. . .

Well, I just couldn't stand to live with that. One of us must go."

Stepping back awkwardly toward the sea, Henri parried Picard's first swing. "You will never get away with this."

Bixmarch swung and the sound of metal echoed off the cliff. "Who do you think will save you this time?"

Henri looked up to the tower of Mont Saint-Michel. At the summit, the very peak of the tower the archangel stood, wings uplifted, sword drawn, a cock standing on his foot. "Oh, God," Henri prayed, "help me in my time of need. Do not forget me, if not for my sake, than for the sake of Renée. Help me, God. Lord, have mercy."

"Praying again," Bixmarch sniped.

"He was always doing that," Picard replied. "Too good for the rest of us."

"Well, if you do get help it must be divine for there is not a knight left in the castle. They all went with the Duke on the hunt and will not be back before evening; by that time your pierced and bloodless body will be washing to sea." Bixmarch then strode in, slashing as he advanced.

Renée ran out from her room through the Knight's Hall, and down into the almshouse. Sitting at one of the back tables were two men-at-arms; judging by their noble bearing and gray cloaks and hoods, they were undoubtedly pilgrims. She had not seen them at the wedding. The first one especially was someone she would have remembered. He had an unforgettable profile: a strong, determined chin and straight nose. Renée had seen many knights, many of them tall and powerful, but none like this one. His every movement spoke power. They looked up from their table as soon as she entered, slowed, and approached them.

"Gentle Sirs, did you see Sir Henri pass this way?"

"Gabriel, this must be the lovely bride Renée," the first one said to his companion, and then they both rose and dipped their heads. "Pardon me, my lady. I am Sir Michel du Jardin and this is my squire Gabriel du Pére. We have but recently arrived. Has he come up missing already?"

"Yes, and I am afraid for him."

"It is obvious," Michel spoke quietly. "We have come on a task of some distaste, but maybe when we have finished that we can be of assistance."

"Then it might be too late. I don't know. But I thank you."

"You suspect danger then?"

"I am not sure, but that is what I fear."

The first knight looked to his squire. "Shall we intervene?"

"I am, as always, at your command, milord, but she seems to be a God-fearing, Christian woman."

The knight paused and surveyed her from head to foot and back before answering, "Yes, I think so." At that the knight reached over and picked up his bow from beside the table. He handed it to Renée. "Do you know how to use this?"

Renée nodded. She took the bow. It was magnificent, light but very strong. Gabriel handed her a quiver. It had only one arrow. This was very odd, very peculiar. She smiled wanly. It was obvious they knew more than they let on, both of them, but especially the first one.

"Now, hurry," Sir Michel said. "Go to the beach. We will get our horses."

Renée hesitated as she walked away. She looked over her shoulder. Why the beach? What did they know? Who were they? Then catching up her white bridal dress with her left hand, she ran faster than ever.

Henri caught Bixmarch's strokes as he retreated and circled to his right. He tried to maneuver in such a way as to allow only one knight access to him at a time. The three were in no hurry. They took turns advancing and backing away, always steady, never letting Henri catch his breath. Nor did they ever allow him the opportunity to concentrate on one person. Their plan was to wear him down—cut by cut, wound by wound— and drain his strength, drain his blood. He glanced back up at the cathedral. In which room did she sleep? Through which window did she rest unawares?

"O, God, watch over her." He mouthed the words without speaking.

"And again praying. You know personally I am not a believer. Never saw any need for it." Bixmarch worked his way to the left while Henri blocked Picard's blade. Galahad held back.

What did this strategy imply? Was Galahad holding back in case Henri should injure one or both of the others?

Picard charged. Henri knocked Picard's blade out of his hand, but only after taking a glancing cut on his shoulder. The sword skidded on the sand.

"You have drawn first blood with the blade," Bixmarch encouraged Picard as he kicked him his sword.

Picard picked it up with a shaky hand, unnerved at having lost his sword.

Taking the momentary reprieve, Henri climbed a nearby boulder. He could fight the three of them better from here. For several minutes he held ground at the top, that was, until Galahad charged. When Henri jumped over a low swing, Galahad bowled him over. They both fell to the ground behind the rock. Henri landed on the arrow, still stuck in his calf, and cried out in pain. Galahad jumped to his feet. Henri rolled underneath him and cut out his legs. That gave him a chance to regain his feet, but now Picard was on the rock behind him; Bixmarch had come around to his right, and Galahad was on his feet to his left.

In this position Henri found himself unable to fully stop each stroke. He ducked under Picard's slash, but his parry of Bixmarch's lunge was a little slow, and it caught his side. Galahad's next foot-ripper he only partially blocked, and it cut into the calf beneath the still-lodged arrow. It was only through grit that he kept his legs from crumbling. With Henri weakened, Picard smacked Henri's head with the flat of the blade.

"Well, this is it." Bixmarch paused as he surveyed Henri's faltering position. "It all comes to this. What was it St. Patrick said? 'Christ before you, Christ behind you, Christ beside you.' Except in this case it is I in front of you, Galahad beside you, and Picard behind you, and we are here to slay you. Anything to say? Any last words?"

Henri gasped in pain. He felt faint; his strength was fading, and the blood flowing from his brow clouded his vision. He looked back up toward the grand tower of the cathedral.

Bixmarch and Picard nodded at each other as they prepared to apply a simultaneous death blow from before and behind.

Suddenly a voice interrupted them. "Sieur de Bixmarch, you are damned to hell. May your burning start now."

Henri looked past Bixmarch to the cliff. Renée stood alone on the edge, her dress blown by the wind, her bow now empty as an arrow sped straight for the mark. Bixmarch, his arm raised, about to administer the coup-de-gras, turned. Horror filled his face.

Henri saw that the arrow would pierce Bixmarch's throat, and without forethought, purely by instinct, he directed his sword away from blocking Bixmarch's blade to block the arrow. The arrow struck his blade and shattered harmlessly to the ground.

A long paused ensued. Bixmarch stopped his swing, looked at the arrow, then back at Henri, and then back at the arrow. Sir Galahad dropped his sword to his side. Picard stepped back.

"That arrow would have shriven me through the neck. It would have killed me." Bixmarch's voice trembled. "I don't understand you, Henri. I really don't understand you." His sword rested limply on the sand. Bixmarch looked to Galahad, and then to Picard.

"To our horses?" Bixmarch asked as he backed away.

His face turning red with anger, Picard looked at both of his partners and then at Henri. "What? Are you going to let him escape? Are you going to let him live? Finish him. Now! Sieur de Bixmarch, behead him. Claim his head as a trophy. We cannot let him go, not now, not when we finally have him buckling at our knees." Seeing Sieur de Bixmarch turning away, he appealed to Sir Galahad. "You sir, where is your honor, sir?"

Sir Galahad looked at Picard. "It is not a trivial thing to kill a saint. Consider it carefully, Picard. Are you sure this is what you want?"

"This is absurd," Picard appealed, but he followed the other two toward the horses.

Renée had dropped down off the ledge and was warily passing Bixmarch, heading for Henri. Bixmarch nodded to her. "He is a better man than me." He jerked his head toward Henri, who was kneeling in the sand.

The three mounted and began to ride away. It was obvious they were in a passionate debate. They were just about to pass out of sight when Picard turned and charged. Galahad followed shortly behind, and then Bixmarch.

Renée screamed and tried to assist Henri. He wobbled onto his feet, but he was too weak to make it to the hills and safety. She took up a position in front of Henri. As Picard came by she grabbed at Picard's tunic. He kicked her to the ground, twirled his horse and cocked his sword back to behead Henri. The next moment he was slumped over his saddle by the bolt of a crossbow that went through his back and pierced his heart.

Renée turned to see Gabriel du Pére sitting on a black horse every bit as glorious as Le Noir. A moment later Sir Michel de Jardin thundered by. Sir Galahad and he collided, and Galahad crashed to the ground.

Sacré
Damned and double damned I am,
Have always been.
The holy I profane;
Christ's name I take in vain
Just for the sake of jest
And venial sin.
I gave no mercy
And ask none in return
Save this: that I may take
One guest to hell's fiery lake.
- Abbess Elaine de Morvan
(In memory of Sieur de Bixmarch, brother and only friend)

This left Sieur de Bixmarch an open lane straight through to Henri. Renée pulled Henri to his feet, threw his arm around her neck, and began dragging him away from the beach. Sir Michel had turned his horse quickly and was right behind Bixmarch, slowly gaining. Henri fell to the ground on top of Renée. He reached for his sword. It felt so very heavy. She pulled him across her lap. He tried to push away from Renée, but when he tried to stand his left leg gave way. He had no strength left and collapsed back onto her lap, into the softness of her satin dress.

They were still fifty yards away. Bixmarch looked at Sir Michel as they raced side by side. Sir Michel was arrayed in black and scarlet with white trimming at the edge. He rode a dappled gray charger, a breed of horse unfamiliar even to Henri. The heraldry on his shield was of a red cock perched at the tip of the crusader's cross.

Bixmarch looked over at him. "I know who you are. I know who you *really* are."

"I damned you once and granted grace," Sir Michel answered.

Bixmarch pulled his horse to a stop and looked at the knight. Sir Michel halted as well. The dappled charger reared as Sir Michel thrust his sword into the sky. "Should I damn you again there shall be no mercy."

Bixmarch looked back and forth from Michel to Henri, back to Michel, and one more time back to Henri. Both of their horses stamped the ground with their large front hooves.

"Damn me, then. Damn me and him," Bixmarch cried.

With that, Bixmarch raised his sword and charged Henri. He was on the near side and had the advantage. Henri raised his sword and tried to steady it. His arm was so weak. Michel tapped the flanks of his great horse. The horse bolted forward with alacrity. Who would reach Henri first? On they came, Bixmarch screaming with fury and Michel seated firmly in the saddle. Renée tried to pull herself on top of Henri to protect him, but Henri pushed her back with his left arm.

On they came. Bixmarch threw off his helmet and dropped his shield. He had one intention and one intention only: kill Henri. Then they were upon them. Bixmarch jumped from the saddle with his sword ready to strike. Sir Michel struck him with the flat of the blade on his back. Bixmarch stumbled, spun completely around, and then fell. Henri braced his sword with both hands. Bixmarch fell on it; he fell on Henri's Damascus forged sword. He fell on the point. He fell heavy and hard. The sword pierced through the mail habergeon and impaled him. The tip came out the back. He slumped on top of Henri, his face upon Henri's face. Henri felt the roughness of Bixmarch's beard and smelled the foulness of his breath. His eyes were open and staring at Henri's.

Not yet dead, Bixmarch reached for his dagger at the belt. Renée grabbed it first. She pulled Bixmarch's head back by his gray hair and slit his throat. She slit it deep. She slit it with one rapid stroke, and then she raised the blade to show Michel and Gabriel. They had taken off their helmets, and they now looked at her and then at the knights lying on the ground. Picard was dead. Bixmarch was dead. Galahad was not. He had pulled himself back into the saddle and was riding away.

There was no exaltation on either Michel's or Gabriel's faces. They just turned and rode away toward the sea.

Renée struggled and pushed Bixmarch off Henri.

"It's over. Bixmarch is dead," she said.

Henri nodded weakly.

The wound from his side was bleeding again. She needed to stop the blood flow. She could tear Bixmarch's tunic and cape for dressings, but that thought repulsed her. Nothing of Bixmarch's should foul Henri's body. His wounds needed clean dressings, and nothing was as clean or as pure as her bridal dress. Taking the dagger she cut long strips; then she bound these around his head, his leg, and his abdomen. Taking her veil she folded it up and pressed it in Henri's abdominal wound.

"Hold on, Henri."

Henri nodded.

She laid him back on her lap and stroked his hair. "Don't go, Henri. Don't go."

Henri closed his eyes.

Above, in the monastery, La Rouge began to howl.

Postlude

The jarring of movement aroused Henri. There were men all around him. It was evening. The sun had declined to the horizon where sand and water merged. They were lifting him, placing him on a canvas litter. At his head were his grandfathers: Duc de Montfort and Paul of Brest, at his feet were Petro and another man, by his left side was Ishmael, by his right was Renée.

"Careful. We do not want to restart the bleeding," Ishmael was instructing them. "All together, one, two, three, lift and lay him down."

Across the sand, Comte d'Auch was kneeling beside his brother Picard. "What a needless waste." He rose when Constance came to his side. Seeing Renée looking at him, he pointed to the bolt in his brother's back. "Henri's or yours?"

Renée shook her head. "Neither."

Comte d'Auch buried his head in his hands. "My brother, my brother."

Ishmael strapped Henri to the litter. "All right, all lift together. We must get him away quickly. His life depends on it." Then seeing Renée's concern, he added, "You did a fine job Mirriam, no one could have done better."

As they lifted, Henri groaned. Instantly Renée was by his side. "It will be all right, Henri. Ishmael is here."

Henri opened his eyes and squeezed her hand.

They climbed the trail up the rock. More men helped. They took him to a house at the base of the monastery. La Rouge bounded back and forth a step before the litter-bearers.

Renée lifted her eyes to Ishmael's. She could read the gravity of Henri's condition.

"Henri, don't leave me. Not now, don't leave me," she pleaded.

Henri beckoned her to draw closer. She bent down. "Remember what I told you that morning on the beach?"

She swiped the hair out of her face. "No, I don't remember."

He took a deep breath and whispered, "Je ne te laisse pas."

Benediction

*Now ends this simple tale of sword and steel
And passes on to lore the tenacious love
Of Henri for his youthful bride.
Now bow before the LORD and faithful kneel,
All you gentle readers who acknowledge him above,
With Renée, ever standing by his side.*

*See that he who upon the blade did rise,
Who leaned his strength on sharpened steel,
Hath fallen—
Blood washed the tides turned red —
Hath fallen —
Doth join the company of the dead —
Hath fallen—
Shall nevermore be fearing fled—
But in justice is his demise.*

*So say I now to you who read,
Who on this earth still breathe,
There is beauty. There is rest;
It remains amidst us blessed.
There is the word. There is the book,
And though by some forsook,
I lay it open and bid you look.*

*For though the company of men
May with foul and evil intend
To do you ill, with malice and harm,
I say to you, I say to all, be not alarmed;
For there is joy, and there is love,
And there is God in heaven above.*

*So farewell, fair friends. I bid you peace,
Though it may not come such as this to you.
Still, like St. Michel's spire ascending to the blue,
I am and will always be your humble servant*
- T.S. Beckett

To God
Be the glory,
and if not before we'll
see all of you in heaven
Dr. Brauer

Un wasserfall cristal (A crystal waterfall)

Quelque chose d'emprunt, quelque chose bleu, quelque chose aigu
(Something borrowed,   Something blue, Something sharp)

Postlude
Benediction
Appendix
Epilogue

Epilogue

Six weeks later, Henri and Renée were sitting on Le Noir and Fallaire, saying goodbye to friends. Henri's hound, Le Rouge, was lying down by the large hoofs of the Frisian warhorse. Sir Petro de Lomange was taking his leave but not as Petro de Lomange, for he was now Sir Petro d' Ayes, Steward. Lord Henri and the Lady Renée needed someone whom they could trust to watch over their holdings in Ayes, and who better than Petro?

"I always said you were lucky for me," Petro said as he prepared to ride away. "As the Lord, so the servant."

"God be with you. Give my greetings to Maria."

Then, turning to Ishmael and Simeon, who were riding in the same company of knights, he said, "Goodbye, my friend. Peace be with you. Give my greetings to Jehudah."

Ishmael nodded at Henri. "Your wounds are well-healed. Though I admit I am afraid to leave you. Montpelier is a long ways away, and if you should need help, none could help you like me." He turned away from Henri to look at Renee. His face softened with a smile. "My dearest maiden Miriam, even more do I hate to leave you. Your face, your smile are sunshine for an aging heart."

"Dr. Ishmael, I can never repay you for all you have done."

"To the contrary, your beauty is repayment many times over."

Renée smiled. "Well, you know, we could use a court physician. You could come and practice here. I am, after all, your most miraculous case. Surely we can find a nice little library for you to write your memoirs in, don't you think, Henri?"

"Of course we could use you, Ishmael. Think it over."

Ishmael replied seriously, "I will do that. I will think it over. Why not? Indeed, really why not? Still, I do need to gather my books, but do not be surprised if you see me come spring."

The last to go were Comte d'Auch and Constance. There was an awkward pause. "I. . . I am glad to see you have recovered. Milord Henri, acc. . . accept the apologies of the house of Gascony. We have harmed. . . harmed you, but God has seen you through. There is one last thing that we wish to return to you. It. . . it came last week, and I have been waiting for the time to return it to you."

At that Henri heard a hawk's cry above him. Little Henri looked at the Comte d'Auch for confirmation. "My hawk? Can he fly?"

"His wing is mended. He is ready to meet the world, as are you."

Henri whistled and held up his arm. The hawk descended and landed on his outstretched glove.

- Finite -

Printed in the United States
80631LV00002B/178-186

9 780977 445202